THE *EAGLET* AT
THE BATTLE OF MINORCA

THE *EAGLET* AT THE BATTLE OF MINORCA

John Mariner

The Book Guild Ltd
Sussex, England

First published in Great Britain in 2001 by
The Book Guild Ltd
25 High Street
Lewes, East Sussex
BN7 2LU

Copyright © John Mariner 2001

The right of John Mariner to be identified as the author of this work has been asserted by him in accordance with the Copyright, Designs and Patents Act 1988.

All rights reserved. No part of this publication may be reproduced, transmitted, or stored in a retrieval system, in any form, or by any means, without permission in writing from the publishers, nor be otherwise circulated in any form of binding or cover other than that in which it is published and without a similar condition being imposed on the subsequent purchaser.

Although based on fact,
this publication has been enhanced
with imaginary characters and incidents.

Typesetting in Baskerville by
SetSystems Ltd, Saffron Walden, Essex

Printed in Great Britain by
Antony Rowe Ltd, Chippenham, Wiltshire

A catalogue record for this book is
available from the British Library

ISBN 1 85776 547 8

In Memory of
David Bernard Peter Lardner
(Died at Sea – 12th January 1972)

CONTENTS

1	A New Beginning	1
2	Admiral Byng	22
3	A Distasteful Business	30
4	Madeleine	43
5	*Corinne*	54
6	The Quick and the Dead	64
7	'Santander'	75
8	Admiral the Lord Hawke	88
9	A Tragic Error	101
10	A Hero's Welcome	115
11	On Enemy Soil	134
12	No Death for a Soldier	150
13	Intransigence and New Orders	159
14	To Have and to Hold	170
15	A Perilous Prospect	180
16	The Rescue	194
17	The Capture of *Vraiment*	209

18	A Glimpse of the Grim Reaper	222
19	The French!	243
20	The English Fleet	254
21	Form Line of Battle!	266
22	The Aftermath	282
	Epilogue	293

1

A New Beginning

The waters of the Carrick Roads at Falmouth glittered as if sprinkled with a million diamonds. The bright January sun hung low on the horizon in the chilly afternoon. So bright was the dazzling haze that even the wherries, plying between Flushing and the Falmouth Quays, seemed to disappear beneath the sheen and then reappear as if cleansed in a baptism of fire.

Behind the Quays the clatter of iron-shod wheels across the cobbles brought life to Church Street. The air was filled with the discordant voices of traders in full throat, fisher-folk, labourers, hat-tipping passers-by and those who came for other reasons to the busy Cornish port with its deep-sea harbour.

The sturdy building of Wynn's Hotel, with its bottle-glass and bow-windowed front protruding onto Church Street, housed a crowded coffee room laden with the smoke from a dozen clays. The noises from the street had caused the level of conversation to rise within. In the granite stone fireplace, a fresh log, damp and bearing the moss of a hundred winters, crackled and spat, sending plumes of steam and smoke up the spacious chimney. The large room was alive with the chatter of seamen, mainly captains and mates from the Dutch and English boats, exchanging mails, anchored in shallower waters in the mouth of the Fal. Men who conversed in haste, constantly aware of both tide and wind.

By the rear window, overlooking the Roads, Post-Captain Daniel Winchip sat in full uniform, his two golden epaulettes denoting his rank. They rated a certain path to high rank should he not be killed in battle or fall prey to a fever. He was ready, yet again, to go to sea, waiting only for the messenger who would pass the word that the ship's boat was at the steps. At the next table sat old Jonathan, Winchip's coxswain of years past, his wooden leg sticking out between the tables for all to step over. With greying hair and a bearded face of tanned leather, Jonathan kept silent, crouched in the chair and hugging his pot, ready at a moment's notice to escort the captain's daughter back to the house.

Opposite Winchip sat his only child, his dearest Emma. He looked at her with a sorrow he found difficult to cover with a smile. At eighteen, she was beginning to look more like her mother; just as beautiful, just as forthright. Even now, sitting demurely with her hands together, the ties of her bonnet hanging down across her bosom and a cheeky grin hovering on her face, she couldn't hide the characteristics she had inherited from his beloved Maria. How much he wished Maria could be with them now.

He was struggling to find different words with which to say goodbye. He hated trite repetition, the expected rote of a traditional farewell. She deserved better. In the end it came out as it always did.

'I have no idea how long I shall be away, my dear. This is a new command. It could be weeks or months – perhaps longer. The navy is not only short of ships, she needs her captains, too.' He knew full well that frigates were in high demand. He put a light pressure on her hands, neatly clasped on the table before her, as was proper. '*Eaglet* has had her sea trials. Now it is time to put her to sea properly, and to work.'

'I know, Father.' Emma inclined her pert little head, the ringlets of her hair framing her pale face as if carved in black Italian marble as they sought to escape from beneath the blue silken bonnet. Her face lit up, only the hidden sadness in her eyes betraying her true feelings. 'Then you shall write to me on every possible occasion. Tell me where you are and all about the places you visit, as you used to. I miss you so much when you go away, not knowing when you will return.' She lowered her head at her own boldness.

'You have Jonathan and Beth, my dear. They have tried so hard since your mother . . .' The sentence died on his lips. Winchip wished he hadn't started it. Maria, and their son to be, had died together at the birthing five years previously and yet it seemed like only yesterday. Now, Jonathan, with his wife, Beth, looked after 'Santander', his house on the hill behind the church. In his heart he believed *he* needed Emma more than she could understand, but that smacked of greater decisions, steps he was not yet prepared to make. At least, not until this bloody business with France was done for once and for all time. She was his family. It was just the two of them. Emma was now in all aspects a woman and that, too, worried him. There had been a time when she would cry openly at their parting and let her feelings out. Now, she simply 'understood'.

'Santander' was set in grounds of about three hectares, each acre climbing above the next towards the skyline until the land flattened into Poppy Meadow and the host of dew-ponds settled amongst the boulders of grey Cornish granite. Jonathan husbanded all of it. The sheep grazed the pasture, while the vegetable field, manned by a few local workmen, supplied the household and brought in a weekly income from the market. Emma kept the accounts, using the task to give her both an interest and keep her occupied. Winchip was not so devoid of feelings that he refused to face the fact she would be thinking of marriage. There were possibilities in the making but he was not likely to interfere in a matter that required a delicacy not given to his nature.

He turned his eyes towards the anchorage, his gaunt and tanned rugged face creasing into a smile. Even the medley of mail boats, nodding to each other in the choppy shallows, were dwarfed in the presence of his new command. His Britannic Majesty's Frigate *Eaglet* squatted in a sea of shining pink pearls that were disappearing one by one as the sun sought to take its final plunge towards the low hills to the west.

Winchip looked up as a floorboard creaked and a polite cough came from the shadows at his side. Lieutenant Pardoe stood beside him, his hat beneath his arm, his eyes on Emma expressing far more than the fatuous grin on his handsome features. His face may have had the olive hue of many a Cornishman but his hair was as fair as straw, blanched by sun and wind alike.

'Aha! Mr Pardoe – the boat, at last!' It was a normal, shipboard reaction, Winchip's smile disallowing any thought of reprimand. He drained his cup, adjusted his sword from between his legs and reached for his hat and cloak, well aware of the looks exchanged between the fair-haired lieutenant and his daughter. His liberal attitude in the matter spoke well of his regard for Pardoe, who had served with him in *Capable*. It would not pain him if Pardoe sought to call on Emma, but that was a matter that rested in their hands. He was aware that Pardoe's 'interest' provided a good allowance and that his navy pay would be in addition to that but he knew little else. He knew about the *man* and for him that was sufficient.

Emma had brightened, the moment Pardoe came up to them. 'Mr Pardoe! It *is* nice to see you again.' If her expression was meant to be coy or demure, there was no sign of it. The shaking of hands took on a degree of permanency.

'And I to see you, Miss Winchip.' The grin had become a fixture.

'Are you come to take my father away, Mr Pardoe?' The question could not have sounded more innocent, any response neither forthcoming nor expected. Emma slowly dragged her hand from Pardoe's grasp and rose to her feet. She knotted the ties of her bonnet, smiling demurely enough when Pardoe handed her the dainty pair of gloves from the table.

'Time we were gone, young man!' Winchip's voice was unequivocal. He turned to Emma. 'I shall take my leave, my dear.' He took her hands in his and raised them to his lips. 'It is better we part here. The quay is no place for a lady and besides, it is cold in the shadows.' He bowed his six-foot height down to her level and kissed her briefly on the cheek. 'Take care, my child,' he whispered. His hands pressed hers, conveying the love he found difficult to express in words. Winchip nodded to Jonathan – all that was necessary – and, with that, he followed Pardoe. Together they took the steps to the quay, to the sudden and incessant noise of seagulls, screeching as they swooped among the fish baskets, then rising to settle on the slate roofs, their beaks opening wide in defiance as they inspected and then gorged their pickings. Around them the narrow brick chimneys with clay pots emitted spirals of smoke that were whipped to a flatness as each was caught by the wind.

Walking on newly sand-gritted planks to the steps, his cloak wrapped about him in the chill wind, Winchip savoured the fresh air that had been absent in Wynn's. He used the moment to face into the onshore breeze and glance across the water towards *Eaglet*, now sitting in a sea of blood, the sun reflected on the great bulge of her hull that was her tumblehome. With sails furled into harbour gaskets, her bare masts towered above her like lances of fire in the last of the sun. He gave an imperceptible nod, as much as to acknowledge his luck as his appreciation of the new frigate. It didn't seem possible that three months had passed since his last command, *Capable*, had been shot through beneath him. It had been a chance meeting with no hope of escape, following orders, away from the Inshore Squadron. He had been seeking out the French ships that were secreted in port and inlet alike, ships that would carry the troops when the expected invasion of England eventually came. He had been on just such a mission, returning from an inshore reconnaissance of Rochefort with an offshore wind when fate had overtaken them.

The huge sixty-gun *Frenchman* had appeared out of the departing mist like a ghost. The exchange of fire, at a distance of two cables, had been both vicious and relentless. When the two ships had finally drifted apart in the almost lifeless air, the only sound had been that of the dying. Damaged in the tops and badly holed at the water-line, *Capable* had struggled north, jury-rigged, her boats behind her, back in tow like a clutch of ducklings. The battered and dismasted *Frenchman* had been drifting, left to be dealt with by the squadron ships-of-the-line.

'The steps, Sir!'

Winchip stopped in his tracks, his mind clearing in an instant, aware of Pardoe's hand on his arm. 'Thank you.' Winchip lightly brushed the hand away. Gathering his sword he stepped nimbly down into the cutter, watched by the massive Hellard, his new coxswain who had stayed by his side as *Capable* had been hit time and time again. Winchip sat in the stern sheets with his sword between his legs and tugged his hat down in deference to the wind yet to come from across the open water.

'Make way!' Hellard's stentorian voice brought instant compliance as the boat leaped away from the grey and weeded steps.

Winchip's thoughts went back again to *Capable*, as they so often did. A good ship, now no more than a memory. In company with a squadron sloop, which had investigated them on sight, she had eventually given up the fight to stay afloat. He had ordered her beached on a sand bar north of L'Orient and once the wounded, stores and powder had been transferred – the guns had long since been thrown overboard – she was burned. The immediacy of her presence remained until the pillar of smoke had disappeared below the horizon.

It had been like losing a limb. Suddenly having to do without what had been a part of him. No! More than that – she had been his whole life. Winchip gathered his cloak a little tighter in unconscious anger. There was the crew – his people. They, too, had made *Capable* their home. Suddenly, for them, their home and all their possessions had become a mere smudge on the shore of a foreign land.

Winchip had been forced to take the philosophical view. The crew would find new ships, new dunnage and new friends. Never would they forget those who had died so suddenly and so violently at their sides. Their sense of invulnerability would be diminished but even that would return. Their one weapon against fear – their only source of courage.

He found no reason to dwell on the court martial. They had exonerated him. Praised him, even. He laughed quietly at that. It had been a matter of life or death! He thanked God that the *Frenchman* hadn't been a seventy-four. His innocence, however, had not been without cost . . .

A sudden spray of spume brought Winchip back to the present. The choppy water splashed against the gunwale and sprayed his face as the cutter turned towards *Eaglet*. The squeal of the thole-pins became more hurried and the beat more urgent. Hellard had overseen her thus far into a head sea. Now, with the small wavelets on her beam, the price had to be paid.

Eaglet gained in size as they approached. A Fifth Rate, new from the yard, she represented a new type of frigate. Built at Rotherhithe, after a design by Sir Thomas Slade, she carried twenty-six twelve-pounder guns on the upper deck and a half dozen six-pounders on the quarterdeck. Enough authority to meet any challenge short of a ship-of-the-line. Her twenty half-pound swivels – eight more than were originally allotted – were strategically placed, with mountings of twice that number for speedy repositioning. Even her four boats were fitted with mountings, only needing the swivels to be taken on board to make each a force to be reckoned with during boat actions. Her six-hundred-and-forty-eight-ton burthen required a crew of two hundred and ten, to eat, sleep, work and fight in a space almost a hundred and four feet long by twenty-nine feet wide. The bow and stern chasers, on reinforced decks, had come later, at the last minute. She was an experiment. A forerunner to what was to become a new era of frigates, the first of which, the *Southampton*, was already displaying her ribs at the Rotherhithe yard.

Eaglet was a ship of which any post-captain could be

proud. As to the crew, that was a matter for the immediate future. They would need knocking into shape. Melding into a single fighting unit. That would be the task of the first lieutenant, the same Lieutenant Niven who had served with him on *Capable*. There were others, too, he had been able to keep, all of whom had arrived during the commissioning. It gladdened him to know he would not be truly alone with so many familiar faces still about him.

'Toss oars!' Hellard's order was enough to jerk him upright. He remained seated while hands snatched at the chains to prevent the cutter racing under the tumblehome in the last of the incoming tide. 'Ready, Sir!'

'Thank you, Coxswain.' Winchip grasped his sword to his side and stepped out for the battens and the knotted handrail. A fine arrival should he slip and plunge into the racing current. With a dexterity gained from practice he was up and through the entry posts like a squirrel, his hand already reaching for his hat to exchange salutes with Niven. Niven, thank God, had had the courtesy to wait until he composed himself.

'Good afternoon, Sir.' Niven went through the motions with a welcoming smile and two curled fingers to his hat, worn fore and aft in the new style of the younger officers.

'Good afternoon, Lieutenant.' Winchip glanced down the deck, always his first action on coming on board. It gave him a sense of things, and satisfied his mind. There was little to complain about, and neither would he have expected there to be, except perhaps the smell of her. The new timber, the newly tarred standing rigging, paint, tallow and new cordage that any seaman would recognise, even blindfolded. Men scuttled and tasked at every point, some seeing him for the first time, peering at him askew, the man who held their lives in the palm of his hand. There were other smells, smells that emanated from below and which would get far worse with the passage of time if allowed to. He glanced at Niven, nodding his approval. 'My cabin, in ten minutes, if you please. In the meantime, prepare to weigh anchor.'

He strode aft, glancing at the nettings as he passed, giving a nod of satisfaction at the neatness of the slip-knots and the uniformity of the hammocks, an additional protection in times of trouble. Beneath the poop he was momentarily blinded by the contrast of darkness against the brilliance of the waning sun. Fortunately, the marine sentry opened his cabin door after saluting. One large boot slammed down on the deck to meet the other, his sword blade resting idle on his shoulder. There was no room for a musket in the tight confines of the short corridor.

Ducking low to enter the great cabin he immediately swung off his cloak and removed his hat, placing them as always on the old sea-chest, the wood and metal trunk with his father's initials blazoned on the top in gilt. With a sigh of relief he flopped down on the cushioned stern seat. The smell of new timber was still present, now mixed with that of paint, tallow and damp, and many things in between. With his arm stretched along the thick sill of the windows he gazed out towards Flushing and the myriad masts and spars flashing in turn as they dipped and rose like the pikes of a marching mediaeval army in the last of the sun's rays. The stern seat was his place of refuge, the place where he could sit and think and, if the truth were known, come to some of his better decisions.

It was the first time since reading himself in (the task of every new captain) that he had found time to lounge as he was doing now. Then, it had been a matter of relief from formality. Standing with his officers at the athwart rail of the quarterdeck, exhorting his people to their duties and responsibilities, at the same time warning them of the penalties should they fail in either. Necessary it may have been. In his book it was far better to want to do one's duty than be threatened with the wrath of the captain and an unforgiving admiralty if one didn't.

Eaglet had come down the coast to Falmouth in fine fettle, despite the calamities of those still learning the ropes. There was hope for them, he would say no more than that. The journey to Falmouth had ironed out a few problems but he suspected there would be more. Only time could tell.

Winchip rose from the seat and sat at the small Gillow table that oozed the odour of beeswax. Here and there were scattered many of his personal items – silver pen tray, quill knife, quills, writing pad, and a miniature likeness of Emma in a silver frame, all rescued from *Capable* by Hellard.

He was looking forward to Niven's report – copperplate and no smudges – daring to hope they had a full complement. His wry grin gave emphasis to his doubts, allowing his angular features to burst into a shower of weather creases, belying his forty-one years, but certain evidence of many long watches in troubled waters. His light olive-skinned face and long thin nose, of Cornish and Spanish origins from the time of the Armada, were framed with hair as black as a tar brush, tied by a black ribbon neatly topping his queue. As he opened a drawer to extract his journal, he heard footsteps under the poop. The knock on the door was exactly on time.

'Enter!'

'The First Lieutenant, Sah!' The marine was there with the stamp of a boot, and then gone in a flash, leaving Niven – with the same problems brought about by height – to duck through the door.

'Come in, Mr Niven. Sit yourself down.' Winchip waved a desultory arm towards any of three chairs.

'Thank you, Sir.' Niven placed his paper on the desk and then perched on the edge of the nearest of the three seats. 'You asked for my report, Sir.'

'Yes, thank you, Lieutenant.' Winchip smiled – it was good to be back. 'I spy a grin on your face. One that heralds good news, I trust.' It was easy to be facile with Niven. To be unguarded in everyday conversation and let the best come out in each of them without fear of regretting it later.

'I hope so, too, Sir.' Niven sat upright in the chair, his grin developing into a smile. 'Our lads pressed eighteen bodies in the area and . . .' he hurried on, now enthused '. . . we had to use the yawl as well in the end. We have three rated able and one who claims he's a company man but, judging by the man's tattoos, for my money he's a runner, Sir.'

'That may have been some time ago, Mr Niven. This is 1756. Many of those serving today are doing so because they want to, or are looking to escape from something far worse.' Winchip thought for a moment, at the same time smiling at Niven's enthusiasm. 'Let him prove himself. Keep an eye on him.'

Niven nodded. 'I worry about dissension, Sir. Runners frighten me. I find they tend to be infectious.' He swivelled in the chair, brightening as Booth, the captain's man-servant, entered with the wine.

Winchip stood, indicating that Niven stay seated. Striding to the stern window he held up his glass against the light and inspected the deep red Madeira. 'I should like us to be back in Plymouth tomorrow. If we can weigh on the turn we should clear the shore before dark.' He sipped his drink, his head bowed in deference to the proximity of the deck above. 'I am to report to the admiral at Plymouth. I have no doubt my orders will be ready and waiting.'

'It will be interesting to know what is expected of us, Sir. Apart from squadron duties we shall have to go much further afield to see any real action – India or The Americas perhaps.' Niven sipped his wine with relish, raising his eyebrows in anticipation.

'Aha! With Lord Hawke, and now Admiral Byng, playing skittles with the French merchant fleet in the approaches and with the continuing problems in the colonies, I have no doubt we shall be at war with France within six months.' Winchip dropped onto, rather than sat on the stern seat as if to emphasise the point.

The crash of a utensil behind the screen betrayed the presence of Booth in his cubby-hole. It would be round the ship within the hour.

'War, Sir? Do you really think so?' Niven stared moment-arily into space as if his mind was suddenly on distant horizons and ambitions still unrequited.

'One can never be sure. The French will not take our truculence for much longer, of that you can be certain.' Winchip could read the thoughts of glory and promotion in Niven's eyes, just as they had been in his own when his command, *Piquante,* had been involved off *Finisterre* in 1747. He had come to know Niven well. He was a man's man, with his dark and handsome countenance and dashing ways.

'A toast, Sir!' Niven held his glass high. 'To the French – may they continue to be confounded!'

Winchip raised his glass. 'May they also wait until Their Lordships are prepared.' He looked Niven in the eye. They both laughed, the sound carrying through the deck light, no doubt to the watch above. 'Very well, Lieutenant. If we are to catch the turn, I suggest you get to it. Let me know when you are ready to weigh, if you please, before we lose the light altogether.'

'Aye, Sir.' Niven jerked to his feet, draining the last drop from the glass as he did so. At the age of twenty-six he still managed to keep his cheerful and enthusiastic smile, his handsome and open features always seeming to inspire confidence. His brown hair was plaited at the back, tied and then doubled under to form a ring, 'to thwart the sword' as he would say. 'There is just one other matter, Sir.' Niven held his hat in both hands, close to his stomach.

'Well?' Winchip searched his mind for something he'd missed, or was it to be some problem yet to be declared.

'Er ... the officers, right down to the gunroom, have expressed their pleasure at the court's decision, Sir. You did everything to ... yet ...' Words failed Niven. He stood agape, as if praying for rescue.

'I thank you, all of you, for your support, Lieutenant. Captain Rance saw things one way, and I another. The court was gracious enough to see my point of view. That is the truth of it, Mr Niven.'

'Yes, Sir, but Captain Rance – '

'One's senior officer is correct in all things. Only when he is mistaken or misinformed can there be a difference.' Winchip held up a hand to prevent interruption. The matter had to come out, but he would have rather been the one to choose the timing. 'You must remember that he lost his son in that action, Mr Niven. Lieutenant Rance was a good officer, a loss to us all. Captain Rance's point of view bore no relation to the fact that his son was serving in *Capable*, I am sure. Let that be clearly understood.'

'Yes, Sir.' Niven waited for dismissal, his face crestfallen, matters of good order and discipline well known to him, as they had to be with every serving officer.

'Then we shall say no more on the matter. Time to weigh, I think.' Winchip allowed the crease of a smile to appear on his face as he dismissed Niven with a flourish.

Winchip suddenly felt tired. It was an accumulation of worry and sleepless nights catching up with him. Niven's oblique reference to Post-Captain Rance's blatant lies at the trial had awakened thoughts that frightened him. To be held directly responsible for the death of his son had been unreasonable, and yet those were the words the captain had used before the trial, when they had been alone together, before others had gathered in that bleak coach next to the great cabin. Lieutenant Rance had been cut out of the tops by bar shot, as had two others beside him. No one should have to account for that. Rance's eyes had bored into him from a face filled with loathing. His verbal threat of revenge had been a private one, punctuated with blasphemies, doused in hate. Winchip had recoiled at the time, controlled anger welling inside him. When the lies in court about his unwritten orders, given in the spirit of what Lord Hawke was practising in the approaches – 'Sink anything you find!' – had been given to him, Winchip had asked if a declaration of war had been made. The captain's reply of 'Do as you would be done by – but do it first,' had left him with no doubts. In court the captain had denied having given such orders. And now? Winchip shook his head in despair. The court's decision had all but called Captain Rance a liar. Their conclusions had been tempered towards the captain in terms of words like 'mistaken', 'misinterpreted', even 'misheard'. Palliatives, becoming his rank and the court's esteem.

Winchip could see his cot, swinging in the sleeping place. The wooden bed that could just as quickly become his coffin should he fall in action or be struck down by disease. He dismissed the prospect as he opened his journal and selected a goose quill. He wrote a short sentence: 'In all respects, ready for sea.' It said very little. What it encompassed warranted volumes.

Niven was still in Winchip's mind as he pushed the journal to the back of the table. The first lieutenant had been a tower of strength during the fitting out and, it had to be said, had ensured *Eaglet* received the best that was available in the way of supplies and victuals. His name was probably a blasphemy with those who would take advantage in the confusion of commissioning a new vessel, minions of the Navy Board who would rid themselves of doubtful foodstuffs, rotten meat or weak cordage. Anything that wouldn't be discovered until the vessel was a thousand miles to sea.

His thoughts turned to the ship herself. *Eaglet* was to be more than a ship. She was to be home to every man jack on board. The men – his people – had been thrown together by circumstance. Common sense, seasoned with a common bond, would soon draw them together. Winchip knew their true worth would come out when it was needed most, when all the training and practice would come to bear. When the survival of the ship – and their very lives – would depend upon that training.

Eaglet, her stuns'ls set, lacked only an audience to witness her beauty as she shaped a course south-west by west, coming away from Plymouth, the sun on her larboard bow and a moderate breeze coming off the Cornish shore. Fifteen miles south of the coastline she would have the weather gauge on anything beating up the channel within sight, whether broad-reaching or on a larboard tack.

Eaglet dipped her bow into the light swell, white horses galloping past on either beam, to be lost and then found again, then lost for all time in a welter of foam, passing astern, breaking in the gusting wind to become spindrift. Her pristine sails, white against the shoreline clouds to the north, bellied out, throwing out her breastplate to celebrate her first taste of the true sea.

'A fine day for sailing, gentlemen.' Captain Winchip's tall figure appeared behind those on the quarterdeck, pulling the collar of his cloak about his neck, feeling the contrast in the weather from out of the north-west and guarding against the liberal amounts of spray thrown up by the bow.

'Indeed, Sir.' Niven moved to one side, ceding the deck.

Mr Ramblin, the portly and ageing sailing-master, called out from his place beside the wheel, his greying whiskers catching the brisk air. 'Course sou'-west by west, Captain.' He peered down at the binnacle and then up, towards the tops. 'Wind is from the north-west but won't be for much longer, I'll warrant. She'll veer a bit soon, I fancy. Lee helm on – just a mite.' The monologue ended with a beaming smile.

'Thank you, Master.' Winchip found Mr Ramblin's smile infectious. As usual it was more of a speech than a report. 'We are well past the Lizard, so let her fall off to south by west as soon as is convenient.'

'Aye, Captain. South by west, Sir.'

Winchip blinked his eyes as he looked upwards. The huge mass of hard canvas, full-bellied and holding taught, was covered by a sheen of water droplets, one moment invisible and then offensive to the eye as the sun was reflected from them in a blaze of light. Even the spray itself displayed a rainbow, an order of colour that hung in the air with the same ethereal and capricious mystery as the crock of gold beneath it. In contrast, his eyes, yet to accustom themselves to the bright sun, could only see the hollows and corners as black depths, giving dimension to the ship, turning her into a living thing, riding the shallow swell as if eager to be about her business. From forward he could hear Sergeant Haggler drilling the marines on the forecastle. The tramp of boots, punctuated by the occasional blasphemy. He could just see them, a splash of red, a bright contrast to the sombre dullness of timber, cordage and black iron.

'Top men are up, Sir.' Bowes, the chubby duty midshipman on the quarterdeck, touched his hat to the first lieutenant, delaying his departure, as if allowing himself to linger for a moment in such exalted company. The son of a rear-admiral, the seventeen-year-old Bowes knew his father's position would never help him in *Eaglet*; and neither would he want it to. His soft but heavy features, more that of an artisan than a warrior, were deeply tanned by the sun and wind, his brown hair weathered to a contrasting lightness. He sought nothing but the sea.

'Thank you, Mr Bowes. Return to your post, if you please.' Niven glanced at the master. Mr Ramblin had heard the message.

'South by west, Zur.' The small, ageing helmsman added without thinking, 'We'm afore the wind!' He stood agape in his innocence, his teeth like leaning tombstones amongst the gaps, the grin of a simpleton.

'Then steer small, damn you!' Mr Ramblin showed the less cheerful side of his nature, turning his head away in embarrassment and sucking feverishly on his hollow tooth.

Winchip walked forward to the athwart rail, resting his hands on the cold and wet timber. Things were taking shape – the past coming back to greet him. The rigging had changed its note. It had taken on a higher octave, persistent now in the changing, soon to fade into the background of noise around him. He felt a need to be at one with the ship, get to know her and discover her best points of sail. It would all come with time. It was a moment for feeling proud, as any captain would. In the greater scheme of things it would be practicalities that mattered. Most important would be *Eaglet*'s fighting fitness and speed, her sailing qualities under pressure and the abilities of his people. Fighting strength required practice until they dropped, if they were to stay alive. Something he was prepared to provide in plenty. He gripped his hands behind his back and stared out across the open water to the south where their destiny awaited them all.

It was to be a new beginning.

2

Admiral Byng

Events had come full circle. It was almost as if they were back on *Capable*, returning from Rochefort. Standing on the quarterdeck next to Niven, with the wind at his back, Winchip found it almost easy to dispel the time that had passed since then. Only those who had died on that fateful day had cause to argue, and they, like the ship, were gone forever.

He considered his orders from Plymouth. The Western Squadron should welcome him with open arms, especially with the provisions in the hold, although the pigs would be in a sorry state by the time they got there. Little piglets, to be fattened on board until hunger got the better of patience. As for duties, well, under normal circumstances 'messenger boy' would come to mind, maintaining a link between the Inshore Squadron and the admiral. Worse still, it could have been relay work or patrols around Brest, waiting for the French to burst from cover at the first sign of a change from the everlasting westerlies that penned them in their own harbours. It could have been any damned thing! He allowed his momentary anger to subside, memories tumbling in on him faster than he could deal with them. He knew Niven would be puzzled at his silence – in fact he was probably even now conjuring up different destinations in his mind, coming to conclusions far removed from the truth. Winchip gave a wry grin. Niven would know the truth all right. He had only to consider *Eaglet*'s stores, cargo and direction to get some idea. What Niven *didn't* know was what had transpired at Plymouth. The Port Admiral had been quick to inform him that he would be required for special duties and immediately detached from the Western Squadron. Winchip had received orders of a secret nature; orders which could test them all when the time came, but what then? Patrols and messenger duties sprang back to mind like an unwelcome guest.

'I shall be in my cabin, Lieutenant.'

He sat at the stern window writing in the journal on his lap. There were things he would have liked to put to pen, but he knew they would be the product of a lonely mind. It was a captain's lot to be lonely, solely responsible for his ship, his officers and crew, as was his God-given right and Their Lordships at Admiralty's command so to do. This was a different loneliness. His thoughts again were of Maria, now gone these five years, together with the son he had wanted so much. Also of Emma, coming to womanhood with all that entailed. He thanked God for Jonathan and Beth. They would look after her, of that he was sure – but age was a relentless foe, a creeping thing. The responsibility he felt for Emma was returning back to him but, for the moment, there were more immediate matters. He dismissed the accusing voices that constantly sought his attention.

Putting his journal aside, Winchip stood with care as the ship came up to meet him. Gathering his old boat coat in his arms he went up through the companion to the quarter-deck, breathing in the keen air as if to drive out the melancholy within him. It would pass, as it had passed a thousand times before, and would do so again.

'Good afternoon, Sir.' The senior midshipman, 'Sandy' Pope, was acting officer of the watch. No doubt with Niven or Pardoe within hailing distance. He stood expectantly, his eager face with its enigmatic expression and his sandy hair tousled by the wind. He seemed to suffer a moment of panic as he glanced at compass and tops in one wild sweep. 'Course south by west, wind out of the north-west, Sir.'

'Thank, you, Mr Pope. Have we any sightings?' Winchip sounded casual.

'A bark to south'ard, Sir. Beating up the channel, I'd say. No colours.'

'Good. Then clear for action, if you please and reduce to fighting canvas.' He added as an afterthought... 'Guns loaded.' Winchip turned away, aware of the shocked and perplexed expression on Pope's face. His own eyes creased in a smile. The midshipman would not be caught again so easily.

Winchip stood with his back to the taffrail, affording himself the best view of events; the collar of his deck coat pulled tight about his neck. Hatless in the brisk north-westerly, he watched with studied interest as the guns were once more run out on the port side. Even in the keen air the men wore very little, some even barefoot and most wearing bandanas or scraps of cloth wound about their ears to deaden the noise. The shouts of the gun captains could be heard above all else, the order of loading, now almost emblazoned on the men's minds as they moved like automatons, shouting, competing, determined to have the first arm pointing to the sky in readiness. The arms rose, one by one, eager faces, wide-eyed, looking towards Niven at the binnacle in the hope of a look or a gesture. Either would be reward enough. Pardoe and Bowes strode the length of the ship, back and forth, encouraging and admonishing in turn, their swords glistening on ramrod shoulders.

'*Fire!*' Niven screamed the command through the 'hailer.

The eruption of sound still took Winchip by surprise. His hands increased their grip on the rail and his body leaned backwards as the guns discharged almost as one, emitting thick and yellow acrid smoke, billowing outwards, pierced with orange and red spears of flame. *Eaglet* seemed to lean to one side as she absorbed the shock of the recoiling twelve-pounders. His eyes went to the flag-topped cask two cables out, bobbing on the swell like an empty jollyboat, the white rag stiff as a rod, fluttering in the breeze. It disappeared in a welter of foam and water – the third leaky water cask that day. His hands slapped down on the rail as he involuntarily shouted, 'aha!' They were good, of that there was no doubt. He had kept his promise and so had they. The question was, would they be so good when the iron was flying and men were dying about them? For that, there could be no practice, only ghastly experience.

A squadron cruiser had sighted them as the forenoon watch dispersed below and the midshipmen carried their quadrants to the master for the noonday sightings. With numbers exchanged, *Eaglet* came to due south, as directed, towards the flagship, the wind on her starboard quarter and the log-ship reading nine knots. The squalls came tumbling down on them from the north-west, each seeming to select *them* when all about them the low sun shone coldly in a clear blue sky. The showers were encouraging colder air and, with that, the threat of worse to come. The tranquillity of Falmouth was quickly becoming a far off memory. It was at the beginning of the first dog watch that the cry came from the tops.

'*Deck there!*'

'*Where away?*' Niven used the 'hailer.

'*Low, off the larboard bow.*'

Winchip, keeping attendance with Niven, officer of the watch, stood wide-legged aft of the binnacle. He had been expecting the call and was not surprised to see Bowes appearing from behind him, hand over hand down the backstay, the quickest route.

'It's the squadron, Sir.' Bowes addressed the captain as a matter of course, with no sign of a shortage of breath.

'Thank, you, Mr Bowes – back to your post, young man.' Winchip nodded to Niven. *Eaglet*'s number would be on the halyard as they spoke.

The prospect of coming up with the Western Squadron, no matter how brief the visit, had a different meaning for some than for others. Winchip, not even sure he would be called upon to see Admiral Byng, was aware his orders would take him onwards, to perform a different task from that of blockade duty. As for those who wondered what lay ahead, they would have to wait – it would come soon enough.

It was another hour before Winchip could discern the flagship with her few consorts. Other ships would be below the horizon. There would be signals aplenty, he had no doubt, and work to be done if they were not to disgrace themselves.

If there were a need to demonstrate the wealth of a nation in one dramatic gesture, the Western Squadron was well equipped to do it, although a closer inspection might reveal the ravages of blockade duty, keeping the French bottled up in port in the face of the prevailing westerlies. Not only were the French prevented from leaving harbour, they were also losing sea time; time in which to train their sailors for the expected invasion of England.

It was from *Ramillies*, a ninety-gun Second Rate, that Admiral of the Blue, John Byng flew his flag high on the main masthead truck. Keeping attendance was Rear-Admiral Temple West in the *Buckingham*, a sixty-eight-gun ship of two decks. A few lesser ships were scattered to leeward, facing into the wind as if waiting for orders, swinging like pendulums in the choppy sea. Sails were against the mast, white in the slate-blue greyness of the horizon.

Winchip passed through the ornate entry port, set into the tumblehome of *Ramillies*, with his coat tails flapping in the wind. He was met by the flag-lieutenant, head bowed beneath the deck above, with the look of a man who preferred to be on the quarterdeck than the confines of the gun deck below.

'Welcome on board *Ramillies*, Sir.' The benign smile was probably reserved for post-captains.

'Thank you, Lieutenant.' There was little else to say. Winchip handed over his orders and despatches. A moment later he was looking at the man's back as he led the way upwards.

Winchip stepped into the bright contrast of light from the blackness below, as would an actor onto a stage. Suddenly he was among the bustle of a great ship-of-the-line, the very innards of a leviathan with no time to take it in. Just glimpses of great guns, of men, cordage and furled canvas. He saw Captain Arthur Gardiner at once – the weather-beaten face with the slightly lopsided grin and the self-effacing expression that was his style in any conversation. The hair was greying a little more but, other than that, it was the same welcome face of an old friend. He was standing by the huge double wheel, with that certain grin already brightening his face.

'It is good to see you again, Sir.' Winchip stepped forward, his hand outstretched. Their last meeting was when Gardiner had been flag-captain to Admiral Rowley in the Mediterranean. He all but pumped the man's hand.

'And I to see you, Captain.' Gardiner's grin had become a beaming smile. 'Shall we go through to the stateroom – where we can talk in peace? I think the admiral is sure to want to see you. He has your orders and despatches, hungry for news, as always.'

The stateroom was set aside from the great cabin like an ante-room. A place of many uses, it was sparsely furnished with a low table and a scattering of comfortable chairs; nothing that couldn't be removed in an instant should the ship go to quarters.

They talked as friends, recalling and reminiscing, Madeira in hand, Gardiner bellowing his delight at the news of the victuals, presently on their way across. They filled in the time with a will until the admiral was free. It was when the flag-lieutenant appeared, nodding his head to Captain Gardiner, that they rose. Winchip followed the lieutenant – like a lamb to the slaughter.

The door opened to a cabin basking in a backdrop of light from the row of stern windows stretching from one side of the deck to the other and the quarter windows that billowed out from the corners. Under the centre windows the admiral sat at the great table. Byng was studiously writing, the scratching of the nib in the silent cabin akin to a dog pawing at the door. Sitting at such a huge expanse of polished wood, the loneliness of the admiral's rank came immediately to Winchip's mind. Striding the few paces across the stark black and white chequered floor, his hat tucked neatly beneath his arm, he stood before the table, his palm resting lightly on the pummel of his sword. His eye cast briefly aft through the stern windows, towards the *Buckingham*, wrestling with the breeze merely to retain her position. His eyes jerked downwards as Byng spoke.

'My apologies, Captain. Be seated if you will and oblige me for a minute longer.' The admiral waved a hand that gave Winchip license to sit where he pleased. 'What would we do without the written word, eh?' The pen resumed its attack upon the paper.

Winchip, only able to consider the benefits of life without the written word, sat in a chair that offered him shadow from the light. An opportunity to take in his surroundings without the glare.

He was immediately struck by the difference between the great cabin of *Eaglet* and that of *Ramillies*. The wide expanse of flooring, unembellished by coverings, did something to enhance the quality of the ornate woodwork about the walls, the carved knees and even the ribs, where exposed, all painted and rubbed to a shining black. The furnishings, although short of Spartan, had been chosen for their practical use rather than ornamentation. They were the choice of a man who held no notion of bettering his peers, nor impressing them. There were no signs of affectation. What he could see was there for a purpose and little beyond that. It was a habitation befitting his rank and no more. The great table, surrounded by chairs, laying bare and unused, save for the admiral, seemed to be waiting for occupancy – sprawling figures, brandy and the haze of smoke in the air. With Admiral Byng it had assumed a baser use, a simple desk, silent and practical, the sheen of its polished surface reflecting the light. Beeswax and tallow, the expected aroma of the place, was relieved by an open sash window looking out onto the gallery, a walkway for the use of the occupant, accessible by a door through which his privacy was assured. Perhaps Byng's gallery was Winchip's stern seat.

At last the admiral finished writing and sat upright, wiping the quill and replacing it in the small oak and silver stand with deliberation. 'Ah! Captain Winchip – my apologies for keeping you.' Byng gave an imperceptible inclination of the head. 'Captain Gardiner has told me so much about you that I feel I know you already.' Byng leaned forward, his total attention devoted to Winchip. 'How was Plymouth?' The question seemed perfunctory.

Winchip laid his hat on the table. 'Busy, Admiral. In the Hamoaze there were fewer ships in ordinary than of late.'

'Hmm, I'm delighted to hear it. Perhaps someone has recognised England's need for ships at last.'

The question had not been so casual after all. Winchip kept his gaze as Byng looked up at him, knowing he would need his wits about him. There was a depth to this man he had yet to fathom.

'How do you find the new frigate?'

'She handles very well, Admiral, even if a little slower than I was led to believe. However, I know she will give a good account of herself, if and when the need arises.' Winchip tumbled out the statutory reply as he chose claret from the steward's tray. He could understand Byng's interest. Already, England was looking to such vessels in earnest. The admiral had obviously read the despatches thoroughly.

'I am sure she will, Captain. The first, perhaps, in a long line of new frigates. Stronger, faster and more heavily armed.' Byng leaned back and took a sip of wine. 'The business of *Capable* was regrettable, of course.' It almost finished as a question.

Winchip's response was immediate, as it had to be. 'She did her duty, Sir, as did my people.'

'Of course she did, my dear Winchip. I have a feeling *Ramillies* might have found you a hard nut to crack! To cripple a ship twice your size . . .' Byng spread his hands, leaving the sentence unfinished.

Winchip smiled, the crow's-feet round his eyes bursting into life.

Byng looked at him directly, a slight grin on his face. 'I am aware of the circumstances of the court martial, Captain. We are not totally isolated out here, you know. I can only say that many of us have been caught in a similar situation, yet here we are, struggling on, the matter closed and long since forgotten.' He tapped his fingers on the table. 'Learn to forget, my dear Winchip, let the Almighty sort it out. Not only does He have the experience, He also has the power, but in His case He knows how to exercise it fairly, if you take my meaning.'

For a moment Winchip was speechless. 'I understand perfectly, Admiral.' He was not sure that he did, unless the admiral had had dealings with Captain Rance in the past.

'Good. Then it may surprise you to know that Captain Rance has been attached to the Western Squadron. He is due here in a few days, after his visit to Their Lordships at Admiralty.' Byng raised his eyes without lifting his head. 'I shall dwell no more on the affair except to say that the matter is done with and, it will *stay* that way.' He adjusted himself in his chair and shuffled the papers before him with unnecessary vigour before selecting Winchip's despatches and peering at them closely.

'I understand, Sir.' There was little else to be said. That Byng had mentioned the matter at all had come as a shock. Affairs between mere captains were not usually discussed at an admiral's table.

Winchip had been looking closely at this man who, in the short space of time he had been off Brest, seemed to be continuing with relish the war of attrition being carried out by Lord Hawke against France. It was, in Byng's case however, the continuance of another's initiative, not his own. Even in his periwig, which he seemed to wear reluctantly, as did many others, Byng's face could change from pleasure to severity without losing the effect of his penetrating eyes.

Or the raised eyebrows that helped to form and maintain that expression, learned no doubt during his many years of experience. It seemed to be an inborn reluctance to become transparent before others. Rather that his expression said nothing; nought to fear and nought to encourage. His mouth, when relaxed, was a thin line, his nose long in proportion to his heavy face, which itself was drawn in by the start of a double chin. He was rather, one could say, heavily built but not seeming to be tall for all that, even from a sitting position. Winchip had taken a liking to him on face value and, for him, that was enough. What was beneath would be revealed with time. Was this highly respected admiral a man who sought stability, who liked things to be orderly? Preferred to act through consensus perhaps, rather than his own instincts? It was a moot question, the answer allowing only hindsight to reveal the truth. His record would seem to deny these things, but Winchip was not convinced.

'You mentioned the lack of a surgeon in your reports.' Byng read it as a statement of fact. 'I have allocated you a good, qualified assistant who should be boarding your vessel as we speak – name of Pollard, looking for a berth.'

'That is most kind of you, Sir.' It was certainly a relief, although the crew might think otherwise. A surgeon was the last man on earth a jack with a wounded leg would want to see.

'I am informed that he is one of those new breed of radicals who think that fresh, new air is better than that which is warm, tested and proven.' Byng waved an arm as if to brush away a fly. 'I am no physician, but – ' Another sentence left unfinished. 'He also has ideas about cleanliness, a subject with which I wholly agree. It keeps the lice away, don't ye know? You may find it more prudent to indulge the fellow than argue but that is for you to decide. They do, of course, have certain inviolable rights, which we are bound to respect, but then, so do we, do we not?' Byng seemed gratified to hear a short laugh from Winchip.

'I am obliged to you, Admiral.' Any surgeon was better

than no surgeon at all. A good one was a bonus, radical or not.

A creak in the woodwork prompted Winchip to glance towards the stern windows. The wind had veered, just as Mr Ramblin had predicted. The ships were either turning on their cables or working hard to keep position, giving each captain a fresh view. He took a further sip of his claret – another French contribution to the admiral's table.

'Now, as to your orders.' Byng was holding the paper up to the light from the stern windows. 'This man Foche you are picking up from Rochefort is a spy. Let us get that clear before we go any further. He has been of great service to our country over the years, I am informed.' Byng looked at Winchip directly. 'Do not be overawed by all this clandestine stuff, Captain. No confidences, eh? Do we understand each other?'

'I understand perfectly, Sir.' Winchip was gratified to realise that Byng had no more liking for spying than he did. This was the first time Foche's name had been mentioned. He had a suspicion it wouldn't be the last.

'There is another thing you should know.' Admiral Byng tapped his fingers on the table, trying to find the words for what he was about to say. 'We may not be at war with France yet, Captain, but I have to tell you, had you been privy to the activities on this station you could be forgiven for thinking otherwise.'

'Your successes have not gone unnoticed at home, Sir.' Winchip wondered how many French prisoners were at that moment whittling away at scrimshaw as they languished in an English prison.

Byng smiled, standing as he did so, at the same time indicating that Winchip should stay seated. He moved to the end of the stern windows, looking obliquely towards the spot where *Eaglet* should be. 'She is a fine vessel, Winchip. It would be a pity to lose her, especially if it were because we were forced to play to the rules.' He turned and faced Winchip. 'Do you understand my meaning?'

Winchip understood better than most. 'I understand you

perfectly, Admiral. The problem is that we English find it difficult *not* to play to the rules. It will take a brave man to fire the first shot – in a time of peace that is.' *Capable* sprang to mind, waiting with dread to see if the *Frenchman* would fire upon him.

'The answer is to put court martials out of your mind.' Byng smiled again, as if glad that the meat of the subject was now ready for carving. 'In the time it takes you to consider the consequences, your fate could be sealed. Yours, and perhaps two hundred others!'

'You put a powerful argument, Sir. One thing that you can be sure of is that when the time comes, I shall do my duty, as will my officers. I cannot see them worrying about court martials when there is a promise of promotion in the offing.'

'Well spoken.' Byng returned to his chair at the table. 'Be careful. Trust no man, and be prepared – always prepared.' He said the last in a quieter tone, as if recalling some past event. Byng raised his cut-glass goblet, his smile broad and resigned as if to expunge a sombre memory. 'I wish you luck, Captain. As I say, we are not at war. Should you be fired upon, however – log it. Then do as you damned well please!'

Winchip nodded slowly, a sardonic smile creeping across his face at the irony of Byng's statement, knowing full well where the blame would lie if things went badly, as he had found out, almost to his cost. Byng rose from his chair, prompting Winchip to do likewise. The meeting had been brief, as he would have expected. It seemed that for the few words spoken, a great deal had been said. Perhaps his additional orders, if any, would say even more. One thing was for certain – he would soon know.

3

A Distasteful Business

Winchip gazed out of the cabin windows, watching *Eaglet*'s wake as it disappeared into the vague greyness of the rising swell. The last ship of the Western Squadron had long since dropped below the horizon, leaving only memories of an interesting meeting. He separated the tails of his coat and sat at the stern seat, drawing a chart of the French coast towards him. He placed a weight on each corner and then took out his orders from the top drawer of the small Gillow desk.

Admiral Byng's comments had inferred that war with France was even closer than Winchip thought. The block-ading of French ports, the wholesale capture of merchant shipping and the confrontations in The Americas, had all contributed to a high degree of hostility, requiring only the stroke of a pen to turn it into a reality. He wondered whether the task he was about to perform would bring things even closer to a head.

A small change in the ship's attitude brought Winchip's thoughts back to the present. Raising himself from the seat, he put on his deck coat and hat and went to the companion, the short way to the quarterdeck.

Ignoring the officer of the watch, conferring with others down at the binnacle, he strolled up to the taffrail. The wind had changed but a mite and yet hands were already in the tops with others gathering to starboard and larboard, ready to haul the yards round if called on to do so. All was well. There was no need for his guidance, even though he knew his presence had been noted. He allowed his mind to go back to another war, in another time and place. He had been eighteen when news of his father's death had turned his world upside down, leaving his mother almost penniless. While Vice-Admiral Vernon had been completing his capture of Porto Bello, in Panama, his father had been struck down with yellow-jack on a rescue mission in the lakes above Balboa. It was his father's sponsor who had helped Winchip to sea, albeit to a cruel ship with memories to match.

Winchip knew he was suddenly gripping the taffrail with white knuckles, looking down the wake of the ship as if it were his past life spewing out into nothingness. A midshipman at eighteen, his late entry into the navy was virtually a declaration of problems in the family when even the age of fourteen was considered late in life to start a naval career. His only consolation lay in the fact that he was never bullied. Sought out, perhaps, by midshipmen who lived in fear of the gunroom, giving help and encouragement to them as best he could. The captain had been a hard man, a disciplinarian, prone to extravagances of punishment. If it had been hard for the common seaman, then it was even harder for the midshipmen who found themselves paying frequent visits to the 'gunner's daughter' – strapped unceremoniously across a gun and then caned until the blood dripped.

He took a deep breath, ridding himself of the memories and the hardships, vowing no ship would suffer so under his captaincy! He slapped his hand down on the rail as if to reaffirm that vow, sending a gull screeching from the window ledge below him.

There had been another side to things. His rise to command had been swift, for reasons unknown. Perhaps he had been in the right place at the right time. Whatever the reasons, he had found that each new responsibility, each new command, had sat well upon his shoulders. Even the temporary commands, bringing back captured ships to England. That was how he had been confirmed into his first ship, his beloved sloop, *Pipette*.

Winchip stood upright, gripping his hands behind his back. Maria's death and that of his unborn son had been a blow from which he thought he could never recover. It had been Emma who had brought him out of his melancholy, had seen in him a father too long torn with grief. When he was sad, so she would be. When he mourned she would lapse into silence. He had begun to see a reflection of himself in her, as if his attitude was affecting hers. From that moment, the mourning had stopped. Only the good moments had been allowed to surface. Now, Emma was suffering a sadness of her own. She was at an age when she needed her mother, needed a mentor of greater wisdom than dear old Beth could provide. He paced across the camber of the deck. It was a problem for which he knew he had no cure.

The cold and steady easterly was bringing the surface of the sea alive with spindrift, flying from the crests of precocious wavelets breaking before their time. There was no beauty in the scene, a colourless void that brought no hope of warmth and only a damp coldness to those who sought anything better.

'Good morning, Sir.' Niven came up to Winchip's side, a glass tucked neatly beneath his arm. 'We have a sighting. Two French merchants, heavy laden by Costly's account.' Niven pointed over the starboard quarter, his finger high to indicate distance, handing the glass over in one movement.

Winchip peered through the glass at the inverted image of the two vessels. 'Straight into the arms of Admiral Byng. They'll make a fine catch.' He looked more closely. 'Out of The Americas I would say.' Winchip lowered the glass. 'All that distance to finish up in an English prison.' He shook his head as if already suffering the plight of her captain. He returned the glass to the first lieutenant.

Niven staggered and looked down at his feet as *Eaglet* dropped into a trough like a stone. 'She's rigid with the holds so full, Sir, and the roll doesn't help in this quarter sea.'

'The ship is a living thing, Lieutenant, not beyond a little artifice when the mood takes her.' Winchip turned to leeward, taking the chill from the side of his face. 'I shall go below. Ask Mr Pope to attend me in my cabin, if you please.'

'Eight bells' was clearly audible from forward. Niven hurried down the quarterdeck in time to hand over the watch. A tipping of cocked hats and a brief exchange of words, fashioned by tradition.

In the great cabin, the cold and dampness seemed to permeate the very vitals of the place. The unwelcome but brief easterly was, for now, remaining constant and, if anything, even colder. The damp had turned to blatant rain as Winchip and Senior Midshipman Pope pored over the chart of Rochefort, the sound of the weather beating and rattling against the stern windows giving them cause to raise their voices.

'This, Mr Pope, is the Island of Oléron. You will see it hides the estuary of the River Charente on which stands Rochefort.' Winchip moved to one side, allowing Pope access to the chart and the light of the lamp to see it by.

'Yes, Sir, I see where you mean.' Pope peered down at the chart. 'Is this the spit of land, north of the estuary, pointing north-west?' Pope looked pleased with himself, chosen above others to take part in his first boat action, no doubt. He was not to realise that Winchip was testing him; giving him a chance to prove his worth.

'That is the one, young man. That is where you will be going.' Winchip sat down in his chair. 'I have every confidence in you, Mr Pope. Remember what I said earlier. On no account are you to be led into conversation with this man. Do I make myself clear?'

'Yes, Sir. Quite clear, Sir.' The midshipman's sandy hair brushed the deck above as he straightened.

'Good.' Winchip stood again. 'In that case, that will be all until nearer the time.'

Winchip waited until Pope had left the cabin before returning to the chart. He sought a likely place for an anchorage. He had suspected his best option was the small islet of Aix. A busy little place with many scattered fishermen's dwellings and a small, white church. There were two forts, south and north, known to him on previous excursions. He considered his options, drumming his fingers lightly on the table. He decided that at night, displaying a French ensign would be the sensible course. He dwelt on it, seeking options before making up his mind. It was worth the risk. It was also a place of tidal rocks, with shoaling but offering sea room. He would also have to anchor with bare poles, or be seen. It was not a good choice of rendezvous, but that was out of his hands. Small French forts were scattered about the place like raindrops on a pond and the small town of Fouras threateningly close. Fortunately, only the ship's launch would need to venture into the shoals.

He suppressed a feeling of doubt about Pope. It was too late. His mind also considered the possibility of a trap. He knew nothing of the man called Foche. This, too, he dashed from his mind. Orders were orders. Others would be left to worry about the consequences.

A sudden realisation came to him. It was because of his knowledge of these waters that he had been given this task. The loss of *Capable* had brought him to the attention of Their Lordships at Admiralty, and now here he was, the reaper of his own misfortune. He shook his head in despair, seeing his future laid out before him, each chapter dependent upon the last, each event triggering another, *ad infinitum.*

At three bells into the second dog-watch, the master, Niven and Pope sat in silence in the great cabin as Winchip outlined his orders. The small confines were already becoming humid with the heat from their bodies, each of them clutching a hot toddy to his chest, as much to warm the hands as the inner man. The yellow light from the lanterns was playing upon their faces, moving with the motion of the ship, their shadows giving the illusion of fiendish plotters or a macabre dance.

'I'm almost tempted to say that this crew is as ready as it

ever will be. However, that can lead to complacency.' Winchip smiled at the trickle of nervous laughter. 'Mr Pope will be in charge of the boat, supported by four marines with Corporal Basson. As for *Eaglet*, she will lie to the north-east of Aix where we can catch the offshore wind at dawn if we need to depart in a hurry.' He looked at Pope. 'It will be a long haul, Mr Pope, but a steady pull will see you there and back *without* any unnecessary urging, if you understand me?' Winchip was aware of Pope's tendency to make life harder than it need be for those in his charge.

'Aye, Sir.'

'Very well.' Winchip gave a nod of satisfaction. 'Lastly, gentlemen, we shall have a visitor in the morning. He is a Frenchman who wishes to speak with Their Lordships. While he is on this vessel he is to communicate with no one. I hope that is clear.' Winchip caught the eye of each. 'Having said that, he is to be treated with courtesy. After all, he is supposed to be a friend – for the moment.' He waited for the laughter to subside. 'If our visitor wants any information, and these people seem to thrive on it, then he is not going to get it from us! Thank you, gentlemen, that is all.'

Winchip stood as they gathered to go, watching them as they passed out of the cabin. Both lanterns were swinging in unison, keeping time with *Eaglet* as she pitched to the head sea, yawing as she rose and then plummeting again, close hauled, towards her rendezvous at dawn.

Eaglet tacked smoothly between the islands of Ré and Oléron, with the night as dark as soot. As eight bells rang out to end the middle watch, Niven winced, convinced that the sound had been heard for miles around. With fore-jib, fore-tops'l and reefed driver the ship barely made headway.

'By the mark, seven.' The cry was subdued, the presence of the French shoreline intimidating in its darkness and mystery.

Winchip stood on the bulwark, wedged firmly against the

shrouds. The pre-dawn darkness was lingering, indicative of heavy cloud cover, the air now slow moving and heavy, a precursor of weather yet to come.

He rested the night glass on the ratline and peered ahead. Winchip could make out the island of Aix, a faint white line of breakers giving her away. He decided to anchor on the north-eastern side, within a few cables of Fort Liedot yet in sight of the spit, with a large French ensign decorating the gaff halyard, despite its whiteness. No ship's captain, other than the French, would be in their right mind doing such a thing.

'By the mark, seven.' The call had become a hoarse whisper.

Winchip cocked an ear. The quicker, slapping sound coming from the bow meant shoaling. Raising the glass he peered forwards, looking for the spit above the mouth of the Charante – and then saw it, confused but there, melting into the dark mass of land about it.

'This will do, Master. Bring her up.' Winchip looked to Niven. 'We can see the spit from here.'

'By the mark, five – less a bit.' The information came in hushed tones, man to man.

'Get the sail off her!' Winchip said it with some urgency. 'Then ease the anchor.' Too far and all would be lost. Stuck on a bar like a mess of flotsam. Winchip raised the glass towards Fort Liedot. A single twinkle of light showed modestly, probably a fisherman's lamp. He nearly slammed the glass shut. 'This seems to be ideal, Mr Niven. We have the sea room and a light breeze to hang onto, providing the wind doesn't change and turn it into a lee shore.' Winchip knew it was unlikely, but the thought of being embayed lived in dread with him as it did every captain afloat.

They waited for thirty minutes before the signal came: two lights, one above the other, just above the surface line. The lights were constant, judged by Niven to be on the northern tip of the long spit, the best part of a mile away, leading down to Fouras and then on to the estuary of the Charante and Rochefort.

'I see them!' Winchip lowered the glass and looked eastward, seeking a dawn that wouldn't come. 'Have the launch manned – cutlasses and pistols, loaded at the last moment. I want no accidents.'

Winchip watched as the launch sank below the bulwarks with a series of jerks and too many squeals. A seaman was on board, clutching at the chains, fending the boat off as it started to swing.

'Remind Mr Pope, he is to leave at the first sign of treachery, or if he is in the least bit unhappy about the situation.' As an afterthought, Winchip added, 'Send down Mr Piper – for the experience.' He smiled as the youngest midshipman on board, his mouth agape, no doubt wondering if he had heard a'right, scuttled over the bulwark and disappeared into space. It would give the lad confidence; give him a feeling of belonging. Winchip was glad he had thought of it.

Winchip watched as Midshipman Costly showed the lantern for a brief moment, glad to see the lights on the spit respond and then flicker out. He stared into the darkness, seeing the last glimmer of stern water turn to nothing as the boat disappeared into the night. At least the four marines and the stocky Corporal Basson would provide a degree of protection.

The time passed slowly, the hands on Winchip's timepiece taking an age to journey from one minute to the next. Frequent glances at the dark shape of Fort Liedot, benign and yet still menacing some three cables distant, did nothing to calm his fears. Lights were appearing there in turn as the fort prepared to greet the new day. The tinny sound of a trumpet turned his blood to water for a moment until he realised it was the reveille.

Winchip paced the quarterdeck. An hour and still the boat had not returned. He could hear the leadsman passing his findings to the next in line until the sounding reached the first lieutenant. By the whisper, he deduced that the tide was still on the make. It would be a backbreaking exercise at the oars for the returning boat. He heard Niven dismiss the leadsman. At the same time a mate came to report four bells, the bell itself long since silent.

Winchip glanced to the sky in the east. On the landward horizon, low to the ground, a thin copper-red line could be seen – a shepherd's warning.

'Ahoy!' The faint call rasped out of the darkness.

There was sudden movement amidships and the sound of padding feet. The entry port hand line was flung over, clattering alarmingly as the knotted ropes struck the tumblehome. It was then that Niven came panting aft.

'The launch has returned, Sir.'

'Come!' Winchip strode to the entry port. The boatswain was close by, not sure if salutes would be required, looking for guidance. Winchip caught his eye, shaking his head to tell the man what he needed to know, allowing him and the marines to melt away into the background.

Senior Midshipman Pope came first, struggling clumsily through the entry port, his sword clattering across the step. His face was a white mask in the pre-dawn darkness. Even his salute was forgotten as he stood stock-still, mouthing words that refused to come.

Niven stepped forward, standing with purpose between Pope and the captain. 'What the hell is wrong, Mr Pope? Speak, man!' Niven's words came out in a harsh whisper, a mixture of anger and confusion.

'There's a . . . a lady on the b . . . boat, Sir. Sh . . . she said she was expected, Sir. I . . . I didn't know what to do.' Pope's confusion was absolute, his confidence in tatters.

'Is she the only person on the boat?' Niven's voice was a harsh whisper.

'N . . . no, Sir. There's a . . . a Frenchman, Sir.'

'Thank the Lord for that!' Niven stared at Pope, knowing the whole deck was hanging on his next move. 'Then let us have them on board – *as quick as you damn well like*!' He spun round to speak to Winchip, his face flushed with suppressed anger. 'Sir, the Frenchman is on his way up.

There is also a lady, Sir. We cannot take her back so I have ordered them on board.'

Winchip nodded, his thoughts tumbling one upon the other. Niven was right, of course. There was no way in which the woman, whoever she was, could be taken back. He knew his face looked like thunder but he didn't care. He said nothing. He merely stepped back and waited.

Niven moved aside as Piper came through the posts. The diminutive midshipman turned back to help a struggling figure over the bulwarks, pushed from behind by Corporal Basson.

Winchip waited for the small, dumpy man to put himself to rights. Having decided that decorum had long since left the proceedings he took two paces down to the dishevelled and puffing Frenchman.

Foche looked up at Winchip. 'I am Gaspar Foche, Captain. At your service.' The man was shivering in the cold wind and out of breath, his hands tucked under his armpits, accentuating the lack of any baggage or effects. His attire was dapper, silken green in both breeches and jacket, his head topped with one of the newfangled pork pie hats, now askew and looking the worse for a trip or two to the boat's scuppers no doubt. His expensive ruffle was awry as were his stockings. The result was not impressive.

'Good morning, Sir. I am Captain Winchip of His Britannic Majesty's frigate, *Eaglet*. Welcome on board.' He turned to Niven as if the spy didn't exist. 'Get us away from this place! North-west until we are clear of the land.'

'North-west aye, Sir.' Niven waited. There had to be more.

'When the woman comes on board, have her put in the care of the surgeon and prepare a space for her in the stateroom.' It was at that moment she arrived on the deck, tall and with bearing, wrapped in a modest cloak and carrying a small valise, looking about her with the fear of a fallow deer, yet trying not to show it. Her pale, frightened face was framed in locks of long dark hair. He found himself struck by the woman's manner, especially under such trying circumstances. For a moment they locked eyes and Winchip saw only fear and despair competing with pride and dignity, a mess of conflictions.

He turned away, back to the waiting Foche. 'If you would care to accompany me to my cabin . . .' Winchip strode aft, leaving Foche to follow in his wake.

Once in the comparative warmth of the cabin, Winchip threw his cloak onto the old chest. The sound of *Eaglet* preparing for sea disallowed any immediate sensible conversation. The need for quiet was now past. Through the stern window the first dull orange streaks of dawn were on the horizon, offering little light, merely prefacing the day yet to come. Through the deck light the ordered tread of the men on the braces was like thunder, coming closer and closer. He rounded the table and sagged into the stern seat, letting his pent-up rage dissolve, as he knew it must.

'So, Monsieur Foche, you have something for me, I believe.' As Winchip spoke so Booth entered with hot coffee. He appeared flustered, an harassed expression which aged even further his careworn face. Winchip ignored Booth's plight of having a woman thrust upon him and simply nodded to his questioning eyebrow, at the same time holding up a hand to prevent Foche speaking, waiting for the servant to scuttle back through the curtain.

'Captain, the information I have is for Their Lordships alone, and is here . . .' Foche pointed a finger at his own head. 'I cannot afford to commit anything to paper.' He took a sip of the coffee, savouring the first taste, gripping the cup with both hands for the warmth, his attitude seeking to assume dominance of the conversation now that he was gathering his wits and composure.

'That seems a precaution fraught with danger, Monsieur. Should anything happen to you, then the . . .' Winchip stopped, suddenly seeing Foche's reasoning. He was quick to realise he was dealing with matters he knew very little about.

'Exactly, Captain! Exactly!' Foche leaned back in his chair, a self-satisfied expression on his face. 'Alors! It is my only protection!' His free hand described a foppish circle. His expression had become smug.

Looking at the problem pragmatically, Winchip decided that further discussion at this stage would serve little purpose. That Foche was adamant, was obvious. As far as Winchip was concerned Their Lordships could have him. He rose and turned to look aft where the darkness was beginning to turn into light. The island of Oléron was slipping past to larboard. In fifteen minutes they would be on the open sea.

'What about the woman, Monsieur? Am I supposed to guess about her as well?' Winchip carried on staring through the stern window, his back to Foche.

'She is English, Captain – a Miss Loxley.' If Foche expected a reaction he didn't get one. 'Her brother, James Loxley, has been found guilty of spying for the English. He has been shot to death. As for Miss Loxley, I was in a position to help her escape lest she, too, should be accused.'

Winchip turned to face Foche, his voice rising as much in anger as surprise. 'Shot to death? Accused? Of what, surely not of spying?' He didn't give Foche the chance to confirm his statement. He couldn't imagine that proud face and magnificent English bearing being guilty of anything, let alone spying. 'Sentry!'

The door opened almost immediately. The sentry took one step into the cabin. 'Sah!'

'Pass the word for Lieutenant Gray.'

'Sah!' The sentry slipped from sight.

Winchip sat at the table and waited, quite content to allow the silence to weigh down the atmosphere until it was leaden. He wanted rid of the man until his own thoughts cleared. The knock came soon enough.

'Enter!'

'You sent for me, Sir.' The sharp features, dark moustache and bright red tunic of Lieutenant of Marines Gray brought both colour and sanity to the cabin.

'Yes, Mr Gray. This gentleman is to be taken to the first officer's quarters where he will remain until we reach England. He is to be given every courtesy and ablutions, but guarded at all times and will communicate with no one but yourself or your nominee.'

'Very good, Sir.' Gray waited, his eyes taking in every detail of Foche, any feelings well hidden.

Winchip turned to the little Frenchman. 'My first lieutenant has been gracious enough to turn over his space for your use, Monsieur Foche. It is small, but private.' He abandoned the man to Lieutenant Gray, ignoring the first hint of blusterings as Foche was politely but firmly removed. Grabbing his cloak, Winchip made for the companion, denying Foche his moment of conversational ascendancy. What he needed was air – a great deal of it.

4

Madeleine

Madeleine Loxley sat across the desk from Winchip. Her modest green dress was very becoming, even if somewhat crumpled from her recent ordeal. Her neatly combed, shining black hair, tied back and falling like a pony's tail, exposed the full contours of her beautiful oval face. Her nut-brown eyes would have increased her beauty further had they been wide open and innocent. As it was they were half closed, argumentative, smouldering, expecting the worst and on the defensive. It was as if her attitude were a continuation of events, as if the boat trip had been a mere interlude. Winchip, wondering what had taken place immediately prior to her coming on board, was totally perplexed. Imperceptibly, he shook his head.

She had transformed herself and completed her ablutions in the stateroom, small as it was. The large cup of coffee, embraced by her long pale fingers, seemed coarse and brutal in her delicate hands. She was, in all respects, a beautiful woman.

Whatever his initial thoughts and feelings, he felt uncomfortable about her. Her general attitude, despite the situation and her genuine anger, gave him one impression, while beneath her façade there was something else, something that was beyond her control – that, and an abject fear of something or somebody.

Winchip had mellowed in the hour she had been on board. He had no liking for surprises but her distress had plucked a chord in him that had found an instant response. As she drank her coffee, his train of thought steered towards the unfortunate Pope. For a moment he almost felt sorry for the midshipman, his first boat action turned into chaos before his eyes, a circumstance both unexpected and beyond the limits of his wits. He would soon put it behind him, just as Winchip knew he could not bring him to task because of it. As for Madeleine Loxley, well, better by far to hear her side of the story and then make his decision as to what to do about her. He had assessed her age at about thirty. Old enough to be responsible for her actions and yet young enough to give little thought to the consequences. He leaned back in the chair and looked at her directly.

'My name is Daniel Winchip, Ma'am. You are on board His Britannic Majesty's frigate *Eaglet*, of which I am the captain.' Winchip gave the faintest bow of the head, enough to satisfy the niceties.

'And I am Madeleine Anne Loxley, Captain. I . . .'

Winchip raised his hand, cutting her off before it became a speech. All would come to light in good time. 'So, Miss Loxley, I think you had better start at the beginning, don't you?' Winchip afforded her a smile, seeing her shoulders relax a little and her eyes close momentarily as if in relief at his congenial attitude. She had looked as if she expected him to be angry and yet had seemed quite prepared to defend her position.

'I'm not sure where to begin, Captain.' Her eyes seemed to fill with water as the time came to recall events. With each idle swing of the dying lantern, they glistened brightly. She took the handkerchief from Winchip's outstretched hand and dabbed her eyes hurriedly. 'Thank you.' Raising her head, she looked at him and continued. 'My brother, Stephen, and I have lived in France for a number of years. Stephen is – was – a marine architect and had been helping the French with commercial harbour construction for all that time, including the improvement of the salt production around this area.' She took a sip of her coffee and then, after a deep breath, continued. 'We have known Monsieur Foche for some time. He came to lodge with us a few years ago and has returned to do so many times after his travels abroad.' She took another sip and pulled herself upright as if to confirm her composure – or to speak of something she knew she couldn't keep back. 'Two weeks ago the French took my brother and he was accused of spying for the English. I protested his innocence, insisted upon it but it was to no avail. He has since been tried, according to Monsieur Foche, and has been found guilty.' She bowed her head. 'Last night Monsieur Foche told me he had been shot to death.' The tears came freely, her slim body wracked with anguish. She was obviously overcome by events she couldn't believe possible. Her composure was reduced to a state of utter despair.

'I am so sorry. You have my deepest sympathy.' Winchip rose from his chair and went round to her, wanting to comfort her, to put his arms about her, and yet he could not bring himself to do it. Instead, he laid a hand tentatively on her shoulder.

'Thank, you.' Madeleine Loxley closed her eyes and bowed her head, the handkerchief pressed against her eyes as if she was trying to blot out all that had happened. 'I . . . I'm so sorry. I tried so hard to be brave but –.' She looked up at him and covered his hand with hers. 'I have embarrassed you, haven't I?' She removed her hand and stared into her lap.

'Of course not. You have done no such thing. I . . . I find it hard to know what to do for the best, that is all.' Winchip found himself floundering. It was the same with all things outside the perimeters of shipboard life. 'My heart goes out to you, Miss Loxley. You must bear in mind, however, that I have to make a report as to what has happened and to do that I must have answers.' Winchip saw an avenue of escape. 'Is Mr Pollard seeing to your needs? It is not easy to accommodate a lady aboard this vessel, as you must realise.' He used the little brass bell to ring for Booth as he spoke.

'Yes, thank you. He is the perfect gentleman.'

'Then we shall talk later, at dinner, if that suits you?'

'Thank you. I look forward to it, Captain.' She rose to her feet, doing her utmost to recover her composure. 'I am so sorry to have burdened you with my problems but I had no other option, no other recourse.'

At that moment, for the first time, she looked directly at Winchip. Even with the redness of her eyes as a result of what had been genuine grief, he could discern a cry for help. More than that, her whole being was racked by something still left unsaid; something she was frightened to reveal to him.

Before another word could be said, Booth appeared as if from nowhere, ready to show her back to the tiny stateroom where he had seen to her needs.

From the stern window Winchip could just see the Isle de Ré slipping past to starboard in the faint light of dawn. The tiny white houses of Ars appeared with each trough and then vanished as the next rolling crest obscured them from view. At least they now had sea room and deep water. Room to manoeuvre whatever the eventuality. Satisfied, he grabbed his cloak and hat and made for the companion ladder.

'The offshore breeze is still with us, Sir. Mr Ramblin thinks the weather may deteriorate shortly.' Niven moved aside as Winchip approached the binnacle.

'Very well, Lieutenant. Keep sharp lookouts in each quarter, if you please.' Winchip's caution was heightened by the ease with which the mission had been accomplished. In his book, for every success a price had to be paid.

Easterly or southerly, either wind would serve their purpose. To the east, above the land, the copper-red strip that Winchip had seen earlier was now the colour of watered blood, higher in the sky, denying even the first glimmer of the sun as the black clouds of the night turned to thunderous clouds by day. The whole eastern sky gave promise of dire weather yet to come. The moment he had formed his conclusion the ship gave a sudden lurch to leeward. He staggered towards the weather side and looked instinctively to the tops. The weather-vane was prancing about like a conductor's baton.

'I think the master may be right, Mr Niven.' Winchip

nodded towards the approaching weather from the land and then caught Niven's eye. 'Mother Nature seems to have something in store for us. If she has the goodness to warn us, I think we should have the courtesy to listen. We shall bring her down to tops'ls and fore-jib, Lieutenant, if you please.'

'*All hands! All hands to shorten sail!*' Niven stood next to the master. He was on the 'hailer in an instant.

Even as bodies crammed the ratlines and spread to the yards in response to the call, another powerful gust sent them reeling. Men appeared from every orifice of the ship in the haste to take in sail. Above them the sky turned an inky black and to the east even the sanguine sky had succumbed to the lowering cloud.

'Secure the guns, Lieutenant. We can manage without a loose cannon today.' Winchip realised that this would be *Eaglet's* first taste of inclement weather. He stood back as Lieutenant Pardoe arrived on the quarterdeck.

'*Deck there!*' The cry came faintly from the tops.

'*Where away?*' Niven replied immediately, his head laid back, the trumpet to his lips, his words addressed to the indiscernible lookout.

'*A sail – dead astern!*'

'Mr Pardoe. To the tops and tell me what you see!' Niven sent him off and then relaxed, assuming the air of a man unperturbed by anything. He turned to Winchip. 'I fear it must be a Frenchy, Sir.'

Winchip didn't bother to answer the obvious. Instead, he nodded ponderously. He knew the area well, so where had she come from? There was precious little shelter on the east coast of Oléron, so she must have been hiding around the southern point of Ré to be so close up to them already. Was this the springing of some devious trap, or a ruse to send him into the arms of French ships yet to be encountered? It was beyond his immediate concern.

'She is a frigate, Sir!' Pardoe's breath was laboured. His dash to the mizzen-top and back had taken the breath from his body in the rising wind. 'She's on the same course –

about two miles – gaining on us I would say.' The words came out in staccato bursts.

'Thank you, Mr Pardoe.' To Niven, Winchip said, 'Come to north-west by west, if you please. Send up the colours and then the challenge – sharply, please.'

'North-west by west, aye, Sir.' Niven once more took the 'hailer to the athwart rail as Bowes reached for the colours.

Winchip gave a nod of satisfaction. What he needed was more sea room, the nearby shore too alien to risk. The new course would allow him a better choice of action.

'It's as if she knew we were here, Sir. Just as if we were expected and now the trap is sprung.' Niven hooked up the 'hailer as he spoke. 'I see shades of *Capable*, Sir, and I don't like it.'

'I must agree with you, Lieutenant, although for the life of me I can see no reason for all this elaboration. As for a trap, she may find she has bitten off more than she can chew.' For reasons he could not explain, Winchip worried for Madeleine Loxley should *Eaglet* go to quarters.

'No response to the challenge, Sir!' Bowes made his report, his eager face a mixture of excitement and apprehension.

'Thank you, Mr Bowes.' Winchip drew the midshipman to one side. 'I want you to find Miss Loxley and take her below. Find somewhere safe and away from the orlop. Do you understand me?'

'Aye, Sir. I know just the place.' Bowes dashed to the poop.

Winchip strode aft to the taffrail and looked closely at the *Frenchman*. With a full suit of sail she presented a gallant sight, her bow dipping gracefully into the swell and then rising with an arrogance seen only in sleek French vessels. Winchip nodded imperceptibly. She was fast all right and would be up to them well within thirty minutes. He returned to the quarterdeck where the small group of officers waited, wide-eyed and expectant. No doubt waking to the thought that this was to be *Eaglet's* first action. He approached Niven with a studied calm.

'I would like Mr Bowes to attend the stern chasers, Lieutenant, when the time comes. Not a shot is to be fired until we are fired upon. Then, Mr Niven, we shall go for her sails – that is the only area where she has the better of us. After that, we shall see.' He allowed himself a fleeting smile. 'Remind the gun captains how well they did at practice and that we require accuracy as well as speed of handling.'

'I'd rather be in *Eaglet* when the iron is flying, Sir.'

'You and I both, Mr Niven, I assure you.'

'Is this anything to do with our passenger, Sir?'

'I would say it has everything to do with our passenger, Lieutenant. I shall have a word with our little French friend. In the meantime, if that ship fires upon us then please ensure that it is logged. I think we had better come to quarters in case there are any more nasty surprises. Load with bar shot – starboard guns and stern chasers only. Round shot in the rest, then have the gunners protect their slow-match. We are in for rain – a great deal of it.' Winchip turned aft, holding a hand in the air, knowing his officers would be saluting his retreating back.

'*All hands! Hands to quarters!*'

Winchip found Foche in the orlop, sitting on a pile of old hammocks, no doubt unaware of the reason for their grisly presence. If things went against them, those hammocks would find new owners, together with a brace of twelve-pound shot and a journey to the deep. He sat on the arms chest and removed his hat, placing it by his side.

'You may wish to know, Monsieur, we have a French ship on our heels.' His dark eyebrows knitted together. His eyes were mere slits. The ensuing silence turned the statement into a question.

'It is of no concern to me, Capitaine.' Foche was almost aloof. 'Your duty is to take me to Portsmouth.'

'I do not need to be reminded of my duty, Monsieur. All I can say to you is that if your countrymen fire one shot at a king's ship, then, as far as I am concerned, France and

England are at war – and you haven't won one of those since 1066.'

As if by an act of providence, from a distance, the sound of gunfire permeated below decks, one report after the other, giving emphasis to Winchip's words.

Gaspar Foche clambered to his feet rigid with fright, his eyes bulging. A small man, he seemed to shrivel even further, his face assuming the pallor of death in the semi-darkness below decks. He sank slowly down onto the hammocks, tugging at his little beard, oblivious to the sound that could only be trucks tackled up the run of the deck as Bowes' stern chasers were run out somewhere above them. His mouth gaped open once or twice before words came out.

'You must run from this frigate, Capitaine, before it is too late. She is too fast and too powerful.' Anger seemed to replace his fear as Winchip turned away. 'You will kill us all with your damned English stubbornness!'

Winchip turned away in disgust, his mind racing as he put the pieces of this floundering French scheme together. Monsieur Foche had some explaining to do, but it would be to Their Lordships, not to him. For now he had a French frigate to deal with and by God, that was just what he intended to do. He strode to the gangway and took the stairs two at a time.

As he stepped up onto the quarterdeck he was glad to see it was at least daylight, even if the sky seemed to deny it. The wind, no longer gusting, had become strong and steady, rocking him on his feet, sending a continuous howl through the rigging and a clattering of dancing blocks above his head. Lines were slapping against the mast in discord, adding to the din.

'*Deck there!*'

'*Where away?*' Niven had grasped the 'hailer in an instant, at the same time sending Costly to the tops.

'*On the larboard bow! She'm shyin' away!*'

Niven acknowledged and then waited until Costly came panting down to him.

'She's a frigate, Sir. She tacked before the man got a good look.'

'Thank you, Mr Costly. That was a good sighting. Tell the man so, if you please.'

Winchip exchanged nods with Niven. 'Log it, Mr Niven.'

They stared back at the French frigate. She was a grand sight against the dark backdrop, full-bellied, her sail as white as snow, confident of catching *Eaglet.*

'She seems determined, Sir.' Niven had appeared at Winchip's side. 'If I had any say, I'd get some of the sail off her. Her captain doesn't realise he's protected by the land at the moment. Another few minutes and . . .'

Winchip slapped his thigh. 'By God you're right, Lieutenant. Get Bowes to attack her fore-top and rigging. Smartly now – bar shot all!' He watched Niven go aft, a large but careful stride, giving no hint of urgency.

The two four-pounders fired as one, leaping back on their breechings, water spurting from the thick rope windings as they snapped taught. The thick, yellow discharge of smoke was whipped away and dispersed by the angry wind.

'She's been hit, by George! Her jibs'l's a'flutter!' His last words were unheard as a cheer rose from the deck.

A sudden crash above their heads cut the cheer off like a knife. The mizzen-mast had been struck a glancing blow. The woldings had been ripped apart, the charred ends of the cordage that bound the mast were hanging like giant hooks in their tarred stiffness. Where the ball had gone after that was evidenced by the sorry bundle of flesh and rags beneath the poop rail, against the bulkhead. A top man who, seconds before, had been on his way up to his work, ready to knot or splice. Before Winchip could speak, Niven was down there. He directed two men at the twelve-pounder to bundle the top man's body through the port. The seaman was stuffed, limp and lifeless, through the aperture, his leg left turned up his back, broken at the pelvis and streaming blood even as he disappeared like a sack of offal.

The rain came again as a few heavy isolated drops,

becoming heavier still with each moment. Astern, the downpour enveloped the French frigate like a shroud as it passed over her, churning up the surface of the sea as it hissed its way between them.

The crashing rain came up to them like a rolling peal of thunder, an all-consuming rain that poured down on deck and sails alike. Winchip and Niven braced themselves on the quarterdeck as gust after gust of rain-filled wind hammered relentlessly at their backs, trying to push them forward where they stood.

'She hasn't reduced sail, Sir.' Niven shouted above the weather, his face streaked with rivulets of water. 'Surely she must realise the danger by now!'

'Her captain is too busy with the chase and repairs to her jib, Lieutenant.' Winchip shouted the words. 'He's blinded to caution because of his apparent success. I also believe he is exceeding his orders.'

'I beg your pardon, Sir?'

'No matter, Mr Niven. I have had enough of this! We shall round-to, starboard side and give her a drubbing!' He shook his head and held up his hand to deter Niven from speaking. For a moment he stood silently, the rainwater beating down on him and pouring out from the crease of his hat like a church gargoyle. He was calculating the time it would take for the *Frenchman* to emerge from the shelter of the land. He looked towards the east and the lower edge of the thunderous cloud where the sun could appear at any moment and then at last he spoke. 'She will come into open water in about fifteen minutes, Lieutenant. We shall come round sharply and pass between her and the land.' He ignored the expressions of concern, knowing that for some *Capable* was coming sharply into focus. 'Her captain will find it hard to contend with his canvas *and* man his guns. Something he was never instructed to do in the first place!'

'How so, Sir?'

'Wear ship, Lieutenant.' Winchip turned away, fearing his anger would surface.

'Prepare to wear ship!'

The rain stopped. As if his decision had been blessed by The Almighty himself, the sun peered out from beneath the blanket of cloud. It was half a sun – a sun awakening – a morning sun, low and dazzling, throwing shafts of bright light across the deck straight into the eyes of the French as they sighted their guns. His plan had worked – a blessing indeed.

'Wear ship! Let go and haul!'

'She's reducing sail, damn her!' Niven stared astern, the trumpet dangling from his fingers. 'Good God! He's started with the t'gallants'ls, she must be manned by landsmen.' He scanned her with shaded eyes. 'Her starboard ports are still closed, Sir.'

'A tribute to the Western Squadron, Mr Niven. Keeping them bottled up has made them rusty. Let us hope their gunnery is just as bad.'

Eaglet was coming round, ploughing into the swell, spray leaping from her bows as her beak head found water. Men stamped their way, forward and aft, leaning into the haul, the braces held over their shoulders like a gang of sack carrying labourers in line astern.

'I don't think they ever expected to use their guns, Lieutenant.' Winchip looked at Niven directly. 'I think we were supposed to scuttle off, our tail between our legs, her mission completed.'

Niven shook his head as if confounded by events, the whole matter beyond his understanding.

Eaglet's sails had expressed their confusion by slatting with demonic fury as the ship came round, almost close-hauled, the sails cracking and banging until the leading edges found the wind once more.

With courses brailed and the wind before her beam, with only the *sauve tête* netting above their heads to protect them from falling blocks and rigging, *Eaglet* was suddenly facing her enemy.

5

Corinne

The *Frenchman* was drawing towards them, her rigging dotted with the scrambling shapes of seamen, hacking, clawing and heaving to relieve the masts of torn sail.

Winchip stared at the frigate, suddenly realising the great responsibility he had placed upon himself and the crew. He felt a coldness come upon him. He had acted upon instinct, just as before. He forced the thought from his mind. *Eaglet* was committed.

'Run out, starboard side, Mr Niven.'

'*Starboard side! Run out your guns!*' The 'hailer rose and fell like a bugler's salute.

The moment had come. Winchip knew that some believed it never would. Others, older men, would realise that it must. Men, some in action for the first time, looked at each other, their looks expressing fear – or bravado. Others touched hands, their only means of expression. All eventually looked to their front, wide-eyed, shuffling into position for the task ahead.

The hands of the gun captains rose almost as one, eyes towards the quarterdeck, staring at Niven's glistening and upraised sword as if mesmerised. At a nod from Winchip it dropped, flashing in the brilliance of the sun, so low on the horizon.

'*Fire!*'

The thunderous roar jerked the deck beneath them. The shouts of the gun captains, the hiss of swabs and the urging of divisional officers, all contributed to the sound of a ship-of-war in action. The smoke was a separate thing. An acrid, rancid, yellow cloud that blinded and choked, its last vestiges gripping the rigging with its tenuous strings before departing like a theatre curtain, its presence lost to mind as the stage was revealed. It draped itself along the surface of the water, trying to become part of it, changing the colour of it.

A cheer rose slowly from *Eaglet*'s tops, working itself into an unbridled roar as the fore-top of the *Frenchman* slowly pitched forward. It hung by the stays for a moment before plunging over the spit, to hang there a second longer before that, too, collapsed beneath the tangled mess of top hamper.

'*Fire!*'

The crash of *Eaglet*'s guns was enough to bring the cheering from the tops to an instant stop. The twelve-pounders rebounded in their breechings as the second broadside discharged its chain shot into the *Frenchman*'s rigging. Even as the French frigate slewed round the sheet anchor of tangled canvas and cordage under her bow, her main-mast canvas was blown inwards under the impact of *Eaglet*'s shot.

'*Reload! Roundshot all!*'

Winchip stood beside Mr Ramblin as *Eaglet* passed down the *Frenchman*'s side. Together they viewed the damage done. Not only had she lost steerage-way, she was in no position to manoeuvre.

The master nodded sagely. ''T'would be better if she struck her colours, I'm thinking, Captain.'

'We are not at war with France, Master.'

'Is that a fact, Captain?' Mr Ramblin stared out to sea, his face expressionless, his tongue sucking greedily on the hollow tooth.

Winchip smiled his thoughts, knowing the master as he did. He looked closely at the frigate, remembering what she had been half an hour since. He was aware that whatever he did now he would be required to answer for in another place. Their Lordships would have no truck with the heat of the moment, or that *Eaglet* had been fired upon first, or for that matter the size of the butcher's bill at the end of the day. The frigate was dead in the water, veered to starboard and settled like a mute swan on its nest of spars, sails – and corpses.

Winchip made a decision, not sure that it was the right one, but made in the knowledge that the *Frenchman* still had her guns intact. By not carrying out the attack to its ultimate conclusion he would, at least, avoid Their Lordships' wrath by submitting something in the way of mitigation. He was, in effect, putting up a spirited defence. He remembered the words of Admiral Byng as they had parted company: 'Should you be fired upon, well, that's another matter . . .' Grand words from a grand man in a grander place, unrepeatable before any court martial.

Having made up his mind, he walked over to Lieutenant Niven. 'We shall give this *Frenchman* a bloody nose, Mr Niven, a broadside from King George and a kick in the rump from us. Enough, I think, to get us home in peace.'

Niven cocked an eyebrow. 'I think our people were expecting something a little more conclusive, Sir. Some with *Capable* in mind.'

'If only life were that simple, Lieutenant.' Winchip laid a hand momentarily on Niven's arm. It had occurred to Winchip that Niven was seeing the possibility of a command slipping through his fingers, but he dismissed the thought; it was not Niven's way. 'The crew can never be allowed to control how we conduct our affairs. We are not at war and there are dire penalties for sinking the ships of so-called friendly nations. That, you must surely understand.'

'I apologise, Sir. I should have realised the, er . . . sensitivity of things. It is just that the crew have worked so hard . . .'

'Our people think only in terms of immediacy, Mr Niven. They have no conception of wider implications, or of being restricted by orders.' Winchip steered Niven round to face him. 'It will be your lot in the not too distant future, God willing, to command a vessel of your own. When that happens you will know exactly what I am talking about. Until it happens, you will have to accept my word for it.'

Winchip rested his point with more of a grin than a smile – enough to put Niven at his ease.

'Thank you, Sir, for reminding me.' Niven looked suitably contrite.

Winchip nodded, grunted, then looked away, glad that Niven had understood. It was important that he did. The men would get their chance soon enough, of that he was convinced. Having said that, the matter of the *Frenchman* still remained. From where he stood he could see the French crew hacking and yanking at the tangle of knotted rigging draped from the stump of the fore-top to the tip of her broken jib.

'We shall round her stern, gentlemen, and loose a broadside into her for good measure.' Winchip looked at Niven, already drawing his sword. 'Run out the starboard guns, Lieutenant.'

The rumble of trucks across the lay of the deck was like thunder. To the French it would be their death knell. Their own private Armageddon.

Winchip, standing erect at the binnacle, his hands gripped together in the small of his back, surveyed his command. Nodding, he allowed events to take their course. As *Eaglet* settled into her new tack with the lessening breeze tickling her coat tails, he could only wonder whether it was at this point, when making his final attack on *Capable*, that he should have run in his guns, filled his sails and set a course for the squadron. There would have been no court martial and no recriminations. No deaths for which he could be held to blame. No Captain Rance, looking for *anyone* to blame for *his* son's death. Right or wrong he was about to take the same decision as before.

'Sir. We are about to come onto the firing point – Sir?'

Winchip held up a hand. 'Wait!' He continued his train of thought, reassessing his decision before it was too late. The reasons for discontinuing the attack now were manifold and all possibilities of aggression in his actions would be discounted on the spot in another place. He heaved a deep sigh, silently cursing Their Lordships at the Admiralty for the dithering old greybeards they often appear to be. It was the crew – his people that mattered. Had he brought them together as a well-trained fighting force – a family, even – for them to scuttle away from the first sign of danger? No, he had not! He looked at Niven with a soft smile, belying the fury to which this situation had brought him. 'Carry on, Mr Niven, but remember, this is a day for chastisement, not revenge.'

'They're opening their ports, Sir!' Bowes suddenly stood before him.

At Bowes' shout, Winchip's eyes flashed to *Eaglet*'s starboard guns. Already the snouts of the great guns were out and, as he watched, Niven's sword flashed downwards in the bright sun, his stentorian order carrying the length of the ship in the crystal air. It would be a race to the touchhole. Almost as one, the roar of the guns blocked out all other thoughts. The ship rocked with the power of them and the brailled courses hanging above shivered and shook in the blast. The smoke billowed away from the ship in a huge yellow cloud, passing across the water like an avalanche towards the *Frenchman* and then like a rolling wave as it levelled all before it. As the sound died, so came the crash of bursting timbers from out of the smoke. The cries of dying men and the screaming orders of the French officers went on and on, a high pitched monotone, coming across the water as from a great distance, rising and abating in their fear and panic.

Winchip leaped to the mizzen shrouds and peered through the thinning smoke at the beleaguered vessel. Her bulwark was missing in places. Her tumblehome was pocked with black-smudged holes and many ports appeared as gaping holes where the frames had been driven inwards. He stared, momentarily mesmerised, as balls of smoke suddenly bellowed from her side. The crash of guns came almost instantly, causing Winchip to pointlessly turn his head away from the approaching black metal in an act of futile protection.

The French sporadic broadside was more obvious for its

accuracy than weight of iron. The shot arrived with a low growl, indicating chain, too low to damage the rigging for which it was meant. It hurtled around in all directions as it caught onto shrouds and timbers alike, whirring like banshees in their random passage until suddenly it was expended.

Winchip groaned in despair as Mr Lunt, the gunner, was picked up bodily and hurled overboard, tossed into the air like a rag doll and thrown over the bulwark nettings, arms and legs akimbo – lost forever.

A marine, kneeling on the nettings, waiting his turn to do his bit, took a ballchain in the chest. Smashed bodily against the larger of two bitts, he bounced in the air to be flung against the mizzen mast. He landed on the quarterdeck as if he had no form or substance, leaving a trail of unwinding and steaming entrails in his wake, his musket spinning overboard like a sycamore seed in a gale. He came to rest as a shapeless bundle at the foot of the binnacle, the blue of his trousers merging with the red of his tunic and his blood spreading into a pool around him.

Eaglet's guns discharged once more. Her final chance before a change of tack. It was a ripple of sound that commanded attention, the acrid smoke hesitating before slipping astern. It was no surprise to Winchip to see Pardoe striding quickly up the deck.

'The Master reports a change of wind, Sir. The offshore has eased and has veered to southerly.'

'Thank you, Mr Pardoe. Inform the first lieutenant, if you please and ask him to attend me.'

The smoke had passed on. Winchip took a glass from the rack and inspected the *Frenchie* where she lay. Her captain had certainly paid for his folly. He assessed her condition, hearing the pops as belligerent Frenchmen discharged their muskets in *Eaglet*'s direction in a futile gesture. The damage was extensive; as much as could be expected from two full broadsides. It was the damage betwixt wind and water that interested him most, but he wasn't to be offered a view of that. He had determined that if he were not at liberty to sink her, then he would put her out of commission for a long time to come. The deaths he had witnessed on board *Eaglet* had smitten his conscience like a hammer blow, knowing he could have left off the action with but a single word.

He returned to the binnacle, aware that the remains of the marine had been disposed of and some effort made to clean the deck – the last mark that man would leave on this earth. He didn't even know his name.

'You asked for me, Sir.' Niven tipped his hat.

'Yes, Lieutenant.' Winchip nodded towards the French frigate. 'Do we know her name?'

'She is the *Corrine*, Sir. Forty guns.'

'Is she, indeed? Then you did even better than I thought, Mr Niven. Well done.'

'What do we do if she strikes, Sir?'

Winchip smiled. It was an interesting hypothesis. 'Ignore her, I say. Let their captain explain it to his crew. A task I'd not relish.'

'Or to his masters for that matter.' Niven spoke caustically, the prospect too horrifiic to contemplate.

'How did the marine go, Sir?'

'He was struck by a chain-shot. Nothing else could have hit him so bodily. He felt nothing, of that I am certain.' They were words he would use to tell Lieutenant Gray. Memories had to be correct – precise!

'There's always a price to pay!' Niven struck his palm on the wooden top of the ready signal locker.

Winchip went towards the companion but broke his stride to speak a last word to the first lieutenant. 'The master has his orders, Lieutenant. North-west when you have finished with her. He pointed a desultory arm towards the frigate. A broadside into her stern and then take us away from here.' As an afterthought, he said, 'Keep the lookouts alert. We are, after all, in French waters. I shall be in the orlop if required.'

*

Every orlop smelled the same. Every ship in which Winchip had served, no matter its size, the orlop was one temporary area that never changed. Hated by many, dreaded by all, the dull red paint reminded rather than concealed the presence of blood. The smell was universal, never seeming to depart once ingrained; a bittersweet tang, once experienced, never forgotten. When the scene of carnage, terror, death and despair was returned to its normal use, when the young gentlemen repossessed their table, soiled with blood, that too, was when the orlop was hated.

Winchip could remember the sounds of the place. The gurgle in the throat of the dying, or the last panting breaths before the end, which never seemed to come and then were unnoticed when they did. There were also those who wouldn't stop breathing, men without legs, without arms or burned beyond recognition ... and men who refused to die.

There were also the wounded, demanding attention, screaming in a demented stupor or waiting for the saw, leather on which to bite, the grin of their bared teeth and wide eyes accusing, pleading – even threatening.

As Winchip came within the circle of yellow light afforded by the cluster of smoking lanterns above the table, he had to urge those who would stand in his presence to sit, to stay where they were.

'Sir!' Lieutenant Gray appeared before him, out of the gloom and out of breath. 'Marine Peters, Sir. A sad end. A man well liked. A moment of stupidity.' The sentences were clipped, as was Gray's way. Never a word wasted.

Winchip nodded. That Gray was already aware of Peters' death and the details of his going was of no surprise to him. 'I am ashamed to say, Mr Gray, that I came down here to find out Marine Peters' name among other things. He has been on the side party so often. One takes people for granted, you know – a habit worth breaking I'd say.'

'If Mr Peters had heard you say that, he would have forgiven you anything, my word on't, Sir!' Gray turned and was gone before Winchip could reply.

A rumble of trucks over Winchip's head drew him to the companion; to the deck where the air would be fresh. He had hoped to see Madeleine Loxley. Truth to tell his shame was in his hope to see her, a desire that could never match swords with his worry for the wounded, but was there all the same. In the end he accepted the outcome.

As he stepped onto the gun deck the roar of the twelve-pounders stunned him into awareness. He stood against the boat tier and let events take their course. The pungent yellow cloud of smoke clung to the surface of the water, rolling towards the frigate as if to consume her, swallow her up and shield her from her shame.

Lieutenant Niven tipped his hat as Winchip came up to the binnacle. 'The deed is done, Sir.' He stared at the smoke shrouding *Corinne* as he spoke.

'You have done well today, Lieutenant.'

'As did our people, I'd say, Sir.' Niven's grin was the width of his face. Praise was a rare commodity in His Britannic Majesty's Navy.

Winchip turned towards *Corinne*, unwilling to allow Niven to turn a word of praise into a melodrama. 'She is a sorry sight, Lieutenant – a sad sight indeed.'

The smoke that had permeated *Corinne*'s rigging had drifted downwind. The fine frigate of the early dawn, cutting through the water with nearly all sails set, cutting a dash with her fine display, now lay dead in the water, reacting only to the wind which left a calm patch of water to show her leeway track. The seagulls had found her, wheeling and darting, finding opportunity as it came, resting, walking on things that were floating, pecking at them and screaming at intruders.

She had no transom. The ornate windows of the cabin, her taffrail and the upper parts of her counter were all gone. Frame timbers poked through the wreckage like the bones of carrion, her crew like flies, black upon her carcass, wandering aimlessly, trying to do the impossible, all assuming they were about to die.

'Should we offer aid, Sir? She has lost her colours, so we must assume the day is ours.'

How quickly Niven's urge to kill had turned into compassion. 'No, Mr Niven. She has enough canvas and crew to reach the Ile de Yeu. Were she down in the water I would consider it, but she isn't, and for my money she can rot on that island's beach, if they can find one.' Winchip looked Niven in the eye. 'Think how pleased they will be to know they are not to die today.' He felt his anger rising yet could not stop it. He knew now what was afoot. This stupid charade – Foche and the frigate, so well timed and yet so disastrously executed. Suddenly he needed to write his reports to Admirals Portsmouth and the Western Squadron alike. They would not make for happy reading but, by God, it would make them sit up.

6

The Quick and the Dead

Winchip relaxed into the relative comfort of the stern seat. The noise of hammering still continued to permeate every corner of the ship. Above him the new woldings being wound onto the mizzen-mast brought a different misery – the stinging and pungent stench of hot tar as loggerheads were dipped. The flames brought forth a smoke that smarted the eyes and sought out every space in the ship. That, and the continuous scrape of heavy cordage across the deck light and the deck above him.

The silence during the committals had been a precious few minutes despite the sadness of the occasion. Marine Peters and Mr Lunt would have no such treatment, their demise requiring their disposal before they were seen by those who could be affected by the horror of their passing. Two other seamen and little Archie the powder monkey, popular with the crew, had each been given their two minutes of attention. Slipped into the water, wrapped in a hammock, their weighted feet pulling them silently downward, they slid into the depths, almost as if they had suddenly found a need to hasten on their way.

The morning watch had been busy in other ways. The reports from officers and mates alike had found their way to Winchip's desk as if someone had dealt them like a hand of cards. He had dwelled on them in turn, most finding their way to First Lieutenant Niven, who no doubt saw them in the same light, hoping there were no jokers in the pack.

At least the dawn heralded a fine day. The south-westerly brought a touch of warmth and a constant sun that scuttled around the cabin like the light of an errant lantern with every pitch and roll that *Eaglet* made. The expanse of bellied sail gave air to the ship and brightness worthy of a summer's day.

The only blight had been another two sightings of the strange sail, the frigate that seemed to be dogging their every move. They had challenged twice, only to see it tack and sink below the horizon.

Winchip, his coat removed and the plain lace ruffles of his blouse dusting the desk with every move he made, was about to continue with his journal when the knock came on the door.

'Enter!' He couldn't avoid the irritation in his voice.

Only the sentry's head appeared round the jamb. 'Miss Loxley, Sah!'

'Thank you. Ask her to come in.' Winchip's voice abated to suit the circumstance. He looked down at his scanty attire and shrugged his shoulders. His coat lay on the chest, too far to reach.

She wore the same green dress with a light shawl cast about her shoulders. Her black, lustrous hair was as he remembered it, hanging in that tail which he found both enchanting and provocative – no doubt in the current style of the French. It was her smile that was missing. Instead, her eyes were red. It was if she had been weeping – or had been deprived of sleep. He adjudged the latter.

'Please come in, Miss Loxley.' Winchip stood and held the back of the Gillow chair, encouraging her to sit where the sun would be least likely to dazzle her.

'Thank you, Captain.' Her smile brightened her countenance; but stayed for only a moment. 'I came to thank you for finding me a safe place. It was thoughtful of you. Mr Bowes told me you had sent him.'

'Mr Bowes has much to say for himself.' Winchip allowed himself a beaming smile, finding new weather creases that seldom emerged. 'I hope it wasn't too frightening for you. Below decks may seem safer but it is only marginal to what happens above. I am relieved that you came to no harm. That is all that matters.'

'Eight bells' sounded out from the belfry to end the morning watch, high pitched against the thud of mallets.

Winchip sat and rang the small bell for Booth. 'Will you share an early coffee with me?'

'Thank you, I would like that.'

When Booth had placed the tray on the desk, Winchip said to him, without preamble, 'Thank you, Booth. You may find employment in the galley until you are called for, and close the deck light on your way out.' He waited until the ageing Booth had gone, surprised to find Miss Loxley already pouring from the jug.

'Thank you for that, Captain.' She sat and smiled at him from above her cup.

The attenuation of noise from above allowed what he had to say to be said without being overheard. 'I . . . I need to make . . .' Suddenly he was lost for words. For a moment he had felt discomfited by her smile – totally besotted by it and yet desperate not to show it. 'I need to make my reports to my admiral and I need to be clear on the facts of your arrival on board, for my own protection as well as yours.' He gathered his wits, knowing that directness was the only way he would get the answers he wanted.

'Captain, I have no wish to keep anything from you, but . . . well, there are some things I cannot speak of lest you feel ill will towards me. That, in turn, would cause you to think ill of me in *all* things and that would be neither fair nor reasonable.'

'Miss Loxley, it would be very difficult for me to feel any ill will towards you. The opposite would be more likely.' Winchip had no idea why he had uttered the last few words. He gathered himself. 'Unless I am mistaken, there is something you are not telling me. This is neither the place nor the time for secrets. I *must* know the truth.' He mellowed quickly, half spreading his arms as if to support his appeal to her. 'What is it you are frightened to tell me, or must I guess?' His brow knitted together in concern as her whole being seemed to tense. She lowered her eyes, quickly finding the handkerchief that Winchip had given her.

'I . . . I told you a lie, Captain.' She looked up at him and then straightened in the chair, assuming that certain demeanour and expression that only women, surfacing from an embarrassment or seeking a perfect composure, are able to attain. She dabbed her nose and then blinked her eyes in an attempt to regain her composure into the bargain. 'It . . . it was not my brother who was the spy . . . it was I.'

'You?' Winchip sat aghast at the sudden and shocking revelation. It took a moment for him to recover himself. 'I cannot believe that!' He shook his head in bewilderment. 'But your brother . . . how could you allow him to be shot if . . .?'

'Monsieur Foche. He warned me that should I speak the truth we would *both* die.' She looked Winchip directly in the eye. 'I know from my experience with the French that what he said was true. Faced with a choice they would kill us both without another thought – their best option and the problem solved.' She was becoming more composed, more sure of herself.

Winchip shook his head, shocked at what he had heard, knowing it to be the truth. If nothing else, he had learned through life that pragmatism came hand in hand with necessity but in this case it seemed that love and loyalty had gone out of the window. He took a sip of his coffee, allowing the drink to hold his attention while he considered this new revelation. In the end he decided that he needed to know more, needed to know everything about her.

'I cannot see you as a spy – it makes no sense.' He spread his arms wide. 'There has to be more to it than that. People do not just become spies.' He spread his hands in despair. He was trying desperately to compete with the evidence. Overhead, the hammering continued relentlessly and the stench of hot tar offended the nostrils.

She held her coffee cup in both palms as if seeking comfort from it. 'It is not exactly what you think, Captain.' She placed the willow-pattern cup down on its saucer but still retained her grip on it like a beach anchor. 'While my brother was working at Rochefort I had a visit from an Englishman who said he was a naval captain. He told me that the Admiralty were concerned about the work Stephen was doing for the French.' She looked directly at Winchip. 'It was a reasonable concern but his work was all commercial – he did nothing but commercial docks and tidal control for the salt flats – how could that be of use to an enemy?' She paused as if her thoughts were running ahead of her, not expecting an answer. 'The captain agreed with that but said the Admiralty needed to be convinced that that was all he did. He suggested that there was a way to convince the Admiralty by reporting the number of naval vessels in the Gironde, a place to which we often went with Stephen's work. He gave me drawings of the ships in which he was interested.' She pulled a folded paper from a small purse and handed it to Winchip.

Winchip, glad of the enforced silence, studied the drawing with interest. He had seen a similar drawing many times. It was that of a troop carrier; almost a collier in its basic concept, even wider across the beam perhaps, but a trooper for all that, three-masted and lightly armed. He looked up. 'And you agreed?'

'Of course I did. Would you not, for someone near to you, and for your country?'

'Without a doubt.' Winchip replied immediately, as the question demanded. 'I am, however, interested to know to whom you passed this information. Was it Gaspar Foche?'

'Yes. Yes, it was.'

'I see.' Winchip rose from his seat and turned towards the stern windows. As he looked out at *Eaglet*'s wake, stretching like an arrow to the distant horizon, he could see the situation in its entirety: Foche using a colleague to recruit a likely candidate to use for his own purposes – another string to his bow and more money for his coffers – at far less risk to himself. He could see now that Madeleine Loxley had been duped. He now realised she was an innocent party in all this. He turned back to face her, seeing in her expression a plea for understanding, a hope that he now understood what she had been through. He certainly would not tell her of his other conclusion – that Foche had sacrificed her brother to enhance his position with the French and had helped Miss Loxley to escape, to do the same for the British. He was a double agent then. Something Their Lordships at the Admiralty would need to know.

'Do you have relatives in England? Someone to whom you can go once this wretched business is done with?'

She blinked twice. 'Our parents were lost some years ago, on the Dieppe packet.'

'I am very sorry to hear that.' Winchip could almost feel the grief she must have suffered then.

'Thank you. They are dearly missed. I have a sister but she now lives in Gibraltar. She is married to a navy captain.' Her brow furrowed for a moment. 'I can't be sure he is still there. He was on the staff of the Governor, I believe.'

'What is his name?' Winchip reached across for his Navy List, eager to grasp anything that would indicate her innocence, let alone her pedigree.

'His name is Munro. Douglas Munro.'

Winchip vaguely remembered the name. He ran his finger down the column, stopping wide-eyed as the name suddenly stared back at him. 'Captain Douglas Munro.' He laid the book down. 'Well, I never . . .'

'May I see?' She reached out for the book, taking it in her slender hands as Winchip passed it over. Finding the name, she stared at it, finally running her fingers across it as if trying to gain some sort of contact. She passed it back, her eyes fixed upon it as if reluctant to let it go.

For Winchip, that was the moment that belief turned into certainty. With that certainty had come a feeling of wretchedness, knowing he had been too severe with her. He had been too willing to think the worst. Now he had an anchor stone to secure his faith in her and that affected him in a way that brought a light-hearted feeling upon him, akin to something he dared not think about, let alone put into words. Her voice penetrated his thoughts.

'Am I still in trouble regarding all this – or am I free to pick up the pieces? I have a certain amount of money, enough to provide a roof over my head until I can reorganise my life.'

'I think you are safe from blame, Miss Loxley, but your movements will have to be restricted until I have spoken to the admiral at Portsmouth. After that you should be free to do as you wish.'

'Thank the Lord! That, at least, is something.' Madeleine Loxley let go of the cup, maintaining her eyes upon it until her hands rested in her lap. 'You have been very good to me, Captain. If I have been a nuisance to you, then I sincerely apologise.'

'You have nothing to apologise for, Miss Loxley. As you have sought self-preservation, so I have merely done my duty. I can only say how glad I am that all has turned out well, despite your sad loss.' Winchip rose from the chair. 'I trust that Booth is still taking care of all your needs?'

'He is almost tripping over himself to accommodate me, Captain. He is a true gentleman.'

'Then, at present, there is little else I can do for you. I do have to complete my reports and despatches.' Winchip offered a broad smile and escorted her to the door. 'Incidentally, were there any ships in the Gironde?'

Madeleine Loxley looked at him in surprise. 'None that I could see, beyond the fishing boats, the usual traders and two small navy vessels. It is over thirty miles in length, however, though where else they could have been – the Gironde is so open, you know.'

'And that is what you told Monsieur Foche?'

'No. I told him there were lots – dozens and dozens. That is what I thought he wanted to hear.'

Winchip smiled. He might have expected it. It would be interesting to know the contents of Foche's report to Their Lordships. He quietly closed the door.

*

Winchip remained standing at the entry port deep in thought. The dampness of the early morning sparkled on the standing rigging like dewdrops on a spider's web. The woodwork of the entry post had the polished sheen of wetness in the morning sun. He watched as the Western Squadron sloop, *Skipper*, still keeled over as she disappeared, close-hauled, became a silhouette against the clearing sky. The meeting with her had been fortuitous and a great saving in time. As he climbed the few steps to the quarter-deck he replaced the glass in the rack, thankful that his comprehensive report to Admiral Byng was now on its way. He had found it difficult to translate the course of events into a report fit for the eyes of the admiral. He knew his greater problem was with the admiral at Portsmouth. It was from him that the word would come for Madeleine Loxley to be discharged. Blameless in all that had happened. He hoped the matter would fade into nothing in comparison to his report concerning Monsieur Foche. Therein lay the makings of trouble all round, as he had been quick to point out to Admiral Byng. His assumptions concerning *Corinne* made sense and offered some interesting theories as to her purpose and intent. He had written down his thoughts on the matter to the admiral – that she had been there under orders to frighten them off, never expecting *Eaglet* to turn and challenge her. Her purpose had been to keep *Eaglet* away from the Gironde, to give the impression that troop ships were massed in there, waiting to be manned and moved to the north to meet up with the invasion force. To persuade the English that their search for the troop ships was over and ensure that ample English ships were deployed to keep them there. Now, the truth was known. So, where were the ships? The options were being pared down to guesswork. What was done with the information would be made clear on his return from Portsmouth. Secretly, he hoped that *Eaglet* might be involved in whatever action Admiral Byng decided upon, but he doubted it. Other captains, senior to him and with greater claims would see to that. He hoped that his words did not fall on deaf ears, as was so often the case – but he thought differently.

'*Deck there!*'

'*Where away?*' Niven, standing at the binnacle, bent over backwards to direct his voice through cupped hands.

'*'Tis the* Lizard – *dead ahead!*'

Niven raised a hand in acknowledgement and then walked down to Winchip. 'The Lizard, Sir.'

'Thank you, Lieutenant. Shape a course for Falmouth, if you please.'

'Falmouth, aye, Sir.' Niven gave no expression to the feelings he must have had with the sudden change of destination. Instead he nodded to a spot behind Winchip's left shoulder before walking purposefully away.

Winchip turned.

Madeleine Loxley completed the final step up the short side ladder and stood erect on the quarterdeck, one hand gripping the nearest solid object to steady herself. She looked at him with a smile. 'So, this is where all the decisions are made.' She screwed up her eyes to look to seaward, beyond the larboard rail, raising her head to the wind. 'How romantic this place could be were it not for the very reason that *Eaglet* is here. I think I might have been a sailor – had I been a man.' She took the crimson silk scarf from her head letting the locks of her raven hair sweep around her shoulders, her pony's tail for the time being abandoned.

Winchip, devoid of any suitable reply, said, 'Good morning, Miss Loxley.' He cocked his hat and afforded her a smile wide enough to show the whiteness of his teeth, a smile that worked every crease of his face. He looked at her through slitted eyes against the sun, the crow's-feet adding to the harsh weathering. 'I was hoping to have a word with you this morning.'

'Nothing that will spoil the day, I hope.' She mocked him with the relaxed ease of a burden removed.

'Not at all.' Winchip guided her to the lee rail, between two of the six-pounders, where the wind was more relenting and where they could not be overheard. Above them the huge gaff sail strained at its tacks and clews, sending up a discordant groan from the taut cordage. 'I have been thinking and have a suggestion to make.' He gathered his words on the instant, unprepared for this early opportunity. 'I have a house in Falmouth where you might like to stay for a while – until you can sort out your affairs and ... and make any future plans.' He hesitated. 'My daughter, Emma, will be there, together with my housekeeper and her husband – my manager. If you – '

'And your wife, Captain?' There was no harshness in her voice, no expression that suspected any contrivance on his part. It was asked respectfully, as if she was interested to know.

'My wife died, some years ago in childbirth, my son with her.'

'Oh! My *dear* man ...' She placed her hand on his arm. 'I am *so* sorry. You must think me so thoughtless. I would never—' She stopped as Winchip raised a hand, her eyes almost closing under the furrowing of her brow, her fingers flying to cover her mouth to stop any words that could only increase her embarrassment.

'It is in the past.' He dragged the words out. That her loss was also in the present, clawing at his heart with each day that passed, was of little consequence here. 'I thought you might like a place where you can recover yourself, have time to think with no pressure upon you. You might even find Emma to be good company in such times. She, too, has lonely moments and unrequited ambitions.' He said the last tongue-in-cheek. A reckless comment, one which he hoped would not be misconstrued. For a moment she dwelled on his last few words, as if realising suddenly how he saw her and cared enough to have had a genuine concern for her.

'I think you had better call me Madeleine; if I am to be your house guest, that is.'

'A house guest! Yes, I like that.' Winchip hoped his next words didn't shatter the small understanding that had come to each of them. 'I shall be asking Mr Pardoe to accompany you and act as your protector until my return in a few days. He is familiar with the house and is acquainted with Emma – together with Beth and Jonathan.'

'Then I shall be in good company.' She looked at him directly, a smile playing on her lips. 'I am under guard, aren't I?'

Winchip hesitated for the briefest moment. 'I would be in breach of Navy Orders were I to release you. Monsieur Foche has also to be interviewed. His evidence may differ from yours, in which case you will be asked to present yourself. Were you not available then I would have a great deal of explaining to do.' Winchip chanced a smile. 'I am sure you can see the logic of that.'

Madeleine Loxley nodded in understanding. 'Then I had better prepare myself.' She turned with a smile and took the few steps down to the main deck.

Winchip moved to the binnacle, totally nonplussed as to the ways of providence. As events changed his life, so they would change the lives of others. He hoped and prayed that the changes would be for the better – for all of them.

7

'Santander'

Madeleine Loxley looked out of the great sash window. The view from above the church was almost certainly responsible for the siting of the house. The whole of the Carrick Roads was laid out before this large, dressed granite dwelling with its huge windows and grey slated roof, its chimneys stretching to the sky. As it was, her eyes were upon *Eaglet*, seeing only the stern of her as her gay blue ensign passed out of sight, to round Pendennis Castle on her way to the sea. The break from the ship and the parting from Daniel Winchip had become another shock to add to a dozen others before it.

How was she to tell him – as tell him she must – about Stephen? About the crooked dealings when money became short? How his honest living as a naval architect had taken second place to the suggestions of his drinking friends and how he had lost even those when the inheritance money ran out? She smiled as she stole a glance at Lieutenant Pardoe sitting in the wicker chair, reading avidly from one of his captain's naval books. He and his captain were men indeed, men who held honour in high esteem with self-respect paramount.

'*Eaglet* is on her way, Mr Pardoe.'

The young lieutenant raised his head from the book and gave her a blushing smile. 'Indeed, Miss Loxley. The captain says it will be a few days before he can return.'

'Please, call me Madeleine. Miss Loxley sounds so stuffy.'

'As you wish, Ma'am – I'm sorry – as you wish, Madeleine.' Pardoe's blush lingered a moment longer.

'Have you a family, Peter? It is Peter, isn't it?'

'Yes. My real parents are dead. They passed away some while ago. I have a stepfather who has been very kind to me. He lives in Truro.' He remained looking at her, no doubt expecting the conversation to continue.

'I am truly sorry to hear about your parents, but glad to hear you have someone who cares.' She wished she hadn't asked the question. It had been forward of her. 'My parents both died in a storm on the way to France. It was a great loss so I know how you must have felt. I have also just lost my brother, killed by the French.'

'Oh, Madeleine, that is terrible!' Pardoe turned in the chair to face her. 'Was that the reason for your wanting to leave France?'

'I am afraid so.' Madeleine tried to shake off her sudden melancholy. 'Captain Winchip – all of you – saved my life, and I shall never forget it.' She felt a need to change the subject – the conversation could never be allowed to finish on such a sombre note. 'Your captain is a fine man and very understanding.'

'He commands the respect of us all.' Pardoe looked at her directly. 'His wife died a few years ago and it was a very sad time for the whole ship's company.'

'Indeed, it must have been.' Madeleine turned her head to the window. She suddenly felt very sad. Everybody about her seemed to have found their niche in the world, whether it was the dashing life of Peter Pardoe or the more mundane and waiting existence of Emma with all before her. How she envied Emma, just as she had resented her brother, despairing at the number of times Stephen had destroyed any possible relationship she might have had, afraid it would cause her to leave him.

In Daniel Winchip she had found that promise of security that comes to but a few. It was, however, a security she had done little to deserve. She had been a burden to him at every turn. Even *she* realised that. That he was attracted to her had become obvious. That he had shown it was incredible. That the feeling had become mutual, under the circumstance, was nothing short of a miracle. Her feelings towards him were honest, of that there could be no doubt. That she was taking advantage of the situation, left with nothing and no one to whom she could turn, would spring to Daniel's mind as easily as it had come to hers. She had no defence, only her feelings. Now, sitting in his house, at his window, looking at the view he would have seen a thousand times, perhaps different on every occasion, she took comfort in still feeling his presence about her. It was with that realisation that she at last felt safe, and with that she burst into tears.

'Miss Loxley!' Pardoe dashed to her side at the window-seat, his book dropping to the floor. 'Are you all right, Madeleine – what can I do?'

'Nothing, thank you, Peter.' Madeleine raised a hand and kept her eyes averted. 'I'm sorry, but everything seemed to tumble out at once.' She shook her head and dabbed her eyes. 'A glass of water perhaps.'

She shook her dark tresses and dabbed her eyes once more. She had not meant to cry, had been determined not to but the events of the past few days had caught up with her. She heard the lieutenant go to the door and was glad for the moment she would have to herself.

The arrival of Peter and herself at 'Santander' had startled everyone. Beth fussing about – now gone to prepare her room. Emma, recovering from the shock of unexpected guests – now changing out of the culottes, boots and battered straw hat, the clothes she had appeared in, dressed for the orchard. It had been a moment of chaos. A panic short lived once the introductions had been made. A rush of joy and incredulity when Emma realised that Peter, too, was staying.

Madeleine blotted the last tear from her eyes and gathered herself together, just as the door opened and Emma pattered into the room like a summer breeze, now wearing a light blue morning dress with a dazzling white collar. Her feet were bare. She would know nothing of the tears.

'Now that looks better, Emma.' Madeleine smiled. 'The orchard's loss will be our gain.'

'Oh, Miss Loxley. What must you have thought of me? The last of the apples, you see. If they are not picked now then they will all be lost to the birds and to the worms and . . .'

'Emma. It was lovely to meet the earthy you – a rare privilege, I think.' Madeleine cocked her head and found a beaming smile. 'This, I take it, is the beautiful Emma whom your father described to me, now in all her glory?'

Emma curtsied. 'At your service, Ma'am.' She did a twirl. 'Do you like it?'

Before Madeleine could answer, Pardoe came in with the water, only to stop short at the sudden change of events. He placed the water on the sewing table by Madeleine's side and stood, awkwardly.

'Thank you, Peter. You don't mind my calling you Peter, do you?'

Pardoe brightened. 'Ma'am, if I am to be the centre of your attention, albeit briefly, then you may call me what you wish.' The words rushed out, his face reddening as they died on his lips.

'Now, now, Peter. You will embarrass me with all this attention, let alone Emma.' Madeleine gave Emma a wink, her face breaking into a smile as Emma looked at her coyly and then glanced at Peter. In those few seconds she realised that there was an unspoken understanding between them, unrequited under the circumstances of their brief meetings, probably never alone. What an opportunity these few days would be to them. She resolved not to spoil their chances of getting to know each other; neither would she worry about those things left unspoken. She felt they could both be trusted. Madeleine suddenly became aware that Daniel Winchip had, unspoken, placed upon her the responsibility of chaperone. It was going to be a very interesting time.

Winchip sat huddled in the corner of the stern sheets of the jolly boat, one hand gripping the planking of the seat and the other grasping the gunwale. His sword was stowed beneath the seat where it could do no harm. The collar of his coat was wrapped firmly about his neck in protection against the vicious westerly. For four days the gale had raged, forcing *Eaglet* to remain firmly anchored within the confines of Portsmouth Harbour. There was a studied silence as the oars dipped and rose, broken only by an epithet from Hellard as the rhythm was disturbed; an oar pulling air in the choppy and turbulent water.

For all his discomfort Winchip had reason to be pleased with events. Foche had remained on board *Eaglet* until Winchip had been to Admiralty House. His report to the admiral and the written statement of Madeleine Loxley had sufficed to persuade the admiral that she was an innocent party to all that had gone on with regards to her brother's execution. Shortly afterwards, the subdued little Frenchman – who had much to explain – had been whisked away by a sergeant at arms, complete with escort.

The matter of *Corinne* had caused the admiral's jaundiced eyes to brighten somewhat, although what thoughts went through his head were beyond speculation. A series of little nods as he had read the meat of the report gave Winchip hope to assume that all was well.

Now, his orders and despatches were firmly tucked deep within the inner pocket of his coat. He was ready to return to the Western Squadron and Vice Admiral, the Lord Hawke, having resumed his command of the Western Squadron. He hoped that Emma was recovering from the shock of an unexpected guest and that she was not reading too much into it, but he knew she would be. Whatever the answer, he would soon find out. The presence of Pardoe, he knew, would lay any problems to rest in their infancy. As to his proximity to Emma for a few days, he thought little of it. A trust assumed was trust indeed. He marvelled at the way events moved on apace, how things never seemed to stay the same and how fickle were man's best laid plans.

' *'Tis* Eaglet!'

Winchip jerked upright at Hellard's call, answering the hail from the ship. Bending, he recovered his sword and then checked his inner pocket, all the time rising and falling with the boat as it approached the tumblehome of *Eaglet*. The battens running horizontally up to the entry port seemed to rise and fall in the mammoth swell, like the action of a long saw in the shipyard sawpit, beckoning him towards disaster.

The westerly wind allowed *Eaglet* free passage from the harbour in the uncertain light of dawn, although the ever changing and ever devious Solent with its sandbanks and shoals, waiting for an errant pilot to make but one small mistake, was not so generous. Even Ryde, usually appearing so close, was hidden by a haze of rain, allowing only the white spire of All Saints Church, high on the hill, to act as a landmark and reference. It was not to be the easy passage for which he had hoped.

With the ship on a starboard tack that was taking forever and in a blow that had turned south-westerly, Winchip was trying to bring his journal up to date. At the same time bearing in mind the threat of the Bill of Portland. He dipped the quill and then held it, poised above the inkwell. After a moment or two he wiped the nib and laid the quill back in the tray. His thoughts were straying to Madeleine. He recalled his unease when he began to see her in a light totally divorced from her reason for being on board, remembered his concern that he was taking advantage of his position and her plight. He had cast the thought from his mind in the vain hope that the problem was of his own making and that his unfamiliarity with the art of courtship was making him shy. Aha! He had never been shy in his life and he knew it. His first thoughts still stood their ground, accusing him each time they surfaced – and he was well aware of it! He smiled to himself as he realised that those he had left at 'Santander' had already had four days in which to become acquainted with the household. Either his house was a scene of bedlam, or one of great change. He feared the former but expected the latter, which brought him sharply back to his original concerns. With a flourish he regained the quill and dipped it in the well . . . three times.

Winchip strode through the bustle of the quays with his sword clamped to his side and the westerly tugging at his coat-tails. Already the yawl, with its brown lugsail hard before the wind, was bobbing its way back towards *Eaglet*, in Hellard's hands, cleaving a way between the incoming fishing boats.

He passed through an ope, up onto Church Street, and strode past the customs house with scant regard for his surroundings. It was only when he reached the corner beyond the Parish Church of King Charles The Martyr that he looked up to see the house as he had done so many times before, but this time it would be different – she would be there.

Blackie, Jonathan's old Border Collie, was the first to hear him as he came through the iron gate. With head held low and tail brushing the ground, the act of deference was belied by his bright eyes and lolling tongue and a burst of barking, fit to waken the dead.

'Father!' Emma picked up her skirts and clattered down the steps towards him. She ran up to him without an arm to spare and dabbed a kiss on his cheek, her eyes sparkling, then took him by the arm to lead him to the door, the integrity of her dress suddenly forgotten. Her words came out in an excited rush. 'Madeleine is here with Peter – I can call him that, can't I?' She took a deep breath as Winchip gathered his sword to his side to avoid a calamity. 'She is wonderful, Father!' Emma came round to his front and urged him to a halt, her voice reducing to that of a confidante. 'Are you to marry her?'

Winchip stopped and looked into her wide enquiring eyes, a smile creasing his face. 'Things are a long way from that, my dearest.' He put a finger to his lips. 'Not another word about it, lest you frighten her away.' After all the agonising he had gone through, trying to visualise Emma's reactions should such an event be possible, she had put the matter to rest in the time it took to utter those few happy words.

Madeleine stood in the doorway, her hands held loosely in front of her. In a light green dress and dark green jacket, flared at the hips, enhancing her figure and the smallness of her waist, she looked so beautiful. The white lace trimmings about her throat emphasised the darkness of her hair and the beauty of her smiling face.

As he approached her he looked into her eyes, seeing her anew; seeing in her expression all those things that had been left unsaid. It was if their parting kiss had opened a door, allowing them to be freer in the expression of their feelings. He was in love with her. He could no longer doubt it.

'Daniel!' She moved down the steps towards him, her beaming smile filling him with pleasure and a delight he had not experienced in many years. She reached up to kiss him on the cheek. 'I have had such a welcome. I feel I shall need rescuing all over again.' She took his arm and led him into the darkness of the entrance hall, out of the brilliant sunlight, almost as if he were the guest and she were the hostess – a wonderful ambivalence.

Emma clung to Pardoe's arm as they walked on the upper slopes of the garden. They stopped on the high path by Poppy Meadow, under the rowan trees and the two small whitebeams at the edge of the peaty dell, where small granite boulders formed a witches' ring, and where the old buckthorn shrubs gathered where water lingered.

In the short time they had delighted in each other's company they had chatted about a thousand things, yet still they had formed no spoken bond. Their affection for each other had grown out of small things, as if their silent meetings under the eye of Emma's father had encouraged a form of association that was nurtured only by facial innuendo and brief remarks, never through personal contact or with freedom of expression. Faced with that freedom and close proximity, the suddenness of it all demanded a maturity they had yet to test.

Pardoe was aware of the trust that had been placed in him. To be alone together, as they were now, had seemed impossible. Now, walking together in the shade of the rowans, he felt as though they had just met. The frequent but fleeting times when they had exchanged glances on meeting had never been qualified by words – words that were hard to find. Words that is, that had meaning. He took a deep breath.

'I can't believe I have you to myself. The times we have met together and yet only now can I talk to you as I would have liked to then.' He hoped he wasn't being too bold.

'And what would you have said to me, Peter?' She looked up at him, her mouth forming that lovely smile he found so warm and provocative.

'I suppose I would have said how pretty you looked and how much I admired you.' His heart was twisting into knots, his mind telling him he had but the one opportunity. A foolish word and it could all end.

'That would have been nice.'

'It *was* nice – to think about, that is.' For a moment he was tongue-tied. 'It is so difficult for me, you understand? With your father being the captain.'

'Then you must write to me.' She laid a hand on his. 'It would be lovely if you did; and then, perhaps you could ask father if you could call. I'm sure he would say yes. He speaks very highly of you.'

'Does he?' Pardoe was surprised that the captain thought that highly of anyone.

'Yes, he does. He says you are very brave and that he is lucky to have you with him.'

'That doesn't sound like your father.' Pardoe knew he was blushing. 'I shall write to you at every opportunity, I promise ... and I *shall* ask him if I can call on you. I promise that, too.'

'Why don't you ask him this afternoon? Then I can look

forward to your letters and to your home-comings.' She seemed to be holding her breath, eager for his reply.

'I *shall*!' He would. Though he would find it hard to tell her it would be the only place he could call 'home'. His uncle and patron would have a great deal to say if he assumed residence with him. *Eaglet* was his home now, just as other ships had been.

'Oh! That is *wonderful*, Peter!' She laughed out loud, clasping her hands together.

Pardoe gripped her hands in his, shielded from the house. 'I do care for you, Emma.'

'And I care for you, Peter. Very much.' She looked away, surprised no doubt by her own boldness.

'Come! Let us go down to the house. The wind is chill up here and I have no wish to remember this spot for that reason.' Pardoe took her hand, his heart doing somersaults and his hopes multiplying with every step he took.

As they walked downhill their hands were tightly clasped, each holding to themselves the feelings they would have gladly shared.

Winchip had often known time to stand still, usually when danger threatened. For hours to pass in the space of minutes was a new experience for him. He told Madeleine of the admiral's decision and shared with her the feeling of mixed elation and sadness that that evoked. They had relaxed and talked, eaten and then talked again, trying to fit two lifetimes into as many hours. When it seemed they had begun to discover each other they strolled in the garden. Both wrapped against what had become a cool breeze, they climbed towards the point where they could see over the buildings of Church Street, across the Fal to Flushing and the width of the Carrick Roads.

With the tide beginning to flow, filling all the defiles and forming little islands as it coursed its way along the mud banks of the Fal, *Eaglet*, in deeper water towards Pendennis, sat on her own reflection. Around her, like ants around a jam trap, trading vessels were plying and buying, trading as if at a country fair. As they watched, one of Falmouth's 'ladies' was being slung aboard, swinging on the hoist like a rum keg, crewmen lining the bulwarks as if at a market sale.

From above them, where the land flattened and the treetops jostled in the winter air, the sound of Emma's laughter came and went like distant music in a fitful air.

'They seem happy together.' Madeleine pulled her shawl a little closer to her neck. 'Emma seems to be quite the little lady.'

'I think Beth has to take much of the credit. She has been with us since Emma was born. And I, far more often at sea than at home, can hardly be considered the best of fathers.' He left it at that, suddenly realising he had broached another reason that argued against their relationship. To be at sea for a year was more commonplace than he cared to remember. He felt the pressure of her arm, linked in his like a cable round a bitt, as it should be, as he wanted it to be. How he envied the romantic articulation of the young, adept at securing most things in the matters of love, and yet pliant enough to recognise the impossible and spend no time being hurt by it. For a while he and Madeleine were quiet and content to be so, each aware how brief his visit would have to be. There seemed no time to talk of meaningful things. Things that had to be approached with care and needed time. It was Madeleine who broke the silence.

'Come, let us go into the house. It is getting colder by the minute.'

They rose together, Winchip offering his arm, speaking as he did so. 'It may be some time before I am home again. Shall I find you here or do you intend to move on – pick up the pieces as you once said?' He waited for her reply, his heart hanging upon her answer.

'That depends upon what you want, Daniel.' She stopped and looked at him. 'For a navy man there seems little enough time to consider anything that smacks of the domestic. I think it all depends upon you, unless I have misread the underlying meaning of all those words that have been left unspoken.' She smiled and held him closer. 'Do you want me to stay?'

'I want that more than anything in the world.' The words tumbled out. 'I cannot bear the thought of you leaving and yet...'

'And yet you think you are taking advantage of me when I am at my lowest, is that it?'

Winchip stood erect. 'Am I that transparent?'

'Have you stopped to consider that the opposite might be the case, that I might be taking advantage of you? You have all that a woman could desire and I have nothing.' She looked into his eyes. 'Oh, my love, you are the most transparent man I have ever met. If you wish me to stay here and wait for you, then I shall. Perhaps, then, we shall have more time to get to know each other, as others do who think they may be in love.' She kissed him gently on the lips. 'You go to sea and do what you have to do. When you come home we shall know exactly where we stand, just as Emma and Peter will, of that I am positive.'

Winchip looked at her and sighed. 'I never thought I could be so happy again.'

'It is good to hear that. Come, let us go indoors before we die of a chill.'

The time for parting arrived like a lee shore – always there, and the more intrusive the quicker it came. As Winchip settled his sword and donned his coat he wondered how long it would be before his return. He could sense danger ahead – was convinced of it; and yet after the few private hours they had enjoyed together he knew he would be back, to return to the woman he wanted more than anything in life.

In the privacy of the hall, lit by two single candles, on wall brackets reflecting before a mirror, he held her face gently between his hands, his expression of feeling too obvious to be denied. 'I shall miss you and think of you with every day that passes.' He would have said more but knew he would stumble on the words. Instead he kissed her on the lips, allowing the kiss to continue as if trying to seal his promise. When he felt her return the kiss, her hands gripping his arms as if to prevent his going, he knew it had been an exchange of promises – an unspoken understanding.

8

Admiral the Lord Hawke

In driving rain and a brisk north-westerly, veering with every bell, *Eaglet* weathered Ushant. It was a flat, grey slab of an island. Rising two hundred feet out of the sea it lay like a huge cornerstone, guiding those who would seek new waters, south to the Baltic and beyond. The high cliffs lost their grandeur as *Eaglet* gave the island a wide berth, unwilling to contribute to the many wrecks littering the northern shore. The land appeared and then disappeared as successive squalls chased one another across the approaches.

Winchip, aware of the lashing rain beating on the deck above him, was intent on completing his reports for Admiral Hawke, now back in command of the Western Squadron. He had had occasion to visit the *Royal George* once before but he doubted Lord Hawke would remember him. Captain Campbell, the Admiral's flag captain, was another matter. Winchip had served under him at a time further back than he cared to remember, his first berth as a young and aspiring lieutenant.

A knock on the door destroyed his thoughts.

'Enter!'

The first lieutenant came in, the fresh wetness of the deck filling the cabin as if a window had been thrown wide open. 'We have just come to west by south, as you ordered, Sir. The wind is erratic to say the least.'

'Thank you, Lieutenant.' Winchip laid down the quill.

Niven made as if to depart but Winchip bade him sit. It was not in Winchip's nature to explain his orders to his officers. In the first lieutenant, however, he often found a foil for his own ideas, serving to set off his thoughts and, by that, his decisions. On this occasion it was none of those things. He had thought long and hard about Foche, his purpose and his motives. He might have dismissed his own nagging thoughts as prejudice against the man, had it not been for *Corinne*. Now, he was convinced he was right and if his suspicions were correct then the French would move heaven and earth to ensure he didn't proceed on to Gibraltar after reporting to Lord Hawke, as he knew his orders dictated. Winchip reached into the desk drawer and retrieved two despatch pouches.

'You will be pleased to know we are not destined for blockade duty after all.'

'Two pouches, Sir?' A book of words could not have given more meaning to the question. The implication gave promise of two destinations, one far removed from the other.

'Yes. One is for Admiral Hawke who has now resumed command of the Western Squadron, the one that we expected. The other is for the Governor of Gibraltar.' He knew Niven's eyes would light up and he was right. 'We are to act as messengers, probably because we are better able to look after ourselves, inferring there is some special importance to the despatches we carry.'

'I see, Sir.'

'I doubt you do, Lieutenant.' Winchip replaced the packages, but this time in the weighted bag, placing them gently in the top drawer, unlocked, ready for quick retrieval and disposal should things go against them. 'I can tell you now, Mr Niven, I do not expect to get to Gibraltar without incident and I suspect Lord Hawke will think likewise.'

'Incident, Sir?' Niven sat forward in the chair, no doubt, like Winchip, seeing the man Foche as a ghost, leaping out to haunt them at every turn. 'I thought this spying business was done with as far as *Eaglet* was concerned.'

'Wishful thinking, Lieutenant.' Winchip wagged a finger. 'It seems we are about to reap the harvest of our endeavours and put the lie to Foche's words.'

'At Gibraltar, Sir?'

'Perhaps beyond.'

'Sir?' Niven's eyebrows were doing somersaults.

'I was merely speculating, Lieutenant. A foolish thing to do in our business, I'd say.' Winchip had said enough. He still couldn't come to terms with Foche's masters going to such lengths to tell them what they already knew; let him think the information was important enough to send a frigate into treacherous waters to try, half-heartedly, to stop Foche in his tracks. No wonder he had been so scared when things turned into a débâcle. Winchip knew he was right, was convinced of it. His worry was for Their Lordships at Admiralty – sucked into the trap like huckster's bait! 'I shall be up directly, Mr Niven.' Winchip rose from his seat. 'Keep the lookouts sharp. I find satisfaction in being the first to challenge.' He raised a hand in acknowledgement as Niven left.

Winchip stared through misted stern windows, translucent with the rivulets of water trickling down to the frame. He was thinking of Madeleine, drawn tragically into Foche's scheme. What he didn't believe was that Foche would go to such lengths in his act to rescue an Englishwoman when, according to him, he had enough problems protecting his own interests, unless ... He turned and retrieved his coat from the chest, suddenly aware that the rain had stopped and a weak sun was trying to lance through the broken cloud – much the same as his confused mind.

He heard the call from the tops as he came up through the companion.

The ships of the Western Squadron, scattered well apart in a rising sea, all pointed into the wind, tugged at their cables like impatient dogs. The larger seventy-fours and the lesser sixty-gun ships dipped their salt-stained bows into the rolling head sea, each in its own time, as if controlled by some infernal machine. All about them lesser vessels and heavy boats scurried to and fro, like paper boats on a millpond, all plying their respective trades or competing for it. A barquentine with ensign at the flutter, probably from Plymouth, kept attendance on a Second Rate, a succession of boats passing between them.

Sitting four square, almost too solid to be affected by mere water, sat the flagship. A broad pennant stood out as stiff as a pike from the masthead truck. The *Royal George*, an hundred-gun First Rate, flagship of Admiral of the White, the Lord Hawke, symbolised the strength of England's Royal Navy. A leviathan among ships, she embodied the essence of naval might.

As Winchip had approached, sitting in the stern sheets of the jolly boat, the ship seemed to engulf him in its shadow. The bulbous tumblehome towered above him, only a few eager faces looking down from the entry port giving him scant encouragement as he prepared to climb the ladder.

Safely on board, his knees weak with the experience of surviving the climb, he was saluted by a young and eager flag-lieutenant who took his despatches and guided him up a spiral staircase to the quarterdeck. Winchip saw the decks in much the same way he had appreciated *Ramillies*. The difference was the brass cannons. With their white breechings crossed at the trunnions and their colour that of burnished gold, they brought atmosphere to the topside, feelings of both invincibility and clinical deliverance, the one complementing the other. He tipped his hat to Captain Campbell amidst the twittering of pipes and a cloud of pipe clay.

'It is a delight tae see ye again, Captain. Welcome on boord the *Royal George*.'

'And I to see you, Sir.' Winchip saw the man as he had done the day he had boarded his first ship as a lieutenant. Certainly, he was older, but as Captain Campbell had once reminded him, the things that mattered in a man knew no age . . . they endured.

'Come! We'll awa' tae somewhere quiet, where we can talk.' Campbell led the way past the great double wheel and into the shadowy depths beneath the poop. They sat in the stateroom and discussed Winchip's progress since they had last met. Thirty minutes and two glasses of claret passed before Campbell mentioned Captain Rance, at the same time giving his approval of the verdict. 'He's here, ye ken. On patrol duty with the Inshore Squadron, sniffing oot the French traders coming and going tae the colonies. Och, 'tis a sad matter all round. Obsessed with the death of his son and now dishonoured in court – 'tis sad indeed.'

Winchip nodded his head. Campbell had summed the matter up in those few well-meant words but he had no time to reply. The young flag-lieutenant stepped out from a doorway and stood to one side, beckoning Winchip through the door.

Like that of Admiral Byng, the great cabin yielded to practicality, yet the quality of the furnishing lent little to economy. The smell of beeswax and tallow still prevailed, except that here it was tainted by the tang of new paint and not a little tar – the expected pervasion after every refit.

Winchip waited, hat in hand, until the admiral looked up from the papers on his desk. Among them, no doubt, his reports, beyond those he had already received. He had heard that Hawke could be touchy about indiscretions. Winchip wondered how he would react to downright folly. Since his meeting with Admiral Byng he had seen death, avoided it and dispensed it. A matter that would not go unnoticed by the admiral, he was sure.

'You have been a busy man, Captain.' Hawke had taken Winchip's reports and despatches to the harsher light of the stern windows, to a chair around which papers were literally scattered on an ornate eastern rug where it was obvious he had spent the last hour, perusing and digesting.

Winchip took the moment to refresh his recollection of the man responsible for destroying enough French sea traffic to bring France and England close to war, every ship and prisoner taken being in retaliation for the French attacks on English outposts in The Americas.

Hawke looked like a man at home in matters of attrition. His strength was not in his height but in his majestic corpulence and strong features – the square contours of his face and the thin line of his lips below a proud straight nose. His eyes were dark and deep, missing nothing, but reflecting the sharpness of his brain with their small but quick movements as thoughts resolved themselves into direct and uncompromising speech. 'You will want to know that *Corinne* is now an abandoned wreck, looking plundered into the bargain.' Hawke had not looked away from his papers. 'I don't know exactly what you did to her but my frigate captain, who reported her demise on Yeu, said she looked as though she had been blown up!'

'*Eaglet* did put up a spirited defence, My Lord.' Winchip relaxed. So she hadn't sunk, along with his career. 'Plundered by locals more like.'

'Hmm.' Admiral Hawke looked at him at last. A studied look, making an assessment, judging his man. A crinkle of a smile developed at the corners of his tight-lipped mouth. 'As you say, Captain. A spirited defence.'

Winchip waited for the sting in the tail but it didn't come. He had refrained from speculation or embellishment in his reports, just keeping to the facts. He knew that were his own little confrontation to be compared with the activities of the admiral in the approaches, taking commercial shipping by the dozen and sending prisoners back to England by the boat-load, he would have little to answer for. Had he gone outside the bounds of his orders, that would have been a different matter.

The admiral selected another sheet from the bunch. 'All Foche has told us, we know already. We are also aware that troop vessels are being prepared at Brest.' He struck the papers with the back of his fingers, a dismissive gesture. 'We have also received ample reports of troop movements. All this insistence – this confirmation! At the cost of a ship and many French lives, I might add.' The statement said it all, requiring no comment from Winchip. Hawke let the paper fall to the deck to join the others. 'Something is afoot, Winchip, as you suggest. Of that I am certain.'

'Not necessarily at Brest either, My Lord.' Winchip had spoken his thoughts. He, too, was unconvinced of Foche's credibility, and having met the man would believe nothing he had to say. At the moment, however, it was for others to decide.

'Did you have something specific in mind, Captain?' Hawke spoke without looking at him, presumably seeking a foil for his own train of thought.

'On my last visit to the Western Squadron, My Lord, Admiral Byng was quick to remind me that Foche probably dipped his spoon in both camps.' Hawke's silence prompted him to continue. 'His masters are going to a great deal of trouble to convince Their Lordships that, for now at least, the blockade here, in the north, should continue. I submit, Admiral, that it begs the obvious question. What else are they doing and where?'

'Carry on, Captain. You have my full attention.' Hawke returned to his chair, his hair and the edges of his frock coat like gossamer in the harsh light from the windows. He took a sip of his claret.

'I believe, My Lord, that something is imminent.' Winchip took a breath. '*Corinne* was employed to chase us off, giving the impression that there was something going on in the Gironde. Were we to be fooled into believing him, it is likely that we would employ valuable ships and time to blockade the place. If Miss Loxley is to be believed, the Gironde is empty – not a vessel worth a mention – too wide and too obvious. Whatever it is we are missing, Admiral, I would suggest it has very little to do with the invasion of England but will be as far from this area as possible.' Winchip took up his glass by the stem, inferring he had little else to say and knowing the dangers of protracted speech.

'Please, don't stop now, Winchip. I'm warming to your case.' Hawke rested his glass on the small table at his side.

'I would call it speculation based on very slim evidence, Admiral.'

'Please let me be the judge of that, Captain.' Hawke gave a wry smile.

'My Lord. When I first took Foche on board he was both

arrogant and cocksure. The arrogance born out of familiarity and the swagger out of over confidence. When I told him about the French ship on our heels, *he* mentioned a frigate – not I.'

'You mean he knew it was coming?' The quill in Hawke's hand began to scratch on paper.

'Yes, Admiral. *Our* friendly spy was party to the whole deceit.' Winchip sat back in his chair feeling that he had said enough, yet he knew there was more to come if the whole matter was to be resolved.

'Is there more?' Hawke was leaning forward, his elbow on the arm of his chair, a hand on his knee.

'What else I have to say, My Lord, is pure guesswork. Until last evening I would have let my thoughts rest there. Now, I cannot. I am not given to speculation, Admiral, but on our return from Aix we spotted a sail to seaward. It was a good sighting and reckoned to be a frigate. We have seen that sail twice more since we came into the approaches. We challenged twice but each time she made off. One of my middies thought it to be a frigate and I believe him above any lookout.'

'She could have been trying to get home by circling to the north. Had you thought of that?'

'Yes, My Lord, I did and it is in my journal. There is one other possibility, which I have only just come to realise. It could be that in the event of my rising to the challenge of *Corinne*, I was supposed to face the combined attack of two frigates. It just so happened that a bad squall passed across the area prior to the engagement. I believe this other frigate was caught in it before she could respond and then took flight when she saw the demise of her partner.' Winchip hesitated, surprised when Hawke failed to intercede. 'This second frigate still has her orders – to prevent us going south.'

'Hmm.' Hawke stroked his chin. 'Has it not occurred to you, Winchip, that *Corinne* and this unknown vessel may have been ordered to avenge the loss of er ...' Hawke retrieved a paper from the floor '... the er, *Valeureuse*? Most of Europe was aware of her demise, dammit; and at the hands of a frigate. And, by God, it didn't go down well with the French as you must have found out at the court martial. Your capture, or worse, would make good reading.'

Winchip was stunned. He had heard nothing of all this, neither had he considered it that important. It was now obvious that the French had made an official complaint – but revenge? He was surprised he hadn't been sent, like a lamb, to the sacrificial altar of politics! He jerked himself together and replied. 'I had no knowledge of this, My Lord.'

'Well, be that as it may, the possibility is still there.' Hawke sat back in the chair as far as his figure allowed. 'It still doesn't answer the more serious problem, does it?'

Winchip paused. 'There is something about to happen in the south, Admiral. I am sure of it. It has to do with Toulon. There is nowhere else. It certainly isn't to do with the Spanish and, as I have said, it has little to do with the invasion . . . at least, not directly.' Winchip relaxed and took a sip of the claret.

'Toulon?' Hawke's eyebrows arched, but not with surprise.

'I believe so, Admiral. One has to consider Minorca or Gibraltar. Toulon is well equipped to build ships, as I am sure you are aware. Troops may also embark from there. What better place? Those ships, having been used at Minorca, could then be used for the invasion of England. They could move north with a fleet escort or use the Atlantic to come in from the west – ideal for Ireland.'

Admiral the Lord Hawke, his expression thoughtful, relaxed into the chair, gently tapping a seal knife on the surface of the arm. 'I was expecting some homespun philosophy, Winchip. All you have said makes perfect sense and I thank you for it. What you have deduced from a single incident, Their Lordships have just come to realise after many months of good intelligence and the loss of quite a few English lives.' Hawke let his words sink in.

Winchip's surprise was absolute. With a cold dampness on his spine he suddenly realised what was coming next.

Someone would be required to run the gauntlet and find out exactly what *was* going on at Toulon.

'We shall discuss this further. I may want to adjust your orders accordingly. Be that as it may, I feel that whatever the outcome, I shall finish up taking a hand in it – perhaps you and I, both, eh?' Hawke inspected his claret and raised it, causing the light from the stern windows to give it luminescence.

Winchip inclined his head. He would do as he was ordered. His mind went to Madeleine for a moment, only to be quickly banished, knowing the depth to which his thoughts might go.

'The French are not fools, Captain. They are obviously aware of *Corinne's* fate.' There was a pause as Hawke paced the cabin, loosening the buttons of his elegant waistcoat to relieve his ample figure.

Winchip waited. The flagship seemed like dry land, solid and immovable. Outside the clouds scudded past the windows, driven by a wind which had backed to south-westerly, bringing the weather back to resume the order of things and keep the French tied to their moorings.

'We are faced with a terrible prospect, Winchip.' Hawke stopped his pacing and returned to his chair. 'At this moment the French will be wondering if we have discovered their plans and are assuming the worst.' It was as if Hawke was thinking aloud. He looked up, staring Winchip in the eye. 'Their first priority will be to stop us getting to Toulon and finding out for ourselves.'

'If you could get a message to the Governor at Gibraltar . . .'

'Lieutenant General Fowke, the Governor of Gibraltar, is well aware something is in the air.' Hawke spoke the governor's name as if there was a rift between them. A lack of confidence perhaps.

'A fleet requires an admiral, My Lord, as does an army a commander.' Winchip's statement of the obvious was offered more for continuity of thought than constructive comment.

'Quite so. The French army forming at Toulon is commanded by the Duc de Richelieu; and Roland-Michel Barin, Marquis de la Galissonnière commands their fleet.' Hawke turned to face Winchip. 'It is lack of evidence of intent and the intransigence of . . .' He stopped as if having gone too far, a sudden anger rising and ebbing in a moment. 'All I can say, my dear Winchip, is that if it can be proved beyond doubt that the French have a specific target in mind, Gibraltar or Minorca, then something can be done.' Hawke sat and stared at the desk as if waiting for providence to supply the answers.

'If it were possible for General Fowke to send a small observation party into Toulon, My Lord . . .' Winchip was thinking about the problem as he would a cutting-out party. He knew better.

'No Captain!' The words were sharp. 'You have little knowledge of politics.' He stretched his neck – a nervous gesture. 'Were General Fowke to organise a landing party, then, whatever was discovered, would be connived to indicate that Gibraltar was the target – his precious Gibraltar! Minorca could go hang!' His anger subsided, his next words more conciliatory. 'What England requires, my dear Winchip, is an independent view. A report on just the facts, as you have presented to me about *Corinne* and all other matters. That is what I require. I want *Eaglet* to undertake the task!'

It was as if Hawke had read his mind. In the time that the admiral had been speaking, Winchip's thoughts had passed through fear to that of duty and the quality of his crew. The whole reason for his being, who he was and what he was.

'Getting there is one thing but getting back is another.' Hawke spoke with slitted eyes as if he were planning the exercise – seeing the dangers in his mind's eye. 'They will take every precaution to hide their intentions.' He nodded violently to emphasise his words, as if seeing disaster from every point of the compass but knowing he had no better option.

'*Eaglet* will do her duty, My Lord, you can rely upon it.'

Winchip knew the words sounded obligatory but they could be said no other way.

'I know she will, Captain. I know.' Hawke spoke gently, not in regret but as if he could see the impossible task he was placing on Winchip's shoulders – the awful responsibility. He suddenly braced himself as though he had made up his mind. 'I shall think on what we have discussed, Captain. In the meantime, I have decided to give you an escort, the frigate *Adept*. It will give you more chance and another pair of eyes.' Hawke looked down as if knowing it was the last thing Winchip wanted.

Winchip's heart dropped, yet he saw the sense in it. 'I shall await your orders, My Lord.' Such fatuous words, leaving volumes unspoken and speculation rife. He stood and set his sword.

'There is one other thing to which I think you should be privy, Captain. God knows, at least you should be told what is happening.' Hawke stood and came round to him, lowering his voice as he continued. 'We have a fleet in the making. Who will command it and where it is to be sent may rest with you, Winchip. I have given you a certain amount of latitude with Captain Rance of *Adept*, although he is your senior. Also with General Fowke and both of them will, I know, respect my wishes. Until you return you are to be your own master. You will act alone and be responsible only to me.' He looked Winchip in the eye. 'Is that understood?'

'Perfectly, My Lord.'

Hawke smiled. 'Whatever orders I send over to you, my dear Winchip, I wish you God's speed and a safe return. Just make sure that I receive a copy of the report that goes to General Fowke – he will want one, mark my words – but nothing about a fleet. Not a word.' His hand came out, gripping Winchip's as if he wanted part of himself to go with *Eaglet*, to transfer all the weight of his command into what he knew to be a dangerous enterprise.

To Winchip, the quiet and airy spaciousness of the great cabin suddenly seemed like another world. The chessboard of world affairs where moves were made, one seemingly unrelated to the other, for reasons known only to the mover, the results unpredictable for the pawns that fell along the way.

Winchip stood with Captain Campbell at the entry door, the perils of the tumblehome steps still to be faced. 'Thank you for your courtesy and hospitality, Sir. It has been a pleasure to see you again. After *Corinne* I thought I might have more difficulty leaving than arriving.' Winchip and Campbell laughed in unison. 'I trust the fresh meat and vegetables have all been delivered safely?'

'Aye, they have and grateful we are, I can assure ye!' Campbell bent closer and spoke quietly in Winchip's ear. 'I know something of what is expected of ye and I wish ye every success, mon.' He offered his hand.

'Thank you, Sir.' Winchip felt his hand grasped in a vice-like grip.

Campbell said wryly, 'Flag-lieutenants lead a more sedentary life nowadays, I'm afraid. I shall be with ye in spirit and look forward to yeer return.' He stood back and uncovered.

Winchip had no chance to reply as the crash of hands on pipeclay threw out a white cloud, and the shrill of the pipes committed him to that perilous drop.

9

A Tragic Error

The journey south, in a lusty north-westerly, had provided a good start for *Eaglet*, the wind on her quarter and her progress swift. With stuns'ls set, ten knots was recorded with the log-ship. *Eaglet*'s best speed to date.

The nature of Winchip's mission brought with it the possibility that he might not return. The prospect was unimaginable. As he found himself dwelling upon it, so he had dashed the thought from his mind – blanked it out as if his survival and that of his crew were not in question.

The strange sail had appeared once more on the evening of the second day, well south of Ushant where the land drifted further away to larboard with every mile. The setting sun had reflected from the stranger's fore-top gallant like a red beacon, causing the shout from the tops.

'Not the *Adept* then, Sir?' Niven lowered the glass.

'No, Lieutenant. She will be waiting for us further south, I am told, close to Raz Point. Whoever this one is, she has the patience of Job.'

'I wonder how she will feel when she sees the two of us.' Niven closed the glass and put it carefully back into the rack. 'Whoever she is, she is going south, Sir, so we may not have seen the last of her.'

Winchip smiled. 'We shall deal with that when the time comes. I want clear water between ourselves and Corunna, day and night, after our meeting with *Adept*, Lieutenant. This is one passage I would like to make without mishap, if you take my drift. I shall be below if I'm required.' He stepped beneath the poop with his hand before his mouth, yawning. His cot beckoned.

Four bells signalled the end of the second dog watch. An uncomfortable night lay ahead with the first wet flakes of snow settling insistently on the deck. It deadened all sound, bringing a form of grace to the line of great guns, dormant and benign, bedecked in a thickening veil of crystal white.

The windows of the cabin were clouded long before Winchip and Niven had finished their coffee. Of the snow floating down outside there was little sign, except where it gathered incessantly in the corner of each window-pane. Periodically, a creak in the woodwork confirmed the presence of a fitful wind, while the tremulous sinking of the stern spoke of an ever present following sea.

Winchip and Niven paced fore and aft on the quarter-deck, turning inwards at the taffrail and retracing their steps. Each was cloaked, with collars secured to the chin against the snow and the cold.

'Well, Mr Niven. If both the stern lamps are shining to the west and we have our best men in the tops, where can this damned escort of ours be?' The question was rhetorical; Winchip wished he knew the answer.

'We have been plodding along since before dark, Sir. I fail to see what else we can do.' Niven was quite distressed. He was changing the lookouts with increasing regularity, the burden placed mainly upon the midshipmen. It was bitterly cold and the tops were no place to be for any length of time.

'We shall compromise, Lieutenant, and lay to while we can.'

'Aye, Sir.' Niven touched his hat and waited for the captain to disappear through the companion.

Niven rose and fell with the deck as the ship wallowed in the shallow swell. It was a bitter coldness that reached the vitals, penetrating every part of the body. He refrained from stamping his feet with the captain below, eager to get two hours sleep before the beginning of the morning watch. Instead he raised Bowes and put men to clearing the decks.

He watched the snowflakes that danced within the yellow light of the deck lantern, only to be dismissed back into the obscurity of the night.

He noticed the flash rather than saw it. It had been a momentary thing, apparent in the corner of his eye, due west. Niven stared into the whiteness, waiting for it to come again, needing to persuade himself that he hadn't imagined it. A faint rumble reached him, so quiet as to remain unheard except that he was alert. Another flash, a long one, far away and close to the surface of the sea, convinced him.

'Mr Bowes!' He used the 'hailer, startling the helmsman and a mate into jerking upright. Niven faced them. 'One of you raise the master – the other can prepare to come about!'

'*All hands! All hands up to wear ship!*'

The shrill of whistles sounded throughout the ship, each vying for attention and, from the shouts below, getting it. A surge of bodies poured through the hatches, those that had been asleep cursing the snow and all it entailed. Top men rushed past Niven, the after-guard to the mizzen-mast. The midshipmen arrived in their turn, each tipping his hat with red-ringed eyes both vacant and wide.

'What is to do, Lieutenant?' Winchip tightened the collar of his cloak, the weariness on his face worn like a gaunt mask.

'Gunfire, Sir, coming out of the north-west. The flashes and sounds were faint, but definite.'

'Thunder and lightning, perhaps?' Winchip had greater faith, but the question had to be asked.

'No, Sir. I'm sure it was gunfire.'

'That's good enough for me, Lieutenant.' Winchip stared into a white void. It could only be *Adept*. Who then was her opponent? Winchip's thoughts went back to the stranger. Had she mistaken *Adept* for *Eaglet*?

Eaglet fell away to westward, the boom of hardening canvas almost deafening as the topsails caught what little wind there was. The yards were well back, the main course angled towards the entry port.

'Our course is due west, Sir – wind out of the north-north-west.' Niven touched his hat and then stood behind his captain's shoulder, relinquishing the deck.

The ship that had hitherto been so quiet was now coming to life in a maelstrom of noise and activity. The plodding lines of seamen and marines pulled round the last of the great yards. They slipped and cursed in the downpour of snow dropping from the disturbed rigging as from a tree in a sudden thaw.

Winchip turned to Niven. 'Hurry the snow clearance, Lieutenant. I want this snow cleared completely and then the decks sanded. The boats can go over and towed later, as we get closer.'

'Mr Bowes has it in hand, Sir.'

The flash came again, as *Eaglet* was coming round, the rumble coming at the count of nine, faint but distinct.

'*Deck there! Gunfire – dead ahead!*'

'Better late than never, I suppose.' Winchip shook his head wearily.

'*Make fast and belay!*'

Eaglet settled on her new tack, close-hauled, as the wind backed. Winchip thanked God for Niven's brave decision. The gunfire had been too protracted for practice and too spasmodic for anything but a sea action.

'Nine-pounders, those, I'd say, Sir.' Niven was cupping his ears, trying to read events.

'Ah! There are the twelves! Much deeper.' Winchip could see what was happening in his mind's eye. 'Someone is losing that fight, Mr Niven. I have the feel of it.' He shook his head, a moment of sympathy for the loser under such conditions.

Three bright flashes made Winchip close his eyes and look away – always too late, his night vision suddenly destroyed in a moment.

'We are closing, Sir.' Niven looked at the captain.

'Then beat to quarters, Lieutenant.' Winchip clasped his hands behind his back. 'Breakfast will have to wait after all.'

'*Hands to quarters! Round shot all! Boats over and tow!*'

'*Top men up! Prepare to take in courses!*'

Niven bent over the log, making his entries. Another long, bright flash was followed by a deep rumble as the semblance of a broadside was discharged, immediately repeated as the other ship replied, a more erratic response without the authority of the first – the tipping of the scales.

'*Take in courses – battle canvas!*'

Winchip lowered the 'hailer. He turned to Piper, the little midshipman at his side, shaking in his shoes but with his head held high. 'Signal locker, Mr Piper, if you please. Raise the battle ensign!' Winchip smiled as the little fellow scuttled away, no doubt delighted to suddenly be doing something of importance.

Eaglet pitched in what was now a bow sea coming on to her starboard bow. A bad platform for the gunners and Winchip knew it. It cast a shadow on his first intentions but confirmed his alternative. He would close with the enemy, when they knew which ship to attack.

Niven lowered his glass and turned to Winchip. 'I have them, Sir. They are alongside each other facing south-west.' He smiled. 'The nearer one is the *Frenchman* – her ensign, from here, is pure white.' Niven raised his glass once more. 'She is a small frigate of twenty-six guns, Sir, I'd say.'

'Thank you, Lieutenant. We shall come up to them from astern. Get Bowes to load his bow chasers with grape, and the same for all the starboard swivels – it may lessen the odds for us. I'm surprised they haven't yet seen us.'

Eaglet turned onto her new course, her sail reduced to reefed tops'ls as she crept towards the combatants, her stern rising and falling with a gentle action in time with the sea. There was a tenuous silence. Men stood, some holding boarding spikes, others crouched like statues, pistols from the arms chest in their belts and cutlass or axe to hand, each waiting for the order that could mean life or death. Some grinned at each other in wild anticipation. Others cowed, their pale, gaunt faces staring aft towards the quarterdeck. Aloft, marines lodged themselves in the cross-trees, ready with their muskets, to shoot the French officers as they appeared. Even the slopping of water beneath the counter sounded loud. The snow eased to the lightest of flakes, as if giving way to events yet to happen.

The ships were suddenly close enough for the noise of battle to intrude. A fierce engagement that told of hand-to-hand fighting – a mixture of shouts, shots, screams and the clash of steel.

At the distance of two cables, Winchip made his decision. He turned to Niven. 'We shall board her, after we have sent a broadside into her vitals. Run out!'

Niven shouted his orders.

The ship suddenly came alive. With the enemy now clearly in sight and with musket balls humming about *Eaglet*'s rigging, men clambered to their stations, lining the starboard side armed to the teeth.

'After the broadside, let the swivels do their work – they'll halve the opposition.' He patted Niven on the back. 'You board at the bows. I shall take the quarterdeck!'

'You know the other ship is *Adept*, don't you, Sir?'

'I do, Mr Niven – she can be no other.' Winchip turned to his side as Hellard arrived, holding his fighting sword. He raised his arms as the coxswain adjusted it round his waist. 'Thank you, Hellard – I think it may come in useful today.' He flashed his coxswain a wry smile.

The moment was almost upon them. The time when Winchip would normally revert to an icy calmness, when his fears would depart like a summer mist and he would be prepared for whatever was to follow. This time it was different. He felt angry; angry that circumstances brought about by folly could deprive him of his life when it was so important that he stay alive. He thought of her but could bring no substance to his thoughts, not even see the image of her face. His naval code was directing his every action, his need to deal with the task in hand, as it should be. As it had to be.

'Your pistols, Captain.' Hellard held the two weapons by the barrel, allowing Winchip to see they were loaded and primed.

Eaglet was drawing closer. A solitary port in the *Frenchman*'s side opened with a flutter and then slammed shut. Somewhere a trumpet sounded. The noise of the fighting had stopped, a sure sign that *Adept* had succumbed. On the nettings of the enemy, faces appeared, staring at *Eaglet* as if mesmerised, seeing her final approach as the harbinger of their own demise. The panic came with the first cry of warning, at the sight of *Eaglet*'s ports gaping wide and the snouts of the twelve-pounders pointing their intent.

'*Fire!*'

The guns fired as one, immediately after the swivels. At the range of a few yards the balls burst through the planking of the French frigate, smashed open her ports and came up through the decks as they careered off the latent and unmanned larboard guns. As bodies were tossed into the air so the thick acrid smoke rolled back over *Eaglet*, the yellow cloud carried on a wind reluctant to release it.

'*Boarders away!*'

The shouts of the charging *Eaglets* as they leaped across the void was almost drowned in the resonant ring of the swivels. The grape they discharged cut swathes through the packed ranks of Frenchmen rising to repel them, as Winchip knew they would. Men, one moment standing, defiant and with a forced bravado, pitched down between the two ships or were thrown backwards onto their own deck, maimed or dying, blowing bubbles of blood, their eyes wide and questioning.

Winchip climbed onto the bulwark and raised his pistol hand with a rallying cry, and then leaped for the nettings of the *Frenchman,* urged on by the watery chasm that appeared beneath him. He flopped onto the hammocks, hanging by the fingers, and then scrambled onwards, only to tumble onto the foreign deck in an ungainly heap. He stood to rally those about him . . . to find himself alone.

'We'm comin', Sir!'

Winchip heard the anguished cry. He leaped to his feet, feeling naked fear as a small knot of French seamen broke off from the main body of defenders to deal with him. They stopped for a moment, intimidated by his pointed pistol and then leaped forward as one.

''Old on, Sir! We'm comin!'

Again the empty words. Winchip wanted to look round, hearing the voice behind him, wondering why no one was appearing at his side. He fired a pistol, shooting the largest man in the eye, throwing him screaming onto his back, his huge cutlass rattling past his feet. Another and yet another Frenchman fell, each with a pike embedded in him, cast from *Eaglet*. Throwing the empty pistol into the face of another, Winchip drew the second, firing it aimlessly, satisfied as another body sprawled under the feet of his companions. He stared another in the eye, wondering as he did so why he hadn't been shot. He drew his father's fighting sword, hearing the singing of the Toledo blade as it escaped the scabbard, and pointed it at the man's throat. Making a feint, he caused the man to jerk back in alarm and then laugh in his face as he compared his cutlass with Winchip's slender weapon. Winchip knew the signs and relaxed – this man was dead already. He took the two steps necessary to confront the man while his friends watched and then adopted the *en garde* position, to the big man's amusement. He then thrust the sword through the man's throat, his rear knee almost on the deck with the depth of the lunge.

'*Eaglets*! To me!' Winchip withdrew his bloodied blade, turning, gladdened by the sight of Bowes leading the pikemen, waving his hanger above his head to rally his men. Behind him the cocked hats of the marines bobbed among the mass, clamouring to cross the gap.

A volley of musket fire alerted the defenders to the new threat from the rear, some of them collapsing to the deck, clutching at their bodies, their screams adding to the chaos. Winchip knew that on the other side of the packed ranks of French seamen, Niven and his party were fighting their way towards him.

Winchip caught a man in the groin with his sword and prepared to defend himself, cheered by the sound of Gray's voice behind him. He had his marines with him, Corporal Basson at their head. He thanked God for it.

Many of the Frenchmen turned on their heels. No longer a solitary officer to contend with but something much more. A small number, cut off from their companions, turned towards them, their faces maniacal in the cold light of the coming dawn, confronted, not by men worn out by fighting but by fresh seamen and the dreaded bullocks, eager for a fight, struggling to reach the thick of it.

Winchip lunged forward, taking a man in the stomach, almost losing his footing in something slippery and anonymous. Shots rang out, the dull but vicious bark of muskets, heard above the screams and cries of those fighting for their lives, killing and being killed. Two of the pikemen at Winchip's side sank quietly to the deck, one of them denying the blood that spurted from his side, trying to regain his feet but getting weaker by the second. Again, Winchip found himself cut off, only his delicately curved fighting blade between him and the awesome weapons of the enemy.

A man lunged at him from the mass – a big man. A seaman with the demeanour of a petty officer, but no artificer – a deck man, with the animal cunning and basic instincts that all that implied. He wore a sneer of pure hatred, his eyes wide with confidence as he made his move, others behind him, glad of his leadership. Winchip hurriedly adopted the best defensive stance he knew; the last resort his father had called the '*petit coup*', knowing he could never stop the man by strength alone. As the man rushed forward to within Winchip's range, his cutlass directed at his chest, his sword arm was locked in the style of a cavalryman.

'Stand aside, Sir, I beg you let me take him!' Gray's voice was pleading and then demanding. How much Winchip wanted to turn away. How impossible it was to even think about it. Time had run out.

Winchip swayed his body to one side, knowing the man's cutlass could not possibly change course in time. At the same moment he lifted the point of his sword from chest height to the level of the man's nose. He flicked the tip of the blade from left to right and back again across the man's eyes, in a move so fast that the man hardly knew it had happened. As the seaman blundered past him Winchip lowered his shoulder and rammed it into the man's side, beneath the armpit of his sword arm, sending him reeling across the deck and crashing into his oncoming companions, totally blind from that moment on. The cry as he lay on the deck was more of a howl that could be heard above the sound of battle. It was an unnerving cry for help that went on and on.

For a moment longer the cry continued until it ceased with the suddenness borne of mercy. The seamen about him stopped in disbelief, a little cameo of men, thrown together to witness the stark reality of life and death. No longer led and suddenly without the surreal security of those who gave them strength.

The arms began to rise, men backing into their companions, stumbling over bodies, seeking to shrivel into the obscurity of the mass. Weapons clattered to the floor as men backed away as far as they were able, in fear and resignation, exposing the large form of the petty officer lying in a pool of smeared blood, a knife jutting ominously and mercifully from his back.

Seeing the plight of their fellows, the French seamen facing Niven and his men in the bows let their weapons fall to the deck with a clatter, some thrown at the English feet in disgust. They raised their arms in the air reluctantly, angry and sullen at having to surrender their recent victory, their abusive mutterings only subdued at the sight of Gray's marines in their red jackets. The few bullocks left in the charge of Sergeant Haggler started to collect the arms, throwing them into untidy heaps in the scuppers, discharging loaded pistols into the air.

'We couldn't get through to you, Sir!' Bowes stood before Winchip, distraught and angry that he had been physically unable to cross the gap to the *Frenchman*. 'The ship swung away, Sir!' He hung his head, his fists clenched, shaking his head as if bewildered by such a quirk of fate. He murmured, 'It was just too far to jump.'

'It is over. Let us deal with the present. You made it eventually, Mr Bowes, and you did your duty. That is all that matters.' Winchip laid a hand on the midshipman's shoulder as he spoke, before bending to pick up a scarf from the deck with which to wipe the blade of his sword. The weapon slid into the scabbard after several attempts, his hand suddenly unsteady after his brush with death. 'See to our wounded, young man. Get them below into *Eaglet*. They shall not be allowed to bring satisfaction to the enemy!'

'Aye, Sir, aye!' Bowes ran to do as he was bid, as if with the fresh heart of absolution.

Winchip looked aft as something caught his eye, almost shouting as he pointed at the halyard. 'Remove those damned colours!' He waited until they had crumpled to the deck, suddenly aware of Niven at his side.

'Sir.' Niven looked exhausted but with the glint of the victor in his eye. 'I have the French officers separated. The captain is in his cabin, under guard. He has disposed of the ship's papers, I'm afraid.'

'No matter, Lieutenant – it is his duty.' Winchip gripped Niven's arm. 'Well done, Mr Niven. Someone will know of your actions this day!'

'Thank you, Sir.' Niven smiled and raised himself to his full height. 'I have many duties to perform, Sir, repairs and the like. I came to make sure you were not among the wounded.'

'My God, the wounded. I should have asked, Lieutenant. What is the bill?'

'Five dead and fifteen wounded, Sir. One or two have cuts and bruises – nothing of consequence. Earning the rest of the day in a hammock is reckoned to be a fair price to pay.' Niven was trying to smarten himself, arrange his stock and cover a small tear in his coat. Blood was on his sword hand – but none of it his own.

'What about the captain of *Adept*, is he hurt?'

'I am told he is in his cabin, Sir.' Niven lowered his eyes. 'In his cups by all accounts.'

Winchip sighed. There would be a reason – there was always a reason. 'I shall go to him, Lieutenant. I take it Mr Pardoe is attending to the prisoners.'

'He is, Sir. They are being taken below. The officers have given their parole so as to attend to their own.'

'Thank you, Lieutenant. Off you go now.' Winchip looked about him. There was much to do and decisions to be made. Winchip leaned for a moment against the ship's belfry, fingering the edges of a sword cut in the polished woodwork. It was then that he saw the ship's name, cast in the bell. It was *Caprice*.

The steady chant of the boatswain urged *Eaglet*'s sprit away from *Caprice*'s bulwark and ratlines with the minimum of damage. *Eaglet* gave a sudden lurch and then curtsied before slipping away from her victim. The holding lines sprayed water as they tightened and then held her fast. The snow had stopped, to be replaced by an icy cold coming out of a star-studded sky to the north-west.

Winchip entered the great cabin of *Adept* without ceremony. The captain was sitting with his back to Winchip, his periwig askew, with protruding tufts of true grey hair seeming to give it extra size. The two epaulettes gave him post rank, warning Winchip to take care.

The manservant looked at him wide-eyed. Turning to the huddled shape in the chair, the man said, ''Tis the captain of the other frigate, Sir.' He took two steps backwards, as if he disowned his captain rather than in any deference to Winchip.

Winchip signalled the man to leave. Walking round the table littered with crockery and empty glasses, he looked into the face of this man who found release in the bottle. For a moment he didn't recognise the reddened and relaxed features, the watery eyes and the stains of dribble on his chin and wine on his stock. When he did recognise him, he backed off a step, shocked at the change in the man and the circumstances in which he had found him. Post-Captain Charles Edward Rance had reached a new nadir in his life. He was unable to speak and had no knowledge of what was going on about him.

Winchip called for the manservant and continued calling until the man burst into the cabin.

'Fetch your first lieutenant immediately and ask him to bring another officer with him – Go, man! Go now!'

Winchip waited until the lieutenant burst into the cabin. Behind him, much to his relief, was Pardoe. Winchip summed the man up quickly. Here was a decent officer seeking escape – he could tell it at a glance. 'Your name?'

'Charles Barriclough, Sir. First Lieutenant.' Barriclough was hatless with a stained bandage wrapped round his head.

'Your captain is ill, Mr Barriclough. I think it would be prudent if you put him into his cot.' Winchip nodded towards Pardoe. 'Mr Pardoe will be pleased to help you.'

'Thank you, Sir. We shall do it immediately.' The lieutenant hesitated. 'What about command, Sir?'

'We shall talk of that later, Lieutenant. In the meantime, look to your captain's interests.' Winchip strode out of the cabin, wanting to know everything yet not trusting himself to ask anything.

Winchip's sympathy towards Capitaine Louis Montesquieu was of a different nature. When he had been offered the man's sword he had gladly allowed him to keep it. The guns of *Caprice* were no match for those of *Adept* and yet he had carried out his orders with a fearful determination. How he must have felt, at his moment of triumph, to hear his lookout report the arrival of a British man-of-war, in the middle of the night, in a snowstorm, was beyond imagination. On top of that, her captor was the *Eaglet*, the very ship he thought he had captured.

Unlike the French captain, Winchip was faced with a problem that seemed to dog him in this time of pseudo war when battles were fought with no prospect of a conclusion.

To release the *Frenchman* would destroy the purpose of his own mission. To take the ship would be to risk a second court martial and the end of his career. *Corinne* and *Valeureuse* had taught him many lessons and he could not imagine Their Lordships at Admiralty singing his praises should another complaint come through diplomatic channels. In the end he devised a compromise. He would take *Caprice* with him to Gibraltar and let others decide her fate.

As for Captain Rance, there was little he could do. With his own report, supported by that of Lieutenant Barriclough, the man would probably be lucky and sent back to sea a wiser man. He had not disparaged him, merely put things in terms of an illness, with the surgeon's backing. What conclusions others came to were none of his business. As Barriclough took *Adept* to the north, back to the Western Squadron, he went with Winchip's good wishes.

At the taffrail he let the warm sun play upon his face as he looked to seaward, suddenly glad to be alive. The enormity and the terror of finding himself alone on the *Frenchman*'s deck had driven home how close he had been to death.

As he closed his eyes he could now see her face. He wanted to reach out and touch her skin, tell her all the things of which hitherto he had been so reluctant to speak. He needed to tell her how much he loved her and wanted her – before fate was offered another bite of the cherry.

10

A Hero's Welcome

Gibraltar was dominated by the rock, the result of a violent upheaval, tilted by some cataclysmic, prehistoric event. The weathering and sedimentation of a hundred million storms had deposited a flatland to seaward – a safe haven for the multitude of small dwellings that lined roads and tracks alike. They led down to the great shipyard and the British garrison, all owing their presence to the Treaty of Utrecht in 1713, confirming Sir George Rooke's victory of 1704.

A flock of inquisitive seagulls, whirling and screeching, kept pace with *Caprice* and *Eaglet* as they eased themselves round Pigeon Island and Cape Carnero, then under tops'ls into the bay. The sight of *Caprice*, her white ensign hanging limply beneath the English colours, had already attracted attention as they approached the anchorage, the flash of sun on lenses betraying those who would watch them from ship and shore alike. *Eaglet*'s minions barked out the required salute, which echoed round the anchorage. The hollow, ringing blast launched a myriad gulls into flapping disarray.

Both vessels came onto their moorings by the old mole, directed there by a lug-sailed cutter, complete with an old battle ensign draped from her stern staff like an airing bed sheet.

Winchip inspected the shipping in the anchorage and beyond. It was far more than he had expected – enough to make up a sizeable squadron and then some, all in ordinary. He was puzzled, mainly because he had been led to believe that the Mediterranean Squadron had been much reduced, ostensibly by the withdrawal of several ships.

A sound, no louder than the rigging in a moderate breeze, grew in intensity as he listened. He grinned as it developed. It was that sound that could only be made by those whom the world had forgotten and had found again. The cheering grew until it resounded around the whole of the hard. At the bulwarks of all manned vessels figures appeared as if from nowhere, waving hats and arms, growing in numbers all the time on the hard and at the big jetty. Winchip could understand their joy, living under the prospect of French domination and the terror that would ensue.

'What the hell . . .?' Niven raised his glass and scanned about him. Lowering it, he looked back at *Caprice*. 'Good God!'

'Yes, Lieutenant. At last they have something to cheer about.'

'And will they cheer when she leaves, as free as a bird?'

'Hmm. We had better hope we leave first then, eh?' Winchip smiled broadly and then turned to look down as he felt his sleeve tugged. It was Midshipman Costly.

'Our number's flying, Sir. Captain to the Governor's office, Sir.'

'Thank you, Mr Costly. Acknowledge, if you please.' Winchip moved towards the entry port, around the busy capstan, well aware that the jolly boat would be ready and waiting.

The pipes shrilled above the cheers as Winchip grasped the knotted rope, easing himself down the battens, ensuring his sword didn't incur a disaster. Bowes' hand was a useful anchor as he warped himself gingerly round into the stern sheets, settling himself as the jolly boat skipped away from the tumblehome.

As they passed two sixty-fours, Winchip could see the answer to his dilemma. These great ships were no longer seaworthy. Great tendrils of rich green weed hung from their cables with signs of grass growing between the huge strands. There was a dereliction about the ships, a lack of care that spoke volumes about the condition of the Royal Navy away from England's shores. The fact that they were still in ordinary at a time when they might be needed most was not lost on Winchip. It begged the question as to the state of readiness of the Mediterranean Squadron, a circumstance that might be to someone's cost in the very near future. It would certainly be a matter for his report to Admiral the Lord Hawke. He glanced at the other vessels where he could, seeing many in the same dishevelled state. A sheer hulk stood like a preying mantis over the hull of a Fourth-Rate awaiting a fore-mast, unattended and inoperative, a sure sign of something amiss. Two sloops and a twenty-eight-gun frigate were obviously in service, each riding anchor with attendants of one sort or another gathered about them.

Winchip accepted the jubilation with a wave – he would have been a dead fish indeed had he not. Even so he shook his head, a mixture of emotions assailing him. It was not possible to see into the dry docks but he thought he could guess at the despair as hulls were inspected after so many idle years of peace. At least he knew the truth of things; was able to discount the vessels, short of becoming gun platforms, should they be considered in any defence of the place. The one positive act in the whole scene was the building work being carried out on the new mole and nearby buildings.

Even the sally-port was crowded. As the jolly boat drew up to the steps, so the people surged forward, disallowing the tossing of oars, permitting them only to be hurriedly shipped as Hellard leaped onto the bottom step.

'Back! Back, I say! Make way for a King's Officer!'

'Is it war, Cap'n? Is it war?'

' 'Oo are ye, Cap'n – what's yer name?'

Winchip scanned the faces about him. Dark faces, pale faces, young and old, each vying to catch a glimpse of the captain and victor. Apparent proof indeed that war had commenced and that Gibraltar's future was in question. This was no crowd of idlers. These were people who depended upon the answers he was unable to give them. Yet, ignore the shouted questions he must. He raised an arm and smiled, as if by so doing he answered them collectively, perhaps allaying their fears, for the present. He followed behind his two solitary marines, pressing through the throng, wanting to block his ears to those very questions to which they deserved answers. Questions to which he had no answers.

The comparative peace and quiet of the secretary's office was profound. The place exuded order, dignity and discipline. Three large windows fell down to floor level, pristine white, with large folding shutters boxed into the sides. Opened by sash, they were connected directly to the garden, accessible by taking a single step. The view over the harbour was impressive, allowing a sight of *Eaglet*, squat upon the water, her pristine image ruffled by the wake of a passing hoy.

There was no tranquillity about the ring of boats gathering to protect *Caprice* from those that would approach and hurl abuse. Already the first of many missiles were being thrown towards her from small craft, an outburst of hatred fast growing into hysteria. At the foot of the garden, beyond the tall, black railings, a contingent of militia trotted past, bobbing in unison with muskets at the port, towards the hard in a dash to restore order.

Across the bay, with the rising hills beyond, Algeciras lay hidden. A sea mist, coming and going like bonfire smoke, chastened by the wind, was swallowing the sails of little craft as they plied back and forth, unknowing and uncaring about the affairs of others.

He had been waiting for more than an hour, the flat of his hand beating lightly upon his thigh, a reaction borne of impatience, an impulse he saw no reason to deny.

A door opened and a young staff officer, a lieutenant, strode through with purpose and a great deal of self-importance. He glanced at the piece of paper in his hand as if to remind himself of Winchip's name. His bright red jacket, splashed with gold, brought colour to the place if nothing else. It fitted him like a glove, his powdered wig giving his head luminescence as he passed through a beam of sunlight, dust particles hanging in the air about his head.

'Captain Winchip?'

'Yes, Lieutenant.'

'My name is Waring, Sir. The general apologises for the delay. He has been studying your reports and despatches at some length, the despatches being of some importance, I gather.' A look of more than casual interest accompanied the unnecessary comment.

Winchip stood to his full height. 'I can only say, Lieutenant ... er ... Waring, that a good many men have died in order to get them here.' He paused. 'They were certainly considered important by those who wrote them.'

The lieutenant looked petulant, his pride in tatters. 'Er ... General Fowke should be ready to see you now, if you would care to follow me, Sir.'

Winchip almost laughed out loud when he detected a slight toss of the head by the dapper young man. One month on *Eaglet* would soon put him back on course. They went through into yet another room, large and luxuriously appointed, where Lieutenant General Thomas Fowke stood in the sunlight by a half-shuttered window.

'Captain Winchip! A pleasure to meet you – at last. You have my apologies for the delay.'

'Your servant, General.' Winchip took the proffered hand. The hint of self-criticism, for having kept him waiting so long, was not lost on him and he warmed to the man immediately because of it. He had a moment to look at the general, of whom Admiral Hawke had been all but disparaging. He was of advancing years, medium height and prone to fat. Not a great deal to inspire confidence, but his smile was broad and disarming. He was dressed in a grey frock coat of plain design – a simple item of day wear that seemed to give him ease of movement. He wore no periwig.

'You have caused quite a stir, Captain. I thank God that the circumstances justify it.' He briefly held up Winchip's report.

'There was little else I could do, Sir. I couldn't allow the French to change the facts of the matter to suit their politics.'

'Quite so, although I doubt we have heard the last of it.' Fowke shrugged his shoulders, waving his arm with a dismissive gesture. Looking again at Winchip's report he studied it closely as if to refresh his memory. 'Your comments with regard to the engagement were most interesting.' He looked up with a smile. 'You were no doubt sorry not to have sent *Caprice* to the bottom, eh?'

The disarming smile had come so easily that Winchip almost fell into the trap. 'My actions were just sufficient to save *Adept* from capture, Sir.' Winchip would not be drawn. He knew the general was testing him, seeking impetuosity – or worse.

Fowke smiled. 'Come now, Captain. Don't be so defensive. Most of the captains here would need to be physically restrained from finishing the job!' He didn't wait for a response, instead he selected one paper from the pile and brought it to the top. 'Ah! Here it is.' He scanned it briefly. 'You seem to be well thought of by Admiral the Lord Hawke. It appears that you both agree about the credibility of Monsieur Foche – or the lack of it!'

'As His Lordship pointed out to me, Sir, Foche serves two masters.' Winchip hoped that was enough. Speculation about the man would serve no purpose here.

Fowke brought out another item, important enough to lay the others aside. 'Their Lordships at the Admiralty are of the opinion that an attack on England is not only inevitable but also imminent. Foche seems to confirm this. Do you disagree?'

Winchip had no idea how much the general had been told. He knew he would be eager for information of any sort that constituted news from England, but there was Hawke's confidentiality to consider. He made his decision.

'I certainly believe, General, that it is the intention of the French to attack England. Monsieur Foche simply laboured the point, at the cost of *Corinne* and a heavy loss of life. In short, Sir, he tried to raise suspicions when the facts were already known. Lord Hawke wondered if Foche's instructions were to deflect attention from activities going on elsewhere – down here in the Mediterranean for instance.'

'Carry on, Captain.'

'My orders, Sir, are as you have read them.' Winchip was not aware of how much information Hawke had imparted to Fowke. The orders that mattered were not written down. It was vital that no one should be told of *Eaglet*'s mission.

'If Lord Hawke is right, Winchip, then we have a problem. The Admiral states that Their Lordships will require details of the activity in Toulon . . .'

Winchip relaxed; General Fowke had Hawke's confidence.

'. . . He suggests that you should be sent there with all haste.' Fowke glanced at Winchip, assessing his reaction and then read on. He glanced again at Winchip, this time wide-eyed, presumably to check whether Winchip looked as mad as his orders seemed to suggest. 'What about you, Captain Winchip?' His eyes were searching. 'What are your feelings on this matter?'

'My belief, Sir, is that either the garrisons at Gibraltar or Minorca, are likely to be attacked by invasion. It is also my contention that the likely target is Mahon – Spain being the only country with eyes on Gibraltar, despite the Treaty.'

'God help us if you are right, Winchip! I don't have to tell you the state of those ships out there!' Fowke jabbed a finger towards the window, Winchip's last remark regarding Minorca seeming to have fallen on deaf ears.

The entry of a steward, complete with claret jug and glasses, provided a precious lull. There was silence as he poured. Fowke took his to the window and inspected it before tasting. After a pause he turned to Winchip.

'Go to Toulon and find out what you can, Winchip, although I think Their Lordships may have to prepare themselves for a shock. We are ill prepared to defend this place and the whole world knows it!'

'May I make a suggestion, General?' Winchip continued

at a gesture from Fowke. '*Eaglet* will do her best to find out what is happening at Toulon. It would serve our purposes well if it were done with the utmost secrecy. We have the advantage at the moment, provided the captain and crew of *Caprice* are detained here for as long as it takes us to complete the task.'

Fowke turned back to the window. 'I see your point. Politically it may prove difficult but she was the aggressor after all.' He stroked his chin and suddenly looked up. 'You can rest easy on that score, Captain. These affairs are notorious for their protraction.' He smiled, warming to the subterfuge. 'I'm too old to change my ways now.'

'In that case, General, can you issue orders for our return to England – on paper, that is? We shall depart openly and lay a course for home, for all to see. If you are allowing officers to sleep ashore and trusties to spend an evening on land, a few words in the taverns will be enough to let it be known we are homeward bound.'

Fowke walked back to the table and gathered up the papers, handing back to Winchip those that applied to him with a smile of satisfaction. 'I shall send word for you to collect your orders – better that way, eh?'

'Thank, you, Sir.' Winchip would have turned to the door but there was something else he needed to ask. 'May I ask your indulgence on another matter, Sir?'

'How can I help you?' Fowke's *bonhomie* had taken in a reef.

'I wish to look up an acquaintance – a Captain Munro. May I make enquiries of your secretary?'

'Douglas Munro, late of my staff and now back at sea with the Mediterranean Squadron?' Fowke beamed and grabbed Winchip's arm, steering him to the window. 'There! The twenty-eight, off the hard. That's Captain Munro – just in for a refit, God help him.'

Winchip turned to the general with raised eyebrows, enough to prompt Fowke into explaining his comment.

'We have precious little of anything here, Winchip. A refit at Gibraltar means collecting limited stores and scraping your bottom. Not a lot is it, for a major naval dockyard?'

'I didn't realise, Sir.' Winchip went on, taken aback. 'I had expected to do some minor repairs . . .'

'They'll do what they can, but don't expect too much.' With that Fowke left the room, leaving only the echoes of his chuckle, which to Winchip sounded more like the tolling of a death knell.

He passed through the large black door onto the street, the reflected sun from the white buildings about him dazzling to the eyes, a fitting contrast to the heady gloom of the governor's residence. He strode down towards the hard, one hand gripping the smooth pommel of his dress sword and in the other some charts that he would certainly need. He negotiated the cobbles, still damp where the sun had yet to reach.

The cheering had reduced to groups of chattering observers, chewing over the event, no doubt seeing in the demise of one French man-of-war the threat of other, larger ships, still at large. In the taverns, the speculation would increase as the beer flowed, discussions robbed of context as questions failed to find answers.

The challenge came from *Mordacious* as the jolly-boat carrying Winchip approached her tumblehome. The frigate, smelling of crusted salt and fouled timber, had lost her sparkle. Great tendrils of weed, attached to her bottom, seemed to float freely in the water like attendant fish to a monster of the deep.

'*Eaglet!*' Hellard's bellow seemed to echo round the anchorage.

Hellard's shout was enough. Already, the knotted rope was being flung down. A seaman climbed swiftly down to the chain plates to beckon the jolly-boat in. Above the bulwarks, Winchip could see the rapid movement of heads – a sure sign that he was about to take the officer of the watch by surprise.

He came through the entry posts to a different scene. Even as he cocked his hat and the pipes twittered, he could tell the vessel was in good order, merely from the feel of her and the smartness of her fittings and rigging, and the cleanliness of the deck beneath his feet.

'Welcome on board, Sir.' Captain Munro was a mountain of a man, tall and broad, even seeming to dwarf the hastily mustered marines on the side party. The single epaulette shone brightly on his shoulder. His heavy features produced a smile with the minimum of movement, qualified only by his curiosity at the unexpected visit. As the senior vessel present, until Winchip's arrival, his mind must have been churning with possibilities.

'Thank you, Captain.' Winchip hoped he looked suitably apologetic. He was well aware that Munro would have looked him up in the list within five minutes of entering harbour.

'Shall we go below, Sir?' Already Munro was on the move, used to making the running on his own command.

The cabin was smaller than that of *Eaglet*, as was to be expected. The two nine-pounder guns dominated it, squatting benignly to the sides, waiting their moment when all else would be of little consequence.

Munro spoke as he indicated a chair. 'I am honoured, Sir, although I can think of no reason why I deserve it.' He gave a nod to someone beyond Winchip's vision.

'I come on a personal matter, Captain, and can only apologise for what must be an intrusion.' Winchip gathered his words. 'Through circumstances to do with navy business I have become acquainted with Miss Loxley, whom, I believe, is the sister of your wife, Alice.'

'Madeleine! I thought the gal was in France.'

Winchip took a glass of claret from the servant's tray. 'She was, Captain. Unfortunately, her brother, Stephen, has been killed under rather involved circumstances and it fell to me to bring her back to England.'

'Killed? But how?'

'He was shot by the French – as a spy, I am informed.'

'Shot, by God!' Munro exhaled. For a moment there was silence. 'Well, it doesn't surprise me.' He stood and took two paces aft and back again. 'I'd wish that for no man, but there are those that won't be sorry to see Stephen go, I'll warrant!' He looked straight at Winchip. 'God rest his soul but he was a bad lot, Sir, and I'm not sorry to say it. He dragged Madeleine around with him – never settling, always trying to sell schemes and the like. He professed to be a naval architect but I always doubted it. He could charm the truck from under a cannon, that man!'

Winchip was in turmoil. Munro's words had been the last thing he expected. He also realised how typical it was of Madeleine that she had said nothing of this about her brother . . . if she had known at all! He kept silent, allowing Munro to continue.

'Alice will be upset, by God! Still, Sir, I thank you for bringing the news – not an easy task.' Munro quaffed the claret in his hand and reached for the jug, pouring into his own glass as he saw Winchip's hand covering his as a denial. 'She'll not forgive me for the things I have said about him in the past, either!'

Winchip reached into his inner pocket and handed Munro the letter from Madeleine. 'I think Madeleine has probably explained everything. She hopes I will bring a reply.'

'Thank you.' Munro took the frail missive into his massive hand.

The 'sir' had vanished. Munro looked at the letter in much the same way that Madeleine had looked at the navy list. Winchip realised the news had come as a greater shock than he thought.

'May I ask about your relationship with Madeleine, Sir? Alice will want to know every detail.'

'I can assume nothing at this time. I have hopes; let us leave it at that.'

'Of course, Sir. I shouldn't have asked, but . . .' On an impulse, Munro took up a small sheet of paper and wrote on it. Wiping the pen he handed the paper to Winchip. 'My address, Sir. Alice and I have a small place ashore. If you could manage to visit us sometime during the afternoon watch tomorrow, she would certainly welcome it. That I'll warrant.'

Winchip rose, tucking the address into a pocket. 'I shall do that, Captain, and look forward to it. My visit will have to be brief as we leave in two days' time. I have to report to the attaché in Lagos.' The lie came with so consummate an ease that he surprised himself.

As he went down the knotted rope, his face no more than six inches from the weathered and deteriorating timbers, Winchip had cause to realise the seriousness of the *Mordacious*'s condition. Settling himself into the stern sheet of the jolly boat, he was quick to recognise the truth of things on an overseas station. Munro would get his hull put to rights, even if he had to careen the ship and get his own people to do it. As to the reduced Mediterranean Squadron under the command of Captain George Edgecumbe, how would he fare should the French decide to attack Mahon? Who, then, would be on hand to beat off Admiral Galissonnière and his newly refitted fleet, even if the French crews did lack sea time? He thought about the fleet in the making mentioned by Hawke. It would have to be a large one; there would be no help from this place. Edgecumbe's squadron would be at anchor at Mahon, for what it was worth.

His thoughts now were directed away from the luckless Douglas Munro and turned towards Toulon, the enormity of Lord Hawke's orders and all that they implied.

Winchip, standing at the ante-room window, once more looked down upon *Eaglet*, this time in the early light of dawn. His thoughts were skylarking in the tops, chasing around his head in confusion, trying to sort themselves into some semblance of order. For a while he had seen the possibility of England's supremacy in the Mediterranean coming to a short and bloody end. He had seen, too, failures and politics combining to allow this to happen in the very near – if not the immediate – future. He realised there had to be a degree of arrogance in his own attitude, in that there was no reason why he should be privy to the greater scheme of things; that there must be events in the making to which he was not privy. Had Admiral Byng and Lord Hawke both been left in the dark? Winchip shrugged his shoulders. The only answer left to him was that he had every reason to believe there was an English fleet in the making at this very moment – things moving apace, the destination of that fleet influenced by what *Eaglet* found at Toulon. He settled for that.

It seemed illogical that General Fowke should think that the French would try to take Gibraltar. They wanted no conflict with Spain at this time. Should they take the rock there would be the difficulty – and cost – of keeping it. The French attack would be directed against Minorca and, by that, the fortress at Mahon, there could be no doubt. General Graveney, the commander at St Philip Fortress, had a strong garrison ensconced in a very well fortified position. His only problem would be the geography of the island. He would be forced to take up a defensive position in the fortress at the eastern end until others arrived to relieve him and, by so doing, leave the rest of the island open to occupation – and the fortress to siege.

It seemed to Winchip that the sooner he got his orders, the more quickly he could discover the strength and readiness of the French at Toulon. As he watched the mist burning off in the bay, another thought struck him. Who would relay these important despatches back to the Admiralty? The answer stared him in the face, unless *Eaglet* was expected to hold Gibraltar in company with a weeded twenty-eight-gun frigate.

'Good morning, Sir!' Lieutenant Waring bustled in with a beaming smile, carrying beneath his arm several copies of *Port Signals and General Orders*, a sure sign of ships arriving or others being taken out of ordinary. 'General Fowke can see you now.' Waring was in haste to be about his business. The petulance had given way to healthy respect.

Winchip picked up his hat from the well worn padded bench and followed the lieutenant into the inner sanctum.

The room had lost its quiet intimacy of yesterday. It had the feeling of bustle, of some great scheme in the making – unless the Mediterranean Squadron was coming home to roost.

'Good morning, Captain!' General Fowke acted as if he were trying to do five things at once. Other junior officers and civilians were attending to duties known only to them. He picked up and passed a sealed pouch to Winchip without asking him to sit. 'These are your orders, Winchip. Are you ready in all respects for sea?'

'Barring those minor repairs, yes, Sir. Those, we shall effect at sea.' Winchip continued. 'I would like to depart tomorrow, General.'

'That will be in order.' Fowke sank into a chair as if he had no option. 'Your orders are plain enough and I have given you a free hand in their execution in accordance with Admiral Hawke's request.' He tapped his fingers on the table as if agitated. 'I have to tell you that should you or any of your men be caught, you are to be abandoned. Their Lordships will deny all knowledge of your presence in Toulon. They may even defame you, I do not know.'

An apology was written in the general's eyes but unspoken, a man willing to take responsibility for his own utterances. 'The more information you can obtain, the better placed Their Lordships will be in deciding what is to be done, if anything. Should the occasion present itself, a prisoner or two perhaps...' The unfinished sentence – shades of Byng.

'I shall carry out my orders to the very best of my ability, General. You can rely upon it.' Winchip glanced in Waring's direction. 'Some charts of the Toulon coast and some layout of the town would be very useful.'

Waring said. 'I shall have some sent over as soon as possible, Sir, though I doubt they will be that up to date.' Waring jotted down a note in his little *vade-mecum*.

'Our trust is in you, Captain Winchip.' The lieutenant-general rose to his feet with difficulty, drawing the brief meeting to a close. He grasped Winchip's hand and placed his other on top. 'What England does next may well depend upon what you have to tell us.'

'I shall return, Sir.' Winchip was sorry to see the hint of desperation in those rheumy eyes, a lifetime of trusting no man, now truly believing his garrison of a few battalions was under threat. 'We all have too much to lose, General.' His smile was enough for the old man to straighten his shoulders.

Munro's house was larger than Winchip expected. Built of stone, it was set apart from those about it by a small paddock with parched grass stretched round the place like a horse-shoe. The windows, all small, both upper and lower were set into the stone as if shrinking from the weather on the occasion of a blow. Even the door lent itself to sturdiness rather than ornamentation, oiled to a sheen with furniture heavy enough to secure a castle keep.

He let the large knocker fall onto its striking plate, almost recoiling at the noise he had caused. He maintained his pose until he heard the rattle of a latch from within. For some reason his heart was beating as though he were about to board the enemy. The door opened soundlessly to reveal the smiling bulk of Munro, in uniform.

'You came, Sir!' He stepped back. 'Please, come in.'

'Thank you.' Winchip handed his hat to a small Spanish serving girl who melted into the shadows of the cool interior.

'Come through, Sir – come through. We have talked of nothing but your coming this last hour.' Munro beckoned Winchip through a lighted doorway as if he did everything at full speed.

Winchip followed, only to stop short, taken aback in shocked surprise as he entered the room.

She was standing by the table with her hands held loosely in front of her. She wore a black, high-waisted, informal gown with a dark blue ribbon tied about her bodice. Her dark hair was worn long and left loose to fall about her shoulders with a sparkle of red highlighted in the candle's glow. She was the image of Madeleine. In her face was a great sadness, recently tearful by the slight redness of her eyes. She had evidently read the letter.

'My dear, may I present Captain Winchip of His Majesty's frigate *Eaglet*?' Munro's pride in his wife was as an open book.

'It . . . it is a pleasure to make your acquaintance, Ma'am.' Winchip held the fingers of the proffered hand like a piece of delicate china. 'I regret the circumstances under which we meet. You have my total sympathy.'

'Thank you, Captain.' Her hand fell away. 'Thank you, too, for coming to see us. Won't you please sit down?' Alice found the makings of a smile and indicated the nearest chair. She then sat herself on the end of a small *chaise longue*, drooping her arm lightly over the small headrest.

'Thank you, Ma'am.' Winchip perched on the edge of the seat.

'Please, call me Alice. I feel Madeleine has brought us all together, don't you, Daniel?'

She had Madeleine's aptitude for plain speaking, that was obvious. He was nevertheless glad of the chance to dispense with formalities. 'Thank you, Alice.' He sat back in the chair knowing he would have to relate all the circumstances of his meeting with Madeleine and the development of their relationship. Nothing would nor could be left unsaid, for Alice deserved that. He took a glass of Madeira from the serving girl and settled into his task, relating things as they had occurred and omitting those that had no bearing. She nodded her head in understanding and shook it in sadness as events were recalled. In the end she quietly excused herself and left the room, the letter gripped in one hand, the other to her face.

An hour later he sat with Munro in his private room. It was a man's place, a room converted to suit Munro's needs, a dark place, lit only by two clusters of candles, set before hanging mirrors on the wall to enhance what light came from the small windows. Charts and papers were strewn over an old desk, while books seemed to covet every other available space. In isolation, a small table and two chairs were clear of all effects as if waiting for occupation. It was here that they sat, Madeira to hand, there at Winchip's behest. He had sought information from the one man who could have the very thing he needed.

'Do you have any charts, Douglas?' By the end of his discourse with Alice it had come down to Christian names all round. 'Perhaps of the French coast in the Mediterranean?'

'If you mean Toulon, I have some spares.' Douglas gave him a grin that spoke volumes. Winchip wasn't surprised. Any captain worth his salt was certain to be worrying about the proximity of the French at this time.

'Yes, I do mean Toulon, although I would prefer this was kept between the two of us.'

Their Madeira all but forgotten, Douglas nodded his understanding and reached into an old chest to bring out a medley of charts. He selected one and spread it out on the table.

'By all, that's marvellous!' Winchip looked down in delight, wondering how it could be that the charts at Admiralty House were so dated. He cast his eyes over the flattened parchment. Soundings, fortifications, shallows, channels and depths, it was all there, together with evidence of roads, cliffs and dwellings along the shoreline. To cap it all there was a street plan of the dock area. He looked up wide-eyed. 'May I borrow this, until I return?'

'With my compliments.' Douglas Munro reached for Winchip's glass and handed it to him. 'May I drink to your health and the good fortune of *Eaglet*?' He was warming to events, no doubt wishing he were in Winchip's shoes.

Under the light of the two lanterns Winchip looked down at Munro's chart, stretched out on his small table, staring back at him in all its precise detail. He knew the thing backwards, as now did First Lieutenant Niven.

He took no comfort in sending others to risk their lives in such a hazardous enterprise. To be disowned in the event of capture was a new departure in the language of orders; political expedience balanced against lives. Was this how Foche had started, drawn in against his will? He doubted it. Winchip's orders required him to observe and report – as simple as that. To penetrate and spy would have been a more appropriate phrase, honest and true, even if unsavoury.

The knock came on the door as a release.

'Enter!'

'Young gennelman, Sir!' The sentry gave a loud sniff.

'Come in, Mr Piper. What is it, young man?'

'The first lieutenant's compliments, Sir. Mr Niven says the muster is complete, Sir.'

'Thank you, Mr Piper. Please tell Mr Niven I shall be with him directly.'

Winchip needed to reconcile himself with the nature of his orders. He was annoyed that he was still required to play a part in the despicable game of espionage. He could cope with exchanging broadside for broadside in a stand-up fight, but the covert aspect of spying when, if caught, one could be executed on the spot was not his idea of fighting for his country. He would do his duty but he was not required to like it.

He went to the window-seat, trying unsuccessfully to drown his disquiet in his favourite spot. His anguish was the greater for having to send someone else to do the dirty work. Slapping his thigh in a moment of anger he rose from the seat and threw his despondency to the winds. It was a job to be done – no more than that and that was how it must remain. He donned his boat cloak against the morning chill and plucked his hat from the old sea-chest with a flourish.

'Good morning, Sir!' Niven, brightened by the prospect, no doubt, of a return to the sea, touched his hat as the captain approached. 'We have a light air in our favour, Sir. Mr Ramblin feels we should make use of it before it disappears altogether.' He looked towards the master who nodded in confirmation.

'Thank you, Lieutenant.'

'The coxswain is at the buoy, Sir, awaiting orders.'

'So, in all respects we are ready for sea?'

'Aye, Sir. In all respects.' As Niven spoke, so four bells rang out hollowly from forward.

'Then let us be at it. Carry on if you please. Course due south.'

There was no going back.

11

On Enemy Soil

The Balearic Island of Majorca was sinking into the south-western horizon, the purple haze above it refusing to fade, a skin of thin cloud hanging over her like a protective canopy. As the island had melted into the background, so Minorca had gradually emerged. Winchip found her in the glass to the south-east and gave an involuntary shiver. The beauty and peace of the place was, he knew, soon to be shattered by a fearful conflict. The facts confirmed it and common sense demanded it. St Philip's Castle, for all its strength and strategic position, would be as nothing should it come under a prolonged siege. Its only hope of rescue would be through the arrival of an English fleet and an army to effect its relief. It followed that the French would support the siege with the fleet of Admiral Galissonnière, and there you have it – a clash of titans! Winchip closed the glass and shook his head. The inevitability of it all stunned him with its obviousness. Yet General Fowke and his three battalions, his mind unreceptive to the obvious, could bring it all tumbling down in ruins with his obsession that Gibraltar was the place about to be attacked.

Eaglet heeled over in the gusting westerly on her quarter. Winchip raised his eyes to scan the tops, taking in the subterfuge of the Spanish colours on the gaff halyard. At every masthead keen eyes scanned the horizon. With the toll of every other bell new eyes would replace them, this time seeking lights – any lights, no matter how small or distant. The afternoon sun was moving down to meet the western horizon. That, and the brightness of its track on the water, was dazzling to the eyes. The warmth it was bringing during the day would later fade by the minute. Then, the chill would set in and with it darkness, and with that . . . the approach to Toulon.

Eaglet dipped her bow into another shallow trough and rose up on the other side, yawing slightly in the quarter sea, creeping forward under reduced sail, her Spanish flag now replaced by that of France and the fleur-de-lis. Three lilies or an iris, it was of no consequence to her mission.

'*Wear ship! Let go and haul!*'

Winchip stood at the athwart rail of the quarterdeck, looking down upon events but his mind was elsewhere. The thought of what lay ahead for the four men destined to set foot on enemy soil at Toulon was eating away at his fortitude. The misgivings crowded in on him, growing out of all proportion yet real nonetheless. They had been with him and would remain with him, until every man was returned safely to the ship.

'*Make fast! Look lively!*'

'*Deck alow! Fishin' vessels to larboard!*'

'Aha!' Winchip turned and hurried to the lee-rail, using the glass to find them at a distance. He stared at them for a while and then scrutinised them with care as a plan came to mind. He called to Costly, midshipman of the watch, waiting until he arrived, panting. 'Mr Costly. Listen carefully, this is most important. I want you to fetch your inkwell and make a note of these fishing vessels.' Winchip rose to his full height and pointed to the horizon. 'Make a note of everything about them. Numbers, sails – everything. Is that understood?'

'Aye, Sir. Everything, Sir.' Costly stood poised, ready to run.

'Off you go then.' Winchip watched him dive below like a rabbit into its burrow and then turned as Niven came across to him.

'Anchor's ready to let go, Sir. We've found a sandy bottom.'

'Very well, Mr Niven, let go but have men standing-to, if you please. We may have to weigh in a hurry and I don't want to lose an anchor.' Winchip placed a hand on Niven's arm as the first lieutenant turned away. 'I have a scheme I would like to discuss with you. Come back to me when you are free, if you please.'

'Aye, Sir. Ten minutes at most.'

''Ow's that then?' Olly Oliver, the sailmaker, held up the brown sail and offered it for inspection. 'Is it scruffy enough, I asks m'self?' He dabbed another splash of grey paint where it would show best.

The cutter had been transformed from a smart piece of regulation naval property into a French high-prowed lugger, as dirty and unkempt as it was possible to make it, complete with gaff rig and riding lights, all in accordance with Costly's sketch.

'There must be something we've forgotten.' Pardoe walked round it once more, offering the benefit of his meagre experience. He held the drawing in front of him as if looking for errors. 'What about markings? You know, numbers and things?'

'None that I could see, Sir, and I looked hard, I can tell you.' Costly straightened up as the captain and first lieutenant appeared at his side.

'Then she's finished, Sir.' Pardoe looked directly at Winchip.

'Well done!' Winchip looked the length of her. 'She'll do for me. Does she need those oars?' He pointed down to the thwarts.

'If we do then we're in trouble, Sir.' Bowes looked to the captain for a final decision.

'Leave one pair in, just in case.' Winchip spoke and then turned away.

Before Winchip went down the companion ladder he looked to the west. The sun had gone, leaving only a faint red glow on the underbellies of two long strips of dark evening clouds. The night had fallen like a stone and with it the wind had reduced to a light air, tickling the lines and playing with the brailled canvas. It all augured well.

In the warm yellow light of the captain's cabin, beads of sweat sparkled on Corporal Basson's brow. He was a coarse man, stocky and barrel-chested. Not a man to be crossed. His shaven head glistened in the light of the lanterns and his ears were thick and bulbous, the result of many barrack fights. His light blue eyes had a steely glint and were like globes in their relaxed state. Together with Niven, Bowes and Pardoe he leaned over the table, staring at the chart that to him was upside down. His uniform collar was done up to the neck, the trickles of sweat not confined to his face. A man who had made sergeant twice, only to be broken the same number of times for fighting, was well within his depth. He worried more about the abilities of his comrades. His own prowess was not in question, he was known well enough. As the captain spoke, so he stood erect.

Winchip looked up, his hands still resting on the table. 'With our new found lugger there should be no difficulty in sailing into the bay as bold as brass.' The swell was picking up the stern and laying it down again like a chicken trying to rid itself of a difficult egg. It wasn't violent, merely persistent. He put a finger on the chart. 'If you do have trouble, head for the north shore. It certainly seems to offer the best cover.' Winchip spread his hands. 'I feel very inadequate, gentlemen. All I can offer is supposition born out of guesswork and a damned good chart. What you should have is a reconnaissance report but you know there is no time for that.'

'I think we shall have to take things as they come, Sir.' Niven looked down at the chart and shook his head. 'With respect, I think the right answers will present themselves as we proceed.'

'I hope to God you are right, Lieutenant.' Winchip rolled up Munro's chart and passed it to Niven. 'Here! Fold up the chart and take it with you, together with our thoughts.' Winchip dipped into a pocket and brought out his timepiece. He checked the time and nodded his satisfaction. 'Take this, too.' He handed it to the surprised Niven. 'We shall show a light for ten seconds at every bell after four bells in the middle watch. If you see it, then shine your lamp out to sea.' He patted Niven's arm. 'Every man jack will be looking for it, so don't despair.'

'This is one time you won't be able to send in Mr Gray to pull us out, Sir.' Niven coloured at the laughter as they left the cabin, a hint of nervousness in the sound.

Tackles were being noisily stowed as they reached the entry port dressed in the oldest clothes they could find. Hellard reported the boat ready at the chains, the tone of his voice letting it be known that he would rather be going with it. His face, however, was expressionless in the light of the guarded deck lantern. Four bells rang out – the end of the second dog watch.

'We shall come in for you an hour before dawn but I can come no further than this spot.' Winchip poked the chart with his finger. 'If the wind is contrary then you'll have to come to us, due south.' He shook hands with Niven. 'I know you will do your best.'

'Let us be at it then!' Niven climbed through the entry port and grasped the knotted rope. In a thrice he was into the cutter, his own appearance in keeping with the disarray and apparent filth of the boat.

A block rattled as Bowes hoisted the lugsail up the short sturdy mast. Quickly, he made fast the sheet on a makeshift wooden cleat, securing the tack and pulling the sheet in to prevent the wind from catching her. Pardoe and Basson dispersed the hammock netting around the vessel, adding to the mess, draping it across bows and gunwales to give credence to their presence. Bowes released his grip on the holding line and then let loose the sheet, allowing the sail to fill to full hardness with a sudden crack of taut canvas.

Niven looked upwards as the cutter drew away, seeing only white faces peering down at him as if reminding him that he was on his own, solely in charge with three other lives in his hands.

The boat was almost jaunty as she slapped into the wavelets, her single square of canvas as tight as a drum. He steered for the faint glow of the town lights reflected in the sky above, hidden from their sight by the peninsula of land that enclosed the long bay itself. For five minutes he inspected what lights he could see, trying to find some relativity in their position but it was in vain. He shook his head and turned to catch a last glance at *Eaglet*, only to find that she had disappeared into the blackness of the night.

The darkness was absolute. A few pinpoints of light on the horizon to the north showed them their direction but beyond that, right and left, there was nothing but inky blackness over a choppy sea. Niven found himself inventing catastrophes, seeing sandbars where there should be none, tidal rocks where he knew there were none. If he allowed himself to advance his imagination to being in the town itself, likely to be shot out of hand should they be caught, then panic would surely ensue. He knew himself to be physically brave, to a point; but this was a different thing. It was intangible. It was based upon luck rather than judgement and it placed itself directly in the path of all he had been trained to face during his time at sea. He had no preconception of the task, no plan of battle, no knowledge of the enemy he was about to face and no means of shortening the odds. All in all it was a pretty pickle, as his mother would have said. He smiled at that, one hand on the gunwale as a wavelet bravely tried to broach them. His father, God rest his soul, would have had no such fears. Killed while directing a cavalry charge against the Prussian guns not five years since, he would have taken his chances despite any odds. Niven dropped his head for a moment, seeing fleeting images of his father at home. He remembered, at the age of thirteen, asking his father if he could go to sea. The response had been instant. 'If the sea is calling you, lad, then that is the place for you!' It had been that easy. Those days, walking the cliffs on the family's moderate Devon estate, watching the schooners, barks and even war ships, had fuelled his need to be a sailor. To see other lands, even seek glory as his father had done with such success, as a colonel, in the King's name.

'Lights are lit, Zur!' Basson's voice came from midships where the two recognition lamps now shone brightly, one above the other as they had been with the little fishing fleet.

The displaying of lights, all part of the grand deception, seemed to Niven akin to downright folly. He knew differently, but while they were hidden they were safe. 'Very well. If we meet anything, Mr Pardoe and you, Basson, must seem to be busy with the nets.' The stern suddenly slapped down hard as an awkward wave found them, sending a shock up Niven's back. He discerned the headland as two small lights appeared to his left that had to be from a single dwelling. It offered no threat but he kept the place in mind. They had yet to return. From the same direction a tenor bell clanged without rhythm or timing, its discordant sound heralding the rocky outcrops of the point.

Suddenly the roads were laid open. Clear water, suffused with the reflections of yellow and white lights for almost two miles, with dark, forbidding land on either side. Any lights were concentrated in the distance, at the far end of the roads where the habitation was most dense. Niven knew that the dockyards and anchorage were also down there, waiting for four mad Englishmen in a makeshift boat. The more he stared, the less he liked it. As it was, he had yet to steer through two cable lengths of unknown channel through dangers he knew nothing about; and then find a landing spot. He sighed and trusted in providence. There was no other course. He shrugged his shoulders at the thought of special signals, dismissing the problem as soon as he realised there was little he could do. At least the wind was abeam, allowing them to sail out without difficulty. The dark, rustling shapes to starboard had to be trees, running a good length of the roads and, just as the captain had said, offering shelter for the boat and a sound landing place.

The approach to the town would be on the waterside track shown on the chart.

The clouds chose that moment to release the moon. It hung in the sky like a lantern, cold and forbidding, and then scudded through the thinning clouds in a race to hide itself once more.

'Bring her up!' Pardoe called in a harsh whisper from the bow. He came back to midships to speak to Niven as Bowes pulled in the sheet. 'I think there's a boom ahead, Sir. A row of small rafts right across the inlet, each with a lantern. There's also a guard boat pulling away from us and others patrolling.'

'I should have known!' Niven rose in the stern sheets, spreading his legs for a better purchase in the stationary boat. He realised now what the captain had said about a reconnaissance report. 'Get those oars out. We'll go straight for the shore.' The decision made, he scanned the darkness of the tree-lined bank. 'Over there!' He pointed with his finger to a dark area that had both depth and mystery, trying to keep some calmness in his voice. 'Corporal! Get the lights out once we've turned. The last thing we want is to confuse the enemy.' Niven stared at the bank, not expecting an answer. For a moment he felt useless and inept, wondering how he could even expect to come out of this charade alive.

They came upon the trees far sooner than he expected. They were pines, broad yet shallow rooted, much the same as those to be found in Cornwall, but seeming larger. Growing out from a steep slope down to the water, their branches spread out to form a canopy. Before them a narrow strip of pungent kelp stretched along the shoreline in both directions.

'Ship oars!' The sudden silence of the squealing thole-pins exaggerated the ripple of water from the bows; and then the rush of sound as the boat careered through the kelp. Quickly, Niven fended off. He hurriedly stuck out a foot to stop the boat before it struck the rocks scattered along the waterline. The stern of the boat continued to rise and fall, shallow waves of the high tide slopping onto the shoreline with a monotonous regularity. The stench of marsh mud, released by the passage of the boat, pervaded the air. Niven looked cautiously about him. It was a perfect haven, hidden from sight. His confidence was stimulated by their first piece of luck. At least they now had a spot to which they could retreat in a hurry; run to for their very lives should things go against them. He turned to Pardoe and said in a hoarse whisper, 'Get up that slope, Mr Pardoe and see if the track is there – quickly now! Mr Bowes – hide the tiller and oars!' Niven stepped onto dry land. There were rocks enough, lying on a bed of shale. Here and there fine grasses sought to grow with little success. As he peered up the rise above him, he could see in the moonlight smaller bushes and longer grass but beyond his limited vision there was nothing but silent darkness.

Pardoe slithered down the last few feet of the bank and strode purposefully over to Niven. He stopped for a moment to regain his breath. 'There is a steep climb of some fifty feet, Sir.' He breathed again. 'There is a track at the top, muddy and with deep ruts. It goes down towards the town and it has a hedge on the far side.' He looked at Niven. 'It looks like open country, save for the trees.'

Niven stared into space. 'Are there any dwellings?'

'None that I could see, Sir.'

'Then let us be at it!' Niven could almost hear his own heart pounding. This was as close to a cutting out party as they would ever get.

They stood at the top of the steep rise in a group, regaining their breath. Niven looked about him to get a feel of the place, holding up his hand for silence. He listened intently. The place was as quiet as death itself. Even so he spoke in hushed tones. 'We shall split into two pairs. Corporal Basson and I will go ahead.' He looked at Pardoe. 'You two follow us about fifty yards behind. In that way we have someone who speaks French with each pair and if anything happens to us you can either fade away or come to our aid – your decision.' He added quickly. 'If we fail then you must complete the task and get back to *Eaglet*. I don't need to tell you how important it is.' Their nods were sufficient to convince him. 'If we are separated then we meet here.' Niven realised this would be his last chance to cover the worst of circumstances. 'Speak to nobody if you are approached. Then, I suggest you engage in a friendly argument – no stranger would interrupt that. I can offer you no plan. We must act as we find. Our whole purpose is to find a place from which to observe and then make the best of it. Have I made myself clear?' The nods came again, accompanied by grunts of understanding. For the moment Niven was satisfied.

He gave Basson a cursory nod and together they picked their way towards the town. It would not be long before they came up to dwellings. Already he could visualise in his mind a thousand circumstances that could bring about their downfall. As an afterthought he turned to Basson at his side. 'No more English, Corporal. If you are approached, then act dumb. Just grunt and shrug your shoulders. I'll do the talking.'

Basson's muttered response was beyond Niven's hearing.

They found themselves almost creeping past the first houses. The only lights were lanterns hung by the cottage doors at regular intervals, more as if by local ordinance than the will of the owner.

The narrow road sloped almost imperceptibly downwards, cobbled in the most part, elsewhere beset by ridges of dried mud and intrusive grasses. There was no longer a view of the water. Buildings and foliage obscured any view of it. The lanterns had increased. As they had come across people going about their business, so Niven kept up an incessant chatter in simple French, huddling close to Basson to deny interference. It was as they approached a tavern on a bend in the road that they saw the soldiers. Unarmed, they appeared to be from the same regiment, resplendent in their light blue, pin-back tunics with white facings, crossed shoulder belts and white breeches. Their cocked hats, each sporting a vague cockade, were set at various angles. Most were the worse for drink. It was not just one or two they saw. The place was full of them, moving from one tavern to another, many with women on their arms. From the taverns came an incessant noise of revelry, singing and laughter.

Niven strode out as if on some purpose, Basson following suit, wide-eyed at his encounter with the enemy. A quick glance behind showed Pardoe and Bowes keeping pace. Despairing of even getting a sight of the shipping, he was aware that their options were diminishing by the minute. It had not occurred to him that there could be such an occlusion, a total denial of vision beyond their immediate surroundings.

The air of the place was one of bustle, the soldiers making the most of their freedom. Despite the lateness of the hour there seemed to be no let up in the laughter and carousing. Soldiers arm in arm with their new found and temporary loves were being guided with consummate ease to wherever the women found it easiest to deprive them of their money. They had neither time nor sympathy for the hapless four wandering down towards the dockyard.

Niven, reduced to the situation of seeking opportunity from whatever quarter, surveyed every opening or alley with a view to seeing the docks, which were now no more than a few cables ahead. It was on an impulse that Niven took Basson's arm and steered him through a small arch on the bay side of the street. As he had approached it, he had seen it as promising. Lit by a single lamp, shining dully from within a tangle of creeper, it was a short and curved passage, losing sight of the road and no more than ten paces long, opening onto a small cobbled courtyard. What drew Niven's breath was the inky blackness beyond, a full view of the roads and a presumption that the docks would be equally on view to the right. Between him and the water was a double railing, a barrier to prevent a long fall to the depths below. They walked cautiously forward together in disbelief, into the light of a second lantern, the noise from the hidden street diminishing with every step.

Two doors set in brick walls, faced either side of the place, across which a washing line was suspended from the upper-floor windows, festooned with garments and sheets of all colours, even now flapping and swinging in a fitful breeze. A table at the railing held an earthenware pot containing a withering mass of umber leaves, two small wooden platters and an empty wine bottle. One of the doors was ajar, exposing a flight of curving stairs climbing into darkness.

Every noise and every shadow was now seen as a threat, so great was the temerity of their steps.

Niven dropped his guard. He scanned the whole courtyard with a final sweep of his eyes and then turned away, devoting his whole attention to what lay beyond the railing. He looked left and right. His shoulders dropped and he emitted a prolonged sigh. Before him the whole of what must be the Toulon Squadron lay at anchor. Ships-of-the-line, double-anchored, with lesser vessels in attendance, all with their riding lights twinkling confidently behind the great boom. He dragged his eyes away to peer deeper into the roads. It was a few moments before he realised what he was looking at and, once he was aware, his mouth gaped open. Line upon line of transports lay beam abreast, their myriad mastheads moving and shining like tall birch trees in a restless wind. Each and every one had its masts crossed and sails in gaskets, needing only the orders to be given before making sail.

Niven looked downwards, seeking a place from which he could observe unseen. From below there came the sound of gushing water, accompanied by the stench of effluence as it spewed out into space.

'*Qui va la?*'

The man, a soldier, had come from the open doorway. He stood, swaying from side to side, his hat and cross-belts in one hand and a wine bottle in the other, his eyes seeking to focus on Niven.

'*C'est chez moi, Monsieur.*' Niven spoke quickly, a beaming smile pasted on his gaunt face. He pointed towards the second door. His heart rose as he saw Pardoe and Bowes approaching the man from behind. Basson stood in the shadows where he had been watching the entrance.

'*Merde!*' The epithet dropped naturally from the man's lips. The swaying stopped and his eyes became riveted on Niven. Dropping the hat and belts he spun the bottle in the air and caught it by the neck. He calmly broke the bottle on the step to leave a jagged edge glinting in the light of the lantern and his breeches dripping with wine.

Niven moved forward with arms outspread, hoping to restore the situation he knew was irretrievable. '*Monsieur, je vous . . .*'

The man staggered forward, thrusting out the broken bottle, holding it at arm's length in front of him, swearing obscenely from behind his large, drooping moustache. Niven saw Bowes moving behind the man, his hanger drawn and held at the ready.

Niven circled to his left, his back to the railing, taking the Frenchman away from Basson, standing stock-still, watching events. Suddenly the soldier lunged. He took one step forward, the bottle held high, and then stopped in his tracks, staring at a point above Niven's shoulder, eyes wide, mouthing words that wouldn't come, choking on a gush of blood that splashed on the cobbles at his feet. His expression turned to one of surprise as he slowly fell to his knees and then toppled onto his face with the sickening sound of flesh on stone. The bottle rolled over the edge and fell silently into space. Corporal Basson was revealed behind him, a large bloodied knife held in his ham-like fist.

Basson leaned forward and wiped the knife on the tail of the man's tunic. It was a simple gesture, a means of cleaning the weapon. The muddled heap that had been a soldier lay inert. He rummaged through the man's pockets, stripping them of every personal possession and placing them in his own. He looked up at a horrified Niven.

'We 'ave to look like 'e was robbed, Zur.' Basson spoke hoarsely and quickly in English, needing help but with no idea how to ask that of an officer. He had reverted to type, dealing with what had to be done in the way he knew best. He looked at Niven and then nodded to the rail. ''E's got ter go over. Don't just bloody stand there or we're all done fer...' He tried in vain to lift the man himself, dragging him as best he could towards the empty blackness of the roads.

They all moved at once, Niven and Pardoe to Basson's aid while Bowes stood beside the door, his back flat against the wall, his hanger grasped firmly in his hand, looking about him wide-eyed as if seeing this as his last moment on earth.

The three of them together pushed the soldier's body under the rail, any sound of a splash lost in the noise of the rushing sewage. Basson flung the pieces of uniform as far as he could out into the night, his anger no longer apparent, his outburst and direct insubordination, to him, now forgotten.

Niven, putting himself to rights, was suddenly aware of the shifting shaft of yellow light as it lit up the darkness of the stairway. The clatter of boots on the stairs told all. As one, Niven and Bowes leaped to the doorway, one either side, Bowes with his hanger held loosely in his hand. Niven nodded to him. The soldier stopped in the doorway and gave a deep belch.

'Armand?' The man looked left and right but could see nothing amiss. He took the fatal step into the light.

Bowes stepped out of the shadow and plunged his hanger horizontally into the man's body, beneath his armpit, as the soldier gripped the jamb of the door. With a long, drawn out sigh the soldier slumped to the ground, his accoutrements clattering and echoing in the confined yard. He died with his legs beneath him and in a sitting position, his head bowed forward as if in prayer.

Niven shook Bowes back to his senses. 'Come on, pull yourself together, man. The deed's done, as it had to be. Grab his legs and let's get him over the side.' As Bowes bent to obey, so Niven grabbed his arms. With Basson's help the body this time rolled over the rail and disappeared without a sound. 'The killing's done.' Niven stood, panting. 'Now! Feast your eyes on that lot and start counting the transports.' He pointed towards the shipping. 'Mr Bowes. Make a list of the ships-of-the-line, their ratings and how many. We are not going to miss this moment because of two drunken soldiers!' To Basson he said with gritted teeth. 'Keep guard, Corporal, and in future watch that damned mouth of yours!' He knew Basson would be relieved at his words – saved from the prospect of a spell at the grating. As far as Niven was concerned the marine's action was forgotten.

After ten minutes of high tension, Niven closed his nightglass and put it back into its leather case. 'Well done, all of you.' He looked at each of them. 'We shall return as before, in twos.' He turned to Basson. 'You come with me.'

'What about prisoners, Sir?' Pardoe posed the question.

'It's too risky. We've got what we came for; let us be content with that, lest we finish up losing everything, including our lives.'

In twos they departed, into the bustle of the street, melting into the crowd, ignoring and being ignored, just as they intended.

As they moved out of the lights, their false drunkenness and camaraderie abandoned, so they moved into the haven of the night. Soon they were in the countryside and the welcome feel of the rutted road beneath their feet where not more than a few hours since they had felt their way towards the unknown.

Niven walked in the van, feeling in his pocket every now and again to confirm that the lists were still there. He knew they had plenty of time, if not too much and yet, should the alarm be raised . . . He dismissed the possibility where evidence was no longer available. Once they were on the water they would be safe, due south towards *Eaglet* and safety. That was the way of providence . . . not fate.

The boat was as they had left it. Silently they attached both rudder and tiller and then clambered on board, ready for the pull into the channel and a welcome breeze. Little had been said. The whole mission could have been ruined because of two drunken soldiers, choosing that moment to quit their love-nest. That had not been the way of it. The fate of the two Frenchmen would crowd their minds according to each man's conscience.

'Give way!' Niven spoke in a hoarse whisper as he pushed out with his foot from the rocks. Two long pulls gave momentum enough to clear the weed. In full voice, he said, 'Make sail, if you please, Mr Bowes.' They were through the kelp and away from the stench, a pull on a low hanging branch taking them into clear water – back to the element they knew best.

12

No Death for a Soldier

Winchip had seen *Eaglet* onto her southerly course, knowing there was clear water for as long as it took to reach Algiers and the African coast. Nevertheless, lookouts were sent up, each with a glass to search out any sign of a stern or deck light that could be marked down as the enemy. Then he had retired.

An hour later, his cot untouched, he was still sitting on the stern seat staring out into nothingness. He had wanted to be with them, be one of them, but that had been out of the question in these waters. Although he could find no recrimination in his own behaviour, he felt the guilt of not having done enough to support their cause and yet, what more *could* he have done?

He was reconciled with his conscience by putting himself in Niven's place. A position he would have been glad to occupy had common sense not ruled against it. The job done, he would have preferred to know that *Eaglet* was safe, ready to come in and pick him up at the appointed time. Without the ship there could be no escape and, pursuant to that would come death in its most arbitrary form. Above all, the information would be lost and that, the final ignominy, would underscore his failure. As to the need for a reconnaissance prior to the mission being carried out, Niven would realise that things needed to be balanced. Had the initial foray to spy out the land ended in disaster, then the whole enterprise would have been doomed to failure. The fact that Winchip had sent Niven into Toulon unprepared could only be construed as an act of faith and confidence in his first officer.

He made a decision, more with anger at not having made it earlier than any consideration of safety. Swinging his boat cloak about his shoulders and picking up his hat, he strode to the door, hearing with a grin the hurried movement of the sentry as he put himself to rights.

Midshipman Pope stepped away from the quarterdeck rail and moved hurriedly towards the binnacle as he saw the figure of the captain coming up the steps. Tipping his hat he glanced quickly up and down.

'Course due south, Sir. Wind north-east by east. All's well.'

'Thank you, Mr Pope. All hands up, if you please, and inform the master I wish to come about. Course due north.'

They came out into clear water in a rush, eyes searching left and right in anticipation of disaster. The roads were deserted except for the activity at the boom. The reflections of the lights glistened on the water towards them like probing spears. The movement of the patrol vessels plodding monotonously back and forth across the width of the waters lost their menace as they moved away to the east and the comparative safety of the open sea.

Bowes' makeshift pennant was showing the wind to be north-east by east. It was enough to take a starboard tack, close reaching to weather the point on the way out of the bay. The boat leaned over as the sail caught and Niven moved to meet her. As they gained speed so a chuckle came from beneath her cutwater and wavelets slapped noisily against the weather side.

'Show those lights, Corporal. Smartly now!' Niven scanned full circle about him, an exuberance coming upon him suddenly as he realised the worst was over. He knew the value of the information he held in his pocket, just as he was aware of what his fate would be were he to be caught with the lists in his possession. Despite his relief his knee refused to stop its relentless jerking, bouncing up and down as if to a lively tune.

'Lights are on, Zur!' Basson sat down on the thwart and spat to leeward.

Niven stared at Basson's back. A common soldier indeed. He thanked God for the man's presence of mind. He had seen the large non-regulation knife as Basson had wiped it on the man's uniform. Nodding to himself, he confessed to the fact that the man had been right in his actions – there had been no other way. The morning would reveal two corpses, stabbed and robbed of all they possessed. Evidence, yes, but not of their presence.

'That was well done, all of you!' Niven had to raise his voice over the sound of the sea beating on the bow. 'I shall see Lieutenant Gray hears of your work tonight, Corporal. You have my word on't!'

'Thank 'ee, Zur.' Basson grinned, glancing at Bowes and Pardoe as if they were all conspirators together.

'Ye gods!' The cry came from Bowes. 'Boats on the larboard bow, Sir. They're the ones we saw earlier today – the ones with the big cutter in front!'

Niven leaned far out, peering round the sail to catch a glimpse of the new threat. He saw the cutter and moments later the smaller boats came into view, in procession like a mother duck and her charges.

He thought quickly. 'Wave as they go past but don't overdo it. If they ask questions, say something in French and then ignore them. They'll be past before you know it.' He saw Basson grinning like a fish out of water. 'Get busy with the nets, we're *supposed* to be going fishing!' He grunted as Basson jerked into life.

The cutter passed by with scant regard for them. She had the wind on her beam and a clear channel. Niven had already dismissed her from his mind. She was committed to her course. The smaller boats passed, one by one, a tuneless song wafting across the gap in evidence of a good catch – or too much to drink. He saw the last of them dissolve into the darkness as she obscured her own lamps. On the weather side Niven felt the pressure of more robust waves striking them, sending spindrift across the boat, telling them that the open sea was in the offing.

'There's a straggler, Sir – just the one.' Pardoe watched it with a keen eye.

'She can do us no harm.' Niven saw her, one of the smallest of the vessels. 'Keep an eye on her, Mr Pardoe.'

'What about prisoners, Sir? There's just one man at the tiller.'

'By God, we'll take her. Even a fisherman will know what's going on. Mr Pardoe! Tell him to heave to on the instant. Mr Bowes! Steer us alongside!' Niven winced as Pardoe's shouted orders came out fit to wake the dead.

'She's luffed, Sir. Ours for the taking!'

The boats came together in a rush – hands grabbing at gunwales, Bowes standing with his hanger already to hand.

'Mon Dieu!' The fisherman dived behind a pile of lobster pots with a mournful cry, drawing his legs up beneath him and covering his head with his arms.

'There are three more 'ere, Zur. All drunk, far as I can tell.' There was a pause. 'One of 'em's a sodger, Zur, complete wi' musket. Shall I do 'im?'

'You leave him alone, Corporal!' Niven shook his head. 'Bind them all and place them in the bows.' To Bowes, he said. 'Take charge of that boat, Mr Bowes, and follow us. I want to get away from here while we can. Due south, Mr Bowes. Due south.'

'Due south, aye, Sir.' Bowes' last words already sounded distant as Niven hurried to let out the sail.

Both boats, in line astern, sailed due south for two hours with a single lamp shining out to sea, their course corrected by Niven's small compass and the sight of the pole star low on the horizon behind them. Intermittently they steered south-east to allow for drift. Now they waited, cold and wet, gazing now and then into the southern gloom, both boats rising and falling in time with the relentless snoring of the drunken soldier.

Halfway through the third hour, with a hint of red on the eastern horizon, Pardoe nudged Niven and pointed to the south-west. A light shone for a few seconds and then went out. The action was repeated until Basson responded in kind.

The dawn light brightened every corner of the great cabin. Shadows dashed about at random as *Eaglet* plunged her bows into the Mediterranean rollers, rising and plunging again as she enjoyed the following north-easterly.

Winchip laid the last page of Niven's report and the list of ships on the desk and leaned back in his chair. He looked directly at the first lieutenant, once again in his uniform. 'Well done, Mr Niven.' He spread his hands. 'You have done a magnificent job and I shall say so in my report.'

'Thank you, Sir. I couldn't have had a better body of men.' Niven's face held a self-effacing grin. 'You were right all the time, Sir, about that man Foche.'

'As it happens, yes, Lieutenant.' Winchip changed the subject. 'I shall not forget those who went with you. They will get the mention they deserve, that I promise you.' Winchip nodded his affirmation. 'The French soldier is still in his cups I am told, so we shall get precious little from him for a while. Has Mr Pardoe finished talking with the sober one yet?' The words tumbled out, Winchip hardly able to contain himself at the success of the mission.

'Yes, Sir. Mr Pardoe is outside at this moment if you wish to see him.' Niven suppressed a smile as the diminutive and lugubrious Booth brought in a large jug of steaming coffee and several cups.

'Good. It will be interesting to hear what he has to say.' Winchip tidied his papers as Niven rose, at the same time nodding to Booth who began to pour.

Pardoe, the only one of the team who had a fluent command of French, removed his cocked hat to enter the cabin and moved towards the desk so that Niven could close the door.

'Sit down, Mr Pardoe.' Winchip smiled and waved a hand

at a spare chair. 'Tell us what our fisherman has to say for himself?'

Pardoe settled himself and extracted a scrap of paper from the depths of his coat. 'First of all, Sir, he is a Jerseyman. He met his wife at Toulon when his merchant vessel paid off some years ago.' Pardoe looked up. 'He was quite free with his information.' Pardoe's attention was attracted to the coffee.

'Probably terrified of being pressed!' Niven snorted with disdain. 'I'd muster a merchant sailor as quick as a navy one any day.'

'He speaks French or English equally well, Sir.' Pardoe nodded to Booth as he took the proffered coffee. 'The soldiers in Toulon are a battalion of the Twenty-Third Regiment of Foot. He believes they have been brought in to protect the area but doesn't know if they are to be used in any future expedition.' Pardoe sipped his coffee and turned the paper over. 'He strongly believes more soldiers are due into Toulon shortly – several regiments, coming from Marseilles, he says; but he has no idea of the number.'

'The one we've got should tell us all we want to know.' Niven was perched at the other end of the stern seat.

'Confirmation is always worth having, Mr Niven. It puts the smack of truth on things.' Winchip turned back to Pardoe. 'Why was the soldier on the boat?'

'He was guarding it, Sir. All catches have to be offered to the army victualling officer before being offered on the public quays . . .' Pardoe added quickly, 'There is also the matter of security.'

Niven spluttered, 'Good God! They had as much security as a harlot's draw-string!'

Pardoe grinned. 'As to the transports, our Jerseyman says that a hundred and fifty men were put on one and it sailed the length of the roads and back. He thought it to be some sort of test.'

'One hundred transports, each with a hundred and fifty men!' Winchip stood and turned to the stern windows.

'Fifteen thousand men!' He clasped his hands behind his back. 'More than a picnic, wouldn't you say?'

It was an open question, picked up by Niven. 'There is no doubt about the number of transports, Sir. We all saw them.'

'I am sure you did, Lieutenant.' Winchip was silent for a moment. 'What do the rumours say, Mr Pardoe? Where are they going?'

'The strong rumour is St Philip's Castle and the naval dockyard at Mahon, Sir. In fact it is more than a rumour; they take it for granted.'

'Thank you, Mr Pardoe.' Winchip turned to face the lieutenant. 'Do you have anything else for us?'

'Yes, Sir. It appears that the French are very short of stores. Also, the workmen in the dockyard have not been paid for a long time and there is discontent among them. They are also short of guns for the ships, Sir. It appears they are receiving English guns on board, through Portugal of all places.'

Winchip took the matter lightly, belying his true thoughts on the matter. 'You have done well, young man, as did you all. If you obtain any further intelligence, please convey it to Mr Niven. Let him have it straight away.' He allowed Pardoe a beaming smile as the lieutenant downed the remainder of his coffee in one gulp before leaving.

Winchip sat on the stern seat. 'Sit yourself down, Mr Niven.' Winchip waited. 'Now, Lieutenant, tell me all about these ships-of-the-line . . . and a true account of the death of these two soldiers.'

Eight bells rang out clearly in the fresh morning air. The aroma of boiling lobsters permeated that freshness, eliciting a mood of expectation throughout the ship.

Pardoe pulled aside the canvas screen and entered the limited privacy of his sleeping space with a heavy heart. Dragging off his clothes he fell onto the tiny bunk, needing only to close his eyes for him to fall instantly into sleep. He stared at the deck planks above his head, trying not to think of the innocent French soldiers, killed because they had been in the wrong place at the wrong time. Trying even harder not to see the kicking leg that told of life still remaining in the first as he slipped under the rail into that dreadful filth, the effluence of Toulon.

He knew it had been a matter of self-preservation. Even Basson could not be blamed. He was a simple and ignorant soldier, trained to kill, doing what he knew best if the truth were told. He would always survive among his own kind.

What would they have done had Basson not been with them? The question raised sparks in the burning embers of his memory. Pardoe knew that they would have struggled with the man and subdued him, at the same time waking everyone in the vicinity. Basson had provided the answer, just as Bowes had followed his example with the second.

Pardoe buried his face in the coarse canvas pillow, a far wiser man than when they had set out on that fateful mission. Perhaps, for all their graces, they had all been well served by the presence of the marine.

With that he dragged his eyes from the rough and heavy wood above him and slept the sleep of the damned.

The brightness of the early dawn had succumbed to a cloudy overcast. A light mist hung above the water, obscuring the French coast and bringing coldness to the air. The importance of getting the information back to Gibraltar was reflected in the urgency with which *Eaglet* stood to the south-west, her abundant sail stretching to use every inch of angled canvas in the light breeze from the south-east. The fitful air, coming up from the deserts of Africa, was dry and dusty to the point of being parched. No sooner had the spindrift turned the light timber dark or the white sails to grey, than the air would soak it out and leave it as before. The air parched the mouth to the point of discomfort.

Winchip stood silently by the binnacle. All he could see was water and even that merged with the mist at a cable's distance. All he could feel was the proximity of the French coast still visible from the tops, to the north.

He had been saddened by events in Toulon, but not angered. The marine, Basson, had done his duty. He had acted as he had been taught; no one could ask more of him. The repercussions, had they been caught, didn't bear thinking about.

The information they had gleaned was sufficient proof of the French intention to invade Minorca, with the means to do it. Even General Fowke would find it difficult to deny the evidence of three officers.

13

Intransigence and New Orders

Eaglet's minion barked out the required salute as she was secured to the mooring in Gibraltar's anchorage. The fact that it was barely dawn had not escaped Winchip's notice. He gave a wry grin at the thought of a thousand souls sitting upright in their beds, assuming that the French were on their doorstep.

A veil of thin mist stretched across the water as far as the eye could see. The upper half of the great rock, now showing spring colours among the gorse and rocky outcrops, was bathed in the first of the sun's rays. The shadow of the earth passed slowly down the great escarpment as if presenting it anew to an awakening world.

In the absence of the harbour cutter, Hellard supervised the mooring. *Eaglet* was safely back.

Winchip waited two hours out of decency before going ashore. There were no cheers, no questions and little activity as he mounted the steps to the hard. Except for a few tradesmen's carts, clattering and rattling along the hard, there were few people about. Those whom Winchip passed as he walked up to the governor's residence scuttled about their business without so much as a glance in his direction.

An aged usher, an old soldier by his bearing, showed Winchip into the scantily furnished ante-room where he delivered his report into the hands of a lieutenant of marines.

Helping himself from the claret jug on the solitary Chippendale side-table, he stood before the window, once again looking at *Eaglet*. The mist had already burned away with the rising sun, now shining through the window where he stood. It was a good place to be. It was where, in solitude, he could think without the intrusion of the ship's noise. He lost himself in thought until the door in the corner opened and a different lieutenant returned.

'Captain Winchip, Sir?'

'Yes, Lieutenant.'

'The General will see you now, Sir, if you would care to follow me.'

Winchip followed with good grace. The inner sanctum was still extensively furnished as before. Gone, however, was the sense of urgency that had been present during his last visit.

The general remained seated as Winchip entered. His face had not lost its haggard expression. The air was tainted with the odour of shaving soap and herbal scents, and his wispy hair had recently been watered down to shape. At the end of the highly polished table an ugly and incongruous china vapour bowl and a crumpled cloth awaited disposal.

'Captain Winchip! Please be seated.' The general waved an arthritic hand in the direction of the chairs at the great polished table.

Winchip saw his single report of events at Toulon lying on the table. Only he was aware of the limitations of what was written. There was no mention of the death of the soldiers. He had seen no reason to include it and Niven's admission of it had been verbal.

'You have done well, Captain, and I shall say so in my despatches to Their Lordships.' He looked up, not waiting for any response. 'It should now be evident that my miserable force in this place is totally inadequate for the defence of Gibraltar. Poor Captain Edgecumbe cannot be expected to stand alone against the French fleet and neither should he be asked to do so.' Fowke looked Winchip in the eye. 'I shall be sending over orders to you shortly. In them I shall be requiring you to leave directly and report to London through the Portsmouth messenger.' He maintained what had now become a watery gaze, as though tears were about to burst forth, but Winchip knew better. 'There will be no deviation on the way to Portsmouth, Captain. No stops along the way, do you understand?'

'Perfectly, Sir.' For a mad moment he thought Fowke had been referring to Falmouth and Madeleine. Winchip offered nothing to the one-sided meeting. He knew now that Fowke would not be moved and that anything he, a mere captain, had to say would be as persuasive as a bucketful of air.

'Good. That will be all.'

Winchip left with his brow deeply furrowed. What the general had meant was that he should not call on Admiral the Lord Hawke, and that was a far more serious matter. He knew he was guessing but it had not passed his notice that Admiral Hawke had had doubts, not about Fowke – except his age – but about the general's conviction that Gibraltar was about to be attacked. The general's phobia could become England's embarrassment, with the loss of Minorca to boot. He smiled grimly, realising he had just stepped into a mess of politics.

He walked down to the shallow hill towards the steps deep in thought. It left him with a decision he feared to make, yet make it he must, perhaps at the cost of his own career.

The steady westerly gale had confined *Eaglet* to the anchorage all day, squatting with bare poles to windward of the mole. Winchip noted with a grin of satisfaction that Niven had doubled the cables to the mooring. It would have been a foolhardy captain who tried to venture down to the straits under such conditions. The sudden blow had come to fill the gap as the hot dry air had risen to give it space. The phenomenon was well known. It would be over by the time the sun went down.

Winchip gave way to the noise of daily repairs coming down to him through the open deck light. That and the sound of clumping feet as the marines went through their drills with Sergeant Haggler, as vocal as ever. He wondered if there would ever be an end to it. He had sent a messenger to the Munro residence with a letter for the captain. It would put his mind at rest if nothing else if he read between the lines. He had also suggested that they sent the messenger back with any mail they might have for England. Among the letters brought back to the ship was one for Madeleine. Winchip held it in his hand for a moment before slipping it into the drawer with the others.

Niven, close to apoplexy over the shortage of items needed from the dockyard, had resigned *Eaglet* to a state of make and mend, the scrubbing of hammocks and the airing of sails.

By the end of the middle watch the next morning, the wind had veered to south-easterly and lessened to a healthy breeze – evidence of better weather to the south from Mr Ramblin's experience.

At the approach of four bells into the morning watch the early mist encircled the dark shadow that was the rock. As the first light of day strengthened from the east, *Eaglet* lay peacefully on the sheltered waters of the anchorage.

'The cable is home and stowed, Sir.' Midshipman Bowes' breath was expelled in misty clouds in the early morning air. The last echoes of four bells would mean a great deal to those who had seen the ship brought alive during the last few hours, preparing for sea. Except for Munro's frigate, there would be precious little else to give the misguided people of Gibraltar any hope.

'Thank you, Mr Bowes. Secure the capstan, if you please.' Winchip turned left and right, speaking to the quarterdeck at large. 'Take a last look at the Mediterranean sun, gentlemen.' He looked upwards to the highest point of the rock where the sun's rays had just struck the mixture of rock outcrop and the shrub greenery adorning the surface. 'We have done our best and left our mark. We can do little more than that.'

The signal gun barked out, the smoke obligingly drifting away to leeward, rolling across the placid surface of the water. As *Eaglet* drew away from the confines of the rock, so the air livened, bringing movement to her rigging and a feel of the sea.

The thunder of the filling sails acted as a signal, sending the ship slowly forward. It was a movement that could be felt beneath their feet. The master tested the wheel and glanced up at the stiffening wind pennant.

'Course, south by west, Master, if you please.' Winchip knew the course had been suspected and was not surprised when a small party of men was able to twitch the yards to Mr Ramblin's liking. 'The noon sightings and your westing should coincide nicely today, Mr Ramblin.'

'Quite so, Sir.' The master tugged his beard and sucked at the hollow tooth.

The ship suddenly dipped and rose. Her first taste of unsheltered waters. Winchip turned away with bowed head as a sheet of spray travelled from the forecastle to the quarterdeck, turning the holystoned wood to a shade of chocolate as it absorbed the salt water.

There had been no guarantee of a peaceful passage through the straits. The threat of French men-of-war passing through to join the French fleet had been real. They would have come from colonial duties in The Americas or even from beyond, summoned long since in preparation for whatever was to come.

Eaglet had passed Morocco Point to starboard two days previously without incident, able to steer north of west into clearer waters and retain that course until today, where she was well out into the Atlantic. Winchip's safe return home had become his priority. He had made that clear to his officers and ensured they knew the value of the information in his desk drawer and the reason why *Eaglet* would avoid action rather than seek it. At noon the wind had veered rapidly to the south-west and had settled at that, as if to urge them on their way.

Winchip placed his cloak and hat on the chest and helped himself to a glass of claret from the jug behind the rail on the shelf. He sat on the stern seat and laid an arm along the sill, drumming lightly with his fingers and nodding his satisfaction that the ship was at last pointing to the north and with a favourable wind. What the Bay of Biscay held in store could be a different kettle of fish.

He tried to summarise events as he saw them and how they might affect *Eaglet*.

Gaspar Foche could be ignored, of that he was almost certain. The part he had played had been tantamount to a charade. Winchip suspected that the whole fiasco had been hastily devised by the French to give them time to perfect their invasion force at Toulon. Even Foche must have followed orders knowing that it was a pointless exercise. Unfortunately for him, he had revealed himself as a double-sided spy and would, perhaps, face the consequences of that, or be used, to serve the King's purpose. He could find no sympathy for the man, but by God he had much to be thankful for because of him.

The other enigma was General Fowke. Considering his age and that the twilight of his service was being threatened by unforeseeable events, it was to be expected that he would lose his sense of perception; see dangers where logic demanded otherwise. Admiral Hawke could have been far less considerate in his appraisal of the man. It would be just like him to arrange for the general to receive another three battalions into barracks at Gibraltar to please Fowke and then withdraw them for use at Minorca when the inevitable happened. As it was, and as Winchip had seen for himself, there was no danger of Gibraltar being attacked. Therefore Fowke, too, could be removed from his thoughts . . . for now.

It left little to be considered. The French fleet was at Toulon – how he wished Niven had been able to perceive an admiral's broad pennant on any of the ships – and Minorca waited. *Eaglet* would convey to Their Lordships the latest intelligence. Their Lordships would provide the fleet – as they were already doing – and Minorca would be saved. So it came down to a matter of time – but then, even that had flexibility. St Philip's Castle at Mahon was well manned and fortified and could take a long siege before capitulating. This gave Winchip food for thought. The French could already be upon the island, occupying it and attacking the fortress. The English would then arrive as a relief force with the need to fight a French fleet before setting a foot on Minorquin soil. Something the French had not been required to do. It certainly focused the mind.

Winchip rose and refilled his glass. Through the stern windows he could see *Eaglet*'s wake almost to the horizon. They could do no more. The necessary information would be in the right hands before another two weeks had passed. He suspected he was delivering confirmation of what was already known but even that had value when the scales required tipping, one way or the other.

Winchip allowed his mind to drift back to *Corrine*. He had been staring back at her then, albeit from the deck, seeing the frigate in all her splendour and remembering the consequences of that meeting and his protective feeling for his distressed passenger.

His first sight of Madeleine would always remain with him. Tall and with bearing, with dark hair flowing about her shoulders and brown eyes that were smouldering in anger and yet appealing, her sorrow and sadness blatantly expressed by the wetness of her cheeks. Her dignity had been challenged by the disarray of her appearance and yet her dignity had won through. He wondered at the miracle of their mutual attraction and perceived Madeleine as she would be now, at 'Santander', waiting for him and wondering if that was where her future lay. He hoped and prayed that it would be so. Her sparkling eyes during the moments of happiness they had spent together had endeared her to him. Her thoughts for him as they had parted had spoken of her selflessness, despite her own grief and troubles. Her demeanour and the way in which she had won Emma's heart had flattered him. He loved her dearly and knew that Maria would give them her blessing.

*

After thirteen days at sea, carried through Biscay by a welcome south-westerly, *Eaglet* made contact with a frigate from the Western Squadron. With numbers exchanged, it came as a surprise when the frigate signalled the captain to report to flag, a signal he could not ignore and the one he had prayed for. It was to be the next morning before the *Royal George* was sighted.

Midshipman Bowes, captured by the excitement of the midshipmen at being among the leviathans about them, peered through his glass from his position in the shrouds. With a sudden jerk of movement he dashed the glass from his eye and turned to the quarterdeck. 'Signal from the flagship, Sir. Captain to repair on board.'

Winchip turned to Pope. 'Acknowledge, if you please, Mr Pope – smartly now!'

So much for Fowke's instructions. From the moment Fowke had told him to report straight to Portsmouth, he knew he could not and would not. To have argued on the spot would have led to dire consequences. To defend his action after the *fait accompli* would be a consequence far easier to deal with. Now, the matter was out of his hands. He made no sign of his great relief.

Winchip tipped his hat to the shrill of pipes before going through the entry posts. The boat's crew was smartly dressed and Hellard, his silver buttons twinkling on his deck coat, stood proudly erect in the stern sheets.

The ship's boat pulled away into the south-westerly swell. Winchip, holding his hat to his head in the cold wind with one hand and his sword with the other, thought how easily this simple stretch of water could have been the Styx.

Having overcome the tumblehome of the *Royal George*, Winchip acknowledged the trill of pipes and the lieutenant of marines as pipe clay burst into a cloud at the slap of hands on musket slings. Once again he found himself guided towards the stateroom by a welcoming Captain Campbell and, as before, relaxed in a chair at the senior captain's behest. It seemed such a short time since he was here last, yet so much had happened. In response to a cough at his side, Winchip passed his reports and despatches to the flag-lieutenant.

'It is good to see you back, Captain.' Campbell leaned to one side as he spoke, allowing a servant to fill two glasses.

'And I to *be* back, Sir, you have my word on't!' Winchip's broad smile urged them both into decorous laughter. Campbell's because he was restricted in what he could ask and Winchip's in what he could tell. 'I can say that there is enlightenment in my reports, Sir. Something, I hope, that will be to the advantage of Their Lordships.'

'By all, that is all I need to know! Well done, man! Well done, I say!' Campbell slapped his thigh.

Winchip replied, 'Time is now our only enemy, Sir.' He was well aware that Captain Campbell would be thinking of a diversion from the arduous duties of containing the French. It would not be expedient for Winchip to tell him that had Lord Hawke been selected to take a fleet to Minorca – a fleet already in the making – then the *Royal George* would already be in Portsmouth or the Downs, putting that fleet together.

It also occurred to Winchip that Hawke would have expected to be selected for such an undertaking – but he had not. It was likely, therefore, that the admiral would not be in the best of moods.

It was another interesting fifteen minutes before the flag-lieutenant appeared at his side.

'The Admiral will see you now, Sir.'

Winchip donned his hat and put himself to rights. There was no doubt Hawke was in a hurry to see him.

The great cabin seemed dull compared with the last time he had stood on the same spot, when the sun had filled the place with light. Lord Hawke sat at the polished table surrounded by papers. The tang of tobacco smoke hung in the air and a steward was putting used glasses on a tray, suggesting that there had been others with him until this moment. Winchip removed his hat and waited until Hawke raised his eyes and saw him.

'My dear Winchip!' Hawke consigned the quill he was

holding to the silver stand and leaned back in his chair. 'Sit yourself down, Captain.' He indicated a chair and drew himself closer to the table.

Winchip sat, suddenly aware of all that had happened since he last sat in the same chair. In truth, there had been a moment as he had risen from it those many weeks ago, when he thought he might never return.

'Well, Captain. What can I say?' Hawke spread his arms and his mouth widened to form a smile. 'I have read your reports briefly and have to confess that had they been handed to me by anyone else I would have dismissed them as a fabrication on the spot.' His smile wavered and then died. 'Their Lordships had already been appraised of shipping at Toulon, but never to this extent!' He smacked the relevant page with the back of his fingers. 'As for the troop carriers – and I assume these figures to be correct – then an invasion of Minorca must be imminent.' Hawke shook his head. 'I only hope we can get there in time, Captain.'

Winchip took a deep breath. 'I was concerned that my orders from General Fowke directed me to report to Portsmouth without stopping, Admiral, for that very reason.' He added quickly. 'I was conscious of your wish to know the result of our mission and was therefore glad to receive your signal to attend the flagship.' He hoped that would settle the matter.

Hawke smiled. 'It is never easy to serve two masters. To play one against the other is a solution I have been known to use to my own advantage.' The Admiral looked Winchip in the eye. 'I do not recommend it as a habit, Captain.'

The entry of the steward with a jug of steaming coffee came as a lifeline.

'Your report mentions the presence of a boom across the entrance to the dockyard, as would be expected. Was your first lieutenant able to establish the size of it?'

'I asked him the same question, My Lord. It would appear from the number of pontoons that it was quite substantial.' Winchip could foresee the admiral's next question. 'He felt that fireships were out of the question unless the boom could be broken.' He sipped the coffee and felt its warmth travel to his stomach.

'As I thought.' Hawke drew a page of the report towards him. 'I have noted the names of those you have commended, Winchip. Theirs was a brave act, fraught with danger and fearful in prospect. It shall come to someone's attention, I assure you.'

'Thank you, my Lord.'

Hawke's face assumed a more serious look. He appeared to gather his thoughts before speaking. 'The matter of *Adept* has yet to be resolved.'

Winchip looked suitably grim. The matter had been laying on him with great weight over the last few weeks. He nodded his head in agreement, wondering about the outcome.

'Captain Rance has been persuaded to see sense. The man was ill, as you kindly put it, and hospital would seem to be the best place for him. The matter is now closed. As to *Caprice*, your decision to take her to Gibraltar was the right one. It has saved embarrassment all round and left the French politically sterile. We still have no direct declaration of war but I am sure it is imminent, either by our government or by the French. Perhaps Minorca will free us to do what must be done to rid us of this Gallic menace.' Hawke shook his head and dismissed his thoughts with a short wave of his hand. He started to gather papers about him – a sure sign that the meeting was coming to an end. 'You will remain under my command, Captain. Get your orders off to Portsmouth and then remain at Falmouth while you do shipboard repairs and gather your wits. I shall send your orders to you within the next week.' Hawke stood and offered Winchip his hand. 'You have done well, as has *Eaglet*. Let your people know that, Winchip. They deserve to be told.'

14

To Have and to Hold

Madeleine, enshrouded in a woollen cloak, her eyes watering in the cold March north-easterly coming down the Carrick Roads, had climbed the shingle path to the top of the garden. She sat on the seat where she and Daniel had spent their last few moments together before he had departed. The scudding clouds with dark underbellies seemed to race through the sky, filling the patches of blue and then releasing them to give a moment of sunshine. At her feet lay Blackie, slitting his eyes as he faced the cold blow. Madeleine had made the climb several times, hoping one day that she would see *Eaglet* anchored offshore.

Already she was beginning to understand the lot of a sailor's wife, the separation, together with the fear of one's husband never returning. Not knowing from day to day, or night by night, whether he might already be dead, lying at the bottom of the sea or buried on some distant shore. She shivered and gathered the cloak more closely to her, not so much because of the cold but because of her love for him and the urgent desire to be at his side in all things. Though she yearned for his return and knew the pain of his absence, she could not help but love him the more for it.

The sun gave up the unequal battle, dulling the waters and allowing a mist of rain to permeate the air. She took a last look at the anchorage and reluctantly rose to walk back down the gravel path.

The house had the marks of generations upon it, outside and in. How it must have looked before the wood panelling had lined every room and the windows had been enlarged she couldn't even hazard a guess. Perhaps the personality of the building changed with those who lived within its walls. That was why it now lived to serve Daniel, his mark upon every room, from the fowling piece and boots in the kitchen cupboard to the volumes of naval books and charts in the library where she now stood. There were also his journals, lined along a shelf, propped up at one end with a conch shell – more than that – a delicate piece of scrimshaw. Beyond that was a space, reserved for future journals – a time yet to come? She ran her hand along the uncluttered oak, wondering if she were to be part of that time, see the shelves filled to overflowing.

'Madeleine! Madeleine!' Emma's cries echoed round the house.

'In here!' Madeleine ran to the door and opened it, springing back as Emma ran in to grip her by the hand.

'Father has come home – he's here – coming up the path! Quickly!' She pulled Madeleine along the hall and out onto the porch. Releasing her grip on Madeleine's hand, she clattered down the few steps to the path and ran down to throw herself into her father's arms.

Madeleine drew herself to a stop on the porch, every sense in her body wanting to run forward, yet allowing Emma her private moment. She smiled broadly as Daniel looked at her over Emma's shoulder, his hat dangling from his hand, his sharp features wreathed in smiles. Her moment would have to wait. Emma's need may not have been the greater, but it was certainly the more important.

As they walked towards her, arm in arm, she wondered why she hadn't seen *Eaglet*. Had she been sunk? Was he the only survivor? Her hand went to her mouth, the thought too much to bear. Memories of that terrible battle with *Corrine* crowded in on her. Suddenly there was no time to dwell on it. She held out her arms.

With Emma long since retired to her bed, Winchip and Madeleine sat together in the withdrawing-room, their faces reflecting the dancing flames and jumping sparks of the log fire, their shadows darting about the walls like Valkyries about their sinister business, speeding to Valhalla with their gruesome charges.

He had allayed her fears about *Eaglet*, explaining why the vessel was anchored in another place, in the lee of the eastern shore to protect her from the northerly blow and the possibility of dragging her anchors.

He handed her the letter from her sister and then rose to gather the latest news-sheet so that she could read it with privacy. He knew it would contain fears for her well-being, concerns that Winchip could understand. It would contain a suggestion by Alice that Madeleine make her way to Gibraltar, to live with them and allow herself time to regain her feet. This, too, he knew to be a wise suggestion were it not for facts known only to him.

As he stood at the library window, watching April snowflakes appear and disappear in the light from the room, he knew in his heart that he could not let her go to Gibraltar. There was no guarantee that the French would not press on to Gibraltar once Mahon was taken. Glutted with success and with the means to hand, the toss of a coin represented the odds.

She had laid the letter down and was staring into the fire. Her proud profile was that of Athene, judging her moment to spring from the head of Zeus. He sat quietly next to her, not wanting to disturb her thoughts. In his pocket he had the letter to Madeleine that he had written at Gibraltar. It would have taken the packet-boat while he was at Toulon but it still remained at Gibraltar when they had returned. In it he had expressed his feelings fully, worded from a distance, so easy to pour out one's heart without those nut-brown eyes to throw him off course and pitch him on the rocks of bumbling inadequacy. Now, at this moment, he had the opportunity of speaking his love for her and yet he could not trust himself to utter a sound lest he became tongue-tied, like young Piper with a simple message to deliver.

Before he could commit himself, she turned to him.

'What is it, Daniel? Is it that difficult for you to speak what is in your heart?' She kneeled on the rug and then sat at his feet, draping her arm with a loving intimacy across his lap.

'No, my dear. I have a dilemma for which I have no answer and a beautiful lady with whom it would be unfair to share it at a time so soon in our relationship.' He looked down at her loveliness and smiled.

'I cannot believe you to be a coward. Neither, I hope, would you think that of me.' She smiled up at him. 'I love you, Daniel. I love you with all my heart. To you, I find that easy to say and it doesn't lessen with the telling.'

Winchip took out the letter, holding it out of her reach. 'This is a letter I wrote to you from Gibraltar, after my meeting with Alice and Douglas, at a moment when it was most important that I told you of my feelings. In it, I try to explain their concern for your well-being and good name. I also tell you how they would be happy for you to live there, with them, in Gibraltar.' He took one of her hands in his. 'I also tell you how much I love you and need you.' He handed the letter to her – delivered it into her hands.

Madeleine broke the seal without a knife, spreading the folded quarters to flatten it and then turned it towards the fire. She read it avidly, inclining her head in that affectionate way that women do when they are in love. Her white teeth gripped her bottom lip as she read every word. When she had read the letter she turned to him and put her arms about him, allowing a warm tear to fall on Winchip's neck. After a moment she withdrew her head and looked at him, her eyes swimming and her face so tender towards him that for a moment he feared the worst.

Quietly, she said, 'Then we are of one accord, requited and happy and yet I see no smile.'

She was not to know that it was fear she had seen in his face. He had to tell her she could not go to Gibraltar, yet how could he do so without it seeming as though he was forcing her to stay. He grasped the nettle.

'You cannot go to Gibraltar.' He looked at her earnestly.

'Minorca is about to be invaded by the French.' Her intake of breath was audible. 'I do not think it likely but Gibraltar could be next and I am not prepared to put you at risk.' He took a deep breath himself and waited.

'Minorca? Attacked?' She was incredulous. 'And perhaps Gibraltar? Oh Daniel! What of Alice and Douglas, do they know?'

'I think Munro . . . er . . . Douglas has the sense enough to see the possibility. He would like as not put Alice on a packet-boat and send her here at the first sign of danger. He has this address. Alternatively he could send her out through Spain. I think she would be safe. I cannot speak for Douglas – he has his duty aboard *Mordacious*.'

'And what of you, Daniel? Are you to fight the French?'

'It is possible but these battles are for ships-of-the-line. I may be sent merely to relay signals and carry men and messages. Frigates do little else,' he lied.

'Oh, Daniel! Am I to lose you before we . . .' The end of the sentence was too weighty to be spoken.

'You will never lose me, Madeleine. That, I promise.'

They clung together in a lengthy kiss. Winchip could feel her breasts against his chest. She spoke without drawing back.

'Then may I stay here with you, and remain when you are gone to sea?'

She had spoken in the knowledge that what she had asked smacked of permanency and begged from him a decision he had so far been hard put to make.

'There is your good name to consider.' Winchip held her shoulders in his hands and looked directly at her, knowing his only reason for not saying what was in his heart was wearing perilously thin.

'I fancy that too much is made of my good name, Daniel. It is you I want. I don't give a *damn* what people say!' There was a glint in her eye. 'How much do you love me?' She focused upon his left eye and then the right.

'Enough to marry you – if you would have me.' The words had tumbled out. Once they had been uttered he felt a great release, as though a burden had been taken from him. He was conscious of holding her hands tightly, willing her response.

'Oh, my darling Daniel. If you don't marry me I shall die!'

The sun shone like an omen late the following morning, shrinking the covering of snow on the roofs below and looking next to relieve the sagging daffodils. The sunlight brightened the house, seeking out corners and casting long shadows. There was warmth in it, enough for them to walk in the garden, arm in arm, significantly leaving footprints where once the untouched snow had been virginal.

'Did you speak to Reverend Walmsley?' Madeleine asked the question demurely, her hand slipping into Winchip's with a softness that denied the urgency of her question.

'As there is no time for the banns, we must apply to the bishop for a licence to marry.' Winchip could sense the stiffening of her body. 'The papers for the marriage licence are already on their way to Exeter by special messenger. I have paid him to stay until the papers are signed. It is now up to the bishop whether or not we can marry before I go back to sea.' He raised his hand and gently turned her face towards him. 'There are no guarantees but Edward Walmsley says he is a man of understanding. We can ask no more than that.'

She leaned up and kissed him. 'We have the rest of our lives, yet I am still impatient.'

'No more than I, my love.' Winchip returned her kiss with feeling, still unable to dismiss the possibility that he might be recalled to *Eaglet* before the papers arrived.

'Shall you be away for long?'

'That is out of my hands, but likely.' He found it impossible to deny her the truth.

'Then we are at war with France.' Her sagging shoulders turned it into a statement of fact, with all its implications.

'In all but name.' He turned her towards him. 'At best it

will be a trip to the Mediterranean and a speedy return. At worst it could mean a chase to The Americas and a spell of blockade duty. Whatever happens, I shall write to you, please rest assured of that.'

'I know you will, my love; but I shall miss you with all my heart.'

The Reverend Edward Walmsley stood before Beth as if to remind her of all her sins. In his black frock coat and breeches, his starched fork of linen gleaming white on the sombre, black cloth, he cocked his tricorn.

'Good mornin', Yer Reverence.' Beth withdrew her ample figure and opened the door wide for the rector to enter. 'I shall tell the captain you're 'ere.' She bobbed and was gone before he could speak.

Winchip appeared with unseemly haste, ushering the rector into the library with a smile that was somewhere between hope and expectation. After days of waiting, torn between a desire to make enquiries and dreading a recall to the ship, the moment was upon him.

'I have news from Exeter, Captain.' The Reverend Walmsley accepted the glass of Madeira and managed to part the tails of his coat with one hand before sitting down. 'As I mentioned to you, the bishop is a man of understanding...'

Winchip relaxed. It was not to be expected that the rector should declare himself and then scamper off like a messenger boy. He waited patiently, wanting to run to Madeleine with the news. Instead he sat, cross-legged and reclined, sufficiently interested to look attentive. The Madeira had vanished and the rector was twirling the stem of the glass between thumb and finger, extolling the Church's willingness and munificence in times of exigency.

Winchip, muttering pleasantries and nodding his recognition of the assistance he had received, hurried to refill the rector's glass.

'It is of no surprise to me that, under the circumstances,

great importance was attached to your application, Sir.' Walmsley smiled condescendingly over his glass. 'Would tomorrow morning be too soon – after matins, shall we say?'

Winchip exhaled with relief. 'Tomorrow would be most convenient, Rector. I don't have to tell you how grateful we both are for your kindness and the bishop's understanding.'

It was only after the consumption of a further two glasses of Madeira that the Reverend Walmsley released Winchip's proffered hand. He took the downward path towards the church, his movements akin to a ketch taking a narrow channel into the wind and having to tack two paces while making a forward progress of one.

The thick oak door closed with a respectfully dull thud. Winchip turned, knowing Madeleine would be there. They rushed together in a tangle of arms, each wanting to shout to the heavens. Instead, they looked into each other's eyes, too excited to speak – only able to smile shared thoughts.

Midshipman Pardoe let fall the lion's head of the front door, well aware he was the last person on earth the captain would want to see. He tucked his hat beneath his arm and ran his fingers through his fair hair, suddenly afraid there would be no one at home, gratified when the wrought and twisted iron ring turned and the door slowly opened.

'Peter!' Emma stepped outside and pulled the door closed so that for a moment they were alone. She kissed him quickly on the lips. 'I have missed you. Why haven't you been up to see me?'

'I had no pretext, my love.' He hung his head. 'I have asked your father's permission to call on you. He said "yes", the moment I stopped talking. It was all over in a moment.'

'Oh! That's wonderful. When shall you return?'

'I have no idea. We may finish up in The Americas. I shall write to you whenever I can, that I promise, with all my heart.'

'I love you, Peter.' She rose on her toes and kissed him again. Her expression confirmed it.

'I love you, too, my dearest.' He broke the spell. 'Hadn't I better come in?'

'Oh yes!' Emma put a hand to his chest. 'You can't call her Madeleine any more. They were married yesterday, down at the church – isn't it exciting?'

'Married?'

'Shh! Keep your voice down!' Emma turned and pushed the door open, taking Pardoe's hat and coat with a single movement, leaving him thinking how coarse and ponderous they looked in her sculptured arms.

He rescued the pouch containing Winchip's orders from the coat pocket and followed Emma to the withdrawing-room.

Winchip had heard the front door knocker. It took but a second to realise that it would be a messenger from the ship, Pardoe or Niven. He guessed the former, considering the speed with which Emma had dashed to the hall. The rap on the withdrawing-room door came after a lengthy delay and confirmed his thoughts. He turned to Madeleine who was sitting near the fire and gave her a resigned and apologetic smile.

'Come in!' He was right.

'It's Peter, Father – with bad news, I think.'

'Come in, Lieutenant. Orders, I suppose?'

'Good afternoon, Sir. Good afternoon, Ma'am.' Pardoe bowed his head in the appropriate manner to Madeleine. With that he handed the pouch to Winchip. 'May I offer my congratulations, Sir? It will be wonderful news for our people.'

'You may, Mr Pardoe – you certainly may – and thank you.' Winchip started to unwind the binding and said to Emma, 'Take Mr Pardoe for a long walk, my dear, while I read these in peace.'

It was later that Winchip gathered his papers together preparatory to going down to *Eaglet*. He had written his letters of thanks to both the bishop and the Reverend

Walmsley. Madeleine's letter to her sister was in his bag together with his books. His old sea-chest stood open at his feet, waiting to be packed with all the paraphernalia necessary for a prolonged stay at sea.

From across the hall he could hear the sound of laughter as Pardoe played the gallant with the ladies. He would deny him none of it. The sound brought hope, and with the hope the thought of death diminished. For the first time in many years he was afraid of death.

15

A Perilous Prospect

Winchip sat with Pardoe in the stern sheets of the jollyboat, the sole passengers as it pulled away from the steps. He imagined that Pardoe felt as *he* did, holding to himself with stoic resolution his own reason for wanting to remain, just as each knew he could not. They sat huddled inside their coats, hats pulled well down and their backs to the weather side to avoid the drizzle in their faces. The fine, misty rain had a cold and dank feel to it, causing the gunwales and boards to shine with a steely wetness. It made no mark upon the water, bringing instead a glassy texture to the surface and the smooth undulations of a gentle swell.

Winchip looked across the bow. Even in such grey conditions *Eaglet* maintained her spark of alertness, her strake now emphasised by new buff paint along the line of her gun ports, splitting the sombre blackness of her hull. She looked what she was, a fighting ship, ready in a moment to answer her country's call.

As Winchip came through the entry posts and stepped down onto *Eaglet*'s deck to the shrill of pipes, he shivered in the coldness of the morning. The mist, through which he had waved goodbye to his wife and daughter, still remained. It came and went, now swirling through the rigging and obscuring the water, uncomfortably damp and forbiddingly cold.

'Good morning, Sir.' Niven sported a knowing grin that promised a speech but said nothing more.

'Good morning, Lieutenant.' He responded cheerfully to Niven's salute and pulled his collar about his neck. 'My cabin in five minutes, if that is convenient?' It finished as a question in case Niven had urgent business elsewhere.

'In five minutes, aye, Sir!'

With his sea-chest in mid air, somewhere betwixt the deck and the water, Winchip dropped his hat and coat on one end of the stern seat and sat at the other. The welcome aroma of coffee emanated from Booth's cubby-hole; it would be newly purchased from one of the Dutch mail-boats now standing in the lee of Pendennis Castle. The clink of china suggested that it was on the way. By the time he had extracted his order pouch and removed the papers, there was a knock on the door and Niven entered. The first lieutenant's coat was silver with the sheen of misty droplets.

'Sit yourself down, Lieutenant. Coffee is on the way.'

Niven took the nearest chair and held out his hand. 'May I offer my congratulations, Sir. The whole ship is abuzz with the news!'

Winchip took the offered hand. 'You may, Mr Niven. I feel I am a very lucky man.'

'No more than you deserve, Sir.'

The curtain parted and Booth brought in the tray and started pouring, a rubbery grin as wide as his face stretching across his ageing and toothless visage.

'Speak, Booth, before you split asunder.' Winchip looked up at his manservant, a smile playing on his lips.

'Good on 'ee I sez, Cap'n, Zur.' Booth grabbed an imaginary forelock and maintained the grip walking backwards until he had vanished behind the screen.

'Thank you, Booth.' Winchip nodded. Neither Winchip nor Niven uttered a further sound for fear of hurting the man's feelings.

'We are once again bound for the Mediterranean, Lieutenant. Minorca, to be precise.' Winchip laid down his orders, knowing them almost by rote. 'It would seem that somebody on high has given credence to my reports, unless I am deluding myself. Personally, I think we have Admiral the Lord Hawke to thank for common sense being brought to bear – I can think of no one else.' Winchip sipped the hot and steaming coffee, holding the cup in both hands, enjoying the warmth of it and luxuriating in one of their few pleasures in home waters – or until it ran out.

'Shall we be visiting the Western Squadron, Sir?'

'We shall only be transferring despatches and mail, unless we are called upon to see the admiral. Despatches seem to be flying about like autumn leaves at present. We shall also be calling in at Gibraltar and General Fowke, again with despatches and mail.' Winchip laid his orders on the desk and pointed out a paragraph, underscoring a particular line with his finger. 'Herein lies my problem.' He twisted the paper round to face Niven.

'By all the gods!' Niven read the line again, his eyebrows rising in his effort to correctly interpret what he had read. 'This means we are at war, Sir. There can be no doubt.' Niven turned the paper back to Winchip. 'If it says, "... avoid contact with the enemy unless ...", we must assume that Their Lordships mean the French!' A wide grin spread over Niven's face as if he were glad that the uncertainty was over. 'I don't know what else to say, Sir.'

'"Enemy" is their choice of word, not mine!'

'But, Sir! If I understand you correctly, a war could start with the slip of a pen!'

'Given a few weeks you may have cause to remember that, Lieutenant; and be the first to do so.' Winchip returned the orders to the pouch. 'In the meantime we shall assume that that is what it means. I have no intention of being taken by ruse or surprise.'

Seventeen days out of sight of land, following a path taken many times before, Winchip felt a kinship with the sea around him. He anticipated a call from the tops at any time. From his place at the binnacle the dawn light was getting brighter. In the tops a dozen pairs of eyes were looking to the east, seeking a sight of land before the brightness of the morning sun made the task impossible.

The first rays of the rising sun had struck the masthead

and worked steadily downwards, just as it had done to the colours of the window of the parish church of King Charles the Martyr where Madeleine and he were married. It had been an occasion that would give him many intimate memories. His mind moved to the wedding itself, seeing again the small knot of people best known to him, each glad to sacrifice their time to attend such a happy occasion at short notice. Madeleine had been dressed in a day gown of pure white, which, against the blackness of her hair, seemed to radiate her beauty. Even as he had stared at the book in the Reverend Walmsley's hand and listened to his intonations, he had heard nothing. Her presence beside him had been all consuming, bringing to him a glow of warmth, well-being, good fortune and pride, confounded only by the sadness of the act of providence which had brought them together.

He had stood on the very same spot at the altar rail with Maria by his side, just as happy and so much in love. With Madeleine at his side he had experienced no feelings of guilt, convinced as he was that Maria was looking down upon them all with the same affection and love that she had shown in life.

'*Deck alow! Sail dead ahead . . . Challengin'!*'

Winchip jerked into life. 'Up you go, Mr Bowes.' He watched the midshipman leap to the ratlines. To no one in particular he said loudly, 'Send up our number!'

'Mr Bowes has confirmed, Sir. The acknowledgement is on.'

'Thank you, Mr Niven. Add "Dispatches for flag".' Winchip turned to the first lieutenant with a grin. 'That must be Captain Munro, earning his keep. It can be no other.'

'We seem to have arrived in one piece, Sir, with a full muster to boot. I just hope we can say the same on the next occasion.'

Winchip offered no comment.

*

'Ah, Captain Winchip!' Lieutenant General Fowke extended a hand as Winchip entered. 'Come! Please sit down.' Fowke tidied the clutch of papers that constituted Winchip's despatches, delivered into the hands of the staff officer an hour beforehand. He extracted one sheet that seemed to hold a special interest for him. 'Did you have an uneventful journey?'

'Yes, thank you, General.' Winchip hoped the meeting would not be protracted.

'I might tell you, Their Lordships are placing a great deal of faith in you, Captain.'

'We shall do what we can alone, Sir. You need have no fear on our behalf.' Thoughts of *Adept* came flooding to mind, finding himself alone on the enemy quarterdeck, waiting for the shot that would end everything. The sealed Admiralty pouches he had brought with him had been numerous. Winchip had visions of events gathering pace and that the climax was close upon them. Suddenly he realised that the general was speaking . . .

'. . . The Secretary of War, Lord Barrington, recently ordered that I should receive Lord Robert Bertie's regiment into this garrison as added protection. Also, in the event of Minorca being attacked, I should release one of my four battalions for the relief of that place.'

'I know little about these matters, Sir.' Winchip crossed one leg over the other.

'No. Of course you don't but the despatches you bring to me now change everything! I am not to get Bertie's regiment, yet I am still required to release my battalion for Minorca.' Fowke threw his arms in the air in a gesture of frustration. 'They could not have read my letters properly!' He sat back in his seat and mopped his sweating brow. 'It seems Admiral Byng will have sailed from England by now. He, at least, is man enough for the job, even if he is a stickler for the book.'

'I knew he was fitting out . . .'

'And under what circumstances do I deliver up this battalion, I ask you that?' Fowke drove on, ignoring Winchip. 'I have four battalions here, Winchip, every one of them precious to me. Furthermore, they are required for relief duties and the defence of Gibraltar.' Fowke relaxed in his chair and mopped his brow once more, his eyes wide, dashing sightless glances about him as if trying to find the sense of things in hidden shadows. With a resigned sigh his eyes settled on Winchip. 'I am sorry to burden you with my problems, Captain. It is unfair of me. I only hope Their Lordships come to see my point of view before it is too late.'

Winchip could understand Fowke's reluctance to deliver up men from his own command into another's. No general living could be expected to do that willingly, especially one who expected to be attacked at any moment.

'If it is of any consequence, General, I believe Gibraltar to be safe – for the present at least. My reports of our visit to Toulon must be construed as proof by even the most jaundiced eye. The talk there was of nothing but Minorca. There was no mention of Gibraltar.'

'You realise you could be walking into a lion's den, Captain?' Fowke raised an eyebrow. 'A dead Daniel is of no value to the King's Navy.'

Winchip ignored the unintentional pun. 'As I have said before, Sir. We have a well-found ship, good enough to see off most Frenchmen.' Winchip spoke tongue-in-cheek, keen to instil some confidence into a conversation that was quickly becoming defeatist. He had allowed for a reply, continuing when he received none. 'Our task, as I see it, is to communicate with St Philip's Castle and let General Blakeney have all the information presently available.'

'You make it sound very simple, Captain. What is your plan of action should Mahon already be taken, which may well be the case if you are to be believed?'

Winchip was annoyed that there should be any doubt. 'Then, General, we shall do the opposite. I shall assess the situation and make my report to you accordingly, though I suggest that if the place has fallen we shall more than likely be running for our very lives.' He grimaced as he said the last few words, turning that into a smile as he realised that the general was mellowing; perhaps seeing his point of view at last.

'What can I do to help you, my dear Winchip? My hands seem tied at this time.'

'Sir. We are used to operating alone; it seems to suit us.' Winchip wanted to give the governor a wealth of assurances, none of which would be true, and certainly unfounded. 'I thank you for your concern. I submit there are few risks for us to worry about. If the French are at the doors of the fortress then there is certainly nothing we can do. If, however, the French have not attacked then we shall report to you accordingly.'

Fowke nodded, his approval unspoken.

Winchip leaned forward in the chair. 'May I ask, Sir, why *Eaglet* was chosen for this task? There are bigger and better ships.'

'You were chosen by the Prime Minister, Captain.' Fowke let the words sink in. 'It appears Admiral the Lord Hawke, through Admiral Boscawen, had a great deal to say on your behalf; and he at least has the ear of the Duke of Newcastle.'

'*Eaglet* appears to have been honoured, Sir.' Winchip shook his head, totally deflated. He suddenly wanted to be away from the place. A quick visit to Alice's home and then off to sea where he could think more clearly. 'May I ask when I shall be allowed to sail, General?'

'I have no hold on you in this expedition, Winchip.' Fowke drained the last drop of his Madeira and stood up. 'I have been requested to give you every assistance, which I hope I have been able to do.' A winsome smile was enough to bring a hundred creases into play. The eyes seemed sad and remained so.

'I am obliged to you, General. I have one visit to make and then, with your permission, we shall make sail.' Winchip stood and tucked his hat beneath his arm.

'Of course, Captain Winchip. I hope all goes well and that some clarity is brought to bear at this difficult time.' Lieutenant General Fowke stepped round the table and extended his hand. 'You have a great weight to carry on your shoulders. I only wish I were in a position to help you carry the load.'

'Thank you, Sir.' Winchip gave an almost imperceptible nod of the head and turned on his heel. He wondered how Fowke would fare when things came to a head. He could lose all his battalions if, or when, the French occupied Minorca. Gibraltar might prove to become a desolate possession just when she was needed most. The sight of the derelict ships in the anchorage and the knowledge that the dockyard was of precious little use did little to ease his mind.

The house was as before and, like the previous time, it was bathed in warm sunshine. Being aware that Munro was at sea he thought twice about knocking at all. The letter from Madeleine and the need for his own presence when Alice read it dispelled any nagging doubts, so, with that, he let the iron-cast knocker drop.

When the door opened he had expected to see the little Spanish maid. Instead, it was Alice herself.

'Daniel! Oh, do come in!' She opened the door all a'fluster, gathering her skirts so he could pass her into the gloomy interior. 'Douglas is at sea, I'm afraid.' Her brow pinched up as she spoke, no doubt fearing that Winchip would dissolve before her eyes.

'Douglas and I have just exchanged signals in the straight, so he will know I am here. Besides which you may find my ... our news quite momentous.' Winchip followed Alice into the day room where the windows were larger and the light the greater for it.

They sat comfortably and waited while the maid served tea – a rapidly advancing alternative to coffee it would seem, to Winchip's disappointment. Winchip sipped and scoured the pages of a recent *Gazette* as Alice read the letter. Twice she looked up at him with a smile and twice he was able to catch it and continue reading. At last she looked up, dropping her hands to her lap and gripping the letter in her fingers.

'Daniel. Oh, I am so happy for you both!' She turned away as her voice wavered. She dabbed her eyes hurriedly and turned to him with her face as bright as a button. 'What wonderful news – at last.'

Winchip wondered if the 'at last' had been because of his ethical demurring or because Madeleine was at last married. 'I know Madeleine will be delighted by your approval, as I am now. Things would have been done very differently, as I am sure you realise, if time and distance had not conspired against us.' Winchip spread his hands to support the obvious.

'Of course they would, Daniel. We quite understand.' Alice rose from her seat as though she felt she ought to be doing more than just sitting down with such news to digest. 'Come! We shall go into the garden and I shall prepare lunch. It will give me an opportunity to instruct you in the needs and requirements of a seafarer's wife while her man is at sea. Then I shall write to Madeleine.'

There had been no need for secrecy as *Eaglet* left the anchorage. Once clear of the bay and in a brisk quarter-wind, she had headed north-east, riding the swell as it passed beneath her, the sea as blue as sapphire, touched as it was by the violet reflections of the setting sun.

Now that sun was rising again, this time bringing with it that feeling of apprehension known only to those whose task it is to face the unknown. The Balearic Islands, below the horizon ahead, were drawing closer by the hour.

Winchip stood at the taffrail with his hands behind him, watching the ship's wake stretching out behind like a ploughman's furrow, pushing them nearer and nearer to what lay ahead. The sun was brightening by the minute, clearing the shadows and bringing a clarity to the deck and rigging alike, allowing wisps of vapour to rise from the planking like departing spirits of the night.

'*Deck there! Land on the larboard bow!*'

Pardoe waved his arm to acknowledge the call from

Costly, sitting in the maintop with a glass. He nodded to Bowes who scuttled up the quarterdeck towards the captain.

Winchip met the midshipman halfway. For the last few hours he had been planning in his mind the best way to approach Minorca, bearing in mind that events had a strange way of springing themselves upon the unwary. He had already convinced himself, and reported, that the French were, as yet, unprepared to leave Toulon. When *Eaglet* had left the place there was still much fitting out to complete – cannons to load and provisions to acquire, if they had sufficient of either. Convinced as he was, he found it difficult to decide upon the best plan of approach.

He slapped his thigh with a resounding thwack. He had made his assessment. It was now time for a decision. He went with his instincts and hastened to the binnacle and Lieutenant Pardoe.

'Mr Pardoe. Raise the hands to wear ship, if you please.'

Pardoe unhooked the 'hailer. '*All hands up to wear ship! All hands up!*'

Mr Ramblin came up the steps still tucking in an unruly shirt. He acknowledged the captain and silently surveyed sea, sky and the ship's rigging in one circuitous assessment. Niven appeared from nowhere, looking as though he had always been present.

Winchip turned to Pardoe. 'Mr Pardoe, kindly inform the master we shall come to due east. Let me know when she is wore and any change in the wind. I have no wish to be put on a lee shore.' To Niven, he said, 'My cabin, as soon as you are ready to do so.' He knew Niven would want to see the course change made to his satisfaction. Even as he spoke the after-guard were gathering, silently and with respect in the presence of the captain.

When the last slab of lead had been put into the pouches, Winchip put them in the top drawer of the Gillow desk. There they would lie, accessible and ready to sink to the bottom of the ocean should things go against them. The knock came on the door as he sat on the stern seat.

'Enter!' He almost shouted in the noise coming from the deck above. 'Sit down, Lieutenant.' Winchip waited until Niven was settled. 'My orders are to make contact with St Philip's Castle, if possible. We are to make General Blakeney aware of the position as we see it and also deliver despatches from both England and from General Fowke. It seems a mundane task but we both know better than that. It seems likely to me that Captain Edgecumbe will still be in harbour at Mahon. There are no despatches for him but I think he would like an appraisal of events if we have the opportunity.'

'What about the French Fleet, Sir? Do you think they have sailed yet?'

'Aha! You have your mind on the task ahead and I'm glad to see it. It is unlikely that the French have left Toulon but one cannot be sure, despite what we have heard from our prisoners. They were still fitting out while you were there and it is unlikely that they have received cannon into those vessels still unarmed. I think we must err on the side of caution. We shall keep a vigilant eye on our horizons and make sure they don't slip past us without our knowing. It is the sensible course to take, and on that I think you will agree.'

'I agree entirely, Sir.'

'Good. Our despatches are important and must get through. After that . . .' Winchip raised his hands in the style of a supplicant.

The noisy workings of the ship were diminishing, a sure indication that things were much to Pardoe's satisfaction. As if on cue there was a knock on the door and the sentry appeared.

'Midshipman to report, Sah!'

'Send him in.'

Pope entered, looking far more confident than he had when Foche had been brought on board. 'The ship is wore, Sir. Due east and eight knots by the log-ship.'

'Thank you, Mr Pope.' He looked Pope in the eyes. 'Take the deck, Mr Pope, and ask Lieutenant Pardoe and Lieutenant Gray to attend me here. Any problems and you send Mr Bowes to me immediately.'

'Aye, Sir.' Pope's wide grin expressed his feelings, perhaps seeing it as a return to the fold, his lapse of confidence forgiven – even forgotten.

Booth placed glasses upon the table and poured the wine from the jug. Two fingers pinned down each glass in the rolling motion brought about by the quarter-sea. The officers sat around the table in exactly the same places as they would at dinner. The atmosphere was subdued. It was not a common experience. The practical and protective sailcloth cover was adorned with their hats and the means by which they could take notes. Winchip knew they would be wondering what lay ahead and what part they would be expected to play in events yet to come. Gray, stiffly upright, stoic and immaculately dressed, brought a rich red colour to the sunless cabin. He would obey whatever orders were given, without question. The others would do as they always did, through the chain of command. Winchip waited until Booth had finished and then ordered him to the galley.

'Gentlemen! One of two things will happen tomorrow.' Winchip was glad to see he had their undivided attention, knowing it could take all their courage to survive what was to come. 'We shall either be paying a routine visit to St Philip's Castle and General Blakeney, when we shall attempt to deliver reports and despatches, or we shall be fighting for our very lives.' He let the words hang in the air. If it worried them, then let them be worried. 'We may also be *running* for our lives. Even *Eaglet* knows when the odds are too great.' He let that sink in and waited for the chuckles to subside. 'The fleet of transports we discovered at Toulon may already be at Mahon – or Ciudadela, landing troops and either laying siege to the fortress or looking to possess the whole island before proceeding on to Mahon. Whichever the case, there will be a fleet of French men-of-war to protect them.' He saw them exchange glances and could imagine the unspoken questions. 'This is why I have decided to approach Mahon from the south. I mean to stay out of trouble until our mission is completed and the despatches are delivered. Once that is done, two more things may occur. Either Captain Edgecumbe will have ordered us to join his command, or we shall be free to gain as much information as we can so that Their Lordships at Admiralty will be better informed.

'Now – fill your glasses, gentlemen – get it done! Remove coats if you wish.' The cabin had assumed a warmth over and above the early May sunshine outside and the response was instant. Winchip had no wish to lose his train of thought, but he wanted what he had said to sink in. Four bells rang out from the belfry, the middle of the forenoon watch. A minute passed before he saw Niven's hand patting silently on the table, demanding silence from his brother officers.

'We have, over the last few months, received orders to minimise our contact with the French – .' The laughter came spontaneously, bringing a smile to even Winchip's face. He raised a hand for silence. 'I have to tell you, we are now considered to be at war with France and need to conduct ourselves accordingly. The French are *not* going to shy away from us!' He leaned forward on the stern seat to emphasise his words. 'Our main task is to bring information back to Their Lordships.' Winchip raised a finger and jabbed it towards them. 'I want you to remember that we may be forced to turn tail, obliged to recognise a superior force for what it is!' He let that sink in. 'We are not in the business of taking risks with information others have relied on us to obtain and deliver.' The pause was lengthy. 'Do I make myself clear?'

'Quite clear, Sir!' Niven spoke instantly for them all. He, in particular, would be the loser, once again foregoing the possibility of a command by dint of circumstances.

'At sunrise tomorrow, weather permitting, we shall approach the Mahon inlet and the harbour from the south. We shall know immediately if anything is amiss. If everything is normal we shall anchor off shore to the south. I'll not see our ship taken because we put her in a position from which she could not escape. That is all I have to say, gentlemen – for now. If you have any questions, then now is the time to speak.'

An hour later, Winchip stood, waiting for the clatter and scrape of chairs to subside before he concluded. 'Get what sleep you can – and that applies to our people.' He caught Niven's eye. He gave them a final moment to put themselves to rights and drain their glasses, observing them as they passed out through the door, his awesome responsibility suddenly weighing heavily upon his shoulders.

16

The Rescue

Winchip stood at the lee rail of the quarterdeck. With his hands behind his back, tightly clasped, he looked strained. There was a tension inside him, suppressed, as it had to be.

The Balearic waters were quiet in the gentle southerly air. Shallow and glassy undulations of the sea, rising and fading in their turn, dissolved into spume as the ship's cutwater sliced a path through them. Perhaps the first hint of dawn, already beginning to lighten the eastern horizon, would only bring substance to his doubts, turn his hopes into disasters and his aspirations into ignominy. The rising sun could be the flame to heat the cauldron into which *Eaglet* was blithely sailing.

The dark shadow lying in the moon's ghostly path he knew to be the south-eastern shoreline of Minorca. From where he stood on the quarterdeck it lay to the north-east. It was almost on the larboard beam as *Eaglet* pushed slowly eastward, her t'gallants hung up tight on their brails, laying bare the yards to thwart the prying eyes of the enemy; ready to let fall on the word of command.

Benjamin Cork changed position at the masthead to relieve the numbness in his leg and to retrieve the half-penny biscuit cake, bought from the cook, before his stint in the tops. The beauty of the scene and the gentle progress of the ship were of no interest to his dulled senses. Anything that threatened his safety, however, was a different matter.

He saw the sail against the backdrop of the land, a small patch of grey against an almost solid blackness. With his eyes screwed up and a hand blotting out the moon, he peered to confirm his finding. A moment later, convinced that it could be nothing else, he shoved the biscuit into his shirt and swallowed to clear his mouth.

'*Deck alow! Sail on the lee beam, 'gainst the land!*'

'Mr Bowes! Up with the glass, if you please.' Niven acknowledged the call and turned aft, knowing the captain would be on his way down to the binnacle. The knot had entered his vitals; be it fear or anticipation, it would not go away. Niven had often known fear and overcome it. This time it was real, growing apace and with substance, and would remain so, controlled and unsuspected, not knowing the forces arrayed against them.

Pardoe reached the tops and patted Cork on the shoulder. Without a word he removed the night glass from around his shoulder and wrapped his legs around the tree, attuning his body to the sway of the mast top in the dizzy height. As he raised the night glass to his eye he could feel the warm African air on his cheek. He adjusted the limited focus, his inspection of the vessel revealing all but her nationality. She was a two-masted, brigantine sloop, and a large one at that. Nothing, he surmised, that could cause the captain any concern. If French, then she was a prize for the taking. The vessel came about as he watched, an ungainly operation, her square-rigged mizzen shivering in the moonlight, bringing her back from whence she came, obviously on patrol. Slipping the glass back over his shoulder on its fish-line, he took the back stay, coming down to the deck, hand over hand, in a matter of moments.

'Well, Mr Pardoe?' There was a note of urgency in Niven's question.

'She's a brig sloop, Sir. A big one. Eighteen guns, I'd say. She came about but not with any haste. I think she's patrolling, heading south-west – towards us, Sir.'

'Thank you. Get back up there and keep us informed.' Niven turned to Winchip as he arrived at the binnacle. 'I submit it is probably just as Mr Pardoe says, Sir. It would be sensible for the French to have eyes to the south, so to speak.'

'Indeed, Lieutenant. If she is patrolling we shall have to

come to grips with her, either now or later if we are to approach Cape Mola and the harbour entrance.' Winchip thought for a moment or two. 'She could be English but I think we both know better.' He paused again, his brow furrowed. 'We shall run down on her, Mr Niven. Hands to quarters, if you please. Load with round shot and brail up the courses.' As an afterthought, he added, 'Have our people taken breakfast?'

'Aye, Sir – long since.'

'Good.' Winchip watched the first lieutenant on his way and then turned to Mr Ramblin. 'Let fall the t'gallants, Master, and shape a course to intercept her. We can make chase when she comes about. I should like to trap her against the land if you think that is practicable – keep her in one piece, so to speak.'

'Aye, Captain. I think it can be done, but may the Lord provide if the wind gets up.'

'The Lord save us if it don't, Master.'

'*Deck there! She'm gone about!*'

Winchip strode quickly to the mizzen shrouds with the day glass. So far, so good. He grunted as he saw her colours blossom from the gaff, the whiteness of her ensign dulling even further the greyness of her sails. He dropped lightly down to the deck and returned to the binnacle, the thuds of falling sails and the cracking of canvas catching the light air, resounding around him.

'She is very brave, Lieutenant. It makes one wonder if she has friends hereabouts.' Winchip hung on one foot for a moment as the ship canted over.

'Indeed, Sir. I have to admit the thought never crossed my mind – another lesson learned, I'd say.'

The sudden rumble of trucks across the lay of the deck rendered conversation impossible.

'We're gaining, Captain! Overhauling her hand-over-fist.' Mr Ramblin stared across the three cables that now separated them, his information his ticket to stand with them. 'I do believe we're takin' her sea room.' The master pointed with the stem of his clay. 'And she knows it!'

'The Master is right, Sir. She'll never weather Aire Island, that's for certain! By God, we've got her!' Niven lowered his glass and snapped it shut, his sharp features mellowing into a broad smile.

Winchip said, 'I am not happy about this brig, Mr Niven, unless she is commanded by some wet-nosed youth.' Winchip pressed himself to the rail, taking a final look before sliding together the sections of the glass. The inner tightness he had felt was now gone. It had left him to do what he knew best. It was replaced by an urge to be about the task in hand, get to grips and calculate what might lie ahead.

'She is ours for the taking, Sir. With a squadron will come greater authority.' Niven's voice was almost pleading.

Winchip laughed. 'Have it your way, Lieutenant. I only hope you show the same enthusiasm when her mistress comes round the island with her teeth bared.' Winchip turned and left them, leaving a gap between the master and first lieutenant where he had been standing.

With the sudden sound of cannon fire came a call from the tops.

'*Deck there! She've fired 'er guns!*'

'What was she firing at, Sir?' Midshipman Pope stood to one side, scratching his head.

'She fired for the honour of her flag, young man. That broadside indicates that she wasn't taken without firing a shot.' Niven smiled at Pope and then shouted for Hellard. 'It could also be a warning if there's a Frenchy close enough to hear it.'

Hellard arrived at the run, his huge bulk intimidating among lesser men. 'Yes, Sir.'

'The captain will be requiring the launch and the yawl shortly. Have them loosened off at once!'

'Aye, Sir.' Hellard was gone in a flash.

'*Deck there! She've dropped 'er colours!*'

'This is a strange kettle of fish, gentlemen.' Winchip addressed the deck in general. 'Her captain doesn't want his ship damaged. Do you think it could be because she is expecting to be retaken?' He didn't wait for an answer. 'Go down to her now, Mr Niven.' There was a pause. 'It might be as well to consult the chart. She could be tempting you onto something rather nasty – I have tidal rocks in mind.'

'Not there, Captain.' The master spoke before Niven could move. 'I know this area like the back of my hand, Sir.'

'Well, Lieutenant. It looks as though you may have your own command at last.' Winchip smiled broadly, knowing, as he did, just how Niven would be feeling. As for Mr Ramblin's assurances, he had every reason to trust his knowledge of the waters.

'Who shall I take with me, Sir?'

'One middy and one mate. Confer with the mate to give you a fair mix.'

'Aye, Sir.' Niven consulted the master and then cocked his hat to the captain in a formal salute before diving below for his dunnage.

Eaglet, held up into the wind, her guns pointing menacingly at the brig, acted as guardian to the transfer of men in the ship's boats. Winchip glanced aloft, finding security in the light flutter of the wind pennant. He wished the shoreline were less obtrusive.

Pope was the one he would have chosen to go with Niven, as midshipman. He was glad when that proved to be the case. Perhaps with the responsibility would come confidence and a good officer to boot. As for the twenty-five seamen and five marines under Corporal Basson, they would be a serious loss.

He knew exactly how Niven would feel with a blue ensign tucked under his armpit, being rowed to his first command, albeit a temporary one should he not be confirmed into her. He watched the boats as they bobbed into the shoal waters, getting smaller by the minute, splashes of red tunic and the glint of oars, rising and falling, flashing in the first moments of the rising sun. Distance appeared to diminish the authority of the boats, reducing them in size, and by virtue of that, seeming to increase their vulnerability.

That Niven feared treachery was very likely. As he sat in the stern sheets of the launch he would be tensed with the expectation and the cruelty of it. Winchip knew it would never happen. The destructive power of *Eaglet* would drive out any such thoughts on the part of the brig's captain. He would have to face the remnants of his crew in the aftermath – if he lived. Even so, he was glad to see activity aboard her. Her boats were being lowered on the seaward side, in full view, her crew pouring into them to be landed in the nearby cove. He didn't begrudge them their escape, just as he knew that this was no time for the extra encumbrance of prisoners. The first few of them were already climbing up the escarpment, scrambling through the thorny gorse, the shrubs resplendent with their seasonal, bright yellow flowers. Others clung to the pale limestone rocks like limpets. As he looked through the glass he could see a boat in the water, abandoned, tossing in the surf like a piece of flotsam, no man willing to return with it to the ship, disallowing its use for other members of the *Frenchman's* crew.

At last the boats from *Eaglet* arrived at the brig. The blue form of Niven was up and through the entry port like a squirrel, marines in his wake, clambering up the side from chains and ropes alike. There was no sound of musketry, no sounds of killing – or dying. Winchip let the air go from his body in a rush, his shoulders sagging downwards with the relief of it.

'Mr Bowes!' Winchip waited until the midshipman came from forward. 'Up to the tops, young man. Ask Mr Pardoe to attend me.' He turned to the diminutive Midshipman Piper. 'Bend on. "Take station beyond the Isla del Aire and report." And then add, "Under French colours." She has been given the number "00", Mr Piper. Enter it in the log when you are done.' The young man would have to learn quickly if he were to survive.

'Claridge!'

The young mate by the wheel jerked upright.

'You are now an acting midshipman, if you wish to be?'

Winchip let that sink in. Claridge, another survivor from *Capable*, had been brought to his notice many times. Today he would receive his dues, should he be prepared to take them up.

'Oh yes, Sir! Thank you, Sir!'

'Then assume control of the gun deck under Mr Pardoe when the time comes.' The mate sped off, dashing towards the poop steps as if the devil were at his heels. Winchip grinned and walked briskly up to the taffrail to clear his mind, past the crews attending the six-pounders, three aside, their snouts permanently visible without the screen of ports. He returned to the binnacle as Pardoe arrived from the main gun deck.

'You sent for me, Sir.'

'Yes, Mr Pardoe. You are now first lieutenant. Claridge has been made acting midshipman to assist you.'

Pardoe's grin was self-effacing. 'Thank you, Sir.'

Winchip nodded without expression. 'Stay by me for now, Mr Pardoe. We will have much to discuss and you to learn if we are to survive.'

The sun had cleared the horizon and the eastern sea was alive with sparkling reflections on the calm waters. As Winchip watched, the French brig's yards blossomed into sail. She moved slowly to the west, close-hauled, a burst of spray jetting from her weather bow, her acknowledgement of Winchip's signal still fluttering from her gaff halyard. She heeled to larboard and settled to a short tack to the south-east before coming about, reaching for the point.

'The brig has acknowledged, Sir. Her name is *La Louve*.' Piper's falsetto voice carried in the air.

'Thank you, Mr Piper!' Winchip watched the signal flags coming off the halyard in jerks. It would be only a short time before the view around the island would be open to *La Louve*. She would have sight of St Stephen's Cove, the entrance to the harbour and Cape Mola beyond – the very heart of the activity, Winchip expected.

'*La Louve* is signalling, Sir!' Piper pointed unnecessarily and then scrambled for the signal book, rifling through the pages. At last he looked up. 'Gunfire to the north, Sir!'

'Very well.' Winchip could hear it, a continuous rumble. The direction was consistent with a prolonged bombardment of the fortress of St Philip. He logged it himself, trying not to let his confusion show.

Pardoe raised his glass. '*La Louve* has come about . . . She's signalling. "Enemy frigate . . . double anchored . . . to the north . . . off Mola", Sir.' Pardoe reeled the signal off without need of the book.

'Well done, Mr Pardoe. Better we stay cleared for action, I think. Let the men rest at the guns. I think they will be needed before too long.' So! The brig had not been alone and neither, perhaps, was the frigate, double anchored or not. Winchip knew this was no full-scale bombardment. It was an attempt to test the defences. The attack on Minorca must have already commenced – from Ciudadela, the old cathedral city. He could picture the scene as his thoughts raced: the great square and the picturesque harbour. He could remember, too, the people, Catholics almost all, hating the English, enduring them because they must. He slapped his knee angrily. He doubted if a single shot had been fired.

Pardoe lowered his glass and turned to Winchip. 'Excuse me, Sir. *La Louve* has just rounded-to. There seems to be some activity in the cove, west of the island.'

'Thank you, Mr Pardoe.' Winchip turned away as a call came from above.

'*Deck below! There's sodgers on the beach – they'm marines!*'

Winchip snapped up a glass from the locker and put it to his eye, trying to catch up on events. He could see the marines well. There were many of them, waving at *Eaglet*, beckoning them near. Their movements smacked of desperation and indicated that danger was imminent. He dragged the glass round towards *La Louve*. She was stationary, her starboard side cleared for action. He looked back towards the marines and made his decision. He called Hellard and waited for the boatswain to come up to him.

'Hellard. Put swivels on the launch and the longboat – you know what to do!' Winchip pointed. 'I want you to get them off while we have the opportunity!' He dismissed Hellard with a gesture and then turned to the master. 'Get the t'gallants off her, Mr Ramblin. I still don't wish to be seen by French eyes yet, if you take my meaning.'

'Aye, Captain.' Already the mates were drawing topmen from the guns and sending them aloft. He looked down upon the main deck and watched the lowering of the boats, nodding his satisfaction as he saw swivels and grape being transferred on board each.

He saw them away and then turned to Pardoe. 'We shall load the twelve-pounders with grape on the larboard side. It may come in useful when we see what we are up against. Put your best gunners to the task, Mr Pardoe; we may have to fire over the heads of the marines.'

'Aye, Sir. I shall see to it.'

There was little more that Winchip could do. He took up the glass once more and immediately he could see marines being chased along the beach by French soldiers. At the top of the shallow cliff, behind the cove, blue uniforms were apparent, firing down upon the marines below them. The marines had dug into the sand to form a perimeter and were bringing down the Frenchmen like ninepins. Already, Hellard's boats were drawing near, small splashes in the water near them telling of French musket balls seeking to destroy their new enemy.

A short way along the beach the running marines were now led by a hatless officer, his sword flashing in the sun as he whirled it about his head as he ran, urging his men on towards the main body on the beach and *Eaglet*'s boats, now in full view. The Frenchmen behind them were falling back, lumbering along in full equipment, some stopping to discharge muskets at their escaping quarry.

Hellard had arrived offshore, calling to the marines to come to him. To load the boats in the shallows would have grounded them with the weight of men. *Eaglet*'s sailors remained cowering at the oars as the running marines ran through the light surf towards them. They clambered aboard in good order, their officer ordering the boat away and then turning his back to return to the beach. A red shape fell from the boat, his musket spearing into the water as he released it. His body sank into the foamy surf and then rose again, spreadeagled on the water, face down. There was no attempt to recover him.

Winchip went down to the main deck where Pardoe met him. They stood watching the affray in silence. It was at that moment that a loud cry was heard. It was a continuous and frightening yell as the French soldiers seemed to rise out of the ground and charge down on the marines from cliff and beach alike. With bayonets pointed before them they charged the perimeter of marines *en masse*, their cry now rising in pitch, a triumphant cheer as they rushed in for the kill.

'Now, Mr Pardoe!' Winchip had removed his hat and he swung it down as if it were his sword.

'*Fire!*'

The twelve-pounders snapped wildly back on their breechings. The ensuing roar of a whole broadside snapped the anchor cable taught and sent a wave of water towards the shore as the ship righted herself. The smoke was the stuff of nightmares, choking and blinding and running the eyes to the point of tears and beyond.

'*Reload!*'

The first sound Winchip was able to hear was the ringing discharge of the swivels from the boats. As the smoke cleared, so the damage to the French became obvious. Body lay upon body, in the cove and along the beach. Men in tattered blue uniforms staggered about the beach holding muskets by the barrel, some walking into the sea with neither knowledge of what had struck them, nor recollection of their purpose, only to sag out of sight as the marines shot anything that moved. Others crawled or scuttled back to the safety of the dunes and gorse from which they had come, hatless and without muskets, some clawing at the limestone rocks in a fruitless effort to climb to safety.

Hellard was at the ship's chains, urging men up the side of *Eaglet* by the ropes being flung down to them. With the last man up, he yelled his orders and steered the boat round to return to the shore, passing the second boat on its way towards the ship.

As the last of the men on the perimeter hurried towards the boats, the remaining Frenchmen rose again from their hidden position and charged down the beach but with less panache. *La Louve*'s abandoned boat was half full of marines clambering to safety when a fusillade of musket balls peppered both craft and men alike. The marines on the boat fell from the craft like petals in a frost, cast outwards and downwards until the surf ran red with their blood. The boat seemed to bob up from beneath them before settling in the gentle swell.

'*Fire!*'

Pardoe had shouted the order without reference to the captain. The twelves leaped back, the smoke billowed and the sound remained in the ears like Truro's matins bell.

The broadside had done its work. The grape had sliced through the attacking force like a whirlwind, reducing its momentum to a few dazed figures standing among the dead and dying. A boat lay smashed, the surf water lapping against it as it did upon the newly dead. The final ringing note of Hellard's swivels echoed like a death knell to France's first engagement on Minorquin soil.

The injured marines clambered aboard, tight-lipped and with faces suffused with sweat, their eyes all but closed and with teeth gritted as every movement brought them pain.

Their equipment was removed and their heaving bodies eased across to the boat deck where Mr Pollard, the surgeon, fussed about them like a mother hen. If Mr Pollard pointed, the man was removed to the orlop, his eyes wide and his groans turning into curses and blasphemies. If Mr Pollard merely grunted, then the man went to the forecastle and a barrack hammock, with water to hand. Equipment and muskets were also taken forward. Already the less fortunate were being carried to the gangway, their cries echoing through the ship as they descended into the blackness below. The usually coarse and unremitting seamen softened in their demeanour, seeming to feel only charity in their hearts as they helped, guided or carried the bullocks down into the depths.

The remainder of the marines clattered over the gunwales, panting, sweating and swearing oaths of defiance to cover their self-imposed disgrace at having to run before the enemy. They sat in the scuppers with heaving chests, shaking hands with any that would respond and swearing a terrible retribution on all Frenchmen.

Lieutenant Gray stood solemnly by the entry port, waiting for the officers.

Winchip gave the faintest of nods as he stood behind Gray at the entry port, allowing him to greet his fellow officers. He knew he was watching the culmination of a job well done – a disaster averted. As he had watched the French walking among their own dead and wounded, he held no fears for Minorca's eventual relief. With men like the gallant marines, England had nothing to fear.

A captain of marines and a lieutenant stepped down onto the deck, both looking about them as if they expected carnage where, instead, they found order, discipline and a clean deck. After exchanging respects with Gray they looked at Winchip and uncovered in silence.

Gray turned to Winchip. 'Sir. May I introduce Captain Durrant and Lieutenant Barnes. I have had the pleasure of messing with both these gentlemen in the past.'

Winchip was simply glad that they were alive. He sufficed with a touch of his hat in response to their smart salute. It was no time for niceties. The occasional musket ball was finding the distance to the ship, skipping across the surface of the water to end with a dull thud against the hull beneath them.

'What is the count, Lieutenant?' Winchip looked directly at Barnes, the man who should know. He hoped for his sake that he did.

'Two officers and thirty-three marines present, Sir. Seven

killed and eleven injured.' He stared at Winchip with a dazed expression, his face and uniform smeared with blood and sand. He lowered his eyes. 'The dead lie where they are fallen, God rest their souls.'

'Thank you, Lieutenant.' Winchip turned to Durrant. 'A word with you, Captain. In my cabin, if you please.' As Winchip passed Pardoe, he looked up at the wind pennant and said one word. 'South!'

'*All hands! Hands to braces! Loosen off!*'

As Winchip and Durrant disappeared beneath the poop, the final act that underwrote the bloody fight was the calling of a heave as the boats were lifted upwards on the tackles with a series of jerks.

Eaglet sailed to the south-east with *La Louve* in attendance. The French brig would be *Eaglet*'s eyes, well above the horizon and clear in the glass.

In the great cabin the sun shone obliquely through the stern windows, playing up and down with relentless monotony, dancing with the motion of the ship as she cut through a bow swell. Winchip was seated on the stern seat while Durrant occupied Niven's favourite chair. The claret had been poured.

'My sympathy for your losses, Captain.' Winchip raised his glass. 'To the fallen. God bless them all!'

'I shall drink to that, Captain Winchip!' Durrant held his glass up into the sunlight, giving it a luminescence and an aura, suggesting that the Almighty himself took the same view. Durrant said as he lowered the glass, 'It was a sad business, Sir. It was suggested that the French might be trying to lay explosives under the walls of the fortress. It fell to my marines to find out during a routine patrol.' Durrant shrugged his shoulders.

'Hmm.' Winchip sipped his claret. 'Do you know when the French actually landed, Captain? And, if so, in what strength and where?'

'Yes, Sir, perhaps to both your questions. From reliable

informers we know that a large force was landed at Ciudadela over the twelfth and thirteenth of April, just over three weeks ago. Accounts vary but it seems as though well over twelve thousand French troops are now on the island and have complete control. Yesterday, information was given that stores and munitions were still being unloaded at Ciudadela.'

'Good God!' Winchip stood and looked out of the stern window, finding comfort in the sight of *La Louve*'s topsails above the level of the swell. He suddenly remembered the conversation he had had with Lord Hawke. 'Would I be correct in assuming that the commander of the French Army is the Duke de Richelieu?'

'Indeed you would be, Sir!' Durrant seemed impressed.

'What about the French fleet, Captain? Is there any sign of that?'

'Yes, Sir. Admiral Galissonnière has been patrolling the waters around the island since the army landed. You will be pleased to know that he is to the north at present. He has a responsibility for those vessels carrying stores, coupled with the need to ensure that when the English fleet comes, he has his force in one piece. I submit he is unlikely to split his fleet for any reason.'

'I am sure you are right, Captain.' Winchip held the goblet in the palm of his hand. 'Tell me more about the French fleet, Captain. Do you know anything of its size?'

'Its size is well known, Sir. Twelve ships-of-the-line, including *Foudroyant, Téméraire* and *Redoubtable*; these have been recognised.'

'What do you think we could do to help frustrate this invasion?'

The question obviously took Durrant by surprise. 'Unfortunately, Sir, very little. The French seem to have taken over the whole island without a shot being fired. We were caught in the open and retreated immediately we knew the size of the force against us. We could never have reached the fortress; but even if we had it would be impossible to gain entrance from the landward side.' Durrant took on a look of anguish. Captain Winchip's reasonable questions had, by their subtlety, brought him to a point where he would begin to have doubts about his own part in events. He looked up at Winchip as though what he had to say could even increase those doubts. 'I have a hard decision to make, Sir – one that may cost me dear – but one that has to be made. If you will take us back to Gibraltar, we would at least be available to continue the fight.'

'If that is your wish, Captain, then I shall oblige you.' Winchip drained his glass. 'Frankly, I think you have made the right decision. There is nothing you can do here.' Winchip's hand was striking gently on his thigh. 'I could, however, ensure that no one could talk of your act as a cowardly one, if that is what worries you?'

'How so, Sir?' Durrant sat up with interest, adjusting his bulk in the chair. He ran his fingers through his fair hair in a nervous gesture and his chin hardened, turning the softness of his features into the hardness of earlier days.

'There is a French frigate lying off the harbour entrance, double anchored and with precious little sea room should she have to leave in a hurry.'

'She is probably there to prevent communication with the fortress, Sir and testing the defences into the bargain.' Durrant was beginning to enthuse.

'Even better. Let us recharge our glasses and discuss what can be done.' Winchip spoke loudly enough for Booth to scuttle in with another jug.

17

The Capture of Vraiment

There was no moon, only darkness. Beyond the vagueness of the low, limestone cliffs, where the sea would be, there was now a dark void: emptiness where there had been substance and blackness where once there had been light. Even the whiteness of the sails of the double-anchored French frigate was invisible from *Eaglet*'s position south of Aire Island. Two cables out in the black void, *La Louve* lay silent, the light breeze bringing the occasional squeal of a swinging lantern or two blocks making contact in the mass of rigging. The ship's bell had long been silent.

With muffled oars, the first three boats moved silently towards the French ship. Captain Durrant stared ahead, unseeing, wondering if providence would once more act against him. He started suddenly and let out a soft oath as the bell of the French vessel rang out into the night. A distant sound, peaceful, yet strident on the mind. It marked the passage of the hours for those who rang it. It went unheard by those who slept beneath it, exhausted by their efforts to harass and isolate a harbour and fortress that seemed impregnable.

Fear had no part to play in the enterprise as far as Captain Durrant was concerned. Fear was the one emotion that had nothing to offer him. It stilled the alertness of the mind and attracted doubts instead of resolve. He glanced at the twenty marines crammed into the boat before him, glad to be part of them. In the yawl to starboard he could see Niven. He almost smiled at the incongruity of the sight. The polished and elegant commander sitting among a ragtag bunch of misfit seamen, each hugging a weapon of his choice, be it a cutlass or a pike, an axe or a maul. To his left, Lieutenant Barnes sat upright in the stern sheets of the brig's launch. Like their officer, the marines sat with backs like ramrods, stoically facing forwards, muskets held vertical, each swaying gently backwards as the oars made their stroke. Behind him, in the curled and twisted vortexes that were the wake of his boat, he knew there were yet three more boats in the flotilla, a total of one hundred and fifty men. Durrant's face twisted in a satisfied grin. There would be French widows aplenty when this night's work was done. Beyond that, sent silently ashore, a marine sergeant would now be wending his way through the rocks, taking Winchip's despatches to the fortress.

As the boats slipped silently towards the stern and the fore-chains of the French frigate, Pardoe was conscious of the killing machine that encompassed him. Sitting with set faces, their muskets enveloped in caring arms, they said nothing. The marines were like precision springs waiting to be released. He looked upon the seamen with something akin to affection. In an assortment of clothing and an even greater assortment of weapons, they grinned at each other, touched hands or whispered into a willing ear. Their bond and companionship was their ticket to life.

Pardoe saw the ship appear out of the darkness; the bows were shining in the dew of the night and the timber seemed wet enough to have ridden a storm. A bow anchor was catted and the fore-chains well within reach of the tall marines. He gave the pre-arranged signal for the boats to move in and was gratified to see men preparing to fend off and save the clatter of a clumsy arrival. As his boat came up to the mizzen chains he tapped the man nearest to him on the shoulder and gestured upwards. The moment had arrived; and with it would come all the horrors devised by man against man.

Suddenly he was gripping his sword to his side as he grasped the chain plate and swung himself upwards. Once there, with a push from behind, he scrambled to the rail and heaved himself over.

The naked deck gave him a feeling of unease, bringing into focus memories that wouldn't go away, moments that would have destroyed his confidence if he let them. He looked about him and then lowered a hand for the next man to grasp with gratitude. He was aware of red tunics at the taffrail as marines eased themselves onto the deck and could hear the grunts and bustle of men trying to be quieter than death itself. He even wondered how they had passed the windows of the great cabin without betraying themselves.

'*Aux armes! Aux armes!*'

The cry shattered the night. The man who had woken from his slumber arose from the boat tier, his arms waving and eyes bulging wide, seeing and yet not believing. The shout was cut off as a boarding axe sank itself into his head.

'Marines! Across the quarterdeck rail in two ranks! *Move!*' Captain Durrant's shouted order brought an instant response. Stealth was no longer required.

'Marines! To the focs'l – *at the run!*' Lieutenant Gray, experiencing his first 'cutting-out', was determined the job would be done right. His eyes darted everywhere as the marines crowded up the steps of the bulkhead to control the forward area of the ship. With their muskets at the port they pounded up the treads, their heavy shoes bringing a sound that should have brought fear and dread to those dragging themselves from their hammocks below.

As Pardoe expected, the deck hatches and companions were thrown open at all points of the ship, gratings thrown aside and covers slamming back on their hinges even as the English seamen tried to batten down the alerted crew. At the rail more marines and sailors appeared as the second flotilla discharged its crews.

The French burst through at the main companion, scrambling and wide-eyed with weapons to hand. As English musket balls found their targets so the Frenchmen fell, their screams unheard in the uproar of the fight.

'*To me*, Eaglets!' Pardoe felt the mass of men about him. Pikes protecting them from all but pistol shots. 'Split their ranks, lads. Across the deck with you!' He ran towards the opposite rail, knowing he would be at the mercy of any man with a pistol. His first opponent was a moustached lieutenant effecting a defensive pose. Pardoe shouted to express his anger and hide his fear. 'Come on, *Eaglets* – she's ours for the taking!' He parried a tentative strike and then ran the man through the stomach, feeling the blade go through to the guard as his arm jarred. Suddenly a screaming Frenchman fell at his feet, driving his legs from beneath him and sending him tumbling into the scuppers. His sword hung from his wrist by the lanyard, the press of bodies and scrambling feet preventing him from regaining a grip on the hilt.

Niven had climbed up the stern by way of the pintle and the ornate window ledge. Blocked from reaching any higher, he had crouched on the narrow sill of an open window of the captain's cabin. He could see the lighted lantern hanging from the deck above and the incredulous and moustached face of the captain in his nightgown as he staggered back at the sight of him. Recovering, the captain strode up to Niven and shouted at him in French, apparently still unaware that his ship was being attacked. Niven struck the man in the chin with his fist before he climbed through the opening. He turned to help others through and then sent them forwards, under the poop and upwards through the companion. As they opened the door to the deck outside, so a servant came out of a curtained cubbyhole and shouted at the top of his voice.

Bowes climbed over the bulwark to land in clear space by the boat deck. Panting, he looked quickly about him. Frenchmen, struggling to reach the deck, were being forced backwards at the main companion. On the other side of the deck he saw Lieutenant Pardoe plunge his sword into an officer, only to tumble out of sight as a wounded man fell at his feet. He adjusted his pistols and raised his hanger, rallying men about him, pointing to where Pardoe had fallen. Together they charged across the deck, leaping over obstacles and round the great guns, men grabbing at rammers and worms, anything to clear the way. Bowes saw a French officer preparing to strike someone at his feet. He charged up to him and thrust his sword into the man's side, pushing it upwards until the man was on the tip of his toes, his sword clattering to the deck, a fearful, piercing scream dying on his lips as he sank to the floor. Bowes couldn't retract the sword. It was buried to the guard and had become part of the man. He thrust him aside as *Eaglets* gathered about him, their backs to him in a ring of defence. Thus protected, he reached down a hand and pulled Pardoe to his feet.

On the quarterdeck, Lieutenant Gray shouted in alarm as the captain's companion opened behind his marines. Before he could reach it, French seamen spewed from the opening as if they, themselves, were being chased from behind. As Gray charged up the deck, so two of the marines were hacked down by cutlasses where they stood. Other marines, alerted to the danger, tried to turn but were frustrated by their unwieldy muskets and the need to protect themselves.

Gray, with panic rising within him, hacked and slashed at the Frenchmen until his arm felt too heavy to lift. He cried out in pain as a musket ball struck him in the leg like a red-hot poker, yet kept up his tirade of blows against any that stood against him, giving the marines a moment's grace in which to turn to face their enemy. A marine next to Gray had managed to revolve his body, only to be shot in the face by a large petty officer, himself hacked down by a maniacal Gray whose sword arm found new strength in his anger, fear and hatred. He hacked, thrust and lunged at anything that moved in a burst of uncontrolled fury that couldn't last. As he pierced a seaman through the throat, he turned to face his next opponent, only to see the muzzle of a pistol close to his face. Too late to snatch his head aside, it discharged.

Pardoe, working his way towards the quarterdeck, saw Gray's head snap back as he was shot. He moaned in disbelief even as he continued to thrust and parry in a mêlée that was becoming a series of smaller fights as the number of dead and wounded, lying in their own blood about them, became a danger and an intrusion. He shouted into the air, 'To me, *Eaglets*. To me!' He knew there was a need for him to both consolidate and rally the men before any felt abandoned or alone. For a fleeting moment he wondered what had happened to Durrant or Niven. Had they, too, met their maker? He heard voices in response, assurances and yells of renewed endeavour all around him, separated from the guttural expletives and cries of the French. He used his pistol to shoot an officer who had hung back, allowing others to do his duty, feeling a certain satisfaction in the act of killing him. He could see them coming towards him from more sides than one. He hacked and thrust with an arm like lead and knees like jelly, wondering how their advantage had disappeared so easily. He ducked and thrust the hilt of his sword into a man's windpipe, feeling the larynx crushed to a pulp. The man sank out of sight.

It was at that moment, with a resounding crash, that the ship lurched to one side, throwing English and French alike to the deck, some to be killed in the moment of confusion, others to be saved as victors were thwarted and the vanquished gained new ground. Pardoe fell to his knees and then recovered in one movement, immediately assuming a defensive position. A ship's bowsprit had thrust itself across the frigate's bulwark and settled there. A moment later Midshipman Pope jumped to the deck. Behind him, yelling English seamen streamed onto the Frenchman with weapons raised high.

'. . . We therefore commit their bodies to the deep to be turned into corruption, looking for the resurrection of the body, when the sea shall give up her dead, and the life of the world to come, through our Lord Jesus Christ; who at his coming shall change our vile body, that it may be like his glorious body, according to the mighty working, whereby he is able to subdue all things unto himself . . .'

Winchip closed the *Book of Common Prayer*, a power pulling at the corners of his mouth as he spoke the names he had come to know so well from as far back as *Capable*. Names that were now so much corruption as the Good Book made plain. He had called those names out, one by one, as they had slipped from beneath the union flag, visible for an age before disappearing into the crystal clear depths, even so far from the shore. Marine Lieutenant Gray had been the last to depart, in a silence so deep that the waves could be heard, slopping beneath the ship's counter. He replaced his hat and passed under the poop to the great cabin.

Later, when a knock came on the door, Winchip was glad of it.

'Enter.'

'Excuse me, Captain.' Mr Pollard's round face looked strained and his small body cramped as he quietly entered the cabin. He was still wearing an apron, smeared with blood but with far less than the previous ones he had worn during the day. 'I just thought you might like to know that Captain Durrant is conscious and should be fine in a day or so.'

Winchip looked up at the man. 'Thank you, Surgeon.' He made a sweeping gesture with his arm. 'And have you a cure for those we shall never see again?' He held up an arm as Pollard made to protest. 'I'm sorry, Mr Pollard. That was unforgivable. We all regret their passing, of that I am very sure.'

'It has been a sad business.' The surgeon's ginger, bushy eyebrows came together, his small head nodding in understanding as he retreated through the door.

Winchip stood and looked out of the stern window, taking the opportunity to look at his little squadron. The name of the French twenty-eight was *Vraiment*. Even now her second officer was committing his dead to the sea. With the remainder of her crew being guarded below decks by marines and her wounded being treated by her surgeon, she would soon be ready for what he had in mind. He had considered sending the French ashore but had thought better of it. They could impart information of value back in Gibraltar and that had been the purpose of the enterprise. He now had a formidable force had he the men to man them – but he hadn't. He struck his thigh in frustration, bottling up the more audacious thoughts that had sprung to his mind. He would command three little ships bound for Gibraltar. A mission carried out and accomplished well – better than well – but at what price?

The three ships lay hove-to, a cable asunder and thirty miles due east of Minorca, licking their wounds. They remained there for the rest of the day, assigning seamen and marines to duties, even to ships other than their own in order to achieve a working balance – a chance to survive. The rescued marines, too, were shared amongst the little squadron, the wounded remaining with *Eaglet*'s surgeon in what had become a crowded orlop. Captain Durrant, satisfied that he could be spared from St Philip's Castle, remained with *Eaglet*, keen to report to Fowke on the situation there.

Winchip found solace in the view from the stern window, his face bathed in the copper hues of the sinking sun. The cabin glowed with the warmth of it, drank it in and absorbed it. Almost a benediction, albeit in the aftermath of an unholy coming together of men. He sighed, memories assaulting his senses, too few of them willing to part from his mind. Raising the muster book to the light he saw the annotation 'DD' against too many good names. Discharged Dead. Fodder for the Secretary's bookshelves, too many faces, lost, even to posterity. He lowered the book. His mind made up, he decided to carry out his decision and inform General Fowke of the situation, according to his orders.

Midshipman Bowes swung round as he heard the measured tread of the captain. He cocked his hat and moved to one side in the accustomed fashion. 'The wind remains southerly, Sir. Nothing to report.'

'Thank you, Mr Bowes.' Winchip glanced down at the

binnacle from habit and then towards the sinking sun, already dousing itself on the western horizon, sufficient for his needs. He turned to Piper. 'Bend on a general signal, Mr Piper. "Take station astern of me – course south-west".' To Bowes, he said, 'I would like you to get the French signal book for me, Mr Bowes. In the top drawer of my desk, if you please.' He handed Bowes the little brass key.

Bowes watched the signal being run up the halyard as he departed, knowing the replies would be almost immediate, the tension demanding it.

The moderate southerly breeze had become a blow. Long, white-foamed crests had charged up from the south as if bent on a mission, the spindrift blown before them beating at the ships as if to drive them back from whence they had come. Each vessel leaned to leeward with reefed canvas showing white against a leaden sky. To the north, appearing and disappearing with monotonous regularity, Minorca lost her menace. The events unfolding there were becoming more remote as distance and fading light separated the ships from her threat. The rain arrived without surprise, the dull grey clouds building from the south and passing above, bringing with them a drizzle to add to their discomfort. In the tops the misery was absolute. Men, clinging to spiralling mast tops like mayflies on reed tips, soaked to the skin and with doubtful purchase, they paid as much attention to staying alive as they did to searching the distant horizons. Driving closer to the wind to reduce the leeway, time seemed to stand still as if the elements were determined that the little squadron should not escape.

'I can do no more, Captain, and keep us this far south'ard.' Mr Ramblin shook his head, shouting his conviction, his grey whiskers now turned dark in the wet and sticking to his cheeks as with a theatrical demon.

'Do your best, Master,' Winchip shouted back, the cord of his hat biting into his neck like a Spanish garotte. 'It could be the saving of us.'

The rain stopped as if it had been a squall. Above them the sky turned from the deepest blue-black to a mellow grey, while on the southern horizon, and fast approaching, all was blue, turning to azure. The sea, in an act of neutrality, reflected those self-same colours.

The wind eased to a breeze, backing all the time, allowing no rest to the few topmen that were left. The sea, slow to respond, had lost its stinging spindrift but little of its raging charge to the north.

Mr Ramblin nodded sagely. 'Divine intervention, Sir?'

Winchip grinned.

'*Deck alow!*'

'Where away?' Winchip shouted, his knuckles showing white as he gripped the 'hailer, knowing the answer before it came.

'*Sail on the starboard bow – hull up!*'

Winchip needed to see for himself. He climbed to the cross-trees, squatting on the solid planks with the tails of his coat hanging over the shrouds. He raised the glass and found a path through the rigging.

It came and went with the intruding waves. A square of canvas, dark against the thin strips of light on the horizon to the west. Whoever she was, she was on a port tack, heading towards them. Winchip stared and calculated, realising his first fears when he concluded they would meet within the hour. He glanced at her once more and felt his heart miss a beat. Beyond the sail was another and beyond that yet another and another, rising out of the horizon like ghouls from the grave to haunt him. It was the French fleet, of that there was no doubt. He tucked the glass into a pocket and climbed quickly down over the futtock shrouds. He placed the glass in the rack and brushed down his tails with studied slowness. He had planned for this moment but, now it was upon him, his resolve was weakening with every second that passed. He spoke to young Piper and retired quickly to his cabin, almost collapsing onto the stern seat. With his head in his hands he stared down at the floor, weighing odds, calculating the lives he was risking and trying to see his plan as it happened, as if he were already in action and events were overtaking him. Suddenly he stood up, cursing himself for his own weakness. He had no other option. He opened the bottom drawer of the desk and removed the French ensign taken from *Caprice*, placing it under his arm as he went back to the quarterdeck.

'Mr Piper!' Piper's doe eyes looked at him with a confidence he found hard to bear.

'Sir?'

'Signal *La Louve* to take the rear, if you please.' Winchip stopped Piper's rush to the signal locker. 'Follow that with a general signal to make all safe sail.'

Piper glanced at the French ensign below Winchip's arm before scampering away.

With acknowledgements made, *La Louve* fell away downwind, her square-rigged sails coming and going like a magical show, her foresail filling and collapsing in turn and her gaff sail swinging to and fro like the tail of a dog. She completed her evolution to tack back on a converging course to take position at the rear of the line – a neat manoeuvre, executed with panache.

Niven had acknowledged Winchip's signal but had waited before executing it so that *La Louve* had time to adopt her position. *Vraiment*'s sails dropped and filled as the reefs were loosened. On each of the ships the French ensign stood boldly out, stiff and plain.

Except for a few daubs of deep purple on the underbellies of high and latent clouds to the west, the day was gone to another place. The French fleet was strung out in line astern, twelve leviathans bearing down upon them like geese on the move, their menace eclipsed by their beauty – their presence akin to the axe man coming forward to take his guinea.

Winchip felt gratified that his calculations had been correct. It was now evident that his little squadron would pass in front of the fleet at a distance of a mile and upwind. Any closer, should anything go wrong, they could be blown out of the water before the third ship had even opened her ports.

The challenge came, Winchip praying that Niven would

obey the instructions he had been given. With relief he saw the bunting break free, followed immediately by the crack of unshotted guns as *Vraiment* fired the salute, the flashes destroying night vision. The smoke rolled along the surface of the water towards the French.

The flagship appeared in the centre of the line. An eighty-four with Admiral Galissonnière's pennant flying stiffly at the masthead, her three decks now shrouded in darkness.

Winchip looked again to *Vraiment*, knowing that Niven would soon play his master stroke. His prayer was that it would work. His brow was beginning to crease into a frown when the signal balls burst out on her yard: 'Enemy to the north-east – twelve ships-of-the-line'.

'She has acknowledged, Sir.' Bowes lowered his glass and looked at Winchip with something like awe. He snapped the glass back up to his eye as a further signal fluttered into life. 'It is difficult to read, Sir.' Bowes walked forward and rested the glass on the helmsman's shoulder. Piper held the French signal book. Eventually the words came out. ' "Take station astern", Sir!' Bowes looked at Winchip wide-eyed.

'Acknowledge!' Winchip knew that a delay could raise suspicions. He heaved a sigh of relief as the bunting stood out on *Eaglet*'s halyard.

The first ship in the fleet was now past *Eaglet*'s beam and slipping further behind her by the minute. As the huge ships began to slip astern, so the might and extent of the French battle fleet became apparent. To Winchip's eye the fleet was almost sailing close-hauled and with a wind that was backing all the time. It was the one factor in his plan that would ensure success. In view of his signal, the French might well come about. He gave the matter a moment's thought before dismissing the idea. The French admiral would take time to consider his plans. If Winchip's small flotilla were to escape, then he had to flee immediately or be caught tomorrow or the next day. He made up his mind – he would do nothing.

'Listen, Captain!' The master held up a hand and cupped an ear towards the enemy.

'Listen, Sir!' Bowes had both ears cupped.

Winchip followed their example, a smile creeping over his face as the sound of cheering from the nearest Frenchman came and went in the ragged air.

Winchip stood before the stern window of a cabin bathed in sunlight, seeing his small squadron, sharp against the sunrise, as some sort of recompense for those who had lost their lives. He recalled most of their names, at the same time castigating himself for not knowing them all. Each ship now flew blue ensigns at gaff and main, a sort of celebratory gesture of the living at having come away from the Minorca theatre with their lives.

The small island of Alborán slipped into his sight on the larboard side. The outcrop bathed in the morning sun, giving momentary beauty to a rocky place with dangerous shoals. It sat in the very centre of the Mediterranean inlet, waiting for the unwary.

His journal lay on the table beside the remains of his breakfast. His cup of tea lay cold where he had left it. The coffee had long since been used up. His thoughts turned to Madeleine as they so often did. He had expected to die more than once during the last few weeks but he had survived. He wondered now whether he would be involved any more with Minorca, whether they would be asked to go yet again into the boiling pot. He found himself wanting to go home to Falmouth and to Madeleine but was quick to recognise that as a forlorn dream.

He heard the cry from the tops and was ready when the knock came on the door.

'Enter!'

'Good morning, Sir. The sloop, *Fortune* has just exchanged numbers.'

'Thank you, Mr Bowes. I shall come on deck.'

Winchip made a final entry into his journal and then took up his hat from the old sea-chest.

18

A Glimpse of the Grim Reaper

The anchorage at Gibraltar was bathed in the last light of a blood red sunset. To the west, the hills beyond Algeciras appeared as though they had been put to the torch and the waters of the bay reflected every hue from pink to burnished copper as the sun took its final plunge.

The atmosphere in the great cabin of *Ramillies*, at anchor, was not conducive to small talk, despite the sumptuous dinner and the impressive surroundings of both the rock and the bay. In the fading light the fleet could be seen, anchored well apart, deck lantern lights beginning to twinkle during the second dog watch.

Admiral Byng sat at the polished table, papers scattered before him as though their contents had been discussed and then discarded. Lanterns had been lit, allowing a confusion of shadows to dance with every movement of ship or man. The six senior officers with him had laid their own papers aside, done with the neatness of those unwilling to encroach on the admiral's space.

'The word fiasco springs to mind, gentlemen!' Admiral of the Blue, The Honourable John Byng leaned back in his chair with his hands on the table, one hand fingering the stem of his wineglass. His expression was austere, bordering on an anger he was prone never to show. He expected no response and got none. 'I am arrived here with a squadron ill-equipped, undermanned and some with hulls so weeded I am surprised they are here at all.' He let the words sink in, promising more to come, his face peering out from the mass that was his wig. 'I find a dockyard virtually unusable, buildings in a shambles and stores non-existent!' His voice effected anger and yet his tone seemed to seek sympathy or understanding among the senior officers present, as if the blame had already been placed elsewhere – with those naval contractors who would yet be called upon to explain themselves.

There was a pause, bearing down upon every man present, each feeling it his duty to speak, to give support to the man who was to take them to meet their enemy the very next day. The risks considered, the pause continued into a silence.

'Pah!' Byng slammed the base of his wineglass down on the table, port slopping out, splashing the flamboyant ruffles of his sleeve. 'We are informed – and reliably in my opinion – that Minorca is now overrun with the French and that they are hammering at the doors of St Philip's Castle at this very moment.'

'Overrun, Admiral?' It was Lord Robert Bertie who spoke, no doubt thinking of his solitary regiment of fusiliers and the poor leavings grudgingly given to him by General Fowke, sitting to his left. It had been a measly concessionary detachment of two hundred and sixty men plus officers – after bitter wrangling. He asked his question wide-eyed.

Rear Admiral Temple West, Byng's second-in-command, took up the question. 'Our information comes from a recent reconnaissance by the frigate *Eaglet* under direct orders from Their Lordships at Admiralty. The frigate lies yonder with her two prizes.' Temple West waved a desultory arm towards the stern windows.

'Also more than thirty marines rescued off the beach, including two officers.' General Fowke was determined that the value of Winchip's mission would not be cast into doubt and once he had started he carried on. 'Captain Durrant has given his estimate at fifteen thousand men. This coincides exactly with Captain Winchip's first-hand report from Toulon. Enough to deal with Minorca and then Gibraltar to boot! There can be *no doubt*!' Fowke sat back, his point made.

'Gentlemen! Gentlemen!' Byng raised his hands in the

air, suspecting and instantly forestalling even more wrangling. He was suspicious of Temple West's loyalty. It was more a sense of unease than anything more specific. As for Fowke, governor or not, his every action and every word were directed towards the defence of Gibraltar. *A damned paranoia!* At sea, perhaps things would be different, where orders would be precise – obedience called for and expected. As for the army, they would be masters of their own destiny once they arrived at Minorca. He felt a moment of sadness. His task would have been so much easier had he been given overall command as he had asked – able to make his own decisions and ensure they were carried out to the letter. Now it would be different, councils and debates, nothing unanimous and yet he would still be held responsible if things went wrong. He rose from his seat. 'We have a full day ahead of us, gentlemen. I suggest you retire and prepare yourselves for what lies ahead.'

The others rose as one, compliant in the small things, deferential where it showed, each hugging his own interests tightly to his chest.

Winchip rose from his seat in the coach as the flag-lieutenant entered.

'The admiral is ready for you now, Sir.'

He waited until the last of the senior officers had passed silently on his way out before walking into the smoky and fetid air.

'Ah! Captain Winchip! Come in and sit down.' Admiral Byng was still talking in the loud voice he had used at the meeting. He gathered some papers together as Winchip made himself comfortable and the servant opened the galley door. Shaking his head, Byng continued in a more subdued tone. 'People can be so contentious, just when we need to work together – in unison.' Winchip heard the words, assuming that Byng's mind was still on more important matters.

'You sent for me, Admiral.'

'I did indeed, Captain.' Byng sat at the table, purposefully giving his whole attention to Winchip. 'Firstly, you will be glad to hear that I shall be arranging for your two prizes to be bought in, all subject to the usual conditions of course, but then . . .' he spread his hands '. . . I see no difficulty there.'

'Thank you, Sir.'

'No more than you deserve, Winchip. From this moment on you may consider yourself a rich man and your officers better off than they were yesterday. I have read your reports and frankly I am surprised to see you here at all.' He chuckled. 'To send the French fleet on a wild-goose chase is something I shall dine out on for the rest of my days, though I doubt anyone will believe it.' Byng selected a package set aside from all the other papers. 'These are your orders.' He pushed the package across the table. 'Nothing more exciting than acting as a pair of good eyes, I'm afraid. When this fleet arrives at Minorca I want no surprises.'

'I understand. Are we to be alone, Sir?'

'You may take the French brig, Captain. I cannot afford to release a single cruiser as you can imagine. *Dolphin*, *Phoenix* and *Chesterfield* will accompany you under separate orders. They should leave you to go their own way before you reach Minorca.' Byng's tone denied any discussion on the matter. 'We shall be approaching Minorca from a southerly direction, if weather permits. It will be your task to ensure the French are not in sight to the south – I do not want to find myself to leeward when we meet. It is my intention to lay-to near the Island of Aire, where I can contact the fortress and see what needs to be done to relieve the place. Is that clear so far?'

'Perfectly, Admiral.'

'Good.' Byng looked across at Winchip and without referring to his notes, said, 'If the winds are contrary then you shall find me where they are conducive.' He sat erect in the chair. 'I hope that is clear?'

'Perfectly, Admiral. May I ask when you expect to arrive?'

'The eighteenth or nineteenth, Winchip; and I do not expect to send a ship to look for you.' Byng spoke with a smile.

'I understand, Sir. We shall be waiting.'

'As will others, no doubt.' Byng rose from his chair and started to move round the great table. 'No heroics, Captain. I need all the information you can give me. However, if you can cause disruption, without risk, then feel free to do so – and I have put that into your orders.'

Winchip gathered his hat from the table. 'May I ask if Lieutenant Niven is to be confirmed as the commander of *La Louve?*'

'It has been done. Your Midshipman Pope is also confirmed in the rank of lieutenant – and it is a good job he'd taken and passed his exams. They are both lucky men.'

'Thank you, Admiral.' Winchip nodded his head and turned on his heel. He knew Niven had been lucky. In the flagship alone there must have been a host of officers more qualified for command, and with interest or patrons who could have made the difference. Any one of them would have given their eye-teeth for such a vessel. He would miss Niven, that was for certain. As for Pope – he had hopes.

Eaglet and *La Louve* left Gibraltar together, sometimes sailing free and at other times close-hauled in the varying wind.

The Fifth-Rate and the two Sixth-Rates kept them company for two days before changing course to north-north-east, fulfilling their own orders, seeking information in Palma and scouting to the north.

It was another three days before the noonday sightings confirmed Winchip's opinion that Minorca lay some distance to the north, unless their leeway had been more than the master had calculated.

'We shall come to north, Mr Pardoe.' Winchip was coatless, his blouse billowing about him as he paced about the quarterdeck. He pushed the segments of the glass together and placed it in the rack. Around them the horizon contained nothing but the deep blue-green of the sea. The change in course would bring a different note to the rigging, rid them of the banshee howl that had been with them for an eternity. He nodded his satisfaction, watching as Pardoe went about his business as first lieutenant, sending young Piper to the halyard to signal their change of course. He would certainly miss Niven but he could have hoped for no better replacement. He realised that Pardoe was likely to feature more and more in his family's life and that, too, gave him pleasure. That he had allowed him to call on Emma had been without reserve.

'*La Louve* has acknowledged, Sir.' Even Piper's voice was beginning to break.

Winchip moved across to the binnacle. 'Keep the lookouts sharp, Lieutenant. I shall be in my cabin.'

Winchip stared out of the stern window. The expulsion of water from beneath the counter and the frothy wake as the sea put things back to rights seemed to bring a sense of urgency to their purpose. The relief at being finished with Minorca had been shattered the moment he was aware of Byng's presence at Gibraltar. That he was now to be involved in a clash of titans provided some recompense. *Eaglet* would be playing a part – seeing history made – performing the very duties for which the ship was designed. There was nothing underhand here, no spying or subterfuge – not any longer.

He considered his options with care, his orders resting open on his lap as he sat on the stern seat. Much would depend upon whether or not the French fleet was sighted. He knew his best plan would be to seek it out; keep it in sight for a few days and then run down on the admiral with the news. But what if he didn't find it, or was chasing it in circles without knowing it?

There were alternatives. Absence of the French fleet was information of equal importance. In the meantime, there would be stores and munitions being landed at Ciudadela without interference. Men who would be complacent and lax, more intent upon getting the job done than contemplating attack, safe in the knowledge that they were protected by the French fleet. The more he thought about it the more the idea appealed to him. The prospect of the place being protected by a frigate, or worse, seemed unlikely. The French admiral would need every last one of those. The worst enemy the French could have would be complacency. Something Winchip could use to his advantage.

Almost imperceptibly, the sun sank below the western horizon on a bed of liquid gold. The azure sky slowly deepened to shades of red and then of purple before the afterglow itself began to dull into night. The sea was calm with only a light, undulating swell to give movement to the ships as they lay, hove-to, three leagues to the south of Minorca.

In the great cabin, Winchip outlined his plan to Pardoe and Niven, seeing both enthusiasm and disappointment in their turn as he explained *La Louve*'s role to maintain a watch to seawards as *Eaglet* did her best to disrupt and destroy at Ciudadela, as laid down in his orders.

The chart was a good one, drawn up at leisure. The Admiralty had, at one time, contemplated Ciudadela for use as a naval dockyard and might have done so had the entrance been wider, or capable of being widened. It was neither. Mahon had been preferred. The only legacy was the quality of the Admiralty chart for the old port, the chart being pored over by Winchip, Niven and Pardoe by the light of two lanterns.

Pardoe observed, 'If there are any ships outside the entrance, Sir, they will be embayed.'

'Embayed or not, Mr Pardoe, they could as quickly become floating fortresses, with endless ammunition and powder to boot.'

Niven nodded his agreement. 'With respect, Sir, anything you decide now could be confounded by circumstances. Would it not be better to act as we find?' Niven remembered Toulon, creeping into the town like a bunch of plotters when boldness had turned out to be the better option.

Winchip straightened up with a wide grin on his face.

'You are right, Lieutenant, even if we have to use *La Louve* as a fire-ship.'

Gone was the rush of water from beneath *Eaglet*'s stern. Easing herself towards the headland on the starboard bow, she approached Ciudadela harbour in the early light of dawn. Far out to larboard, *La Louve* surveyed ahead, around the northern point, a French ensign fluttering gainfully at her gaff.

The new midshipman, Claridge, sat in the maintop mast, the signal glass held steady in his hands as he focused on *La Louve*. Above him the masthead lookouts surveyed the horizon, seeking anything that might herald the appearance of the French fleet.

Winchip stood at the poop athwart rail, looking down upon the main deck as the last few men shuffled into position at the guns. The ports were not yet open, needing only a pull on the rope to reveal the muzzles of the great guns as they were run out.

The headland was now astern of the starboard beam, rocky crags below a gorse-topped cliff extending northwards with little change save for the sandy coves. The water around was blue and clear, turning to a shade of yellow where the shoals began. Beneath them deep shadows slipped astern, rocky depths, enough to alert a fertile mind.

'*Deck alow! The brig's signallin!*'

Pardoe acknowledged the call, moving down the deck towards the captain, suddenly impatient as he waited for Claridge to come down the stay.

'She says "ship at anchor – in harbour – a collier", Sir.'

'Thank you, Mr Claridge. Back you go; and with more haste, if you please. One day your speed may determine whether we live or die!' Pardoe turned away. This was not a time to be considerate and the man needed to be told. He turned to a mate. 'Acknowledge!'

Suddenly there was tension in the air, as if the decision had been made and the battle joined.

Winchip spoke as Pardoe joined him. 'She'll be a transport, I have no doubt. What she will be carrying is another matter. Full or empty she will be a loss to the French.'

It was another fifteen minutes before the headland fell away to reveal a large bay some five miles in length, curving round to the other headland to the north from where Niven was keeping station. At the far end, disguised were it not for the grey stone buildings around it, lay the narrow entrance to the harbour of Ciudadela. Before that entrance a bright square of canvas betrayed the presence of the collier, wide across the beam and low in the water. From his position on the ratlines Winchip peered hard through the large glass. Beyond the collier was another, as large but with bare masts. He nodded to himself. The nearer of the two was waiting her turn to discharge her cargo. He closed the glass wishing he had a bomb ketch under his command. The wistful thought was dismissed from his mind as he made his decision. Jumping down onto the deck, he called over to Pardoe.

'Battle ensigns, Mr Pardoe! We have work to do.' He looked over the thwart rail once more to show his face. The men still clung to their guns, alert and prepared, their captains looking towards him for their orders and trails of smoke emanating from slow-matches draped across pans of water.

A cheer rose from the deck as the flags blossomed out, catching the light air and working themselves into a respectable display.

The collier seemed to come alive before their eyes. Stays'ls climbed upwards, higher and higher, her mizzen tops'l dropped like a wet bed sheet off the line and her upper tops'ls appeared as if by magic, knives used when fingers would have been too slow. The boats in attendance suddenly parted from her, oars flashing, scuttling right and left; others were being swayed out as the crew strove to save themselves, get safely away from the imminent threat.

For many it would be too late – *Eaglet* was almost upon them.

Winchip grabbed up the trumpet. '*Run out your guns!*'

Pardoe had been the length of the ship, pointing out the target and enthusing at every gun. He perched on the edge of the boat tier with his sword held high, waiting for the captain's sign.

'*Point your guns!*'

Pardoe looked at Winchip and saw the nod.

'*Fire!*'

The guns fired as one. An imperious crash of sound, the acrid smoke enveloping the decks as it moved slowly forward, preventing a sight of the damage until it was done.

'*Reload!*'

The rumble of trucks went unnoticed. Spikes levered the half-cannons round. The hands rose one by one as the captains showed their readiness and looked to Pardoe.

The collier had taken on the appearance of a pepper-pot. Her hull was littered with holes, some close to the water, others leaving their mark on the shattered bulwarks.

'*Fire!*'

Before Winchip could inspect her in detail the guns roared out once more, the yellow smoke from the six-pounders engulfing him with its acrid smell. The smoke chose to linger, clinging to the clothing and smarting the eyes. Men were dowsing their faces with water from the water-boy's ladles, ridding themselves of the vile stuff.

Already the collier was listing, the weight of her sail pulling her over as the inrushing water rose below her deck. From amidships a whiff of black smoke was rising, increasing by the moment, towering upwards in the still air, in a thin twisting column before breaking away as it found the wind. It was to be a race between the elements, fire or water – fatal in either event.

The brilliant and silent flash of white momentarily blinded all those who watched the demise of the collier. The explosion that followed two seconds later struck *Eaglet* with the force of a whirlwind, heeling her over until her larboard scupper drains jetted water across the deck. The ship remained so for two seconds, almost capsized, before swinging back to the vertical. Before the senses could perceive its origin the blast of noise came like nothing on earth, followed by a gale of hot air that swept all before it.

Winchip had only time to blink his eyes as the light dazzled him. The next moment he was bodily picked up and flung across the quarterdeck to hit the nettings with a sickening crash. The noise of the explosion engulfed him, destroying his senses and confusing his mind as the deck was first taken away and then forced up beneath him as if he were held in the fist of a giant.

As Winchip came to his senses he could hear voices nearby. From further away came shouts – urgent cries, as if in a crisis. He found breathing difficult, only able to gain air with short breaths, as though he had been running. He opened his eyes, his vision blurred and figures indistinct.

'Thank God you are safe, Sir!' Pardoe's concerned voice held a note of relief.

'What happened?' Winchip felt bandages around his head. His chest, too, was bared, bandages wrapped around him like swaddling clothes. 'Am I badly hurt?'

'You are in your cabin, Sir. You have some bruised ribs and a knock on the head. Mr Pollard has seen you and passed on to those more in need.'

'More in need? What happened, man?'

'The transport blew up. She was carrying powder, Sir.'

'Good God! No wonder they left her in a hurry.' Winchip tried a grin at the sound of laughter. He struggled to a sitting position, only then realising his head was resting on Hellard's arm. Events were coming back to him in a rush, foremost being the safety of the ship and the lee-shore that was the headland.

'Get me to my feet, Mr Pardoe – I'm of no use lying here.'

'You should lie quiet, Sir. Mr Pollard says— ' He gave up, taking the captain's arm as he struggled to his feet.

The cabin and all within it moved round in a slow, clockwise circle. Winchip gained a purchase on somebody's shoulder and held on as if his life depended upon it. The ship was still at quarters – the partitions and furniture gone, and the twelve-pounder on the starboard side was still manned with shackles draped about the place like a rope-maker's yard. He beckoned for his blouse and jacket and with assistance put them on. He felt better for it. He turned to Hellard.

'Stay by me, Hellard, I may need your arm.'

The deck was a shambles. Timbers, some charred, lay scattered about the place. Aloft, things were no better: cordage hanging down like forest creepers, tangled and forlorn. Where the fore-t'gallant yard should have been was space – a great deal of it. Winchip's shoulders sagged as he noticed the absence of gibs'ls and the huge rent in the driver above him. Draped across the athwart rail of the quarterdeck was an abundance of sail, being gathered and removed even as he watched. He span on his heel, looking towards the land, relaxing when he saw it on the horizon, desolate and stripped of all that had been there before. Even the buildings were blackened and of people there was no sign. He sighed with relief at the sight of *La Louve*, holding her position, as she must. Many a commander would have run down to them at the expense of safety.

The damage required no explanation. It was enough to see Oliver, the sailmaker, bringing up summer canvas from below. As he watched, so the tarred and twisted cordage, grotesque in its fixed positions, was dragged to the deck. Forward, the great yard was being pulled back on deck, the crowd around it like ants dragging a morsel back to the nest. Winchip went back to his quarterdeck, feeling every step. There were scars and much work to do. His concern was how long it would take to get the ship seaworthy. He looked about him. No cajoling from him was going to get it done any faster.

A large black cloud hung over the scene of the explosion, looking like a giant anvil as an offshore breeze flattened the top and dragged it northwards. Of the transport there was no sign. It was as if it had never been. Between *Eaglet* and the shore the sea was covered with pieces of timber of all shapes, rising and falling with each wave. From inside the harbour more smoke rose quickly into the air, grey and thin with the red of fire reaching up to chase it to the heavens. Winchip slapped his thigh. The other ship was alight and burning well. He prayed she had no powder on board. He turned to the attendant Hellard, still at his side.

'Were there many injured, Coxswain?'

'We lost a topman, Sir. Cox were his name. He came down wi' the yard – ridin' it like a witch 'e were.' There was no smile with his quip. 'We never found 'im, Sir. There's some with broken bones but none that won't mend.' Hellard took a step backwards as Pardoe came back.

'Well, Lieutenant? What is our position?'

'The yard is up and being crossed, Sir. I have recalled the boat looking for Cox – we'll not find him now and we need the hands.'

'Very well, Mr Pardoe. Carry on; and consult the master and let me know the moment we are fit to set sail.' Winchip added. 'What of the ensigns?'

'Away and stowed, Sir.'

Seven bells rang out from the forecastle, half an hour until noon. So far, it had not been an auspicious day.

'Help me down to my cabin, Hellard. I'm in the way on my own quarterdeck.'

It was halfway through the afternoon watch before Winchip was able to tour the ship. It had been an heroic effort. Putting aside the cost of sail and cordage, it was as if the ship had been cast back in time, back to the moment before the attack on the transport nearly half a day since. It had been Pardoe's day. Faced with a tangible problem and the means to correct it, he had driven the crew to impossible limits, urged on by the possibility of a French cruiser – or the French fleet itself – appearing on the horizon at any moment.

As Winchip sat at his desk, quill in hand, his report on the sorry affair staring accusingly back up at him, he made his decision to mention Pardoe's part in the affair. He was about to write, pen poised, when he heard the shout from the tops, unintelligible from where he sat but enough to send a chill down his spine. With a forced determination to complete the sentence on the paper and not rush to the deck, he added the last few words. As a clatter of footsteps heralded the knock on the door, so a panic rose up in him. Here at Minorca, they were alone. It could only mean one thing.

'Enter!'

Piper peered round the door. 'Lookouts report three sail to the North, Sir. Two transports and a frigate . . . a bloody big one!'

'Thank you, Mr Piper. Tell Mr Pardoe I shall be up directly.' Winchip was glad at the relief of hearing Piper's verbatim report, warts and all. He replaced the quill in the rack, gathered up his hat and strode with a studied lack of haste to the companion. His decision had already been made. There was no reason to remain at this place. If the frigate offered battle then they could be reduced to a wreck, win or lose. Fingers had been burned this day, on both sides; and the transports now approaching them could be equally volatile. It was time to turn tail and call it quits.

Winchip came out onto the quarterdeck, stopping for a moment as shooting pains dashed across his chest.

Pardoe was at the weather rail, the signal glass aimed towards the trio of ships, now with their topmasts showing above the horizon. He turned at the sight of the captain and met him at the binnacle, cocking his hat. 'They are French, Sir. Three leagues or more, coming down to Ciudadela without a care in the world.' Pardoe sounded almost indignant, as if the French should be turning tail at the very sight of them.

'We shall wear ship, Lieutenant. South-west by south – give ourselves a few points large.' Winchip turned away, brooking any expressions of surprise. 'Signal *La Louve* to do likewise and take station ahead of us.' He took out a glass from the rack and pointed it southwards, towards the headland and the sea into which they would soon be sailing. The north was done with. It was now from the south that dangers could come, embaying them on a lee-shore, penned up, like sheep for the market and all that that implied.

Winchip remained at the larboard rail until the evolution was completed, content to rest his bones and clear his head, still bandaged to protect the splits in his scalp. He regretted nothing. At worst *Eaglet* had been badly bruised. At best they had deprived the French of two fair-sized colliers and a cargo of powder, let alone the damage to the wharfs and life itself. At least he would not be the only one with a headache, albeit of a different kind.

Another hour brought *Eaglet* into the open expanse of the Mediterranean, the light swell pulling at her forward progress as she took the sea on her larboard bow. The sun was still warm on his face as Winchip scanned the southern horizon. It would require a good ship to surprise them now.

The call came down from two lookouts at once. Winchip waited until Pardoe sent a mate up the ratlines with a glass. In less than two minutes the mate was back, his face full of foreboding.

'Well, Lieutenant?'

'Sir. The frigate that was reported with the two transports is pursuing us. It seems she is a Fifth Rate.'

'Have you seen her yourself, Mr Pardoe?'

'No, Sir. I . . . I thought . . .'

'Get up there and report what you see, Lieutenant. Size, guns and direction.' Winchip kept his voice low. His expression required no interpretation.

He was aware that the French had some larger frigates, as did the Americans. They were known to run to forty-four guns but he had never seen one. If they were that large it was likely they would carry eighteen-pounders. However, there was also the question of sailing ability. It was the lighter ship that could sail closer to the wind and that, at least, would give *Eaglet* an advantage. One thing was for certain. He was not going to risk all by fighting her.

'She is a Fifth Rate of forty-two guns, I'd say, Sir.' Pardoe stood next to Winchip, his breath coming out in staccato bursts. 'She has a full suit of sail, with stays'ls to boot. She is also gaining on us. She is about six points off the wind. She is also alone.'

'Thank you, Lieutenant. We now have an accurate picture of her.' Winchip climbed a short way up the mizzen shrouds and lay the glass along the ratline. He was not to get a full picture of her yet, merely her t'gallants, dragged round to almost fore and aft in her efforts to come up to them. He climbed back down. He made the assumption that her captain was angry at what he had found at Ciudadela. This urge to catch *Eaglet* was personal; he could feel it in his bones. At some moment in the near future the man would regain his common sense. He would realise that whatever he was sailing into could be far more dangerous than he could imagine. It suited Winchip's plans. It had been his intention to patrol to the south of the island once they had harassed and caused destruction at Ciudadela. Now, it had been forced upon him. He shrugged his shoulders and replaced the glass in the rack. Pride had no place in war, as many had found to their cost.

The true realisation of how close they had come to disaster was not lost on him. It would probably become more apparent as he penned his reports. Whereas his journal would include his thoughts and reasons, the report would contain only stark facts, without qualification. Perhaps events yet to unfold would be of sufficient consequence to overshadow the unsuccessful forays of a simple frigate captain.

His thoughts turned to Madeleine as they often did when he was alone, either here, at the taffrail or sitting on the stern seat in his cabin, staring out at the water as it rushed out from under the counter.

On the night of the wedding they had stayed up late, sitting before the fire of logs, shadows dancing across their faces, each seeing in the other the expressions they wanted to see, conjuring each other's thoughts, allowing no other thoughts but those of love to enter their silent conversation.

When, at last, they had gone to bed it had not been the

feverish passion of the young that had seized them. Their lovemaking had been an adventure, a coming together of two people already aware of their feelings for each other, perhaps reluctant to taste the one mystery denied to them until this moment. When, eventually, staring softly into each other's eyes, they had come together, it had brought a rapture beyond description, an act of consummate love, a oneness never to be broken.

In the early hours, lying with their arms about each other, they had stretched naked on the bed in glorious exhaustion. The moon had shone through the window to bring dimension to their small world, the soft glow coming and going with varying intensity as fleeting clouds passed across the pale sky. That was when sleep overtook them, at a moment etched forever in Winchip's mind.

His thoughts were snatched from him as two gulls screeched at each other over a morsel, wheeling down close to the water before lazily drifting along the line of *Eaglet*'s wake.

He opened his personal glass and once more raised it to look at the French frigate. She was neither closer nor further away. As he looked at her he could see her change the configuration of her sails, wearing ship as her captain decided to cut the corner. He would be taking the risk of fetching up on a lee-shore eventually should Winchip decide to turn and fight but Winchip knew that chance had a place in every decision, a chance he would willingly take if he thought *his* adversary was running scared.

'Excuse me, Sir.' Pardoe stood, waiting for the attention of the captain.

'Well, Mr Pardoe?'

'The French frigate has wore ship, Sir. She appears to be trying to gain a march on us.'

'Thank you. Let us go down to the wheel and talk to the master.'

Mr Ramblin touched his tricorne with two fingers as Winchip came up to him. 'Course east by south, Captain. Wind south by east. A touch of weather helm is keeping a straight path.' He looked astern at the frigate. 'She's hardening and then bearing away, Sir. If she catches us it will be because she's faster, not 'cause she's playin' silly games.'

'Thank you, Master. The fact is, I can now see her tops'ls when an hour since it was only t'gallants.'

'Then she's catching us, Sir.' The master sniffed and then sucked on his hollow tooth.

'Stuns'ls then?'

'I think not, Captain.' Mr Ramblin took the clay from his mouth and pointed the stem over the starboard quarter. 'This swell's risin' and it'll be worse before it gets better, and that's a fact.'

Already the swell had *Eaglet* in its palm, lifting the stern and then plunging the bow into each successive trough, spindrift hanging in the air like rain. The moaning of the lashings, holding the great guns as the boat dipped and rose, was akin to the squeal of a hundred rusted gates, tempered only by the tight rigging as the wind strummed it as on a discordant harp.

Winchip raised the glass once more, now aware of the *Frenchman*'s intentions. Her captain was drawing closer, sailing further from the wind, preparing himself for a dash to windward, close-hauled, to steal the wind and force the fight. There were three hours to darkness. Time enough.

As the master had predicted, the swell took on mammoth proportions, rain squalls coming and going with monotonous regularity, each one bringing its own wind and rain, irregular and varied, bringing misery to the exposed topmen. It was at the start of the second dog watch, as the sun commenced its final plunge, that the wind abated and the squalls lost their fury. In the space of a bell the sky had changed from a raging bull to a bleating lamb, now placid, only the swell left to remind them of what had been.

The *Frenchman* had gained her ground but not yet the wind. Less than a league off the lee quarter, illuminated in the orange of the sinking sun, she was ready to make her dash, close-hauled and into a weakening breeze across *Eaglet*'s stern.

Winchip saw the dangers; had known them all along. He knew, too, that night was not going to save them from battle. He raised the glass and peered to the south where *La Louve* showed herself as an orange triangle above the horizon. There was one other option.

'Mr Pardoe!' Winchip waited for the lieutenant to reach him.

'Sir?'

'Mr Pardoe. I want you to make a signal to *La Louve*. Tell her to make "enemy in sight", leave it for three minutes and then raise an acknowledgement. When that is done she is to raise battle ensign and come about to join us. Can you do that?'

'Oh, yes, Sir! Mr Niven will get your drift.' Pardoe dashed to the signal locker, a grin of excitement on his tanned face.

Winchip turned to the master. 'Master. When the battle ensigns go up, I wish to come about and offer battle to the French frigate. We shall sail down to her, as we have the wind at present, and come upon her to starboard. I do not want her to use chain-shot on us and I do not want her to gain the wind. Have I made myself clear?' The master's reply was lost to him as Winchip snatched the 'hailer from the hook.

'*All hands! All hands up to wear ship!*'

Winchip swivelled round, eager to see Niven's response. It was not long in coming.

'The acknowledgement is down, Sir . . . and the battle ensigns are going up!'

'Then raise our own, Mr Pardoe. Let us show this *Frenchman* we mean business.' To the master, he said, 'Come about, if you please, Master; and let us be done with it.' He called to Pardoe. 'The 'hailer, Lieutenant. We shall come to quarters when the evolution is completed!'

'To quarters, aye, Sir! Are we to do battle, Sir?'

'Not if I can help it, Lieutenant.'

The battle ensigns fluttered bravely to leeward in full sight of the enemy, casting long, flickering shadows across the undulating surface of the water in the dying sun. It would mean fear for some, relief to others, glad to know their faith in the captain was justified, even if it were tainted by a touch of madness.

Winchip watched the French frigate, knowing her captain was unlikely to be fooled. His anger about events at Ciudadela would be modified by now, with common sense taking its place. On the other hand, he must surely wonder why a solitary English frigate and an accompanying brig should be foolhardy enough to venture into what had now become a lion's den. In addition to that, the English fleet must surely be expected and a frigate captain would be aware of his responsibilities should it suddenly appear. He lowered the glass. There was no change in the *Frenchman*'s course, nor was she reducing her headlong charge towards them.

'*Wear ship!*'

The commitment was made. As Winchip watched the mates telling off men at the masts, sending them aloft or loosening lines, he wondered at their blind obedience, their willingness to do or die with no hint of the greater scheme of things. Perhaps it was better that way.

With the helm a'lee, her jib and stays'ls let fly, *Eaglet* came about through the eye of the wind, men waiting and then suddenly hauling, bringing the great yards into position.

'*Mains'l haul!*'

The stern came round. It was as if the ship were turning on a sixpence.

'*Let go and haul!*'

The fores'ls' leading edges bit into the wind and suddenly *Eaglet* was on her new course, pointing towards the French frigate with every intention of carrying out the threat imposed by her battle ensigns.

'*Hands to quarters! All hands to quarters!*'

Winchip moved to the rail with the big glass trained on the French frigate. Still she persisted, drawing closer with no more than half a league between them. He was about to close the glass, resigned to whatever fate had in store for them, when he noticed a difference. She was slowing in the water, rising up and then sinking down into the long swell, showing more of her bow and stern. He continued to watch, not allowing himself to believe what he was seeing even though the last of the sun's rays were illuminating her in profile. She was increasing in length, turning down wind, running away, just as Winchip had been doing for exactly the same reasons.

19

The French!

Winchip sat on the stern seat with his journal on his lap, trying to portray the facts concerning the large French frigate without dramatising events. He had been lucky to escape, and he knew it.

He had found it interesting that the frigate had not maintained her course to the north with the wind in her favour. Whilst still hull-up, she had turned to the east and had continued in that direction until she disappeared over the horizon. He had a mind to look in that area for the French fleet. It would be on the move. That was for certain. Considering how long the wind had endured from the south, it would be a wise admiral who sought to maintain a position of advantage.

It was now the fifteenth of May. If he was to find the French and get back to the south of the Balearics by the eighteenth, then he would have to leave now, or be late. He was beginning to regret sending *La Louve* to the west, to Ibiza so that the length of Niven's patrol would be shortened. But it was done and that was that. He sat back and gave himself a moment to gather his thoughts. It would appear from his reports that he had been quite busy since his arrival but he new better. Other than having saved himself from capture or destruction by a solitary frigate, he had done nothing. It had occurred to him that had he taken on board some senior army officers at Gibraltar, he could have landed them at Mahon with ease. They would have been able to assess the situation and bring expertise to bear on the defence of the place and send a report back to Admiral Byng to boot!

He made up his mind in a rush. He rose and picked up his hat from the chest. It was a time for action, not thoughts.

Pardoe stepped aside, cocking his hat as the captain arrived at the binnacle. 'Course north-west by west, Sir. Wind west of south.'

'Thank you, Lieutenant. We will come to due east immediately, if you please. We are going hunting!'

'*All hands! All hands up to wear ship!*'

Winchip watched as the evolution took place, seeing on the eastern horizon a thin streak of bright light, peeking from beneath the cloud as if from under an ill-fitting door. The dawn could herald an interesting day.

Winchip came out of a deep sleep in response to the pressure of a hand on his shoulder. Piper looked down on him with the apologetic look of a man who knew he was unwelcome.

'Well, Mr Piper. What is it?'

'A sighting, Sir. Mr Pardoe says . . .'

'All right, Mr Piper. Tell the first lieutenant I shall be there directly.' Winchip sat up in the cot and reached for his timepiece hanging on the chain. It was four o'clock. He yawned, thinking how two hours could have been four had he been left to sleep.

The sky was leaden and there was a welcome hint of moisture in the air. He approached the binnacle as a mate came down the mizzen ratlines. Winchip nodded at Pardoe's salute.

'I hear we have a sighting, Lieutenant.'

'A suspicion of one, Sir. I should like to see for myself.' He already had a glass tucked beneath his arm.

'Off you go then.' Winchip checked course and wind, noticing the light breeze was still coming off the African shore. The ship looked better for the repairs. The smell of tar tickled his nostrils as easily as did the sawdust. Even the woldings on the mizzen-mast had received treatment. He looked up to the expanse of canvas and could find little that told of *Eaglet*'s close encounter with the powder-ship.

Pardoe came down in a rush. ''I've seen her, Sir. She's big. Her t'gallant says she is a ship-of-the-line, Sir. I'll stake my rank on't!'

'Hmm.' Winchip dwelled on the matter, seeing no alternatives. To Mr Ramblin, he said, 'All plain sail, if you please, Master. I need to know who she is and whether she has companions.' He turned to Pardoe. 'Break out the French ensign, Lieutenant. She may not be so ready to report our presence.' He knew he would be right. There was no other sensible place from which to approach an enemy. The 'hailer blared out from the athwart rail, calling up the hands from below.

With the first bell of the first dog watch, Pardoe told Winchip all he needed to know. It was the French fleet. Twelve ships-of-the-line. With no further ado *Eaglet* came about and Winchip took to his cot.

Winchip didn't realise how long they had been seeking the French fleet. It was dawn of the seventeenth of May when Minorca was sighted to the far north, a smudge of cloud and a thin dark line that was the land. Winchip had already calculated in his mind the direction from which the English fleet would arrive. Admiral Byng would fix his position as he came upon Formentera and then proceed either north of Ibiza, or south, depending upon his disposition. Whichever he decided, he would then come south of Majorca and onwards to Minorca. That was the information Byng had given him and that was the supposition that Winchip was forced to take. It now required patience. A general patrol south of Minorca, east and west with a wind on the beam. He knew it could never be that simple. There would be French eyes watching for the fleet at Ibiza; and at Palma French frigates would be waiting to carry the message to the French Commander, Admiral Galissonnière. Those frigates would take the shortest route, perhaps requiring the very water on which *Eaglet* was now sailing. It was a sobering thought.

At the end of the forenoon watch, the last vestiges of Minorca passed below the horizon. It was time to come about and retrace their steps to the east. The light and steady southerly breeze was bringing warmer air. The grey, colourless sea, reflecting the sky above, was lifeless. Small wavelets, their crests glassy in appearance, passed across the bows in closed ranks, collapsing to nothing before they could break. The weather bow shattered the wavelets into spray that fell upon the water like rain, giving no relief to the increasing heat of the sun.

'Mr Piper!' Winchip called to the young midshipman who abandoned his noonday sighting to run over to him. 'I would like you to visit each lookout in turn, Mr Piper. They are to keep a keen watch to the west. I am expecting to see a sail at any time and it must not go unnoticed. Do I make myself clear?'

'Oh. Yes, Sir! Very clear, Sir.'

'When the lookouts are relieved, they will pass the message on. Tell them how important it is.'

'. . . How important it is. Aye, Sir!'

'Off you go then.' Winchip smiled at his departing back as he dived for the mizzen ratlines.

The call came as a single bell sounded out from the belfry in the afternoon watch. Winchip deferred going to quarters until the sighting was identified. He sent Claridge to the tops with the large glass, hanging on his shoulder from a fish line. The man would hold his opinion until he was sure of his facts. He had proved himself since his promotion to midshipman and found no difficulty with the extra responsibility.

'*Deck there! She's challenging!*'

Winchip acknowledged with a wave as he turned to Piper. 'Send up our number, Mr Piper.'

'She has acknowledged. Number "00", Sir. It's Mr Niven!' Piper's face burst into a wide grin.

'Thank you, Mr Piper. Send, "Captain to repair on board", if you please.'

Winchip had shaken Niven's hand like a leaky bilge pump. Now, as he sat on the stern seat with Niven across from him, it seemed as though time had come full circle.

'Have you seen the fleet, Lieutenant?'

'I have, Sir. *Ramillies* and fourteen others. Admiral Byng has a few frigates in attendance, including some taken from the Western Squadron.'

'And in which direction is the fleet coming?'

'The last time I saw the van, Sir, it was coming wide, around Cabrera, from the north.'

'Ah, as we expected.' Winchip's face assumed a serious look. 'I cannot stand idle, Mr Niven. I have the approximate position of the French fleet and it is important that I get my report to the admiral at the earliest moment.'

'Then I shall not delay you, Sir. Suffice it to say that I am delighted to see you in good health.'

'Thank you, Lieutenant, and I to see you in the same condition. We haven't even had time for a glass of claret.' They rose as one.

Winchip and Niven were at the entry port when the call came down from the tops.

'*Deck! A sail to the east, hull down!*'

At the moment of the call, the warning bark of a swivel sounded from *La Louve*.

'I must go, Sir.' Niven was about to cock his hat and the pipes were about to be trilled.

'Wait! I have something for you.' Winchip dashed away and ducked beneath the poop. He returned within the minute, a package gripped in his hand. 'This is my report for the admiral. Deliver it!'

'Go!' Winchip shouted. 'Stop for nothing. *Nothing! Do you understand?*'

'Aye, Sir. I shall do that.' Niven went through the entry

port, giving Winchip a last glance before backing down the tumblehome.

Winchip turned and looked up at Pardoe at the rail above him. 'Hands to quarters, Lieutenant.'

'*Hands to quarters! Hands to quarters!*' The shout came through the 'hailer with especial urgency.

Winchip stood at the entry port and gave Niven a last wave, unheeded by a lieutenant who would be searching the eastern horizon.

'Are we to load, Sir?' Pardoe asked the question as the captain came to the binnacle.

'Yes, Mr Pardoe, port and starboard, if you please. Double-shotted to starboard.' His supposition had been correct. He thought it likely that the frigate, if that was what it was, had been chasing *La Louve*. She would have seen the brig before Niven could see her, her tops being that much higher. He watched as the brig fell downwind and sped to the north with a complete suit of sail. She could outrun any frigate if she had to and he thanked God for that. He had made out a copy of his report to give to Niven in any event. There was no heroism on his part. It would do Niven no harm if he believed he was holding the only draft.

Winchip would have gone to his cabin to gather his thoughts together but there would be no cabin. By now it would be an open deck, the two twelve-pounders poised for battle.

'*Deck there! She'm a frigate – a Frenchie!*'

'How did you know, Sir?' Pardoe looked at Winchip with undisguised awe.

'There could be no doubt, Lieutenant. As we are reporting to our admiral, so she is reporting to hers. It would be to England's advantage were she not to arrive.'

'Indeed, Sir.' Pardoe glanced down at the gun deck. The gun captains squatted with upraised arms. 'Should we run out, Sir?'

'No, Mr Pardoe. Let them rest at the guns for now. It will be a while before we are upon her.'

Winchip took the large glass and went to the shrouds. He

supported the glass and peered at the frigate himself. She was hull-up. He noted with interest that she was showing no great eagerness to come up to *Eaglet*. In the light breeze he would have expected to see stays'ls at least. This was no triumphant charge on the part of her captain. It was more of a subdued approach – and with caution? He decided to test her – see what she was made of – a risk he would have avoided were Niven not carrying his report.

He jumped to the deck with a spring in his step. 'Hoist battle ensigns, Mr Pardoe, and prepare to reduce to battle canvas.' He rattled up the steps to the quarterdeck and gazed down at the guns. The ship was still. Hardly a soul moved in the moment of tenseness. There was a sudden cheer and a raising of arms as the battle ensigns billowed out in a wind that held them stiff upon the halyards. Their dark shadows danced and pranced among rigging, sails and the waves to leeward. 'Go down to them, Mr Pardoe. Tell our people who she is and what she is attempting to do. It will sharpen their mettle, God's teeth it will! Remind them of their practice and the three casks they blew out of the water!' As Pardoe drew his sword and went to the steps, Winchip turned to the master. 'We shall hold our sea, Master. As she veers, so our guns will be pointing directly at her.'

'*Deck there! A sail dead ahead!*'

Winchip's heart sank. Was there to be no end to it? He walked with a steady pace to the steps and onwards to the bow, speaking and encouraging as he stepped round the gun crews, crouched and ready. He went on to the forecastle and opened the glass. The French frigate was easing to her larboard, almost deferring to *Eaglet*'s passage. She was over a mile distant. He let the glass drift to the horizon behind her, shimmering as it was, as the sun reflected from the shallow waves. He stared at the newcomer, seeing her not as French nor English, but as a ship he knew and recognised, but with doubt in his mind at the possibility of it being so. He took his eyes away and blinked them to rid them of water. He peered again, recoiling at the sight of

British battle ensigns standing stiffly from her truck and stern. It was no apparition. It was *Adept*.

He turned and stopped in his tracks as Hellard stood before him.

'Your sword, Sir.' Hellard made to run the belt around his waist.

'Not today, Hellard.' Winchip pointed forward, across the bow. 'That is *Adept*, my friend. Get to the quarterdeck and make the challenge.'

Winchip returned to the quarterdeck with his heart pumping. The tension in him had been as much as he could bear. The arrival of any English ship would have been shock enough. For it to be *Adept* was an event contrived by the gods. She had obviously been detached from the Western Squadron. He strode to the wheel and spoke to the master. 'We shall wear ship and come up into wind, Master, and lay across her bows. Battle canvas, if you please and hove-to.' He turned to Pardoe as he came up the steps. 'Secure guns until we are come about, Lieutenant; and then run them out, starboard side only.'

The evolution was made and the guns run out. *Eaglet* lay in the path of the *Frenchman* with a row of double-shotted guns pointed directly at her. Behind her, *Adept* bore down with stuns'ls giving her huge breadth; and stays'ls on fore- and maintops. Her battle ensigns stood out as stiff as boards and her mustached bow wave of white water and her probing bowsprit lent her the trappings of a charging lancer.

'*Deck there! She've lowered her colours!*'

The French frigate fired no guns '*pour l'honneur du pavillon*'. The honour of her flag would be of little consequence should her cannon-fire be misconstrued. She simply came up into wind and squatted on the water, her reduced sail pressed against the mast. She was a smart vessel of thirty guns with a fine strake and a proud stern. Age may have dealt well with her but lack of use had found out her failings. Lichen grew between her planks, and weed, now scraped off, had eaten into her timbers, leaving stains upon and within the wood.

Adept also came up into the wind, matching the *Frenchman* bow for bow, her guns run out.

'Put our number on the halyard, Mr Piper, and be quick about it.' Winchip was well aware that the French vessel was his by right. However, Captain Rance had been in sight of the capture and could claim part credit because of it.

Hellard had supervised the putting of boats into the water, crammed with marines and seamen alike, with Pardoe sitting upright in the stern seat of the first. From *Adept* a similar flotilla approached the French frigate with Lieutenant Barriclough playing a similar role.

Winchip prepared himself to go aboard *Adept* as was his duty so to do. He didn't relish the prospect, but he knew Captain Rance had more reason to be disconcerted by the meeting than he did. As soon as a boat was available he made to go through the entry port.

'A boat approaching, Sir.' Midshipman Claridge stood next to Winchip. The response to the hail was '*Adept*'. 'It's *Adept*'s captain, sir.'

Winchip smiled. He knew what was happening, as did Rance; and he respected him for it. 'He will be coming on board, Mr Claridge. Honours due, if you please.' Winchip retired a pace or two as the pipes and four marines took up positions.

Post-Captain Rance came through the entry port to the shrill of pipes and a cloud of pipe clay as the marines slapped the shoulder straps of their weapons in salute.

Rance held his hand to his hat as Winchip strode down to meet him. They tipped in unison before Winchip spoke.

'Welcome on board, Sir.' There was little else he could say, but what he did say was said with the slightest of smiles. He noted with interest that Rance seemed to have changed. He seemed subdued, his eyes without spite or anger.

'Thank you, Captain. Shall we go to your cabin?'

'Of course, Sir.' Winchip led the way, unsure as to whether he had a cabin to go to, the ship still being at quarters. As he moved to go under the poop, so Hellard came out, giving the captain an imperceptible wink.

The cabin was returned to normal. The claret jug sat in the centre of the table on his only silver tray, rescued from *Capable*. Two upturned goblets lay beside it. He beckoned Rance to a chair and commandeered his window-seat, noticing the sharp tang of beeswax in the air and the less intrusive smell of tallow from the newly set lanterns. The noise of the ship returning to normal, the unloading of the great guns and the trimming of sails, came down through the deck light as a welcome background to a conversation Winchip did not relish.

'Claret, Sir?' Winchip leaned forward and poured two glasses, pushing one over the centre line for Rance.

'Your health, Captain Winchip.' Rance raised his glass.

'And yours, Sir.' Winchip took the plunge. 'I was glad to see *Adept*. For a moment I thought it might be the enemy, in which case . . .' Winchip shrugged his shoulders.

'Were it not for you, Captain, I would be on the beach now, on half-pay and you know it. I also have to thank the loyalty of Charles Barriclough, my first lieutenant.' He held up a hand as Winchip made to protest. 'I have been a fool, Winchip. My anger and hate for you was illogical. It had no basis and gained me nothing. I loved my son and had so many plans for his advancement. For some reason I needed to justify his death. Instead I attributed blame, using it as a panacea for my grief. I offer you my sincere apologies and hope that you might forgive me. I was not myself and I wronged you greatly.'

Winchip stared at his glass for a brief moment. 'Indeed you were wrong. But I could never find it within myself to condemn you for your actions. I hold no grudge, be assured of that. It may help if I tell you that I lost both my wife and my son some five years ago. I had no one to blame for that. If I had, I may have nursed that hate for all time. So I do have a degree of understanding.' Winchip held out a hand and gave a beaming smile. 'Better friends than enemies, I feel.'

Rance grasped Winchip's hand in his and placed his other on top. 'You are a good man, Winchip. Not many men would have acted as you have. If there is anything I can do to atone . . .'

'There is no debt owed, Captain. I have a crew out there that would like nothing more than to see us part friends. Many served with your son and remember him for the good things he brought to them and did for them. Others have friends who died with him. He is not forgotten.'

Rance sat upright in his chair. 'Thank you for that.' He brightened. 'May I suggest we return to the fleet with this prize. If they don't buy her in I shall sink her where she floats.'

Winchip rose from his seat. 'You are the senior officer, Sir. *You* must take her in. I, too, shall be reporting to the fleet but I feel my orders will take me onwards with all speed.' Winchip spoke with conviction, knowing Rance would defer.

'Well, we can't stand in the way of orders, can we?' Rance smiled and took up his hat. 'Then I suggest we get at it. My agent will be pleased, as will yours no doubt. I shall get the prisoners safely battened down and find the fleet. The French frigate will certainly give them heart for what lies ahead.'

20

The English Fleet

Adept had been on the point of departure when *Eaglet* was allowed to fall away to starboard to catch the wind on her larboard beam. Winchip had decided to remain until the ships were underway, forestalling any attempt by the French to retake their vessel. He ordered the stays'l booms to be deployed and then returned to his cabin, glad for the privacy of it.

He had been taken aback by *Adept*'s arrival on the scene. A meeting with Captain Rance was inevitable. That it had resulted in apologies and contrition should not have been a surprise. The man had been heartbroken at his loss, intent on revenge and determined to get it. Any rationality had been thrown overboard. As Winchip took up his journal he paused for a moment. Rance had suffered an aberration, of that there was no doubt. Had he, himself, not done the same when Maria and his son had died? His victim had been Emma, left to her own devices, ignored, with only Beth to turn to. On reflection, he found comfort in his attitude towards Rance, content that he had done what needed to be done with no ill will. Perhaps both he and the captain would both be better men because of it. He was content with that. The matter was dead.

Above his head, through the skylight, he could hear shouted orders, stamping feet, laughter and even anger, all combined with the rush of water from under the counter, the swaying of the vessel and the creaking sounds of a ship content with itself . . . and alive.

As he returned his journal to the rack the dawn sun lit the cabin for a moment and then disappeared with the pitch of the ship. Soon, *Eaglet* would be embroiled in greater events. The grand fleet would be with them and what happened next would be in the hands of others. He took up his hat and deck coat and went through the companion to the quarterdeck.

'Good morning, Sir.' Pardoe stood to one side. 'Wind is south by west and our course due west as ordered.'

'Thank you, Lieutenant. It's a fine morning.'

'It is, Sir. There is nothing in sight but I think that may change in the very near future.'

'As it surely will, Mr Pardoe. We are not that far from where the trouble is and that is where Admiral Byng is heading. When he arrives, we must remember our drills. I think it would be a good idea to prepare the bow chasers for the salute. We don't want to be caught napping. I would also like my boat's crew to be extra smart. Perhaps you could have a word with Hellard.'

Pardoe grinned. 'It won't be necessary, Sir. He has had them lined up for inspection already and smart they certainly are. According to the coxswain, their lives depend upon it.'

Winchip nodded. He should have expected that. '*Adept* and her prize are hull-down, I see.'

'Long since, Sir. They both seemed in good order.' Pardoe appeared to want to say more but decided against it.

'*Deck there! Sail dead ahead!*'

'Send up the challenge, Mr Piper.' Pardoe sent Claridge aloft with a glass, slapping him on the back, urging him on his way.

Winchip took a glass from the rack and went straight to the mizzen shrouds. She was a small frigate. As he watched he saw her number flag break out. The blue of her ensign said all and proved nothing. He returned to the quarterdeck to await Claridge's verdict.

'She appears to be English rigged, Lieutenant. We shall wait and see.' Winchip had tucked his Navy List into his inner pocket.

Claridge arrived at the run. 'She's the *Phoenix*, Sir. Captain Hervey, twenty-four guns by the look of her.'

'Thank you, Mr Claridge. Do not run away, *Sir!* Stand by me!' Winchip wanted no evidence of excitement. Both tension and excitement had been building for the last few days. An opportunity to see the fleet or anything connected with it was every seaman's dream. This was a Sixth Rate, not a man-of-war. He turned to Piper. 'Acknowledge and send up our number!' He quickly fished out the Navy List, surprised when he found that Hervey was his senior. He remembered the name – it would all come back to him. He walked to the bulwark and glanced at her again. A smart little ship, fast and lively, now much larger in the glass.

'Captain to repair on board, Sir!' Claridge spoke over his shoulder with urgency borne of excitement.

'Acknowledge and then find the coxswain, Mr Claridge. Then have my boat put over, the moment we have wore ship.' Winchip nodded to Mr Ramblin, ever alert, by the wheel.

'*All hands! Prepare to wear ship!*'

The great cabin of *Phoenix* was as Winchip recalled for Sixth Rates, small and cramped and a little short of adequate. Augustus John Hervey was of average height but with bulk enough to assert his presence. He wore no wig. He was hirsute in that he showed no baldness and wore neat curls to each side of his head. His face, young for its years, had the marks of cheerfulness and that certain roundness to give promise to that conjecture. His eyes were contemplative as he ushered Winchip to a chair in a hurry, enough to suggest he was impatient for news. The Madeira was bundled onto the table and into glasses before Winchip could blink.

'Have you *seen* the fortress, Captain?' Hervey was on the edge of his seat.

'Yes, Sir. We stood off for some considerable time.' Winchip saw no point in mentioning the French frigate. 'St Stephen's Cove is free but the Mola seems occupied; by whom we couldn't tell. The harbour is clear up to Philipet

Point.' Winchip added quickly, 'I think it would be possible to land people below the fortress, Sir, but certainly not an army.'

'So! A message *could* be delivered?'

'Without doubt. The English flag still flies, Sir. Besides which we have recently delivered a despatch from Admiralty, through Lord Hawke.'

'Damn my soul!' The expletive was delivered with vehemence.

'Sir?'

'As it stands, Winchip, I could land a dozen senior officers, were they to hand. Men with expertise and the knowledge to deal with this fiasco.'

Winchip nodded his understanding. He could see what had happened. Attached to the English fleet would be a relief army. Included would be some very senior officers, well qualified to make things very difficult for the French. General Blakeney was an old and sick man, more often confined to his bed than out and about. Those officers would be invaluable in the fortress at this moment, if someone had had the sense to send them. He saw no reason to tell Hervey he had been of the same mind.

'What of the French fleet, Captain. Have you seen it yet?'

'I have, Sir. It is all in my report. It seemed to be patrolling in the south-east, using a steady southerly. It comprises twelve men-of-war plus frigates. It is my belief their admiral will show himself from the south-east when the time is right, if only to keep the wind.'

Hervey acknowledged the information with a nod of agreement and continued to look at Winchip's report. He jerked upright with a beaming smile. 'By God, you're an impetuous devil, Winchip, as your reputation infers. The captain of that French forty was a very lucky fellow in my book.' Hervey handed Winchip's report back to him and tucked the one for Admiral Byng in the top drawer of a small Gothic-style, Chippendale writing table, well scarred with usage.

Winchip wondered about his disposition. Would he be

acting as a relay or remain on patrol? He assumed he was about to find out.

'Well, Captain, Admiral Byng will be delighted with this information. You have done better than well. As for your prize, she will be bought in and fighting for the English before you know it. Your task will be to find Roland–Michel Marin, Maquis de la Galissonnière, admiral of the Toulon fleet and report it back through relays, which should be upon us at any time now. When you have found him, report to the battle area and simply put yourself at the admiral's disposal. You and I are the only frigates he has, save those from Edgecumbe's squadron. He was afforded none by Their Lordships and by virtue of that will look upon us as manna from heaven. I can add nothing to that. Dissuade frigates from their usual ploys and keep your eyes peeled for flag's general signals. You will not be alone this time. I shall be here. Have I made myself clear? I have no time to write things down today; the fleet is on my heels and I have much to do.'

'I understand perfectly, Sir.' Winchip made to rise. 'If there is nothing else . . .?'

'That is all, Winchip. I wish you luck.' Suddenly Hervey raised a hand. 'We declared war on France on the fifteenth of this month. I thought you should know.'

'Thank you for telling me, Sir.' Winchip remembered Niven's comment about a slip of the pen.

Sitting in the stern sheets of the yawl on the way back to *Eaglet*, Winchip felt drawn to the western horizon. Hervey had intimated that Admiral Byng was on his heels. At any moment he expected the pristine line that separated sea and sky to shatter into fragments as the great fleet burst upon the scene. For a moment he enjoyed a boyish thrill at the prospect, soon shattered as he realised the terrible implication of Byng's presence in Minorcan waters.

As Winchip stretched for the battens to the entry port, the deep shadow of *Eaglet*'s tumblehome seemed as nothing compared to the might of shipping yet to engulf the sea around them.

Eaglet made slow progress in the light south-westerly air abaft her beam. With her t'gallants clewed up to thwart detection, she progressed under tops'ls, her lookouts evidencing the plight of a squirrel at the very top of a wintering oak.

The forenoon watch was coming to an end and still Minorca adorned the horizon to the north-west. There was nothing to disturb the dull purple of the land. There were no thuds as the great guns blasted their intentions, nor was there a single sail to give promise of more to come. The island, for the moment, was benign.

Winchip sat on the stern seat, writing letters to Madeleine and Emma. If circumstances allowed them to reach England, the letters would tell them no more than they expected. He knew that if he expressed his true fears he would be putting upon them more than they deserved, upsetting them unfairly. He had no premonition of impending death – and neither would he allow such thoughts to enter his head. Those were dangerous thoughts, more likely to weaken one's resolve when his people needed him most. They were too dangerous even to contemplate. If anything it was life he feared – the possibility of life after the dreaded orlop should he be struck down. He needed to be near his family, perhaps the last opportunity to be with them in spirit, even for the length of time it took for them to read of his thoughts and of his love.

He heard the penetrating note of eight bells through the open deck light as he applied the wax to the letters. He cleaned the quill and replaced it in the pot and closed the well. It was always at this moment that new words sprang to his mind. Other things he could have written yet hadn't.

A cry from the tops jerked him upright. He sprang to his feet and grabbed his hat from the trunk as he sped to the companion.

Pardoe had assumed the watch. As Winchip came down to the binnacle, so young Piper scuttled across the deck from the mizzen shrouds, the large glass bouncing on his back. Wide-eyed, he diverted towards Winchip. 'It's the

French fleet, Sir, to the south-east – the van hull-up! There's about a dozen – perhaps more, sailing north!' Young Piper delivered the most important message of his life without a stammer.

'Thank you, Mr Piper. That was well delivered. Back up there, if you please and keep us informed.' Winchip turned to Pardoe. 'Enough is enough, Lieutenant. We shall come about and return to Admiral Byng with all haste. Keep the lookouts sharp, Mr Pardoe. It is one of our relays we are now seeking.'

'Aye, Sir.'

Winchip took a glass and strolled to the taffrail. Scanning the horizon to the east he could just make out a disturbance where the sky met water. It was a trifle in the scale of things, history seeking to be made. He waited – and counted.

He returned to Pardoe. 'Twelve ships-of-the-line, Lieutenant. Put it in the log.'

'Aye, Sir.'

'Have our people eaten?'

'The watch below are eating now, Sir.'

'Very well. Ensure they are all fed, while they have the chance. I shall be in my cabin.'

In the greater scheme of things there was little he could do. Whereas the sight of an enemy frigate would stir passions and create great activity, the sighting of an enemy fleet was as nothing in comparison. As a mouse would run from a cat, so it could contemplate an elephant without fear. When the clash did come, it would be a meeting of leviathans. It would mean death on a grand scale. Wholesale butchery. Consummate aggression. All soon to be consigned to memory, the dead forgotten, the reasons perhaps obscure.

He needed fresh air, enough to drive the morbidity from his mind and to lighten his soul. Should he ever achieve flag rank he knew he would have to become inured to such things; he would need to be hardened to the point of relishing in the fight to be fought by others. He would have to be dismissive of high principles, endowed with the confidence of people in high places where Jack Tar was forgotten, where only numbers had importance.

He wanted to believe none of it!

A call from the tops sent Winchip back up to the quarterdeck. He met Piper on the way and despatched him back to the deck.

'Where away, Mr Pardoe?' Winchip took up a glass.

'On the larboard bow, Sir. She is a frigate from the fleet. We have sent up our number.'

'Thank you, Lieutenant. Signal "Enemy to the southeast. Twelve ships-of-the-line. Eight leagues. Proceeding northward".'

The signals jerked their way upward on two halyards.

'She has acknowledged.' Claridge's voice bellowed from above their heads. ' 'Tis the *Phoenix!*'

Winchip patted the rail with a satisfied nod. Contact was now made. He looked to the north-west. Minorca had come back into view, the sun reflecting from the rocky face of Aire on the horizon, like a signal mirror held in nervous hands.

'We shall continue this course to the fleet, Lieutenant.' Things were coming together. The protagonists were bunching their fists. It was now a matter of when the battle would commence. Winchip nodded his head. When the time came, they would be ready.

'*Deck there! Ships on the larboard bow – big 'uns!*'

'Up you go, Mr Piper.' Winchip patted him on the back. He knew it would be the fleet. Things were coming to a head.

'The wind is veering, Captain.' Mr Ramblin looked over at Winchip. Already top men were scampering up the shrouds to trim sail.

'I do believe you are right, Master. And lessening, to boot!' Winchip sighed. For a moment Byng had found the wind in his favour. Now, it seemed he would have no wind at all. Over the larboard rail he could see *Phoenix* almost becalmed, close in to the shore and in a dangerous position.

The fleet was now in prominence, easing its way eastwards, coming before the southern aspect of Minorca in line astern. They were well apart.

Ramillies(90), the flagship, was in the van, her admiral's broad pennant unable to carry its own weight in the fickle wind. It jousted with the shrouds like the tongue of a snake. Behind her came *Culloden(74)* and *Buckingham(68)*, each ship adjusting sails, enough to progress but not so much that a gust could put them on the lee-shore. As *Ramillies* signalled and then hove-to, almost in the lee of Aire Island, so the following vessels came up into wind, no doubt watching the sandy bays and the scattered tidal rocks with increasing trepidation.

Winchip maintained his watch on the fleet as *Eaglet* turned into wind, assuming a station from which he would be in full view of the flagship and any signals she might make. The novelty of the fleet's presence had not been allowed to turn into a spectacle. A few harsh words had brought those who gawked back to matters in hand.

There was a great deal of activity aboard the flagship. Signals, understood only by the receiver, were hoisted and lowered with utmost precision. Various vessels answered in their turn. It came as a shock when three progressive puffs of yellow smoke issued from the larboard side of *Ramillies*, to be instantly followed by heavy discharges as the great guns roared. Winchip knew it was a signal, to a fortress unresponsive to earlier attempts to gain contact. The signal guns would be a last resort. During the time that the admiral had been trying to raise St Philip's Castle, the French fleet were drawing nearer and that was giving Winchip cause for concern. He wondered for one moment whether he should send a repeat and remind Byng of the dangers approaching from the south-east. He might have done it if *Ramillies* hadn't let fall her courses.

Signals blossomed on the flagship as on a cherry tree in the first bloom of spring. Replies bristled from other ships-of-the-line while others remained silent. Winchip uttered a sigh of relief when the signal to 'prepare for battle' blossomed from the flagship's truck where it would gather most wind. It would be a case of follow-my-leader when the great ships made sail in turn, not wanting to precede the ship ahead. Winchip judged what their course would be and opted to sail clear. He lowered the glass and looked to the binnacle.

'Mr Pardoe!' Winchip shouted from the rail. 'Make all sail, course north-east.' He looked once more at the fleet, his fertile mind envisaging the frantic activity on every ship.

Claridge shouted again. 'Signal. Prepare for battle, Sir!' The midshipman looked over his shoulder, wide-eyed.

Winchip knew at that moment that the lookouts on *Ramillies* had seen the fleet for themselves. From this point on the battle was joined.

'*Deck there! Phoenix is lowering boats!*'

Winchip dashed to the shrouds and raised the glass. Captain Hervey had done the unforgiveable. *Phoenix* was in danger of going onto the rocks. A gust of wind must have pushed her beyond the point of recovery. His response was instant.

'Wear ship, Master. Bring us close to Aire. We shall drop off boats for her.' Winchip ignored the noise and activity. 'Mr Piper. Find Mr Hellard, if you please.' The ships of the fleet would soon be on the move. All it required was the signal 'general chase' for there to be a scramble for wind and sea room. Hellard would have to be quick.

'You sent for me, Sir.'

'Yes, Hellard. *Phoenix* is in danger. We shall put the cutter and the longboat over, double-banked. Put crews aboard and get them over to Captain Hervey. Strong men only, Coxswain; it will be a hard pull.' As an afterthought, he added, 'If "general chase" is raised you will have to row like the devil or be run down! We shall recover you later.'

'Aye, Sir.' Hellard grinned and then dashed to the boat tier, yelling names as he went.

Time seemed to stand still. There had been no further signal from the flagship. The two boats had made good speed across the water towards the island that was now much closer. *Eaglet* wore ship once more and regained her station. He resisted the temptation to follow the boats with the glass; see them safely through the line of ships.

Midshipman Claridge, oblivious to the sudden activity about him, peered through the large glass at the flagship. 'Signal, Sir! "Frigates to close on fleet".'

The signal, recalling the few frigates supplied by the Mediterranean Squadron under Captain Edgecumbe, flew at the flagship's mizzen. Winchip opted to obey it and walked to the binnacle. 'Acknowledge, Mr Piper.' It was the call he had been dreading. There was no escaping it. Soon, from the ships-of-the-line, boats would be coming to demand men and marines from the frigates.

The three boats approaching *Eaglet* were from *Culloden*. With minimum crews they were expecting to be filled. An officer was prominent in each, standing in the bows, staring towards Winchip as if daring him to object. All three swung onto the chains, oars tossed, and hooked on with purpose. The senior lieutenant cupped his hands to his mouth, directing himself to Winchip now staring down through the entry port.

'Captain Cornwall's compliments, Sir! Thirty of your best people if you please – for King and country!' The man took his hat off and waved it above his head. If he had expected a cheer he got none of it.

Winchip raised a hand in acknowledgement and stood back from the posts, his face like a thundercloud.

'Pass the word for the boatswain.' He voiced the words to the air knowing somebody would react. He walked over to Mr Ramblin. 'I want you, Master, to confer with the boatswain and deliver twenty men over the side.' He was trying not to let his feelings show. 'You will muster every man to his part of the ship and then select those you can best release.' He waited until Mr Ramblin nodded his understanding. 'Very well, let it be done. If any man demurs, then he shall answer to me. Am I understood?' In a quieter voice he added, 'Make sure they have the opportunity to gather their dunnage.'

Winchip returned to the port and leaned over between

the posts. 'Ten minutes and you shall have your men.' He stood back, not waiting for a response. 'Pass the word for Sergeant Haggler!'

He was feeling calmer now that the task was in hand.

'You sent for me, Sah!' Haggler looked as though he had just come off parade. His ginger hair offered a strange contrast to the colour of his tunic, and his freckles denied his age of thirty or thereabouts.

'Yes, Sergeant. You will release ten marines for service on *Culloden*. Have them ready in ten minutes, complete with kit.'

'Sah! I should also like to tell them that they belong here and that we expect them back, Sah!'

'You do that, Sergeant.' Winchip believed him.

He saw them over the side, clattering into boats to go into a battle they would have been content to watch. He acknowledged Haggler's smart salute.

It was done. Perhaps he *would* get them back. For now, though, he was to be short-handed – for King and country.

It was another twenty minutes before the last of the boats found its way back to their ships, all fully loaded, a medley of colours, the oars flashing in the afternoon sun.

Through the large glass he could see progress with *Phoenix*. She was standing free and the boats were holding her against the wind until she could make way. He knew that Hellard would now be absent from *Eaglet*, along with those who went with him. He was now commander of a depleted vessel, hardly able to manage herself, let alone man all her guns.

'Signal, Sir! "General chase"!'

'Acknowledge.'

Winchip afforded himself a cheap smile. He had watched the selected hands as they had clattered down the battens to the waiting boats. Had he made the choice himself the faces would have been much the same. He had seen Niven's 'dissenter' among them. Someone had made a good choice and qualified Niven's opinion into the bargain. Now, as he turned away from the rail, the ship seemed suddenly empty.

21

Form Line of Battle!

Winchip gave the order to make sail as the last of the ships-of-the-line, *Buckingham,* let fall her courses and followed the fleet in grand style, coming to south-east as she left Aire Island.

'We shall make sail, Mr Pardoe. Course south-east, under tops'ls, unless you want us to join the fray.' Winchip had already decided that battle was unlikely. It had taken the best part of the day for the fleet to prepare and already they were well into the first dog watch. The after-guard were padding their way forward, their job done, looking anywhere but at the officers at the binnacle.

With the courses brailed up, the view afforded from the quarterdeck was all embracing, allowing a view of the whole horizon. Already the great ships were tacking in succession, forming the line by dint of habit, despite the order for 'general chase', their captains assuming a course of action which could not be held against them later, should things go badly wrong. The great pyramids of sail cloaked the horizon to the east, sailing like angry swans on a great lake, each ship canted to leeward, blue ensigns stiff in the breeze coming out of the south-west. Signals came and went on busy halyards, the sign of feverish activity on every ship. The thirteen ships-of-the-line were a grand display of might, demonstrating England's claim to the Mediterranean.

'General signal from *Dolphin(22),* Sir. "Enemy in sight. South-south-east".'

'Thank you, Mr Bowes.' Winchip considered the position of the French and just as quickly abandoned any thoughts as to their intentions. Their progression would be designed to obtain the wind gage but already they were too far to the east.

'*Deck alow!*'

'*Where away!*'

'*Sails on the starboard bow – a fleet!*'

'The French at last, Sir!' Pardoe peered forward, relaxing when he saw nothing.

'We shall not be fighting the French this day, Lieutenant.'

'Not a night action then, Sir?' Pardoe's voice had a hint of disappointment in it.

'Good heavens, no! We shall size each other up until darkness descends. There is always tomorrow.' As Winchip spoke, so the French van appeared on the south-eastern horizon, against a lowering sky. They were now standing to the north by east, neither looking to escape nor attack but in line astern, well disciplined and closed up.

'So. Some will live to see another dawn. A sobering thought.' Pardoe replaced the log slate.

From *Eaglet* the two fleets were now appearing as one, distance distorting and confusing the eyes. For three hours the protagonists used the distant horizon to manoeuvre, sometimes coming closer and then drifting away from each other as if reluctant to be the first to engage. It was at the moment when a fight seemed unavoidable that Admiral Byng stood to the west, the fleet tacking in succession, leaving the French to make off to the north-east.

The sails of the returning English fleet reflected the red of the setting sun. The pyramids of canvas were highlighted in a vivid pink, rose petals against the darkening eastern sky. Were it not for their purpose in being there, beauty would have sprung to mind. As it was, Dante's Inferno came with greater ease, the confusion of water in their wake resembling the glowing embers of a dying fire.

Winchip retired to his cabin. He knew that things had concluded. The first skirmish was over, a rattling of sabres. Byng, who knew the waters, would no doubt retire to anchor in the lee of Minorca, to make use of the offshore wind in the morning.

Even in a diminishing wind with the advent of evening, the creak and squeal of moving and straining timbers seemed to pervade *Eaglet*. Reaching to the south-west, the angled yards eased and then stiffened as the fitful air played with the expanse of sail. Beneath the counter the water rushed out with a gurgling regularity, occasionally ceasing as the stern was lifted on an approaching swell.

Winchip pushed away his empty supper plate and took up his second goblet of claret. He moved to the stern seat with a puckered brow, the bowl of the glass cradled in his hand. He had watched the manoeuvring of the fleets during their first foray with studied interest. If nothing else, it had been a useful exercise, an opportunity for the crews to prepare themselves for what was to come. What had cheered him most was his conclusion that no matter what the outcome of the conflict, the French could not win the battle for Minorca.

Should the French win the sea fight, it would be a shallow victory and never to the death. The English would fight like terriers – from dismasted hulks if the need arose. Whereas, for the French, their only hope of dominance over St Philip's Castle was to maintain the sea with sufficient undamaged ships to protect both their forces on the island and the transport of supplies from Toulon. It would need a crushing victory over the English indeed to achieve those ends.

He was reminded of a thought that he had had earlier, one which appealed to his sense of innovation, even if it *was* unorthodox. It would take little more than a battalion of soldiers to create havoc on the island. Landed at night, they could destroy urgently needed stores and powder, weakening confidence and breaking morale among the French forces. It was with a smile that he contemplated the damage a few companies of marines could inflict, dashing to their objectives and then retiring before the defenders had recovered from the shock.

Footsteps prefaced a knock on the door.

'Enter.'

Pardoe stood in the doorway. 'We have a change in the wind, Sir. It is backing by the minute.'

'Thank you, Lieutenant, I shall be up directly.' Winchip finished his claret and rotated the stem of the glass between his fingers. His conclusions about Minorca had lightened his spirits.

The dark night had a warmth to it. With *Eaglet* once again hove-to, her estimated leeway recovered, the heavy air from distant African shores played around her rigging, shuffling lines to beat a soft tattoo on the masts.

Winchip knew that below decks, those off watch would have gone to their messes rather than their hammocks. The conversations beneath the purser's glims, shedding their dull light over men huddled at the hanging tables, would be of tomorrow and what the daylight might bring. Perhaps debts demanded or companionships formed. Much would be spoken in hushed tones – debates as to the qualities of those sent to lead them and exaggerations of their past achievements. Those who did sleep would be the better for it, their minds untarnished, neither tainted by the fears of others nor betrayed by false hopes.

At six bells in the middle watch, the darkness still enshrouded the ship like bed curtains. Winchip, having the watch, returned to the binnacle after a tour of the upper deck. As he looked to the wind vane, an act borne of habit, he saw Costly coming down the backstay. Intrigued, he waited.

'Excuse me, Sir. The fleet is coming alive, Sir. The lights are like glow worms, there are so many.'

'Very well, Mr Costly. See that the lookouts remember the other points of the compass.'

Either the admiral was an early riser or he hadn't slept at all. Winchip hoped it was the former. The latter suggested a lack of confidence. In either event there would be many who had gone short of sleep through no fault of their own.

Pardoe arrived on deck before the end of the middle watch, giving Winchip the hope of an hour of rest before sleep became a thing of the past. His cot had been too inviting. Instead he took a pillow and placed it behind his head as he leaned back on the stern seat, allowing his eyes to close.

His thoughts turned to Madeleine. He had not conjured them – they had come automatically. He thought of her as she lay next to him after they had made love for the first time. He had looked down upon her with great tenderness, seeing her firm breasts shining with perspiration in the moonlight. He had cupped one gently in his hand, smiling as she gave a moan of pure pleasure. They had given their all, each in their own way determined to express their love in the way best known to man or woman. With the consummation had come the affirmation of their commitment to each other. The reasons and questions had melted away as if they had never been. Their personal contract had been made with an abandon that had left them exhausted, pleasured and secure with each other in a way that no words, written or spoken, could ever evoke. They were happy. They were man and wife.

He refused to think of death or the possibility of it. It served no purpose and would alter in no way the manner or the moment of its coming. Yet now he dreaded it. He saw it as an intrusion, an ever present threat to a happiness he deserved to enjoy. He also saw it as a cloud that blighted the day-to-day life of Madeleine, hearing news from the Mediterranean and not knowing the worth of it – worry and concern creeping beneath the surface of every happy thought. Dreading each waking hour that he would not return.

'Sir! Sir!'

Winchip jerked awake, the pillow falling to the deck. 'What is it? What has happened?' The words came out automatically, his reaction betraying his befuddled senses.

Pardoe snatched his hand from the captain's shoulder. 'The French fleet has been sighted to the south-west, Sir.'

Winchip's head cleared in an instant. 'Very well, I shall be up directly.'

Winchip came up onto the deck with the dizziness of

sleep still with him. Snatching a glass from the rack he moved to the mizzen shrouds, climbing upwards until he reached the trees. Lodging himself, he lifted the glass to scan the horizon. Within seconds he saw them, tiny patches of grey mingled with the sunless light of the horizon. It was enough. He was down within the minute, suddenly realising that the dawn was upon them.

'All plain sail, Master, and then let fly the fore-jib. Course due north.' To Bowes, he said, 'Signal "Enemy fleet in sight to the south-west". Bend on the battle ensigns and have a twelve-pounder readied and see it is fired every three minutes, unshotted, if you please.' The wind was in the right direction.

Eaglet, so quiet and benign not fifteen minutes since, was now alive to the sound of orders and preparations. Already the ship was coming about, the fore-course bellying and stiffening, dragging her round with the driver as hard as a drum skin.

The resounding crack of the unshotted half-cannon brought the ship to attention. A reminder of what was yet to come.

'We have an acknowledgement, Sir. Flag is making general signals' – there was a lull as Bowes peered through the glass – ' "Prepare for battle", "Make all plain sail", "Course south-east", "Tack in succession".' Bowes leaned forward with the glass as if to better his view. 'That appears to be all for the moment, Sir.'

As if it wasn't enough! 'Thank you, Mr Bowes. Keep your glass on her.' Winchip relaxed. For the moment their part was done. It only required *Eaglet* to assume her station to windward of the action, prepared to drop down on any event calling for her presence. He turned to Pardoe as the lieutenant arrived from below. 'Wear ship, Mr Pardoe, south by east, if you please.' Winchip had made his assessment and chosen his position to windward of the flagship in the centre of the line. To his starboard, a full mile distant, *Dolphin* had chosen the rear of the line. To larboard *Phoenix* assumed attendance on the van.

'South by east, aye, Sir.'

'We shall go to quarters, Mr Pardoe. Bar shot all. We have precious little else to offer, I fear.' As an afterthought, Winchip added, 'Put two quoins beneath the main guns, Lieutenant. If we are to go for rigging, better we do it properly. Do not run out until ordered.' Winchip turned away and slowly paced the quarterdeck.

So, the day had begun.

The wind was backing towards southerly, the English fleet no more than seven points off the wind. If it backed any more, as surely it must, then it would be in England's favour. The line had clawed its way from Minorca, strung out in ragged succession with angled yards and tight canvas. Only from the masthead of the most southerly ships could the French be seen on the distant horizon, moving across the bows of the English towards a point south-east of the island. It was a ploy to gain the wind. Both fleets were now racing towards a point of intersection on opposite tacks, the French from a southerly position and the English from the north-west.

'Sir. The wind is veering to south-west.' Pardoe would feel the change in the ship's attitude, confirming it with a glance upwards, towards the wind vane.

'Thank you, Lieutenant. Even the wind seems to be on our side today.' Winchip raised the glass and looked towards the south-east. 'Our fleet will continue on its course for the moment, I think. I feel it will be tacking before very long and moving northward.'

'How so, Sir?'

'Because, Mr Pardoe, the fleets will now approach each other nose to tail like a pair of inquisitive dogs. Admiral Byng will come round with the wind, and when our van is level with the French rear, he will tack and reverse our order of sailing. We should then engage the enemy.' Winchip looked wry. 'Before that can happen, however, they will need to approach each other, a process that will take both time and distance – and we shall need to be in attendance.' Winchip glanced once more at the protagonists, judging distances and estimating his next step. 'We shall come to due east, Lieutenant. There is no sense in going south if we are to work our way back to the north in a wind that continues to back.'

'Due east, aye, Sir.' Pardoe was at the master's side in an instant.

Winchip watched through the glass as the fleets slowly converged, each passing the other, the combined length of the two fleets diminishing as they passed each other, at least two miles apart, with the English rear far closer to the French than the van. So far the challenge had been put out and accepted by the French, the wind gage had been won by the English and the coming together seemed inevitable. The English would come about and then go down to the French and the battle would commence. He nodded his head in appreciation of the sailing expertise and yet wondered if the initiative won by the English would be equalled by their gunnery. He knew the French. Their ability to bring down rigging from a distance was well known. Their ability to face cannon shot at close quarters was another matter.

'Aha!' Winchip exclaimed out loud, his voice drowned by voices as *Eaglet* wore. The French van had emerged on the left, the *Orphée* came into view on the right with *Hippopotame* close astern. Winchip waited for the English fleet to tack. As the expectation came upon him so it happened. The weak sun from the south flashed upon the changing faces of the sails as the fleet tacked and came about, putting *Defiance(60)* now in the van and *Ramillies* fourth from the rear. It only required the signal for each ship to edge down upon her opposite number, or to dash down, 'lasking' down-wind, for battle to commence.

'Signal from flag, Sir, to *Defiance*. "Steer one point to starboard".' Costly's flushed face and wide eyes stared up at Winchip.

'Thank you, Mr Costly.' Winchip watched with anticipation, waited with bated breath, seeing in his own mind the inevitable outcome of a close action, ship-to-ship battle.

Yet still he waited, the glass against his eye, his anticipation turning to despair as the ships continued on their course, closing perhaps, no more than the ordered amount, an extra point, sufficient an order to close on the enemy. *Defiance* under the command of Captain Andrews made no move to increase the angle, made no sign that he understood the underlying hint to close. There had been no other signal that could convey the message.

'A *repeat* from flag, Sir. To *Defiance*.' Costly stood, panting.

Winchip merely nodded, enough to send the midshipman back to the halyards.

He raised the glass again, seeing with shocked surprise that *Defiance* had increased sail and was surging forward, no doubt to catch *Orphèe*, his opposite number. It was as though Andrews was following his own instincts, or had misinterpreted Byng's intentions. The ships astern of *Defiance* crowded on sail to keep up with her, the whole of Temple West's division drawing away from that of Byng's. The line was breaking.

Winchip drew down the glass and wiped his eye with his sleeve. He looked upon the whole scene with naked eyes and shook his head.

'General signal, Sir. Red flag for battle, Sir, at the foretopmast head!' Costly's voice had risen an octave.

'Thank you, Mr Costly.' Winchip afforded the lad a smile.

With anger in his heart and a smile on his face, Winchip approached Mr Ramblin.

'We shall close on the fleet, Master, and wear ship one mile distance from the action, if you please. I feel we may be needed.' Winchip looked towards *Phoenix(22)* and then to *Dolphin* in turn. Each was wearing ship as he watched, both, perhaps, of the same mind. He directed the glass towards the centre of the line but was suddenly attracted to the van where volumes of smoke prefaced a rapid discharge of guns as the leading ships made contact. He traversed the glass as *Eaglet* swung round to face the fleet. He could see strikes on the English rigging as the French pursued their normal practice at long range. Each English vessel was coming up to her opposite number in turn, the billows of smoke beginning to obscure the scene as it wavered in the lee of the ships before being released to the north-east.

It was with dismay that Winchip saw the foremast of *Intrepid(64)* collapse and plunge like a spear towards her deck. A moment later her maintop yard swung to an upright position as her canvas was shredded where she stood. The ship swung and then recovered, opening a gap in the line as if a tooth had been extracted from the set. Astern of her, *Revenge(64)* and *Princess Louisa(60)* sat with sails aback, as soon did *Trident(64)* and *Ramillies*.

Winchip watched the opening gap in the English line with a furrowed brow. With *Captain(64)*, the last of Temple West's squadron, drawing ahead, it left options open to the French should Galissonnière decide to split the English forces.

He stared at the opening for a moment longer and then strode over to the master.

He spoke with no urgency in his voice. 'Master. I have a mind to defend that gap in the English line.' He looked Mr Ramblin in the eye. 'Can I have your support?'

Mr Ramblin tugged his whiskers and beckoned a mate, whose eyes opened wide as the master spoke. The mate looked across to the battle and suddenly nodded his head.

Eaglet's courses dropped with a noise like thunder as they caught the wind. As topmen scampered round the rigging and the yards were set, the ship seemed to spring forward, the wind behind her and her battle ensign in full view from the mainmast truck.

Winchip turned to Pardoe. 'I trust the quoins are in, as I ordered?'

'Yes, Sir. They will give you the elevation you want, of that I am sure.'

'Good. We are not going to fight, Mr Pardoe, so have no fear. We shall block the hole and hope it is sufficient to keep an intruder at bay – no more than that.'

'I'm very glad to hear that, Sir.' Pardoe looked away with a smile playing on his lips.

Eaglet approached *Intrepid* with a view to tacking to larboard, to see the ship into her position without any hindrance to the progression of the fleet. The chain-shot could do much damage even though the range was extreme. Winchip toyed with the idea of using larger charges but dismissed the idea with the guns untested for such an action. The noise was growing. Continuous discharges, one upon the other, assaulting the ears. The smoke was tumbling down wind, through the French line and away to the north-east, clinging to the water, the tops of the yellow-ochre clouds clipped off by the wind.

As he viewed the approaching gap through the glass, he was amazed to see a boat leaving *Intrepid* to return to *Revenge*. Had *Revenge*'s captain asked for permission to pass *Intrepid*, the Fighting Instruction needing to be obeyed to the letter? Winchip was aware of the fear captains had for the Fighting Instructions but what he saw was beyond his understanding. He would have to leave room for *Revenge* to pass. He could only hope it would be to her starboard, between *Intrepid* and the enemy. Even thought was difficult in the inexorable crescendo of discharging guns.

The moment had come. Winchip glanced down at the gun deck knowing that all the practice would now come to fruition, when every man would have to do his work to perfection.

He shouted. 'Down to the guns, Mr Pardoe. Tell them how good they are.' Winchip smiled and patted Pardoe's shoulder. He then glanced at Mr Ramblin and nodded his head, words having no sound nor meaning.

Eaglet came about with the wheel being wrenched over at Winchip's side. Two helmsmen, shoulder to shoulder, sharing the moment to check the spokes to Mr Ramblin's liking. Sail was taken in, opening up the ship to daylight as would the drawing of curtains in a darkened room. Winchip gauged the distance between *Intrepid* and *Captain* and then held up his hand. *Eaglet* settled in her place with steerage way, enough to allow weather helm to prevent her drifting towards the French.

Winchip quickly surveyed the centre of the French line and noted that *Intrepid*'s opponent was easing towards the gap, a ship of sixty-four guns, her yards swinging as she sought to test the gap close-hauled. Winchip acted before her profile could shorten. He looked towards Pardoe and flashed down his hand.

The guns discharged as one, as Pardoe's sword swept downwards. The smoke billowed forward. Winchip watched the trajectory of the chain-shot with fascination, seeing them reach their zenith and then curl downwards towards the *Frenchman*. Her topsails blew inwards as if they had been punched, leaving ragged holes and tears where once they had been unscathed. As the crew reloaded, the company cheered and cheered again and he did nothing to stop it.

The guns fired again and once more the French frigate's sails and rigging trembled under the impact. A yard swung upwards as rigging was severed, spilling men into the air to fall, grasping at nothing as they plunged through the putrid smoke and into the sea.

The *Frenchman* turned away, falling downwind until she was pointing away from the battle.

'The English ship is coming through, Sir.' Costly's voice had a note of urgency to it.

Winchip turned. 'Thank you.' He bent to shout in Costly's ear. 'Tell Mr Pardoe to rest the guns.' He turned to the master and shouted, 'That will do, Master – bring her away! There is nothing more we can do.'

Eaglet made sail with her yards well round, to catch whatever wind she could in the prevailing south-westerly as she retired.

Winchip stood next to the master, the large glass tucked under his arm. 'Thank you, Mr Ramblin.'

'My pleasure, Captain. It's nice to know that at least one Frenchy will have some explaining to do before supper.' He looked at Winchip and they both laughed heartily.

The heavy shot struck *Eaglet* a devastating blow. It had ricocheted off the water to strike the ship directly below a quarterdeck gun. It entered the poop, taking away an upper knee and throwing the six-pounder onto its back as if it were a toy, its four attendant seamen smashed down where they crouched as the hot metal passed amongst them. It then came up through the quarterdeck planking and took away the bulwark on the opposite side, taking a further seaman with it. It then splashed into the sea, spent, two cables from the ship, on the starboard side.

The ship heeled over to starboard, sending Winchip to his knees. Mr Ramblin was flung into the scuppers like a sack of wheat. Winchip recovered himself and staggered aft, sending men to attend the master. He called for Bowes and was glad to see the midshipman appear from the steps.

The six-pounder was on its side, the truck shattered into pieces, the small wheels gone. From below the wreckage two legs protruded and blood was spreading in a pool beneath them. Of a body there was no sign.

'Get men up here, Mr Bowes. Get this mess cleared away and secure the gun.' Winchip went to another seaman in the opposite scupper. With his chest caved in he sat in repose. There was no blood nor sign of a wound except the depression in his chest. He had fired his last gun.

Winchip left Bowes to it as soon as he saw Pardoe arrive at the binnacle. Already the lieutenant had put a mate to the wheel and the helmsman was putting himself to rights.

'What damage on the gun deck, Lieutenant?'

'None that can't be repaired, Sir. I don't think it was intended for us in the first place. All the guns are secure.' Men padded aft as Pardoe spoke. Already the two seamen were being removed, water and sand being thrown liberally over the bloodied deck.

Winchip assessed *Eaglet*'s position and course with respect to the wind and relaxed. Mr Ramblin was cursing as he was lifted ignominiously to his feet, his pride hurt and his stature in ribbons. Winchip clenched his teeth and looked around to see the plight of the other two seamen.

'They are gone, Sir.' Pardoe looked down at his feet. 'They were blown overboard. They didn't even come to the surface.'

'That is too bad.' Winchip brushed himself down and recovered his hat. The stray ball had shaken him to his roots. It was not the first time that it had happened to him – *Capable* came clearly to mind – he remembered hoping then that it wouldn't happen again.

'Mr Bowes has charge up here, Mr Pardoe. Let him be. Check below, if you please, with the carpenter.' Winchip stared at the jagged splinters of decking as they pointed to the air and at other pieces driven deep into the mizzenmast like arrows. It had been a narrow escape.

Winchip wound his way through the quarterdeck guns, nodding his approval as he went to the taffrail to watch the outcome of *Eaglet*'s endeavours. His whole frame seemed to be shaking and there was little he could do to stop it. He forced himself to carry on and concentrate on what he knew best.

The smell of smoke still lingered in the air, along with sweat, burned gunpowder and the sharp tang of burning slow-match. All the twelve-pounders had been allowed to play their part. A chance to throw iron at the enemy and say that they were at Minorca. Bowes, securing tackles to lift the upturned gun, worked in breeches and blouse, issuing orders and doing his part to bring things back to normal. He stood upright as the captain approached.

'You did well today, Mr Bowes – as did you all!' Winchip turned to finish the sentence, his loud words embracing the whole quarterdeck. 'This was a freak accident. A scratch as far as *Eaglet* is concerned!' He turned away from the cheers with a wave of his hand and walked unsteadily to the taffrail.

Winchip rested his hands on the smooth oak and studied the action being played out before him. The *Revenge* had made a safe passage past *Intrepid* and was followed by *Trident(64)*. *Princess Louisa* had been mauled in the tops and had the appearance of being shot through as she came suddenly up into wind with her tattered sails shivering and the masts quivering. Winchip looked away in despair, distressed at being unable to quantify the damage to the French. The smoke was too thick and the view otherwise obscured. He took the moment to watch *Ramillies* as she bore down on her opponent from an angle of some thirty degrees. Only when Captain Gardiner realised that his ship had overrun her enemy did he fire his guns at the next ship in line as his guns came to bear. The ship that faced *Ramillies* by mistake suddenly found herself without a maintops'l yard and her sails peppered. Great damage must have been caused below as the ship fell downwind and withdrew from the line.

Winchip noticed that *Ramillies* had crammed on sail to catch *Revenge*. The gap that *Eaglet* had momentarily filled was still redeemable and he was convinced that Byng was racing to secure it. It was then that he saw *Foudroyant*, Galissonnière's flagship. She was emerging from the smoke on a tack to take her to the gap at an angle, to take the wind from *Captain* and by virtue of that, the whole of Temple West's division. Behind her the French centre and rear were cramming on sail to bring them up to their flagship. It was to be a masterful stroke should it work.

Winchip swung the glass to *Ramillies*. Byng had gathered his division about him. Winchip could see the signal on the flagship for his division to fill and stand on. *Deptford(50)*, which had been sent to join the frigates so that each side would have equal numbers at the start of the battle, was making headway in support. He could see the English rear passing to leeward of the stricken *Intrepid*. First, the *Revenge* and then the *Deptford*, followed by *Trident* and then *Ramillies*. Behind the flagship, *Culloden* and *Kingston* kept pace, the *Princess Louisa* doing her best to follow. Already the smoke had passed away as if the battle had never taken place. A faint, yellow haze, like mist over the mud-flats of the Fal, hung in the air on the north-eastern horizon, the only sign that it had ever been. As Winchip closed down the glass he grunted in satisfaction as he saw the forty-gun *Chesterfield* easing her way towards *Intrepid*, no doubt to stand by her and defend her against capture.

The *Foudroyant* and her consorts had gone about, their glorious moment lost to them as Byng re-established the English line. Galissonnière took his fleet to the north-north-west, followed by Byng until the evening drew in, when the English fleet tacked in succession and returned to Minorca in the last light of the day.

Winchip walked to the thwart rail, looking forward along the length of the ship at the men resting at the guns. The loblolly men, ready to heave on lines or fetch and carry, were gathered in a group, as were the powder-monkeys, all waiting to play their part and do their bit for king and country. The few marines that were left to him stood at the shrouds, waiting to gain the cross-trees should the need arise. At the guns the slow-matches glowed. Worms, sponges and rammers lay close to hand. The ports remained open in the quiet sea and the warmth of the evening. Winchip let things be. He walked back to the binnacle and Lieutenant Pardoe. It had not been a good day for England. The engagement had been a brief and bloody one, with more than a few ships in urgent need of repairs to rigging and spars. Perhaps the morrow would bring a day when captains could do what they knew best, without having to find solutions within the bounds of the Permanent Fighting Instructions, and admirals would place themselves in the centre of the line where they could be seen and understood.

'Mr Pardoe. Get our people fed, if you please, turn and turn about. You may also secure the guns.' He didn't wait for a response. Instead, he spoke to the master. 'We shall go down to *Intrepid*, Master, and see how we can be of service.' To Pardoe, he said, 'Take off the battle ensign.'

'Are we not to finish it, Sir? Chase them back to Toulon?'

'I think not, Mr Pardoe. That would require a meeting of the council. By that time . . .' Winchip threw his hands in the air and turned towards the companion.

Four bells rang out in the second dog watch. The thin cloud of the day had faded to a sky of duck-egg blue, gradually changing to pale azure above the spot that had cradled the sinking sun. A few strips of dark cloud hung unmoving above the horizon, their underbellies a furnace red. Winchip knew there would be no more battle that day. Tomorrow was yet to come.

22

The Aftermath

Winchip sat in the stern-sheets of the yawl, feeling the motion as the bow cut into each successive choppy wave on its journey to the flagship. His hands gripped the seat beneath him as the stern rose and then crashed down with sickening force. As they approached the lee of *Ramillies'* tumblehome, so the motion eased, allowing him to release his stiff and whitened fingers.

There were many other boats and barges waiting under the main chains, signs of other captains already on board, probably called to answer for their sins. Looking at the barges he revised his opinion. These were the boats of senior ships. It was to be nothing less than a meeting of the war council, with witnesses to be questioned and opinions to be sought. He knew then that his wait was to be a long one. He closed his eyes in despair, anger rising in him too readily. How Their Lordships at Admiralty, with all their past experience, could countenance such a fragmentation of command was beyond his understanding. It would be interesting to see how quickly the 'council' would act when it came to sharing the responsibility of failure.

'Toss oars!' Hellard's voice transcended thought. His return from *Phoenix* and Captain Hervey had been welcomed that morning, as had the return of the men and the boats and a dozen bottles of Madeira, sent with grateful thanks.

Winchip took the ladder in his stride, his mind racing, trying to find a reason for his presence among such company. Coming up onto the quarterdeck, he was greeted by the ship's first lieutenant. Exchanging salutes, he followed him up to the stateroom.

'I must apologise, Sir. Captain Gardiner may be some while. The admiral has decided to hold a meeting and— '

'A meeting or a council of war, Lieutenant?'

'Er . . . a council, Sir.'

Winchip adjusted his sword and flopped into a chair, one where he had a view of the quarterdeck, even if only to keep his mind concentrated on things that mattered. Men – their people – brave and willing, with the tools to do the job. Valueless if misdirected or ill led by those who would seek excuses for what had passed – or give false reasons for what was likely to come.

Admiral Byng was in a position to make one of many choices. Coming off worst in his encounter with the French, with sail and rigging destroyed by an enemy that fired and then retreated out of range, he would be hard put to find an answer – the Permanent Fighting Instructions saw to that. It would take a brave man to ignore the fate of Admiral Matthews who had chosen to ignore the mandatory instructions in 1744, at Toulon.

There was the option of blockading Toulon and denying supplies to the French Army at Minorca. He could land a large force on Minorca dedicated to destroying stores and supplies and bringing chaos, thus weakening the resolve of the invading forces. The French transports at Ciudadela could be destroyed piecemeal and the port blockaded. The possibilities mounted with the telling, each enough to bring new resolve to an admiral with his fleet still virtually intact and a small army itching to be employed.

Considering these options, Winchip cursed himself for his lack of faith in Byng. Perhaps it was not defeatism being bandied about in the great cabin behind him. In order to do any of the things that had come to mind it would be necessary to plan; and to plan required communication at the highest level. He felt better for having reached such an obvious conclusion, choosing to ignore the twinge of doubt that still remained. He passed what was becoming a long wait by reflecting on *Eaglet*'s involvement.

Today was the twenty-third of May. The third day since the battle, and the third day since they had committed the dead in the first hours of the night.

Keeping station to windward of *Intrepid* and *Chesterfield* had been a slow and ponderous experience. The fleet had melted away into the north-west leaving the small group to fend for themselves. Under a jury rig, *Intrepid*'s weight had been too much for her limited sail. Every hour had been fraught with danger, the threat of attack and fear for the great ship herself. Only on the second day was *Eaglet* able to withdraw as *Dolphin* and *Experiment(22)* appeared on the northern horizon.

To Winchip's surprise, the fleet had been hove-to, busy making repairs some eight leagues south-east of Aire Island. When *Eaglet*'s own lookouts had reported the French fleet lying to the north-west, between the English fleet and St Philip's Castle, his surprise turned to despair. An attack by the French at that moment, with several English ships still unfit for battle, would have gone badly for Byng.

Make and mend had been the order of the day, although from Winchip's perspective the bright new paint in which the fleet had arrived had been sorely smudged.

A succession of barges and boats had come and gone from *Ramillies* like ants toing and froing at their nest hole, their occupants giving little indication as to what was afoot. Whatever activity had been taking place in the great cabin of the flagship, it had nothing to do with renewed hope, or fresh intentions. In Winchip's mind, any thought of completing the task for which the admiral had been sent to Minorca, seemed as distant as John de Wynn's coffee-house at Falmouth.

That day had passed without incident. Still the repairs had continued and still *Eaglet* patrolled to windward, conscious of the French sitting on the northern horizon.

It was on the third day – today – that the signal had come for him to report to the flagship.

A sudden bustle of sound intruded Winchip's thoughts. The doors to the great cabin had been swung wide open, an indication that the council had concluded its business.

If Winchip had expected a hubbub of voices, raised in a sudden freedom of speech, he was disappointed. It was a sombre succession of senior officers who filed from the meeting place, heads held low with little sign of the anticipation one would expect from men fired with a new enthusiasm. His heart sank. Perhaps his worst fears were about to be realised.

He watched them pass through, onto the quarterdeck, forced into stilted conversations as each waited for his boat to come up to the chains. He recognised a few: Captain Henry Ward of *Culloden*, Captain John Amherst of *Lancaster*, Captain Thomas of *Defiance*, whose fore-top had been hewn down; and the luckless Captain James Young of the stricken *Intrepid*. There were others, gathering at the nettings, looking to sea with vacant eyes, avoiding contact and keeping to themselves.

Winchip stood as Captain Gardiner entered the stateroom, followed by a cabin servant who poured claret into two glasses on the small table – a welcome refreshment.

'I am sorry you have been kept waiting, Captain. It has been a busy meeting, to say the least.'

Winchip could have sworn there was despair in Gardiner's eyes. 'We must all bow to the exigencies of the moment, Sir.' The words were fatuous. It was information Winchip hungered for. He needed to know whether Mr Lunt, young Midshipman Piper, Archie – the powder-boy, Marine Peters and Marine Lieutenant Gray, among many others, had died in vain, their deaths to no purpose. Sparked by anger, he relived for a moment the broadside from *Corinne*, seeing in his mind's eye the little cameos as if they were being re-enacted for his benefit alone. He drew himself together at the sound of Captain Gardiner's voice.

'Admiral Byng would like a word with you.' Gardiner stepped back to allow Winchip to gather himself and pass through the door. He placed his hat beneath his arm and his hand on the pommel of his sword. Admiral Byng was sitting in exactly the same place as when he last visited *Ramillies*.

'Ah! Captain Winchip.' Byng's smile disavowed his problems, his face expressing genuine pleasure as he waved Winchip to a chair.

'Your servant, Sir.' Winchip sat without preamble and settled himself.

'We have come a long way since we last met, Captain. Much has happened and more may happen yet.' Byng settled his periwig and brushed the queue from his shoulder. 'I am entrusting you with letters and reports for Their Lordships, Captain. They are of extreme importance and most urgent.' He looked down at the papers before him as if they carried his life in their hands. 'The reason I have asked you here is that your name appears in these reports, as do others.' Byng looked at him directly. 'One can never predict that what one does will have the effect originally intended. You must know that as well as I.' He paused to allow his point to be made. 'Your action of the twentieth in deterring that ship from exploiting an unfortunate gap in our line could have been the saving of the fleet – we shall never know. However, I was witness to that event and, by God, I should like to thank you for it, as would many of my officers.' Byng stood and walked around the table. 'It was a worthy act, Captain.' Byng held out a ruffled hand.

'It was my duty, Sir.' Winchip shook the admiral's hand.

'Of course.' Byng nodded with another smile. 'I wish you a safe journey, with no distractions.'

Winchip's face burst into creases as he grinned. 'Thank you, Admiral.' He turned and left the cabin with Gardiner in his wake.

'Well, my dear Winchip, the admiral is not usually so beneficent. Were it said to anyone else I would say go while you may. It will not happen twice.' They laughed together. 'It will be some time before the admiral's despatches are prepared, so I shall have them sent over to you, as with your orders. I would ask you to sail immediately, if that is possible. I heard about the random shot. Are your repairs completed?'

'Nothing that cannot be put right at sea, Sir.'

'Fine. Then I bid you a safe passage and add my thanks to those of the admiral. It was damned quick thinking!'

With the usual noise, the mist of pipe clay and the shrill of whistles, Winchip descended into the yawl to return to *Eaglet*. He would await his orders and despatches. The yawl dipped and rose with each successive wave, disallowing him any other thought than that they would be homeward bound before the sun had set.

Winchip sat on the stern seat staring at the satchel of despatches lying on the small table. All the way to Gibraltar he had wondered whether they represented a parcel of excuses or a declaration of intent. Had Admiral Byng decided to leave Minorca and the men at the fortress to their fate, or had he re-entered the fray with renewed heart and a keener resolve?

General Fowke had been quick to shatter any illusions he may have had as to the answer. His had been a perfunctory gesture, an acceptance of the situation in respect of his fears for Gibraltar. Without confiding in Winchip, he had made it quite clear by inference that it was Byng's intention to return to Gibraltar, not merely to repair and provision his fleet but to defend the place – as Fowke had wanted.

Winchip had visited Douglas and Alice Munro. Outwardly it had been a happy meeting, tainted only by his inability to even speak of Minorca lest he found himself having to answer for it at a later date. Munro had been understanding, even if a little vexed at not being able to receive first-hand information before his brother officers. With Alice it had been different. She looked so much like Madeleine that he wanted to be gone from the place – back to Falmouth where he knew she would be waiting.

Instead, he dined well, talking long into the evening. When he left, gripping the leather despatch case in one hand and a packet of gifts and a letter for Madeleine in the other, Munro kept him company to the sally port. The clatter of their shoes on the wet cobbles was enough to waken even the heaviest sleeper, but there were no sounds of protest, as they were as likely to be the night watch as anyone else. Munro broke the silence between them, speaking in a harsh yet subdued tone, his arms outstretched even as they walked.

'I am worried about Alice, Daniel. I may be called to duty at any time and I have no means of protecting her – I cannot take her to sea during hostilities as ye well know.' Munro had twisted his body round to face Winchip, almost pleading in his effort get a reaction to his plight.

Winchip stopped and looked at Munro directly, speaking in a voice that was little more than a whisper. 'All I can tell you I have already said, Douglas. In my opinion, Gibraltar is safe for the present. I know how you must feel and it grieves me that I can offer no more help.' There was a pause that fell heavily upon them both, Winchip struggling to come to a decision and Munro with bated breath.

Winchip, his mind made up, rose to his full height. 'This must go no further, not even to Alice. She must do what you ask of her without question, is that understood?'

'My word on't.'

'Good! Admiral Byng is likely to come here, to Gibraltar – to defend this place. He will certainly not offer battle again, not without reinforcements. It is General Fowke's wish that he returns here and Byng's necessity to make repairs that makes me sure of it. Nothing more will be done until new despatches and orders are brought from Their Lordships at Admiralty.' Winchip stood back a pace. 'There you have it. If you think Alice may be in danger, then I advise you to look to Spain for her escape.' Winchip reduced the tone of his voice and became more conciliatory. 'Were I in your shoes I would make arrangements for her to stay across the border until things are clear. Then, you can act decisively.'

'Well, I thank you for that.' Munro's large body seemed to almost shrivel in relief. 'I shall do as ye say and I shall not speak of it further, I swear.' The steps were no more than twenty yards distant and already a man of the watch was swinging a lantern for Winchip's boat. Munro held out his huge hand. 'I know ye'll be returning to England with news of this damned business. I wish ye a safe journey, Sir.'

Munro tipped his hat, turned and was gone into the night before Winchip could even reply.

Winchip was so deep in thought that the knock on the door startled him.

'Enter!'

Pardoe stepped in with the freshness of the quarterdeck still upon him. 'The Lizard is in sight to the north, Sir. Clear as a beacon.' His face was wreathed in smiles, no doubt thinking about Emma and the hopeful resumption of their advancing relationship.

'That is good news, Mr Pardoe. I shall be up directly.' Without realising it, Winchip had shed his despondency, suddenly glad to be home. The early morning sun was streaming through the quarter windows, bathing the stern seat in light. It was going to be a fine June day. Not one to be spoiled by dark thoughts.

At the end of the morning watch the call came from the tops. The grey rock of Black Head was visible off the larboard beam and the promontory that was Lowland Point showed itself through a hazy sea mist, unable to disguise the fresh green of the summer that filtered through.

Winchip moved to the weather rail. With his feet planted apart for purchase and his hat athwart his head, he leaned back into the light sou'-westerly, enjoying the feel of the ship beneath him as *Eaglet* rode the stern sea with the panache of a King's ship in home waters.

He knew it was a time to count his blessings, but he was also aware of how changes could come about so easily – usually swiftly and when least expected. It was a natural time to think of what was to come, with England once again at war with her old enemy. At least the immediate future was taken care of – *Eaglet* urgently requiring a clean and a refit. What happened after that would depend upon many things, not least of which would be the need to blockade French ports. It was a dismal prospect. Dismal enough for Winchip to break off his speculations and return to the ship's business. Falmouth was almost in sight.

Winchip sat tall in the stern sheets of the jollyboat as it made its way towards the quays. Pardoe sat beside him, the leather bag at his feet carrying the total of his possessions. Around them, the quay punts with their stubby masts to take them beneath the yards of the square-riggers in the roads, ferried seamen from the Dutch packet-boats to and from the shore.

It was doubtful that Madeleine had seen *Eaglet* arrive. The deep water round to Pendennis Castle had been a mass of masts and spars, far too many to allow the ship a safe anchorage, where she could be seen. So, it had been the roads and a long haul for the boat's crew, now feathering their oars as the boat approached the steps.

They attracted little attention as they climbed up to the quay in the lowering tide, Pardoe loitering for a moment to slip Hellard a guinea. It would be another hour or two before the crew started back to the ship, weaving a more precarious course than the one that brought them to land.

Winchip took a glance at Wynn's as he approached the steps up to the ope, leading to the street. He remembered how he had thought of the place when they were south of Minorca and had almost smelled the aroma of roasting coffee beans. It held other memories, too.

He had no recollection of the walk along Church Street. Only when they arrived at the gate by the church did he bring himself back to the present. For nearly six years he had come home to a house devoid of connubial bliss. Of course there was his darling Emma, growing a little more with his every return. There were also Beth and Jonathan, now part of his little family. There had been no Maria waiting for him as there had been in those distant days. For a moment he saw her face in every detail, smiling, her head to one side, dependable, loving and always there, waiting for him. Winchip shook his head, shattering the illusion, increasing his pace as a rogue anger built up within him. It was Madeleine who mattered now and as Winchip thought of her, so he knew in his heart that Maria would approve, would be glad for him and selfless in her hope for his happiness.

As they walked up the steep garden path towards the house, so Blackie came down to them, his tail sweeping the gravel, his body low to the ground in a gesture of obeisance as he approached.

It was then that Winchip saw her – saw them both – Madeleine and Emma, standing in the doorway, shocked and unbelieving.

It was Emma who ran down to them first. Winchip turned aside and strolled onto the grass, looking anywhere except at Emma. It was time for them to be more open about their feelings as he would be in a matter of moments. He had made Emma's decision for her. She ran into Pardoe's arms as if they had been married yesterday. A moment later she grasped Winchip by the hand and whispered, 'Thank you' in his ear as she kissed him.

Madeleine remained at the steps, holding her arms out to him as he came up to her, his hat dropping to the ground unheeded. As they came together her tears glistened in the evening sun, her eyes wet with happiness.

'Oh, my dear, dear man.' The sobs came and remained, her head buried in the white facings of his coat as she gripped him with a passionate fervour. She then looked into his eyes, her face childishly happy, her love absolute.

They went into the house together, Pardoe and Emma retiring to the kitchen with Beth and Jonathan.

Winchip held her tightly as they entered the withdrawing-room, only releasing her so that they could sit together on the *chaise longue*. He kissed her softly – a kiss of love. It was a time for tenderness. Passion would come in its time. 'I have missed you so much, my dear. I have thought of you every moment of every day.' He kissed her again, gripping her small hands in his as if he could never let them go.

'As I have missed you, my darling Daniel.' She looked demurely away as if she were keeping the burden of a secret, frightened to tell him – and yet desperately wanting to.

'What is it, my love?' Winchip searched her eyes, hardly noticing as she took his hand and laid it gently on her stomach.

'I am bearing your child – our child.' Her damp eyes looked into his, her smile of utter happiness enveloping them both, bringing them together in an embrace that promised all things. A togetherness destined to last for all time.

EPILOGUE

The senior officers who emerged from the great cabin of *Ramillies* on the twenty-fourth of May 1756, the day of the War Council and four days after the battle, must have known in their hearts that the agreed decision to return to Gibraltar had been the wrong one. They may have been comforted by the fact that their answers held true to the questions put forward by the agenda placed before them by its author, Admiral of the Blue, The Honourable John Byng. The wording of that agenda left no other recourse than to leave Minorca and the sea to the French and return to Gibraltar.

Not least among the questions the agenda posed were whether Minorca could be relieved should they attack the French fleet, and whether the island could be relieved, even if the French fleet were not present. To these questions the unanimous answer had been 'No'. Also, would Gibraltar be in danger should the English fleet meet with an accident? It was agreed that Gibraltar would be in danger and therefore needed protecting. Other options, due to Byng disallowing discussion, were not considered.

When Byng returned to Gibraltar, ostensibly in order to defend that place, a litany of excuses and reasons for his quitting Minorca and the garrison there was sent to England, not least the findings of the Council of War. It was likely, too, that Admiral Byng felt secure in the knowledge that he had obeyed the Permanent Fighting Instructions to the letter – belabouring them almost.

All in all it is doubtful that Byng had a conscience. In his mind he must have thought he had done his best, albeit with an inferior fleet, both undermanned and ill-equipped to perform the task for which he was sent. He was certainly no coward and no charge of cowardice had ever been laid before him. In his despatches he asked for more ships to finish the task.

At home, news of a victory at Minorca was eagerly awaited. When Admiral Byng's first despatch announced his departure from Gibraltar to relieve Minorca, it seemed inevitable that news of the demise of the French would follow soon afterwards.

It was unfortunate that the Prime Minister, The Duke of Newcastle, had received, by circuitous means, a copy of a letter sent home by Admiral Galissonnière. In the letter the admiral described the confrontation with Byng suggesting that the English had been bested and that Byng had not been determined in his efforts to win; had left the sea to him (Galissonnière), and St Philip's Fortress to its fate.

This letter from Galissonnière was received before Byng's own despatches and already it was being accepted as a true record of events. There was anger in the streets, dismay in government and fury in the heart of the Duke of Newcastle.

When Byng's despatches, telling events as they were and giving the decisions of the Council of War, were received by Their Lordships at Admiralty, they were released to the 'Gazette' in a heavily abridged form and not to Byng's advantage. Galissonnière's letter held greater sway over those whose minds were already made up.

Admiral Byng, ordered home, was arrested and charged with not doing his utmost to defeat the enemy. The sentence for which, should he be found guilty, was mandatory death.

At his trial many spoke on Byng's behalf, both inside and outside the courtroom. It was to no avail. He was found guilty and sentenced to death accordingly. The court, however, recommended mercy, to the only arbiter, the King. A clever ploy indeed! Should George II decide not to grant clemency, then it would be he who bore the brunt of the blame for the death of a man who did not deserve to die.

There was to be no clemency. King George II remained silent.

In Portsmouth Harbour, at midday on the fourteenth of March 1757, on board *Monarque*, once Byng's flagship, Admiral of the Blue, the Honourable John Byng was shot to death.

END